Schrödinger's God (5 Stars)

'The best of the series so far. Hugh Greene never fails to deliver thrills and new insights.'

'Greene is one of those artists who manages to make everything seem simple and effortless, but the more you look at it the more detail you see, and the more you can't help but admire those delicate touches. His characters are human. They don't have a storytelling veneer, they are people. Plausible, recognisable, everyday people. An incredible piece of writing. And the more I think about it all the more impressive it gets. I strongly encourage you to walk the path of this book because it delivers.'

'As always the research the author did means the book has more levels than a typical skyscraper. Hugh Greene gives me both pleasure and surprise in his words. He should be a lot more famous then he is.'

'The tension is kept throughout, and there are twists and turns and a well hidden, very surprising final reveal. A murder mystery with a difference.'

The Darkening Sky (4.44 Stars)

'I have read many a crime book, but this book was different. I never for one moment guessed how the story would unfold.'

'Brilliant. Very much enjoyed – a new detective series based in England.'

'This was quite a read. Greene brings a lot to the table in this with great details on psychiatry, forensics, medicine, society, cars, and countless other small details, yet they are delivered with ease and purpose. As for the strengths? For me, the dialogue wins it. It's natural. It has wit without heavy punchlines. Greene handles the reveal superbly and leaves you hanging until the end. Sign me up for more Power and Lynch.'

'It is a good crime and psychological thriller and will keep any reader interested to the end. Well written, with great development of characters; I felt that I knew Power & Lynch personally. I look forward to further volumes in this highly entertaining and somewhat edgy series. Hugh Greene is a writer to start paying attention to in my opinion. Highly recommended.'

The Fire of Love (4.62 Stars)

'Good plot and enjoyable read – away to locate more books in this series.'

'This is a gripping story, I was hooked from the first page.'

'A well written book with a well-thought out storyline, I enjoyed it very much and definitely want to read the next one.'

'There are lots of twists and turns and complex characters to keep the ending from you and difficult to guess.'

'After the first chapter I could not put it down.'

'A good read that I would recommend to anyone who enjoys crime novels and psychological thrillers. The writing is constantly good and interesting.'

The Good Shepherd (4.38 Stars)

'There was drama and suspense and a nice twist at the end. It was quite compulsive, I felt I had to read more to see what happened next.'

'It is a very enjoyable and intriguing read. Well-written, it evokes the spirit of the times, the mid-nineties.'

'I enjoyed this book. The characters were interesting and I felt the book was well researched.'

'The story builds well with excellent attention to detail paid to the places that the main characters visit.'

'The pace of plot was gripping, and makes me want to know what is next.'

'An excellent read, loved it.'

'I was hooked from the first paragraph.'

Dr Power's Casebook (4.3 Stars)

'Hugh Greene the Author conveys the nineties in a way that helps me to look back fondly on that era. Dr Power's character is developing in a way that I am enjoying and I want to find out more. I cannot wait until the next book.'

'This is a little different to the novels but it is entertaining and well worth reading. I enjoyed all the stories but 'The Dark' has to be one of the best short stories I have ever read.'

'The more I read of Hugh Greene's stories the more a fan I become. These short stories are written in his own inimitable way and as always the dialogue flows seemingly effortlessly as the stories unfold.'

'During these stories you begin to get a real feel of the characters the book is based on. I can honestly say I am enjoying this authors books.'

Also by Hugh Greene

The Darkening Sky
The Fire of Love
The Good Shepherd

Omnibus of Three Novels in a Single Volume
The Dr Power Mysteries

Short Story Collection
Dr Power's Casebook

Schrödinger's God

A Dr Power Murder Mystery

Hugh Greene

Illustrated by Paul Imrie

ISBN 10: 1522774041
ISBN 13: 978-1522774044

First Edition Published Worldwide in 2017

A catalogue reference for this book is available from the British Library

Typeset in Cambria
Proofreading and typographic design by Julie Eddles

All characters appearing in this book are fictitious. Any resemblance to real persons, living or dead, is purely coincidental.

www.hughgreene.com

twitter: @hughgreenauthor

Schrödinger's God

Prologue

Maria found the hotel room and settled herself down. The priest had left her in the airport hotel lobby, paid for her room and left, and for that departure she was grateful.

He had given her the usual two pills. They were like two tiny yellow sweets. One was shiny and round and the other was mottled and had an indented Smiley face pressed into its surface. He told her to take these an hour before her new 'father' arrived. He would be there to collect her at four p.m. Amsterdam time and drive her into Germany to begin her new life whenever he chose.

She looked round the room but there was not much to divert her. The furnishings were bland and grey. The windows were well soundproofed and so the jets that she could see outside, climbing in the blue sky as they took off from Schiphol airport, were strangely silent. There was a vague smell of dust and disinfectant. The sun shining through the windows lit up a constellation of dust motes and she watched these for a while, mesmerized.

The room was big, and the double bed it housed was so large it was almost as wide as the room. She tried not to think too much about the bed, although its position and its function were central to the priest's transaction.

He always said, "The nuns have taught you how to please a man by making him comfortable; cooking and cleaning and so forth, and I have taught you how to make him happy in other ways . . ." He always said this after he had pressed his attentions on her; in a tone that implied she should be grateful.

At least, she would never have to hear or see him again. She was surprised to find within her heart the smallest nugget of regret, but she supposed that this was more probably fuelled by a fear of what might be to come. The unknown.

She looked at the clock and decided it was time to take the pills. They would help to take away the anxiety she usually felt. She got a glass of water from the bathroom and swallowed them both, the Smiley pill last.

She sat on the bed in a shaft of sunlight from the window. The drugs were beginning to allay any fears and she was almost beginning to look forward to life with her new 'father'. The priest had tried to reassure and cajole her. She would have money, food and her own flat in the city centre. There was music and fashion and nightlife. Her new 'father' was in a profession where he could certainly protect her and provide for her. Not bad for a girl of fifteen. She could but hope for the best.

* * *

The cellar was dry, but she knew from when she'd been locked in there in the daytime that there were cobwebs in the corners. Where there were cobwebs it logically followed that there were spiders, and this knowledge frightened Lucia.

It was worse now, because it was dark. The moon that shone through the grating was only a thin crescent moon and so the moonlight and starlight from the night sky did not help her much. The spiders could be very close indeed.

Twenty-four hours' punishment in the cellar. That's what the nuns had ordered as a sentence for her disobedience; for her refusal to visit the priest's room.

It was a warm night, though – at least that could be said for it.

She had spread some sacking on the flagstones to insulate herself from the grey stone to make herself a hard bed for the night.

Lucia felt a small feeling of triumph. She was beginning to think that any punishment was worth it; better than the alternative of a visit to his room. It felt comforting to rebel, although sometimes the nun's would slip yellow pills into her food, and then nothing seemed to matter and the priest could lure her into his room and do what he liked. She no longer seemed to care. But the next day when she woke in his empty bed, she would steel herself, and punish herself and the nuns who clucked their disapproval, by refusing to eat anything they offered her, for as long as she could. The nuns would then beat her with the hard wooden backs of hairbrushes to encourage her to eat. She could usually manage about three days without any food and then she would relent.

She tried to keep herself very thin now in the hope that the priest would turn his attentions elsewhere. It didn't seem to work though. He kept asking the nuns for her. Did her refusals excite him and attract his attention she wondered?

She was so thin that sometimes her bones hurt when she lay down for too long. Even though she was thirteen she still hadn't had a 'monthly' as the nuns called it. They blamed this on her refusal to eat properly.

She lay down in the dark and wondered where the spiders were.

PART ONE

Chapter One

August 2000

Beyond the Cloud of Unknowing
Is
Schrödinger's God

"I shall be Don Quixote, the knight of La Mancha. And you can be Sancho Panza, his trusted companion," said Dr Power jovially, as they stood in the middle of the marble floor of the Departure Hall of Manchester Airport. He went on to tease further. "We are going on a quest in Spain after all."

"I rather think that it is a pilgrimage," said Andrew Lynch, Superintendent of Police and friend of Dr Carl Power. "Not a quest, and also, if anything, I would rather be the hero Don Quixote, and you can be the servant sidekick."

The doctor frowned, "Perhaps I didn't want to be a delusional old knight anyway." Dr Power was a psychiatrist. "And only the deluded go on pilgrimages."

The casual listener might conclude that Power was an agnostic at the very least, and that he was arguing with Lynch. However, Lynch was one of his oldest friends and both knew where, as far as they were both concerned, the fine line could be drawn between a teasing comment and an insult.

The conversation was being overheard by Lynch's wife, Pamela. She was familiar with the usual tenor of their conversation, and was smiling. She did not share Lynch's profound enthusiasm for the Christian faith, and sided more with his friend, Carl Power. Pamela had driven her husband to the airport and was waiting to say her goodbyes. Power's girlfriend, Laura, had dropped him off and kissed him goodbye as he unloaded his luggage. She had driven back to Power's Victorian house in Alderley Edge and nestled down in his bed again. There were still several hours of sleep to be had before she had to go to work. Pamela was hanging back though, because she desperately wanted to talk to Power, and preferably alone.

She played for time and looked up into the doctor's brown eyes. "If you can't bear religion I don't know how you will bear a walking pilgrimage to Santiago de . . ." she paused, uncertain of the name of the city that was her husband's ultimate goal.

"Santiago de Compostela," said Lynch, betraying the mildest hint of irritation. "In Galicia. It's the capital of Galicia. In Spain." He fixed her with a look that was almost a glare.

"Well," said Power, wondering again exactly why he had agreed to accompany his friend on the St James's Way, a cross-country walking trek across scores and scores of miles of baking Spanish countryside. "I suppose it's because . . ."

Lynch interrupted. "I'm going to the place," and walked off suddenly towards the toilets.

"It's because . . ." said Power.

"Never mind," said Pamela. She wasn't altogether interested in his friendly reasons for acquiescing to accompany her husband. Her opportunity had come to talk to Power alone. "I wanted to say something while he's gone. He's not right, and I want you to watch over him."

"What do you mean?" Power was taken aback.

"You saw him. He's being snappy with me. It's not like him. Andrew needs a break, I know that and I hope the time away with you does him good. But he's been so stressed by work. They never appreciate him. Never see what a talent they have amongst them."

"Andrew would probably have a Bible quote ready for that," said Power.

"You know him so well. I've been with him so long I can even say which Bible quote he'd use; 'A prophet is not without honour, save in his own country, and in his own house.' Anyway, as I say, forewarned is forearmed, Carl. So, now I've told you, will you look after him, please?"

"Of course," said Power. Over her shoulder he spied Lynch returning. "He's on his way back." He thought about the point at which Lynch had left the conversation. "And so, I thought I needed the exercise, really, some time off in the fresh air. Some good wine, some beer . . ."

". . . and knowing him," said Lynch, as he joined the two of them. "Carl will want some good food to go with the drink. Am I right?" Power nodded. "Listen, Pamela, we need to check in and go through security. I will say goodbye here." He hugged her and kissed her on the lips. She patted his arm and kissed him once more.

"You take care, Andrew. Look after each other, you two." Her eyes were tearing up, and to avoid a scene she smiled and, waving goodbye, turned on her heel and left.

"Right," said Lynch. "Let's check in and stow our luggage."

* * *

The hot August air hit Power in the face as he stepped off the plane. There was a smell of aerofuel, but also something else, possibly spice or incense, he was not sure. Power felt his back instantly beginning to perspire. He bought bottled water for them from a machine in the terminal building. Lynch waited by the luggage carousel. He had organized a minibus from Madrid Airport to take them and their baggage to Leon. The driver took them first to a city centre restaurant in Alcobendas, where Lynch dined on aromatic seafood broth and a whole buttery lobster. Power settled for a plate of grilled vegetables – tomato, peppers, onion and aubergine, with crisp, fresh bread.

They sheltered under a great awning, well out of the fierce mid-day sun, and drank a cold bottle of Rueda Verdejo and two large bottles of mineral water. There was cigar smoke drifting in the air from a gregarious party of the capital's business men. "This is the life," said Lynch, stretching out his long legs. "We have it all wrong in England. The Spanish have a long lunch, and then a siesta afterwards . . ." he grinned.

Power nodded, and sliced a purple fig into quarters and ate it as he sipped strong, scented coffee.

Lynch was suddenly distracted by four people at a table across the restaurant. Power followed his gaze. Three were eating hungrily, whilst the fourth, a decidedly thin young woman, was toying with her food and drinking from a goblet of wine far more than frequently than she was raising food to her lips.

"So thin," said Lynch. "Is she anorexic do you think?"

"I don't know," whispered Power, worried that Lynch's voice would carry and that his friend would be heard and understood. The English abroad had a misconception that the English language was something that rendered them audibly invisible. Because Power was a psychiatrist, others often asked him for opinions on other people's mental state that he couldn't realistically know. "She could be physically ill, or a model, or, yes, she might be anorexic."

"I'm sorry to point it out," said Lynch. "Whatever the cause, she looks ill to me."

Power nodded, "Well you're right, she looks a mite too thin. Did you know that female film stars have only sixteen per cent body fat? And that around twenty-two per cent is needed to have normal periods."

"Why on earth are we discussing this?" asked Lynch, mopping up the butter sauce on his plate with some left over bread.

"Because you brought up the subject of anorexia," said Power, "and because our world encourages women to have body-shapes that are not compatible with normal physiology. Although, I think anorexia nervosa is more of a biological illness and less a consequence of the fashion fascists."

Lynch grunted assent and pushed his squeaky clean plate away.

"So, now we are here, have we officially started on our quest, then?" asked Power.

"No, our pilgrimage starts in Leon, not Madrid. After we visit the office of the Friends of St James in Leon tomorrow; that's when we start, and it's where we pick up our *Credencial*. It's like a Pilgrim's Passport. We start there in Leon. Other people start in France, or Portugal. It all depends. And actually, I suppose the St James's Way could even start outside your own front door. So there are an infinite number of ways to do the Way, but everything ends at the Cathedral of Santiago de Compostela. The journey we all take is called the Camino, and tomorrow we're starting our walk along the oldest route of all."

Their white Mercedes minivan was waiting in the shade under some trees outside the restaurant. The grey-haired driver held open the door and nodded to them. "Did you enjoy lunch?"

"Yes," said Power, climbing into the middle seat, and realising that he didn't know he asked the driver "What's your name?"

"Patxi," said the driver, and after Lynch had climbed in, slid the door to with a clang. Patxi went round to the left of the vehicle and got into the driver's seat. "The name is Basque. I speak English little.

I take you to Hotel Leon tonight. The guide joins us tomorrow. We stop on the way at Uruena."

"How long is the drive to Madrid?" asked Lynch.

"Three hours," and with this Patxi gunned the engine into life and the Mercedes sped off along the afternoon streets of Madrid.

The outskirts of the city did not last long and soon they were on a motorway flanked on each side either by plains of sun-dried, dark brown vegetation or occasional vineyards. Large red spiders of iron pipework stood amongst rows of green vines to water them. "Our wine at lunchtime came from round here," said Lynch, and closed his eyes to snooze. Power looked out over the vineyards to the horizon where the land met the bluest of skies. The late afternoon was sliding into early evening when Patxi turned off the motorway and down a winding side road.

"Are we there yet?" asked Power, mindful of how he sounded like a child.

"Over halfway," said Patxi. "We stop at this village. Walk. Maybe drink?"

He drew to a halt outside a wide sandy-coloured church. Its roofs were shallow and tiled and its walls were arranged around a central octagon with tall, curved bay walls. "I show you this," said Patxi. "It is called Nuestra Senora de la Anunciada."

"Our Lady of the Annunciation," said Power. "It looks like a Romanesque church."

"It looks like a Templar church," said Lynch, as he opened his eyes and surveyed the curved walls. Power and Lynch exited the minivan and Patxi urged them to walk around the wide, dusty yard that surrounded the church.

The two friends walked around the walls of the silent church. In the dark blue evening sky the sinking sun still shone, but now the pale white moon could also be seen as it rose. The air was still shimmering hot and the silence so profound that all Power could hear was the crunching of their feet on the gravelled ground and their breathing. In the distance on a hill was a walled town.

"That must be Uruena, the village Patxi mentioned," said Lynch. "It looks kind of Arabic. Well, I suppose maybe it was. Spain has flickered back and forth between Muslim and Christian." They came upon a plaque about the church, but the Spanish was beyond them. Power could discern something about the twelfth century. "That would fit with the Templar Knights," said Lynch. "They helped rout the Muslims out in the crusades to make the area safe for Christian pilgrims journeying south to Jerusalem." Leaving Power, Lynch began photographing the church and the walled town in the distance. He walked round the church clicking away with his camera, fascinated by the play of light and shadow on the various curved shapes.

Power was thus standing alone when he glimpsed a dark figure near the front doors of the church. His mood suddenly went from a feeling of sunny relaxation, to transfixed panic. His self-confidence disappeared like water running down a sheer wall of glass. Power felt his mouth open, but no sound came out. About a hundred yards away was a priest dressed in a black cassock and zucchetto. His hair was black and he wore an eye patch. His one eye caught sight of Power, and the two men – priest and doctor – simply stared at each other. Dr Power felt a deep coldness in his chest and he thought his legs would give way. The light mood of the evening had turned raven black.

It was the priest who moved first. He moved suddenly, like a fleeting shadow and was absorbed into the darkness of the church. The church doors slammed to, shattering the peace of the evening like a shot ringing out. The birds took flight in a flapping, scattering panic from their resting place in the nearby trees.

Power charged towards the church, shouting as he ran, "Andrew!"

Lynch heard the alarm in his friend's voice and hurried round the church. He arrived just in time to see Power running up the step to the doors and flinging them wide open. For a second time the crashing of the doors echoed across the churchyard and Patxi, standing by the Mercedes, looked up with a frown.

By the time Lynch ran into the cool interior of the church Power had had time to search round inside. Power stood alone, his face and body as white and still as marble. And yet he was trembling. "It was Cousins," he whispered.

"Who was?"

"Didn't you see the priest? It was Cousins."

"But Cousins is dead," said Lynch.

"Didn't you see?" asked Power.

Lynch shook his head. "I was at the back of the church."

They were joined by Patxi, who could see something was wrong. "What happened?"

Power looked around. The interior walls were as simple as the stonework outside. There was an altar with a Virgin Mary dressed up in a silken blue material. An array of flickering red electric candles. But apart from the trio of Lynch, Power and Patxi the church was empty. "Did you see the priest, Patxi?"

"Sorry. I look at the map." Patxi looked around the empty church and shrugged. "Maybe we should go and get some water? A drink?"

They drove up the hill to the walled town of Uruena in silence. Power looked at his hands; they still shook, a visible reminder of his fear.

Patxi drove inside the town gates and parked by the walls. "Let's go, there is a small café still open," said Patxi. He took them along the Moorish walls to a bar, which seemed to double as a social centre for the hundred or so villagers still left in the hill town. There was a patio inside the building. They sat there and Lynch ordered them all some coffee and water.

"Would you like something stronger, Carl?" asked Lynch. "Some brandy or something?"

"Maybe I shouldn't, but maybe I will. Yes."

They brought Power brandy, and strong sweet coffee. Lynch swigged down a full bottle of water. "It was Cousins," said Power softly, almost himself.

"A ghost maybe? A shadow you saw?" asked Patxi, mindful of the emptiness of the church.

Power looked up and saw the concern in his companions' eyes. "I saw someone, a priest. He had black hair, an eyepatch."

"Which eye?" asked Lynch.

"The left, of course."

Lynch nodded. "But Cousins is dead. The injuries he sustained were life threatening. The damage you did to him. The blood he lost. He couldn't have survived."

"He managed to walk away," said Power.

"There is no trace of him surviving," said Lynch. "After Toronto there is no trace. A man cannot hide. Not with the injuries he had. He would have had to receive medical help immediately to survive, and he didn't attend any hospital. He would have died – inevitably. He has been at the bottom of the lake, feeding fishes, for the last three years."

"I wouldn't just imagine seeing him," said Power, irritably.

"And how would he know we were here?" asked Lynch. "Why would he follow us? Revenge?"

"He looked as surprised as I was," said Power. "He ran."

"I have had police keeping an eye out for him worldwide for three years," said Lynch. "Not a trace."

"We recognised each other," said Power.

"Look, drink up and we'll get to our hotel in Leon. Put some miles between the church and us. Whoever it was, he can't possibly follow us. He can't know our plans. We'll put a barrier of distance between him and us. You've got me with you, Carl. I will keep you safe."

Power smiled to himself and nodded. He thought it was ironic that he had promised Lynch's wife that he would look after Lynch. Here was Lynch offering to look after Power. Power reasoned that there was nothing he could do, but follow Lynch's advice. Whoever or whatever he had seen near the church he couldn't change what had happened.

As they left the social club, Power noticed that the men sat playing cards in the room with the bar on one side of the café, whilst the women sat separately in another room. It looked like the women were making some kind of quilt.

As they walked to the car Lynch pointed up at the night sky to try and distract the doctor. Darkness had fallen whilst they were in the café and the stars were out. A vast and elliptical swathe of stars stretched across the heavens. "The Milky Way," said Lynch. "Ancient pilgrims sometimes walked the Way of St James by the light of the Milky Way, and they called the Way the road of stars."

Power looked up and nodded thoughtfully. "It's beautiful."

"The Creation," said Lynch.

After Power climbed into the van, Patxi held Lynch back and closed the door to. From inside Power could see Lynch talking to the driver and surmised that the topic of the conversation was him. Power sighed and looked back up at the stars and tried to ignore everything else.

"Señor Lynch? Your friend. Is he all right? He was scared."

"He's fine now. Maybe it's been too hot for him, Patxi? Look, he was involved in something a few years back. There was a shooting. A man called Cousins shot the person he was with and then turned the gun on my friend, Dr Power. He had to fight to defend himself against the gunman. He thought he saw that man again outside the church. But I'm sure that the man died. It was an illusion, I think."

"Maybe a ghost?" Patxi returned to his previous theory.

Lynch shook his head. "No, I think we are both tired and too hot after our journey. We were up early. We need some sleep."

"Si," said Patxi. "I will get you to your hotel."

Power was quiet in the Mercedes as they left the walled town. To get back to the motorway they had to pass the ancient church. It was wrapped in shadow now, and Power could hardly bear to look, but his eyes searched the gloom for a glimpse of his old adversary. 'Is this what it means to be haunted?' Power wondered.

Chapter Two

Give me my scallop-shell of quiet,
My staff of faith to walk upon,
My scrip of joy, immortal diet,
My bottle of salvation,
My gown of glory, hope's true gage,
And thus I'll take my pilgrimage.

Sir Walter Raleigh,
The Passionate Man's Pilgrimage (1604)

D r Power was glad that the night had passed and that dawn was upon him. The morning sunlight filtered through the curtains of his room at the parador in Leon. The sun gave everything in the room an orange glow. Power went out on to the iron balcony and watched the city awakening. Cars and bicycles flowed round a roundabout carrying the morning commuters. Palm trees nodded in the breeze.

Power had felt troubled physically and mentally through the hours of darkness and this puzzled him for the room was both comfortable and beautiful, full of dark wood and a glossy parquet floor. His bed was sumptuous with drapes and numerous red cushions. The impression was one of gothic elegance. The door's massive iron lock, and equally heavy key, suggested fortress-like defence to keep infidel intruders at bay. A mild aroma of expensive cigars pervaded the atmosphere. The bathroom was majestic with a noble bath, almost so long Power could have swum up and down in it. No, Power couldn't fault the setting, but he had found the mattress cripplingly hard. His hips ached.

When he had managed to drop off to sleep he had been plagued with dreams of his last encounter with the assassin Cousins. The nightmare was a recurrent one and so vivid. The colour red featured throughout. The feelings of fear and anger were still palpable. He recalled the scent of the woman he had been dining with. The sound of the shot usually woke him. Power recalled his hatred for the man and his revenge for the murder of his lunch companion. Only by the Grace of God had Power been spared. So for the majority of the night Power had lain awake. To add insult to injury he could hear Lynch in the bedroom next door, snoring contentedly all the way through the night.

Power ran a deep bath and rested his bones in the tub. He dressed in clothes he imagined might be suitable for walking about the city on a hot day. In the morning light his fears were receding and he, too, found it difficult to credit that he had seen any priest the night before, let alone seen Cousins, a man returned from the dead.

The paradors in Spain are state-run hotels based in old castles or monasteries. The parador in Leon had once been the Monastery of San Marcos. Power left his room at six thirty. He passed Lynch's room on the carpeted corridor. Distant snoring could still be heard through the door. Power grimaced as he passed a vast number of paintings of bulls, bull fighting and matadors in the corridors. Power had been vegetarian for several years. He found the pictures somehow alien, from a different culture – out of place, out of time and distasteful.

He wandered lofty stone corridors, with their walkways and balconies overlooking verdant courtyards and gardens. On an upper floor he found himself in a Library with many oversized picture books and books of botany. The Library had a small balcony which overlooked a truly precipitous drop into the nave of a church. The walls of the church were encrusted with stone scallop shells. A nearby plaque informed him that the balcony enabled nobles to participate in the church services just as much as they wished, or read in the library and chapel. Power thought this was probably an ideal way of attending church.

Power descended to the ground floor and walked round a stone path on the periphery of a garden with trees and shrubs. The leaves were slick and bejewelled with drops of water that shone in the morning sunlight. Power was warming to the day. A nearby statue, set on a massive balustrade, loomed over him and he read that this was St James, apostle and eponymous saint of the Way. Power patted the saint's foot, which he felt was smooth from the touch of thousands of previous pilgrims.

A small photograph on the wall caught his eye. A nearby plaque in the shade described a poet who had been imprisoned in the Monastery in nineteen thirty-six for his affiliation to the labour movement. He had been tortured and seen other prisoners starved and killed. Reading this in the shadow, Power shuddered. All of the hotel bedrooms had once been prison cells. He suddenly realised that the massive iron locks on his bedroom door had not been installed with the intention of keeping residents safe; not intended to keep burglars at bay, but instead had been installed in the nineteen-thirties to immure political prisoners.

Another plaque described how the Monastery had once been a hospital from the twelfth century owned by the Knights of the Order of Saint James (or Santiago) providing hospitality and medical care to pilgrims on The Way. Further still another plaque described how the burial place of St James and his own disciples had been found in the ninth century in a wood under a strange light that hovered in the sky. The bones were now in the Cathedral of Santiago de Compostela.

"There you are," said a voice nearby. The voice echoed in the cloister area. Power looked over to see his friend, Lynch. "Are you ready for breakfast?"

Power looked at his watch and saw he'd been mooching about the parador for hours. "I am a bit hungry, yes."

"Come on then," said Lynch, and the pair set off towards the dining room.

"I've been looking round. The hotel, the monastery, is incredibly old. Eight hundred years, or thereabouts. These corridors have seen knights, monks, nuns, nurses, doctors, prisoners, and jailers. It's like all that history is crowded together here. If we could see them all, if everything was collapsed into one time, just imagine.

"Like in the poem by Masefield:

And this I ask and fain would know;
Will Now be in a day or so?
Is this-time-next-year Now or no?
Or did Now happen long ago,
Long, long ago?

"Do you ever feel that, sometimes, every event from past and future and present is here . . . all in one place?"

"No," said Lynch, with a definite edge to his voice. "I am starving and the only event I want at this time of day is breakfast. I slept like a log, did you?"

"Not quite," said Power, deciding to keep his unpleasant dreams to himself. "But I am hungry."

"You are always hungry, my friend," said Lynch, as he led the way to the buffet.

They met their guide and interpreter at ten o'clock outside a café some way from the hotel. Lynch and Power had sat down at a table in the sun and were enjoying a café solo. They were listening to the local music as it floated out of the café. They were joined there by Mr Delgado. He was slim and dark, and in many ways resembled Carl

Power. Lynch introduced him to his friend. "This is Mr Delgado. He came highly recommended by the Deacon at Chester Cathedral. She had walked some of the Way with him herself. Mr Delgado will spend some of the time with us, but we will have to do most of the walking alone. I think we can handle that."

"But the driver will pick us up between the walks, won't he?" Power sounded somewhat anxious.

"Sometimes," said Lynch, who had masterminded the itinerary. "We must do a lot of the walking ourselves. We can't cheat too much, you know."

"That wouldn't do at all," said Mr Delgado. Power felt aggrieved that the guide was siding with Lynch. He wouldn't have minded rather more travelling in the Mercedes van and rather less walking. "In order to be a proper pilgrim you must walk a full one hundred and twenty kilometres at least. That way we can end properly in Santiago."

"One hundred and twenty kilometres! We're walking that much?" asked Power.

"Don't worry, our driver, Patxi, will be there when you need him. Mr Lynch has planned a clever route. I will be walking with you three days, and four days you will walk alone. You should manage twenty kilometres a day easily, I think." This sounded rather a lot to Dr Power. "And remember, every kilometre you do is a few years off purgatory; that is the deal, as they say. And we are going to the edge of the world, did you know that? The Medieval pilgrims also thought that Santiago was as good as the edge of the world. Beyond the sea at the coast nearby, well there was nothing. They perhaps felt like space travellers, at the edge of reality, no?" he laughed and stood up. "I will just go and make a telephone call, to make sure of our welcomes. You are by the city walls here," Mr Delgado pointed out a slightly tumbledown wall of yellow stone, perhaps twenty feet high.

"You are from Chester, yes, a Roman city?" Lynch nodded. "That is our Roman wall here in Leon. This walk we do is an old, old way; an old Roman road as you will see. And the music you are listening to here. You are enjoying it?"

"Yes," said Power. "Quite lively – I suppose it's local music?"

"By a group called Café Quijano. The owner of this café," he pointed to the café where they were sitting. "He is father of one of the group." And with that Mr Delgado walked off – just half a dozen yards or so and began to make a phone call on his mobile.

Power turned to Lynch, he wondered if he had time to find out about Lynch's wife, Pamela's, concerns – to explore what was troubling Lynch. He had noticed an edge to Lynch – a shortness in his response to some of their conversation in the last twenty-four hours, which was quite unlike his friend. "Something I've been meaning to ask you, Andrew, what is the real reason you wanted to come on this pilgrimage. The pilgrimage is a Catholic thing and you are Church of England. I mean, it's great to be here and everything, and I get the idea of a pilgrimage being good for the soul, but why this, why now?"

"Well," said Lynch, regarding Power somewhat circumspectly out of the corner of his eye. "Well, I will tell you, if you promise to withhold any of your secular snarking." Again, a slight bitterness was evident in Lynch's tone, something that was alien.

"Very well," said Power quietly, and with a reassuring smile. "No snarking. Promise."

"Firstly, I suppose I have to correct you. The pilgrimage pre-dates the split with Rome in fifteen thirty-one. So it is a Christian 'thing' as you might put it. I have wanted to make this pilgrimage for many years and want to do it before I am too old. It is physically quite demanding – walking twenty or thirty kilometres a day – so it's a physical challenge and a spiritual challenge, or a psychological one you might prefer to say. The Way is a metaphor for life – beginning, birth; adolescence, the middle of the journey; and the end of the journey, well that's death. It's all about how you live your life – a symbolic matter from start to finish. And it follows the path of one of the Saviour's own disciples; James and *his* own two disciples. Walking in the apostle St James's footsteps brings you closer to the Lord himself."

He sighed, and suddenly looked older and greyer. "And I need this now, Carl, because, well, I feel so weak, both spiritually and at heart."

"You feel disheartened?" said Power.

"Very much so," said Lynch. "My work has become a thankless task. A chore. To my superiors I am an expensive dinosaur ready for retirement, and that retirement would rid them of having to pay my annual salary, and to my juniors I know I am mocked as a religious zealot, an anachronism in today's world of the Internet and faithless folk who only believe in celebrity and money. My faith is not shared by such people and my loyalty to the Law and my methods of upholding it are despised. So, you can see, after years of living this way, of being a fish swimming against the direction that the shoal is swimming in, my spirit is in need of some refreshment."

Before Dr Power could ask any further questions, Mr Delgado returned, beaming. "They can see us now, have you finished your *café solos*?"

They set off in something of a rush; certainly before Power had been able to respond to Lynch's disclosure and even before he had ascertained their destination. The trio hurried along the bakingly hot pavements of Leon to a street called Av. Independencia. They ducked into a small shadowy hallway where a guard was sitting in a cubicle behind glass. The guard slid open a window and began a long conversation with Mr Delgado. Power was grateful for the shade of the hallway, but he could not understand the machine gun spatter of words between the guard and their guide. He nudged Lynch's shoulder. "What are we doing here?"

"We are visiting the Friends of the Santiago Way. They will give us our Pilgrim's Passports and set us on our way."

"Passports?" asked Power.

"Pilgrim's Passports," repeated Lynch. "Didn't I tell you? They are called *Credencials* and will enable us to chronicle the journey – we get them stamped at places along the Way – and they will prove that we are genuine pilgrims when we stay in the albergues; they are like hostels. Not as grand as our parador, but somewhere to rest our weary bones at the end of a day's walking. And we can't get in unless we prove we are genuine."

"Well, sort of genuine," said Power. "I'm sure you're not allowed lifts in vans like we are doing."

Lynch harrumphed. "I think you will find that we are doing plenty of walking. It's three hundred kilometres to Santiago de Compostela, and we will be doing about half of it, which technically is enough. The full walk from Southern France is over seven hundred kilometres and would take us weeks. We have about eight full days."

Mr Delgado interrupted. He was standing in the lift at the end of the corridor and was beckoning them to follow. Obediently they both got into the lift and stood crowded together in the cramped quarters as they ascended to the fifth floor.

The Friends of the Santiago Way resided in a small office. Power and Lynch were sat down as guests of honour by two smiling volunteers who introduced themselves, via their interpreter/guide, Mr Delgado, as the Chairman and Secretary of the Society. Power and Lynch nodded and smiled when it appeared necessary, but much of the rapid conversation in Spanish was unknown to them. Maps of the Way were brandished and there was discussion of the stages of the walk, facilities available along the way, and sage advice given on clothing, hats, walking staffs and water carriers. Mr Delgado vouched for them as honest pilgrims and Christian men. Eventually, for a small donation, folded card Pilgrim's Passports were filled in with names and addresses and solemnly handed over to Power and Lynch. They were each given a small scallop shell to attach to their rucksacks; a further symbol of the Way. Power looked at his Passport, his *Credencial del Peregrino*. He saw his address, Alderley House, Macclesfield Road, Alderley Edge. There was a blue stamp, the first one already in the Passport, an stamped impression of a scallop shell with a lion in it.

"Every place has it's own logo on it's stamp," said Mr Delgado. "All the places on the Way – albergues, hotels, bars, cafes . . . you can record your progress."

"*The Pilgrim's Progress,*" joked Lynch, smiling. "Like Bunyan."

"I believe that the full title of the Bunyan book is, *The Pilgrim's Progress from This World to That Which Is to Come,*" said Power. "Which is a bit forbidding."

"It depends where you're going, I suppose. Up or down." said Lynch.

The ex-President of the Society had decided to join them to impart his additional wisdom. There was more conversation about the imperative need to wear hats under the sun, to travel early in the day, not to carry too much, to be careful about the road markings (there were apparently yellow arrows painted everywhere), to verify your position on the map every so often and to use Vaseline.

"Vaseline!?" exclaimed Power. "Did he say Vaseline?"

"Si," said Mr Delgado. "Vaseline for between the legs. To stop rubbing. Most important. Also to always take care of the feet. The least pain, stop immediately, inspect, correct the problem. You don't want blisters or worse."

"Hmm, said Power. "Thank you for that. Prudent advice for the soul, mind and body."

Eventually, Mr Delgado and the two initiated pilgrims stood to leave. There were smiles and jokes. There was laughter and hand shaking and even hugs. Then they were out of the Society's office and away to lunch. As a concession to Power's vegetarianism Mr Delgado had located probably the only vegetarian tapas bar in the whole of Spain. They dined on small earthenware mugs of gazpacho soup, egg roll tapas, tortilla de patata, and fragrant stuffed peppers. They quaffed Zerep Tostada beer and commended its nutty brown flavour and Power insisted they drank a bottle of mineral water each. "It's important to keep hydrated," he preached. The guide disappeared for a moment with their Pilgrim's Passports and returned brandishing them with pride. "Look," he said. "I got them stamped for you." The tapas bar owner had stamped their Passports. "You can build up a whole lot. The hotel will stamp for you in the morning." Power looked at the stamp. There was a big, green 'V' in a circle stamped with the name of the bar.

"Well," said Mr Delgado, looking at his phone. "It is time to move on, the museum has opened. We have a schedule to follow if you are to make the service."

"A church service?" asked Power. He noticed Lynch glowering at him.

"Señor Lynch wanted to attend the service in the Cathedral. The Pilgrims' Service. To bless the pilgrims on their Camino, on the Way. We have enough time to tour the museum and the Basilica vaults beforehand."

"No siesta?" asked Power. Again he felt Lynch's glare. Mr Delgado looked puzzled. "Just joking," said Power. In view of Lynch's earlier conversation with him, Power deemed it wisest to conform with his friend's program. However, the thought of any church service simply did not appeal to Power, who was, at best, an agnostic. They got up and started walking. Power tagged along behind Lynch and the guide as they chatted. He wondered about phoning Laura and home.

They stopped off in a row of shops and tried hats on. Lynch snorted when the guide suggested some baseball caps and chose a white cotton hat with a wide floppy brim. Lynch put it on and modelled it, catching Power's look of disbelief in the shop's mirror. "It's not a fashion choice. It is a logical, practical choice. The white will reflect the sun's rays. The wide brim will cast enough shadow to protect my neck. The cotton is a natural and cool material." Power found a similar one and tried it on himself. He supposed it didn't look too bad, and Lynch's argument about practicality was something he could accept. They bought two. Next they sought two walking staffs and bottles of sun block. They stood outside the shops, adorned with hats and staffs. Mr Delgado clapped his hands. He affixed the small scallop shells they had been given earlier to their rucksacks. "Now you are true pilgrims."

With hat and staff, Power made his way self-consciously along the streets of Leon behind Lynch and the guide. To his surprise people now greeted them with the phrase 'Buen camino' to which the guide conscientiously replied 'Buena vida'.

"What is being said?" asked Power.

The guide turned to him. "'Buen camino' means 'Good way'. They are wishing you a good pilgrimage. And 'Buena vida', my reply, means 'Have a good life'."

Power smiled, "Oh that's nice, I like that." He was beginning to warm to his new role as a pilgrim.

Somewhere on the journey between there and the Cathedral, Power became lost in his own thoughts. His meditation was broken only by the realisation that he was standing with Lynch and Mr Delgado in some kind of vault probably under the Cathedral. He had no recall of the journey into the Cathedral's belly. Or was it a Basilica. His consciousness suddenly returned to him and he looked up at the vivid frescoes on the curved ceiling of the vaults. The guide noticed that Power was suddenly taking an interest in the paintings. "They are Romanesque, Dr Power. There is a depiction over here on this wall of the months and seasons of the year – what Medieval people did in Autumn – gathering in the harvest, salting meat and fish, and here you see the snows and thorns of Winter."

Power realised he was also standing by some kind of sarcophagus. "What's this?"

Mr Delgado looked patiently at Power. Hadn't he just explained this to Mr Lynch? "This is the burial place of the Kings of Leon. The Kings established a Benedictine Convent here, on the remains of a Temple to Mercury."

"Ah," said Power. He fumbled in his pocket for a camera, but a custodian nearby shook her finger at him as he brought the camera out. Chastened he replaced it in his pocket.

"Above us, here, is a fresco of Christ seated in a mandorla, look at the vivid blues, browns and yellows. And there, Dr Power is Luke. Specially for you."

Power looked blankly at one of four figures floating round Christ. Mr Delgado seemed to be pointing to that. Lynch leaned close to Power's ear so as not to embarrass his medical friend. "Luke wrote one of the four gospels. He was a doctor, Carl. That's why Mr Delgado is pointing him out to you."

"Ah," said Dr Power, nodding and trying to look as if he had really understood all along. "Of course, of course."

"Goodness," whispered Lynch. "You are a heathen. Luke wrote the Gospel of Luke, hence the figure is carrying a book. He was Greek physician who lived in Syria and he was probably a disciple of St Paul. His symbol was the bull, hence the bull's head on the figure."

"Was he crucified?" asked Power. "A lot of the disciples were, weren't they?"

"No, he lived until he was eighty-four," said Lynch. He died in Greece and his bones went to Constantinople."

Power grunted assent and drifted off to look at a pillar. He liked the carving at the top.

"The carving is Visigoth," said the guide, as he sidled up beside Power. "So many cultures have been here in this place, Roman, Visigoth, Arab . . ."

The guide then took them through a Library with illuminated manuscripts and a stone chamber with an illuminated chalice. "They say that this *is* the Holy Grail," he said. "The cup is that one – you can see the carved brown material and it was quite simple once. The gold filigree and jewels have been added on top. They say that Stephen Spielberg came here to research his films. You know the films with Harrison Ford in?" Power nodded.

Next, Mr Delgado took them to see some paintings. Some were on religious themes with devils roasting evil priests, or torturing monks by unravelling their intestines from their bodies on hand wound spools. One was a portrait of a tall, distinguished man, with curly brown hair, a pointed beard and soulful brown eyes. He wore a white gown with a black tunic. A red cross was emblazoned on this. It looked more like a sword pointing downwards.

"It is a Knight," said Mr Delgado. "He is wearing the red cross of St James. So he is a Knight of the Order of St James. It was a religious order but they were warriors too. They fought for Christ, not symbolically, but actually with weapons. Spain was a Muslim country once and even when things headed back toward Christianity the Christian pilgrims were still killed on the road by Muslims. The Knights' job was to fight and protect the pilgrims. They kept a corridor of one hundred and fifty miles wide free of Muslims so that the innocent Christian pilgrims could travel safely. Tell me, have you ever seen a painting of the Spanish Court by Velazquez?"

"I think so," said Power, who liked to fancy himself as a cultured man. "Doesn't it have a young princess in it, with a huge white dress and dogs?"

"Yes," said Mr Delgado. "That is the Infanta Margaret. There is a reproduction of the painting here, on this wall. See?"

A small reproduction of the sixteen fifty-six painting hung nearby. Power saw it was called *Las Meninas*.

"It is such a famous painting, there is so much hidden in it. There is the dwarf, here a jester. And over here in the mirror drawn at the back? There is a couple reflected in the mirror. They are thought to be the King Phillip and his wife looking on. And of course over here on the left is the artist, the painter himself, Velazquez, portraying himself painting the picture. He has put himself in the painting, looking straight at us, looking back at him. It's like everything collapsing in on itself."

Power looked up at this unusual phrase.

"Do you see anything else in the painting about Velazquez?"

Power looked hard. "He has the red cross of a Knight on his chest too."

"Yes, he was made a Knight, but only after his death. It is said that the King himself painted the red cross onto the painting. Velazquez was a very dear friend to the King. The Order of St James was a very noble Order. Like the Templars, all the Knights were of noble origins. And the Order has lasted for nearly eight hundred years."

"It is still going?" asked Lynch.

"Sort of," said Mr Delgado. "It was disbanded by the Republics. The last time in nineteen thirty-one. But when the Monarchy returned in nineteen seventy-five the Order was restored. But there are only a handful of Knights now, and they are all old and feeble, rich and noble."

They went up to the exit and gift shop. Lynch wandered about looking for books in English. Power sat down and his eyes were immediately taken with two young women. One had very tight and scanty denim shorts, which revealed soft brown skin that he could not help but look at, admiring curves and so on. There was a cough. Power looked up. Lynch was looking at him. "Eyes right, soldier." Power opened his mouth to protest. "I was asked to look after you, and I will," said Lynch.

"Can't I even look?" Power protested.

"No," said Lynch. "They are too young for you. You could be their father."

"I don't think so," said Power in a slightly hurt voice, trying to do the maths to back his argument up.

"Still," said Lynch, beginning to head over to the cashier's counter. "I will leave you with your conscience. You know I'm right."

Power was left wondering about who exactly was going through some mid-life crisis. Was it his friend Lynch or himself? He had never thought of himself as being too old for a person he was attracted to. Maybe he was getting old? Pamela had been worried about her husband Andrew's crisis. Maybe Power's own midlife crisis was brewing up its own storm.

The guide, Mr Delgado, left them outside the Basilica. He gave them advice about breakfasting and rising early to begin their walk. About taking enough water. About where they would meet next. He gave them cards with his number on in case of emergency, and was gone.

Lynch and Power went to a bar and had two glasses of wine, Ederra Rioja Crianza, with some glasses of water. "He does jabber on," said Lynch, about their guide. "But you do miss him when he's gone."

They walked over to the Cathedral, and for a moment spent their time staring at the carvings over the door, wondering what they meant and sorely missing the guide's interpretation now he was gone.

"I think," said Lynch. "They represent the division between the sons of Abraham. To the left we have Isaac's family – Isaac was his son by Sarah. To the right we have Ishmael, his son by Hagar. The two brothers did not get on. And both had their own nations, and the division is at the root of so much . . ."

They passed back into the Cathedral, where other pilgrims were gathering for the daily service held for the pilgrims, to bless them and their Journey.

Power sat in a pew with his friend and was as patient, silent and unquestioning as he could be, so that he did not ruin the experience for Lynch. He flicked through a Spanish Bible and a prayer book, seemingly printed in Latin, and tried his very best not to sigh or fidget. When he looked up the service had begun and he watched the small choir and the priests moving about with detached interest. He understood nothing. Power looked at Lynch and wondered how much sense it meant to a staunch English Protestant. Maybe Lynch was feigning understanding?

The Mass continued in Latin. The droning sound was both soothing and perplexing. The priest was doing something on the altar that Power could not see and he felt frustrated at this. He could not bear the silence and the not knowing any more.

"I feel like a fish out of water," he whispered to Lynch. "What is going on?"

The priest suddenly turned round from the altar and, half chanting and half singing his Latin, continued the liturgy. Power looked at the young priest. He took in the priest's vestments, his outstretched arms, and then Power looked at his face.

His face was fair and his hair was blonde. He had blue eyes. Power gasped audibly and gripped Lynch's arm. "Look at his face, the features. He's the image of Cousins."

Lynch gave Power what could only be described as 'a look', half alarmed and half incredulous. Lynch looked at the priest as closely as his middle-aged eyes would allow and snorted derisively. "Firstly, he has blonde hair and Cousins had black hair," Lynch hissed. "Secondly, he has blue eyes and Cousins had brown eyes. And thirdly, the priest has *two* eyes, and Cousins lost one, as you know. And finally, Cousins is, as far as I and every police force in the northern hemisphere know, almost certainly dead."

"But his features," insisted Power. "He looks like Cousins."

"He's a bit far away," said Lynch. "But he doesn't look like the photographs of Cousins that I saw."

"Maybe not quite," conceded Power, after further study. "But all the same. . ." Someone in front turned and shushed Power and put their finger to their lips. Power ceased talking and looked remorsefully at the stone-flagged floor. Perhaps Lynch was right. He looked up at the priest again, but by now he had turned his back on the congregation. The priest's blonde hair looked natural enough. It didn't look as if it was dyed. His voice sounded nothing like Cousins. The accent was vaguely Irish. Southern Irish if anything, thought Power. He watched the priest as he turned and this time he could see this was not Cousins's face. Power began to feel foolish. And yet, when the priest looked at the congregation his expression was all self-assurance. 'More like a television presenter, than a priest,' thought Power. 'Worldly-wise.' He mused on the point, but decided against engaging Lynch in a discussion about the priest, who seemed to radiate self-confidence to the point of arrogance.

The Pilgrims' Service seemed very long to Power, but at the end Lynch assured him it had only been three quarters of an hour. With difficulty Power made the decision to hold any comments about the service in check, but Lynch seemed happy to talk.

"Thank you for coming along, I know it must have seemed like purgatory to you, Carl."

"Well," said Power. "As long as you enjoyed it. Do you feel better for the blessing?"

"I do," said Lynch. "Despite the oddness of hearing the Latin used. And as far as purgatory is concerned, you can relax. Every mile walked on the Way counts for several years off your time in limbo, I believe."

"I thought limbo and purgatory were different," said Power. "One is for the unborn, or am I wrong?"

"To tell you the truth, I'm not an expert on that. The ideas are not Protestant. Are you hungry? I'm just asking, because you always seem to be?"

"Well, you're wrong again," said Power. "I think I had one too many tapas before and I am quite full."

"Good," said Lynch. "Then we can get an early night for tomorrow's walk. Get up and walking before the sun gets too hot." They started walking across the city towards the parador, The Monastery. Power saw it in the distance. It was dusk now, and the classical façade was brilliantly lit.

They entered the vast entrance lobby side by side; the immense hall resembled some great castle, with a flight of stairs in the distance that seemed to ascend into the heavens. Lynch patted Power's shoulder as they climbed the stairs. "I hope you get some rest, and don't dream about Cousins. He seems to be playing on your mind. Everything's safe. The priest here was just a boring priest, virtuous and bland. Don't worry. Get a good sleep. Tomorrow we walk!"

Chapter Three

Footfalls echo in the memory
Down the passage which we did not take
Towards the door we never opened
TS Eliot – The Four Quartets

Lucia was brought out of the cellar just before evening. She had spent two days and nights there and had finally given in through hunger. She promised to be a good girl, as she always did, to escape the stone cell. She was given food and water to drink. After downing these she toyed with the idea of being awkward and asking to go back to the cellar, but Lucia knew that any new phase of imprisonment would last longer, maybe even three days to punish her for lying about her contrition.

She had sat at the kitchen table and eaten her bread and soup hungrily and somewhat noisily, to the disapproval of Sister Ambrosia. The sister tutted and wagged her finger at Lucia. Lucia deliberately left a few slices of bread untouched. She didn't want to get back to her normal weight. There was no point in looking well or desirable.

Sister Ambrosia said the words that she dreaded to hear. "Father Bruce is asking for you. He wants to talk to you about your behaviour."

"Must I really, Sister? I have apologized to you and the other sisters. I am so very sorry for my disobedience to you."

"And what about your disobedience towards Father Bruce? How will apologizing to me make any difference to him?" Sister Ambrosia had a young face, but her skin was paper dry. Lucia imagined reaching out to her face and plunging her nails into it and tearing the papyrus skin apart.

"Oh, Sister, please. I will do anything you ask. I will scrub the floors and peel the potatoes all week. I will wash the clothes of everyone in the household. I will . . ."

Sister Ambrosia slapped Lucia hard on her face. Twice to underline her point.

"Enough! That's enough of your scheming. Devious girl. We all have to do things that we don't like. Our duties cannot be neglected."

Lucia thought of an answer, but kept it to herself. She held her reddening cheek.

"Father Bruce is a nice, kind man. Hasn't he worked his fingers to the bone to raise the money to keep us all here? To afford us heat and light and food. Without him . . . where else would you be? The dirty, dirty streets?"

"He touches me. I don't like it."

"I will wash your mouth out with soap. Blackening his good reputation with your evil lies. It is you that is a vessel of lust, my girl. And a slut."

This time the blow to her head catapulted Lucia to the floor of the kitchen and the sister aimed a sensible-shoed kick to her belly.

"You don't say such lies to anyone. Anyone! Blackening a priest's name. It's blasphemy."

The nun was red-faced through emotion and a certain guilty pleasure at exacting such physical retribution. She leant down and slapped the girl twice again on the other cheek to feed her pleasure a little more. "Now, do you want to repeat what you said? If I ask you, does he touch you, what do you say?"

"I say nothing, Sister. I say nothing."

"And that would only be the truth, now, wouldn't it?" On the ground Lucia nodded once without making eye contact. "Now, get up off the floor and go and get washed and changed. You smell. I want you back down here in twenty minutes. Do not be late."

Lucia ran upstairs, but once out of the nun's eyeline she had to pause near the top through breathlessness. Her vision was all wavy from the blow to her head. In the bathroom she cried silent tears as she washed herself all over. One of the nuns had put some fresh underclothes and a linen smock and skirt on her bed. Two of the other girls were in the dormitory sitting and sewing the nuns' clothes. They looked up as Lucia came in. They made sympathetic eye contact, but did not speak a word to her lest they be overheard.

By the time Lucia was back in the kitchen there was a tray made ready by one of the other girls. It had the priest's supper on a white porcelain plate, still hot under a silver cover. A bottle of red Rioja stood unopened on the tray with a single glass. It was her job to take it into his lair.

* * *

Maria woke and the bed was cold. Dieter must have left early. She didn't recall when he'd gone. Daylight filtered through the net curtains. The light in Germany was thin and blue and depressing. Maria didn't like it.

She pulled a dressing-gown on and went into the kitchen. There was evidence of coffee having been made. Grounds were scattered in the sink, without care. Toast crumbs littered the work surface. It was as if he didn't care any more.

He had been spending less time with her. He blamed pressure of work. A big case.

Dieter complained about the food she kept in the flat. She remembered his rage when he came back after a long shift and disliked the fish stew she had made. There were still traces of it on the wall where he had thrown his plate. She thought about the nuns. The nuns would know how to remove the stain of his rage. Had she done anything wrong to provoke him? She thought back, and was unsure. She felt unsure a lot nowadays. She missed the other girls at the orphanage. She sometimes remembered Lucia and her rebellious ways. Maria wondered whether the nuns had broken her spirit yet?

One night Dieter had brought a 'colleague' home with him. They had drunk vodka and then both had expected to come into her bed. She tried to forget that night. He hadn't liked her reluctance. She was letting him down all over the place, he said.

No, it wasn't good, Maria thought. She made herself a coffee and curled up on the sofa she had pushed near the plate glass windows. She pulled a blanket over herself and watched the dull city outside beginning its day.

Chapter Four

Leon to Santibanez de Valdeiglesias
Thirty-one kilometres

If faith is unprovable by the intellect then it is impossible to be true
Ramon Llull

They were to start walking just after dawn. Power had found
Lynch praying in the church at the rear of the Monastery. He
was surrounded by his baggage, his staff and hat. Power did not
speak, but respected his friend's silence. Most of the church was in
gloom, but as Power waited for Lynch to come to a close he peered
around the church. His attention was taken by a large painting of St
James. St James was bearded and wearing a floppy brown hat and
red coat. He was riding a white horse and brandished a curved sword
or cutlass aloft. There was a symbolic scallop shell on his hat. The
horse was rearing, however, and under its hooves it trampled several
prostrate men.

Lynch, who had finished his prayers, joined Power. "That didn't
actually happen, said Lynch. "It is a depiction of what happened in
someone's dream. St James tried to spread Christianity in Spain, but
his mission did not succeed and he returned home. He was martyred
by being beheaded in Jerusalem in 44 AD. His bones were somehow
found and interred in Santiago. This portrait of him shows him
slaughtering Muslims, and I suppose reflects the battle between
Muslims and Christians for the soul of Spain."

"Whose dream was that?"

"I don't know," said Lynch. We'll have to ask. But the Order of St James was a group of Knights – like the Templars, who kept the route of the pilgrimage to Santiago safe for Christians. Safe from Muslim attacks."

"I don't know why people can't just get along," said Power. "Religions always seem to divide people."

"I think that is rather simplifying matters," said Lynch. "The holy books of each faith are incompatible, that's one thing . . ."

"Well, can't people get together and merge things, produce a compromise?"

"Syncretism," sighed Lynch. "It has been tried, Carl, and in fusing things from two religions you just produce a new, third belief-system that can be disagreed with by the fundamentalists of the first two."

"And the scallop shell," said Power, changing the subject. "What's that about?"

"The ancient pilgrims liked to go to the shores of Galicia, as far West as they could go, the edge of the World as far as anybody then knew and take a shell as a souvenir. And also, another story, the pattern on the shell is a metaphor. All those grooves on the shell, going to one destination. Like all the routes that pilgrims can travel going to the same destination, Santiago." Lynch gathered up his rucksack and staff. "I'm ready. Do you have everything?"

Power nodded. His stomach grumbled. "Don't we have time for breakfast? We have paid for it as part of the hotel . . ."

Lynch looked at his watch, it was just after six a.m. "No, we would waste too much time. The kitchens aren't open for another hour or so. Come on, we can eat on the way; the Friends gave up a list of villages with cafes in. They must have known you were coming and written it specially for you. We can get croissants and coffee."

And so they began striding out on the Way that passed westward directly in front of the Monastery. A group of early morning pilgrims standing in the square in front of the Monastery waved to Power and Lynch and wished them "Buen Camino!"

Smiling, Lynch answered back "Buena vida!" as they passed by.

The dawn streets were largely deserted and cool. Power noticed brass scallop shells set into the pavement. Occasionally, in a fork in the road there would be a yellow arrow in thick yellow paint on the ground or on a nearby wall. The small metal spikes of their staffs clicked on the pavements as they both paced forward.

"We will be on the outskirts of the city in a few miles," said Lynch. "By mid-morning I hope we will be in open country."

* * *

Lynch walked relentlessly, almost marching his way forwards along the Way. Power, although he was a younger man, lagged behind slightly at times to consult his watch and think about coffee and snacks. He wondered when he could phone Laura next. He missed her voice. They walked along paths by the side of busy roads at first, passing through small grey towns like Trobajo del Camino and Valverde de la Virgen. In time, though, the path broadened out and was alongside broad, brown fields and countryside. Power looked at unfamiliar trees – Spanish holm oak covered in acorns, and twisted, old chestnut trees.

The path passed through the middle of a dairy farm. Power stopped to fuss over baby calves in a nursery area, pulling handfuls of fresh grass to feed to them. Lynch leant on his staff and watched him soberly. In the distance there was a mad honking of a car horn. Power looked up.

"It's an arrival in the village down there, probably a delivery," said Lynch.

"I didn't notice a village," said Power, pushing more grass through the bars of the calves' enclosure. "How do you notice all this stuff?"

"I saw the steeple of the church through the trees," said Lynch. "And village deliveries often announce their arrival in the countryside. It could be bread, or meat, or fish, brought in a van. The local women will hear the van's horn and go and get what they need for the days ahead."

"Speaking of what food they need . . ." said Power.

"It's only eleven o'clock" said Lynch. "Too early for lunch, we've only done a few hours. We've got about ten kilometres to go at least before we stop for the night."

"We shouldn't do too much on the first day," said Power, hoping for a rest sooner rather than later.

"I know," said Lynch. "I've factored that into account. We do need to get to our destination fairly early to make sure we have a bed for the night, though. The albergue only has a limited number of cots. You can't book, it's first come, first served."

"What if it's full?" said Power, slightly horrified.

"We walk on to the next one. Don't worry, they are about every four or five kilometres."

Power stood up, thoughts of further petting the calves disappearing. "We'd better get on, then."

"Don't worry too much, Carl," said Lynch. "I've planned for us to have coffee or beer in the next village. We can re-fill our water bottles too."

And at the next village, San Miguel, they did pause at a bar. Lynch had coffee while Power treated himself to a beer. After their drink, Lynch insisted that they have their Pilgrim's Passports stamped as he seemed to do in every place they visited.

They walked on to have a late lunch in the small town of

Villadangos del Paramo. The food was simple and fresh, and they both had codfish and potatoes. In the bar, a television was showing bull running. Power watched open-mouthed, as a crowd of young men and a few women ran down narrow streets, in open shirts and jeans, ahead of a group of bulls and cows. Occasionally, a person would fall in the dust and Power's heart was in his mouth. The cameras focused on the fallen man, and usually he pulled himself up after the stampeding bulls had passed. The running was amazingly short, and over after a few minutes. The cattle were rounded up into a bull ring where there would be a fight that night. At the end of the running, however, the cameras lingered on one prostrate male figure who did not get up. He lay in the dust of the street, unmoving. First-aiders ran over to his body and the camera view switched to the studio, where two talking heads compared notes on the spectacle. "He looked dead to me," said Lynch.

"Barbaric," whispered Power. "Was that going on? Actually going on – now?"

"I think it's still very popular," said Lynch. "And legal."

"I feel ill," said Power. "It's barbaric – from the point of view of all concerned. The bulls. The people. I can't believe what we just saw. It's the twenty-first century not the nineteenth."

"And at six o'clock tonight, the bulls face the matadors," said Lynch. "Come on, Carl." He stood up and gathered his rucksack, hat and staff. "Much as we'd like to, we can't change a whole country and their attitudes."

"If only we could," said Power.

They walked on through the early afternoon, between hills of dusky, dusty brown earth and dried and tangled rows of abandoned vines. On the edge of a plantation of Black Poplar trees, a man on a bike stopped by them and introduced himself. He spoke broken English and blessed their pilgrimage, explaining that he had been a monk and had studied in a Monastery in Bilbao over to the east. His monastery had been dissolved. Now he lived in a nearby village with his sister, he was taking some flowers in the basket on his bike to the church. He wished them well with the customary "Buon camino."

The day was now very hot, and Power was glad he could hide in the shadow under the brim of his hat. He drank frequently from his water bottle. Occasionally, he wet his hands from the bottle and wiped the moisture over his sweaty face.

They ploughed on through fields of beans, and hops, and corn until they reached their destination for the night, an albergue at San Martin del Camino. They ate a small meal of bean stew and bread. Power drank two pints of beer, thirstily. Lynch drank spring water. Power phoned Laura, showered and tumbled into a cot in the dormitory of six bunk beds. He was weary from the miles he had walked and was snoring within minutes. Lynch read a well-thumbed Bible till he too fell asleep.

* * *

The next day, just after dawn, they walked to Puente del Orbigo. There, at mid-morning, in a café by the Way, Lynch breakfasted on bacon rolls, orange juice and coffee. Power had an omelette with mushrooms.

They walked on slowly through the afternoon, because the day was very hot.

The albergue in Santibanez was full. The shadows of dusk were gathering and Power, being tired, did not feel they should walk in the dark to the next village. The owner of the albergue stood in the arched doorway and apologized for the lack of beds – seeing Power's weariness, he suggested that they use a field on the hill nearby, where there were some tents set up already as an annexe for any overflow of pilgrims. He gave them some mats and freshly laundered sleeping bags on the strict understanding they returned them in the morning. He said there would be no charge – if they would care to eat in the café bar run by his brother? Power avidly agreed. His stomach was rumbling. Lynch smiled at his friend's sudden enthusiasm.

They decided to eat first, in the brightly-lit stone front room of the café bar. They stowed their borrowed bedding and rucksacks by the table and ordered Mahou beer and perused the menu as they rested their weary legs. The menu was simplistic. Lynch chose a tortilla de jamon with some fried potatoes. Power chose a tortilla de queso. Afterwards they had some form of orange custard flan, garnished with fresh berries, which Power ate with relish. The food was good, the evening was warm, and they were both tired after their first day's walk. Power wished there was a bath he could soak his aching legs in. Lynch had closed his eyes and his head was nodding. Power ordered two cafe solos, which appeared strong and tasted vibrant. The caffeine hit Lynch almost immediately and his post-prandial somnolence was rapidly dispelled.

They walked up to the camping field in the dusk. The field was up a cobbled path, at the crest of a small hill, and was shielded from any breeze by a fringe of chestnut trees, which grew around its edges. There were three tents already planted in the field, clustered around a small makeshift hearth.

One of the tents was already occupied. An old man with long grey hair and small, golden-rimmed spectacles, sat at the entrance to his tent. He waved at them and politely got slowly to his feet to greet them as they walked over to the tents.

He offered his hand to shake. "Good evening. My name is Ramon. We are sharing this field tonight, I think. No room at the Inn for you either?"

Lynch introduced them as he shook hands. "My name is Andrew Lynch and this is Dr Carl Power." Lynch put his rucksack and staff by one of the tents.

Ramon shook Dr Power's hand. "Pleased to meet you, Doctor. What are you a doctor of? Divinity? Or physics, like me?"

"Medicine," said Dr Power. "I am pleased to meet you."

"I was just about to light a fire," said Ramon. "Do you mind if an old man warms his bones? It can be quite chilly when the sun goes down. Maybe we can talk a little under the stars, by the fire?"

"A fire sounds good," said Power.

Ramon knelt by some dry moss, twigs and kindling that he had prepared earlier and drew a tinder box from his pocket and struck a flint. The spark jumped obediently onto the dry moss at the heart of the fire and a small flame grew at once. The dry twigs around the flame started to crackle.

"You made that look almost easy," said Power.

"Many, many years of practice," said Ramon. "I've been walking the Way every year, for a long while." Power and Lynch pulled some matting out of their respective tents and sat down by the fire opposite the old man, who asked, "Tell me, Dr Power. Since you are walking the Way, are you a man of religion?"

Power shook his head. "I'm just here to accompany my friend. Are you a priest maybe?"

"I suppose I am more a man of science, at least in recent decades. That is the fashion these days. For some people God is either a matter of faith or a matter of intellectual truth. And for others it is sufficient to say that they think the Bible might not be the literal or scientific truth, and that God is merely 'psychologically' true. Well, it is not just a matter of faith for me. I believe that God is scientifically true. 'If faith is unprovable by the intellect then it is impossible to be true', as someone once wrote."

"But there are so many problems with religion," said Power. "How can it be other than blind faith? Because when you scrutinise the details, a man of science could not take it as a literal truth."

"Surely it depends on your science and your logic," said Ramon. "We have moved far beyond Newtonian physics and simple logic. No-one can disprove the notion of God. It would be futile to argue in an infinite Universe that something does not exist. An infinite set of possibilities must exist in an infinite Universe. Therefore, a wise person would not argue that God can not exist.

"I suppose it is more a set of probabilities. As we exist, and as the Universe is infinite, then it is at least possible God exists. Surely God is more probable than not."

"God either exists or He does not," said Lynch. "As far as I am concerned He exists. He is."

Ramon laughed. "We live in complex times, Andrew. Your view is absolute, but our physics is not absolute, we can't take a simple Newtonian view any more. Things are not as simple as action and reaction, cause and effect. Everything is more elusive. Our certainties about matter have changed. We can agree that, here, we are sitting on an Earth that exists: she appears solid and holds us, as her children, to her skin with a force called gravity. But we know that the atoms that make the Earth's matter, that make up our own bodies are, by volume, mainly empty space. And the electrons that circle the atom's nucleus . . . what are they? Are they particles or waves or something else? We can sometimes locate them, first here, then there, but between times where are they? They are gone. Where do they go? They are intangible. Matter is a mere probability. And dark matter . . . the more we know the less we know. When our certainties are so uncertain, can we really state 'There is no God!' without sounding just a little bit arrogant and ill-informed?

"Our Universe is still so unexplained and full of Mystery. I now think that quantum physics is our route to God, and it fills me with hope that we will find God in the smallest of places. Precisely where we least expect Him. You will be familiar I think with the physicist Erwin Schrödinger who made the first descriptions of our quantum worlds. You know his thought experiment about the cat?"

"I've heard of it," said Power. "He described the experiment where the cat is in a box, and something bad happens to it in the box. I forget what. And the cat is either dead or alive, but you don't know until you open the box. So, until you open the box, the cat is simultaneously dead and alive."

"I suppose," said Ramon. "Like we don't know where the electron is between measurements. Here in front of us? Or hiding an infinity away. There always has been a cloud of unknowing between us and reality, and we have to put up with it. Newtonian physics doesn't work at this very fine level of detail, at the particle level. Our new science teaches us that faith in the probability of things is necessary. In Schrödinger's box, or a steel chamber as he described it in nineteen thirty-five, the cat was subject to a random event, that may or may not happen depending on some atomic event that triggered a hammer – a hammer that might strike a flask of hydrocyanic acid – the unpredictable decay of a particle of radioactive substance. If the hammer breaks the flask, the cat dies. But we cannot know whether the flask has been broken and the cat killed by cyanide, unless we look. Until we observe the living cat or the cat's body there is an equal probability that the cat is alive or dead. Until the matter is resolved, the cat is somehow simultaneously alive and dead. There is a superposition of states. Dr Power, do you hope that cat is alive or dead?"

"Alive," said Power. "Of course."

Ramon chuckled. "Then, forgive me if I extend the analogy to faith and propose the idea of Schrödinger's God. We cannot know

God does not exist. It is not easy to know if He is here with us all the time or none of the time. There is some uncertainty, a superposition. God does not exist or God does exist. Is He particle or wave? Simultaneously here and somewhere else? Popping up at this time and this place and then also at another time and place?"

"He can't be here at one instant and light years away at another instant? How would He travel between?" Power scoffed.

"Embrace the paradoxes, Dr Power." Ramon looked up at the stars above them and lay back on his mat staring at the heavens. "I used to be a conventional astronomer for a while and then distances seemed to matter. Well, I suppose they do, but when you get to really small levels, there is a thing called entanglement, and it seems to offer the prospect of action at a distance, even over vast distances. Imagine particles that are linked in terms of their quantum state. Two particles, twinned say, for properties like spin, or momentum. Imagine a pair twinned so as to say that their total spin is zero. So one particle spins clockwise and the other counterclockwise. Total spin zero. Now, if you separate the particles, and you change the spin on one, say from clockwise to counterclockwise, then the spin on the separated twinned particle also switches (from counterclockwise to clockwise) to maintain the equilibrium – so that the total spin is zero. Einstein called it 'spooky action at a distance', and he didn't like it – well, that's what he said to me anyway. But the effects can be demonstrated in experiments, and they indicate that there is communication, faster than light communication. How is that possible? Embrace the paradoxes, Dr Power! And that's why I believe that physics will develop to show us mechanisms whereby anything we dream is possible. Science will show God can exist. But the irony is, that He would exist whether we proved Him or not, whether or not we looked in the box, God exists. That's Schrödinger's God for you."

"Did Schrödinger believe in God?" asked Power, relaxing back on his own mat. Lynch followed suit and for a moment they were silent as they all stared up at the stars.

"Did Schrödinger believe in God?" mused Ramon quietly. "No, I must admit that he did not. He lived most of his life in two passionately Catholic cities – Vienna and Dublin. But I don't think he believed, although he was buried in a Catholic cemetery. He was a physicist, first and foremost. And he helped consider what was the stuff of life, DNA. He was not a perfect man, though. He had a penchant for younger women. He was not faithful. He had children by mistresses, and he had a grandson, who was brought up without any knowledge of who his grandfather was, who went on to become a quantum physicist. I think Schrödinger would have liked that irony, especially because of his interest in DNA."

Ramon got up and placed a large tarpaulin or ground sheet over the broad hill and threw his bedding on the sheet. In the village below the hill the lights were switching off one by one. The fire was dying down to some glowing embers. Power could smell the woodsmoke. At first the sky assumed an inky blackness, but as his eyes became accustomed, he saw stars emerging out of the gloom that he hadn't been able to see before.

"For a little while – until it is too cold for old bones – I will lie here and look at the stars. Join me – both of you, and we will talk until it is time to go into our tents and sleep? The moon is not full, there are no clouds, and the stars, even the galaxies, are clear. We should take advantage."

Power and Lynch got their bedding from their tents and lay on their matting alongside the professorial old man.

"Oh," said Power, looking at the sky. "I don't think I've ever seen so many stars."

"We are far away from the city and its light haze," said Ramon.

"This is how the night sky should be, how it was for our ancestors. Are you familiar with the constellations?"

"No," said Lynch. "It's all a mystery. I've lived over fifty years and I know nothing about the world around me."

Lying by the old man, Power listened raptly as Ramon explained what he could see. He followed Ramon's pointing finger into the night. "If you look up there you can see Perseus. All these constellations have been watching us here on Earth for billions of years, and we have only been writing about them for thousands. Ptolemy of Alexandria described Perseus and the other constellations at the beginning of this millennium. Over there is the Great Bear, Ursa Major, which contains the youngest galaxy in the visible universe. And there," Ramon looked over at Power and Lynch to make sure they were following him. "There is Cassiopeia, the vain queen of mythology. See the W shape? Five stars . . . so?" Power nodded. Lynch grunted assent. "Over there is Andromeda, the daughter of Cassiopeia. One of the largest constellations. The brightest star, there, is actually a binary star. And the constellation contains the Andromeda galaxy, which has a trillion stars and which is the closest spiral galaxy to our own Milky Way."

"A trillion?" gasped Power.

"A trillion," said Ramon. "And have your eyes become accustomed yet? Can you see all the stars? If you look you will see the Milky Way itself. Which has a hundred billion stars. You see there, like a cloudy band across the night sky?"

"Yes," said Power, sighing at the majestic beauty.

"To the ancient pilgrims, The Milky Way was the Heavenly embodiment of the St James Way," said Ramon. "Our destination is Santiago de Compostela – and *Compostela* means field of stars. They were more in touch with the physical world around them than we are. If you try, you can sense so much more in our physical reality than you ever thought was there. You just have to spend time in it, revel in it."

"His creation," whispered Lynch to himself.

"And where is Gemini? The twins?" asked Power.

"The twins are not here at this time of year. Not in the sky anyway. Over there is Draco, the dragon," said Ramon, continuing his explanation. "And there, Pisces, which also has a galaxy within it. This galaxy has a supermassive black hole."

"How far away is that?" asked Power.

"Don't worry, Carl, it's not going to come and eat us up. It's two hundred and thirty-seven million light years away."

"Lying here, I am thinking of a time when I was very small," said Power. "My father took me downstairs. It was the middle of the night. It was dark and the house was cold, and we wrapped ourselves in a blanket and he turned on the TV and we watched the Moon Landing. The first men on the moon."

"Armstrong and Aldrin walking on the Moon, and Collins orbiting above them, keeping watch," said Ramon. "Weren't they brave? Going into the unknown. It was a magnificent achievement, but it was still a leap of faith. And in comparison to all this immensity above us, the vast distances, we have only taken baby steps into space."

"I remember sitting on his knee," said Power, who was lost in reverie, a million miles away from them. "I remember him reading to me, *The Box of Delights*. I love that, have you ever read it?"

"You know," said Lynch, looking up at the ancient stars. "It is like we are flickering stars on God's firmament, ourselves."

"Mm, that's poetic for you, Andrew," said Power.

"This," Lynch waved at the night sky. "Makes a man poetic."

"The history is all around us," said Ramon. "Like cloth draped over everything . . . clothing us in a many coloured coat . . ." The phrase sounded familiar to Power, but he wasn't sure where he had encountered it.

At that moment there was the sound of a howl, somewhere in the distance. Something primeval in this sound of the night raised the hairs on the back of Power's neck. He sat up and stared around, wild eyed. Ramon noticed his stare. "Don't worry, it was miles away. The sound just travels further at night."

"What was it?" asked Power.

"What do you think it sounded like?" asked Ramon.

"Well, to be honest it sounded like a wolf," said Power.

"You can relax," said Ramon. "The wolves are running, but it was miles away, I promise. They have reintroduced the Iberian wolf in these parts. There are now several hundred in Northern Spain. You don't see them. They are generally afraid of Man and stay clear of our villages and towns."

"Who would do something so stupid as to reintroduce the wolf?" asked Lynch.

"Well, some people like to return things to how they were once upon a time," said Ramon. "You will be safe here in your tent." Power thought that a thin sheet of fabric was not much protection for a sleeping man. "They don't attack unless they are very hungry and they know you are wounded or when, as a pack, they really outnumber you. Attacks on humans are really very rare indeed." The wolf sounded again.

"I won't sleep if that noise carries on," said Power.

"It will be quiet," said Ramon reassuringly. "There have been some attacks on sheep, I will grant you that, the farmers aren't altogether happy. But the wolves are protected. The farmers can't shoot them."

"I would have to side with the farmers," said Lynch. "A wolf is a wolf. We know their character. We know what they can do. We shouldn't fool ourselves as to their danger, deny reality and pretend everything in the garden is lovely."

"Well, they are part of God's creation too," said Ramon, "just as much as these pretty stars in the sky, which are simultaneously really blazing infernos of gas. It's all relative and depends entirely on your perspective." He stood up suddenly and started gathering his bedding together to put it into the tent. "And it's late, the air is growing cold for my old bones and I must sleep. I bid you good night, gentleman, and wish you good rest. Lie here and stargaze all you like. Let me wish you a 'Buon Camino'!" And with that he was gone, before Power could say 'Buena vida!' back.

Chapter Five

Santibanez de Valdeiglesias to Astorga
Eleven kilometres

You can still die when the sun is shining.

**James Joyce, A Portrait
of the Artist as a Young Man**

D r Power woke to the sound of birdsong and bells. A warm shaft of sunlight carved its way into his tent through a gap in the flap. He had slept solidly and well. Partly this was due to tiredness after his long walk, despite the ground he had slept on being relatively unyielding. He was unused to sleeping outdoors and he imagined that he had been woken by the birds and the sun at the crack of dawn. When he stuck his nose out of the front flap of the tent he noted that the sun had already climbed a little in the sky and there was the sound of a group of pilgrims laughing and joking. They were already re-commencing their pilgrimage on the Way, taking the road below the hill.

Power looked at the bright blue morning sky and remembered watching the stars the night before. He had never seen the night sky so clearly and a trace of the awe he had felt still remained with him and inspired him to get up and engage with the day.

The old man's tent opposite was clearly empty. Ramon's bedding and baggage had gone. The tent and field belonged to the Inn and was offered as a form of annex when all the beds indoors were full. The old pilgrim had left silently some time before dawn. Something about the old man had reminded Power of home. For many years there had been a piper at Alderley Edge, whom Power had always taken to be a traveller. The Piper had been the leader at a New Age camp set up at Solstice time when Power first encountered him. The Piper could never be pinned down to plain speaking, however, and always seemed to prefer to speak in riddles. Dr Power, being a psychiatrist and used to listening to all sorts of people, had always enjoyed the Piper's company, but Lynch had found his elliptical style insufferable, especially when he had once been trying to solve a case and had desperately needed the Piper's help. Lynch had paid attention to Ramon though. Ramon had made more sense and Ramon shared Lynch's faith, but for different reasons.

Power fell to wondering whether they would ever meet Ramon again. His thoughts then moved to musing where the Piper might be. He had not seen him about his village at home for months. And finally, he fell to wondering where Lynch was, for Power suddenly realised he was alone with the tents in the field. Lynch's tent was wide open to the morning air too. And Lynch's bedding and rucksack had gone as well.

Dr Power puzzled over the matter. He thought it most unlikely that Lynch, a Superintendent in the Cheshire Police, had been abducted by the old man. It was equally unlikely that Lynch would have abandoned his old friend without a word and left the village. All in all, Power thought the communal bathroom in the albergue or a simple breakfast at a café a more likely scenario for his friend, and so he started to gather his own things together. He wondered about getting a shower immediately himself, but settled on finding Lynch as his first duty. He knew they planned to reach a town soon, where the guide and driver had stowed their main luggage at a hotel. The prospect of a proper bedroom and bathroom in a hotel sounded so wonderful to Power, in an all together fresh and novel way that he would never have thought possible, had he not lain on the ground in a tent all night.

Power tied back the flaps of the tent to air it, as the other campers had done. He hefted his rucksack onto his back and began walking down the grassy hill towards the village. He reasoned that Lynch must be within the confines of the village and that he must find him there.

The village was little more than a linear straggle of stone cottages with terracotta roofs. There were a few larger buildings. These included a kind of Town Hall, a few bars, the albergue – a hostel for pilgrims – a cluster of unknown buildings behind some kind of wall, and an ancient-looking yellow stone church with a rounded end wall. All at once, Power realised where Lynch would be, and remembered that the first sounds that had woken him were birdsong and the ringing of the Angelus bell.

He found Lynch at the church's doorway in a conversation with a white-haired, bright-eyed husk of a woman. Lynch's conversation was hampered by his relative inability to speak Spanish, but he had made some headway by a series of gestures. He looked up at Power as he arrived. "Can you help me, Carl? I think she wants me to do something for her? She looks after the church here where I've just been praying. I thought I'd be back before you woke up. You were snoring away. I didn't want to disturb you,"

Power smiled at the old woman and tried a few hesitant phrases in Spanish. She introduced herself as Isabella and spoke slowly for his benefit. She told him how she had looked after the church for forty years and noticed that Lynch was a religious man. She had stamped his *Credential* document for his pilgrimage to Santiago with the church's stamp and wondered if he would do something for her. Then she told Power what it was. Power smiled and turned to Lynch. "It's simple enough, Andrew, she noticed that you were praying here as a pilgrim and wondered if you would say a prayer for her when you reach the Cathedral in Santiago. She says she has never been herself."

Lynch smiled, "Of course, tell her that of course I will."

They walked across the street to a tiny café on the Way itself and ordered their morning coffee and apple juice and ate fresh baked pastries. They took it in turns to have a wash in the tiny bathroom. Over breakfast they discussed the old man they had met, Ramon.

"I don't know who he was," said Lynch. "Some sort of physicist. He knew his astronomy, I think. I liked what he said about how quantum physics might have a place for God in it – how twinned particles can change in sympathy with each other . . . even if they are far apart. I don't understand how, though. It seemed a bit like a description of magic to me."

"I suppose no-one really understands," said Power. "I am continually puzzled by physics – even everyday things. Although you pour boiling water directly and carefully into a mug with coffee granules in why does boiling coffee climb up and splurge out and over the side? Surely it's defying gravity! And when you open a book with shiny paper, why is there a kind of purple glow along the gutter of the page?"

"No idea," said Lynch. "But I was kneeling there in prayer and I thought about what you said. About time collapsing in, or something? Everything happening at once? And this place is so very old. The church has all the hallmarks of being built by the Templar Knights. That's nearly a thousand years of history in those rounded walls there."

"I thought the Way was protected by the Order of St James Knights not the Templars," said Power.

"I guess there was some overlap. The Templar Knights had property everywhere – Spain, Ireland, England, France – all dedicated to their mission to help pilgrims reach the Holy Land. Maybe they were the first multinational company."

"Didn't it all end rather badly?" said Power.

"Well, they lost the support of the Pope and the local kings eventually. After a few hundred years they had grown rather large and rather too powerful, I think. And there were some scandals. Men will be men unfortunately, and corruption affects all we do. The devil tempts us all. Or maybe it was a degree of jealousy by kings and politicians who sensed the Templars were getting beyond their control. Anyway, as far as the church here goes, St James is certainly in there. On a great white horse, brandishing some kind of cutlass and looking most piratical as he tramples unbelievers underfoot."

Power seemed taken aback. "That doesn't seem right. I don't remember an apostle doing that in the Bible."

"It isn't," said Lynch. "Medieval times were rather strange. It seems that someone had a dream about St James fighting the Muslims, and that was enough inspiration to trigger all these images."

"It's a good thing people don't take my dreams seriously," said Power, as they stood up and hoisted their rucksacks on their backs. "I tell you something, Andrew, I'll be glad to get a good soak in the tub tonight after our walk. And a cup of proper tea. Unless you think proper tea is theft? "

Lynch ignored the pun. He found that this was the best approach to Power's jokes.

"I think you'll like the hotel tonight. We are staying with a Knight. He owns the hotel."

"How Quixotic," said Power. "The thought of that hotel will keep me marching along today." At this point two cyclists whizzed closely past them.

"You can cycle the Way as well," observed Lynch. "It's good for you, cycle-ogically speaking."

Power groaned at the uncharacteristic joke from his friend. "Spare me, please. Come on." And Power set off briskly, staff in hand. Lynch chuckled and followed.

They were soon in the countryside again, striding along the Way through fields of sunflowers or through woods of poplar trees. Occasionally, the dusty Way would give way to Roman stone pavements at the edge of a babbling stream. As they passed the stone gateposts of a farmhouse, they came across a table covered in white linen, with bowls of fruit – bananas, pears and apples – golden and shining in the sun. There was a tower of paper cups beside covered jugs of juice. A painted board said *'Take, eat; Tomad y comed; prenez et mangez; nehmen und essen; buon camino!'* Power took a banana and peeled it. He insisted on leaving a few euros by way of exchange, despite Lynch protesting that the offerings were a gift from the farmer and that no payment was required. "The farmer wants to give something for God. He doesn't expect anything in return."

"I don't like depending on others," said Power.

"We all depend on each other sometimes," said Lynch. "The Way is like life. A metaphor. We started off in Leon. That was birth. And we are nourished along the Way, and grow. And on the Way and in life we are together, all travelling the path together." Lynch smiled, he was enjoying himself.

"I see," said Power. Doctors are trained to look for pathology, and Power was framing a question about the end of the Way. What was that a metaphor for? A metaphor for death? He looked at his friend's cheerful face and didn't feel he could be mean enough to ask. He had sensed a real vulnerability in Lynch when he had been talking about his job earlier. He didn't dare query the ideas Lynch had brought up. Maybe Lynch would talk about the arrival at the Cathedral of Santiago de Compostela being a metaphor for Heaven. Power couldn't bear to ask, because he didn't share Lynch's belief.

He bit his tongue and finished the fruit he was holding. The day was bright, they were ostensibly enjoying themselves, but Power couldn't shake off a feeling of foreboding that had dogged him since Leon.

After that, they walked steadily for a good six kilometres. Their path climbed as they walked and Power perspired greatly under the white-hot sun disc. The brown pebbled path was dusty and the clouds of dust they raised clogged his throat. They occasionally paused, and then Power would drink deeply.

Before long his water bottle was empty. Lynch offered him some of his, but Power pointed to a collection of buildings on a hill over to their left. "Is it a farm? Maybe the farmer will let us refill our water bottles."

They walked across several hundred yards of the scrub-like vegetation to a long driveway that connected the buildings to a distant road, far beyond the Way. Lynch said, "I don't think it's a farm."

A low wall ran around the perimeter of the property. A long curve of black railings sat atop the wall and rose to above the height of a man's head. They walked a circuit of the wall, trying to find a way in. Inside the railings was a flat expanse of a grey, cobbled yard. Several long, two-storey buildings sat on the periphery of the yard. There was a stone cross on the gable end of a taller building, which looked more like a house with tall, green-shuttered windows.

"The place has a bad feeling," said Power. "It's so quiet." He had noticed two children sitting on a low bench at the edge of the yard near one of the buildings. They looked down at the ground and seemed not to see Power and Lynch. "They're not moving about, or playing," observed Power. "They sit still, like old people. Are they even talking to each other?"

"I can't see at this distance," said Lynch. "I can't hear them."

Suddenly, there was a distant shout. In perfect and unnatural unison, the two children stood up and trailed into a doorway that had opened up in the wall of the house. The yard was now empty.

"I think I can see the entrance to the yard," said Power, and led Lynch to a pair of iron gates between two stone pillars. The gates were chained and padlocked. "It doesn't look a very hospitable place," said Power.

"There's a sign on this pillar," said Lynch. "Can you translate?"

Power looked at the small, stained, brass plaque. There were three engraved words in capital letters. "I think it says 'House of the Children', or something like that. Maybe an orphanage?"

"May the Lord help any child sent here," said Lynch.

"You feel it too?"

"It's not a feeling," said Lynch. "It's an objective observation. Have you ever seen a place less orientated to children? Where is the playground? Where are the climbing frames? Where is the minibus to take them out? Where is the sound of laughter?" Lynch rattled the chains in disgust, and shouted out, almost angrily. "Hello! Is anybody there, please?"

After an age, the front door of the main house opened. A black and white figure looked out and slowly glided towards them. Her hands were hidden within her sleeves. The nun stopped maybe ten metres from the locked gates and regarded them. Lynch called out again, "Hello, can you help us, please? We would like to get some water?"

The nun's brown eyes looked at Lynch intently. He felt like he was a specimen being stared at down a microscope. There was a bizarrely protracted silence as the three adults regarded each other through the railings. Then the nun took her right hand out of her sleeves and waved them tetchily away, like she was shooing away a pair of dogs. She turned on her heel and slid back to the house.

"I think that would be a no," said Power.

Lynch was almost speechless with indignation. "That is the first act of rudeness we have encountered since we got here. I can't quite believe it . . . the lack of charity."

"Maybe it's a silent order?" suggested Power.

"I don't think so," said Lynch. "Let's get back to the Way. There's a village in a few kilometres. Maybe someone there can tell us a bit more about this place."

They made their way back to the Camino. The dusty Way stretched before them over a broad hill ahead.

Knowing that Power was thirsty, Lynch offered him what was left of his water.

In was past noon when they staggered into the hillside village of Castrillo San Justo. Low stone buildings with overhanging wooden eaves and broad, green-painted barn doors thronged about the winding cobbled streets. "Pretty place," said Lynch, as they crossed a small stone bridge across a stream. "Looks a bit like Derbyshire." He paused to consult a notepad. "Mr Delgado said that there was a good restaurant here. It's popular, and we haven't booked, but let's try it."

The restaurant was indeed full, bustling with local families, whose smiling children were running about. Power and Lynch were found a table downstairs in an equally full cellar. Lynch had been given a list of things to order, recommended local dishes that he now wanted to try. Power listened to him reel off what sounded a menu's worth of food. Power felt he should chip in and emphasised to the waitress that he was vegetarian. She added, "Si, si."

"What have you ordered?" asked Power.

"I'm sorry," said Lynch. "There are local specialties that Mr Delgado insisted we try. I have ordered you some cabbage soup."

"Cabbage soup!" Power poured them both a long drink from a bottle of cold, sparkling water. "I hope it really is vegetarian."

"*Caldo gallego*," said Lynch. "It's a must."

When it arrived, Power was obliged to agree that the soup was good. It was served piping hot in a deep earthenware bowl with crusty fresh bread – steam rose from a satisfying broth with cabbage, white beans and potato in. Power ate hungrily and with great relish. "I must make this when I get home," he said.

Lynch had ordered an alternate dish with stock, cabbage and vast hunks of chicken, small sausages, balls of meat pudding, pork fat and beef. The meal also sat in a squat earthenware dish, but the sheer quantity of meat had a challenging, almost threatening air as far as Power was concerned.

Power peered at the dish. "I think every animal in the farmyard was invited into that meal."

They drank a bottle of Las Tres Filas between them after the satisfying soup, Power only just had room for a small pudding of ground chestnuts with a caramel topping. Lynch had failed in his quest to finish the meat dish and was unable to contemplate a dessert.

The owner of the restaurant, Senora Coscola, breezed by their table and asked in perfect English if they were happy. Lynch patted his stomach contentedly and smiled.

Power took the opportunity to ask a question. "The food is excellent, but I wanted to ask you something, please. We are pilgrims."

"I know," said the owner, smiling.

"We passed a set of buildings in the middle of nowhere, outside this village. An orphanage? Run by the Church, possibly. There were children, but there were railings and locked gates – it was all locked up like a prison. Do you know anything about the place?"

The restaurateur shook her head and frowned disapprovingly. "No. We know nothing, but we talk about the place. It is often locked up. Sometimes the sisters are there. And sometimes they are not.

They are not of the village. The village people don't work there. They don't go there, no one is welcome. The sisters are not of this place."

"Are there any stories about the place? What goes on?"

"Ah, you have a bad feeling about the place, maybe?"

"Well, yes," said Power. "How did you know?"

"Because no-one has any other feeling than that. Anyway, my friends, I must go, I am very glad you enjoyed your meal." It seemed she did not want to linger talking on this topic. She glided away amongst the tables.

Power looked at Lynch who was sipping a café solo. He was frowning. "An orphanage that is sometimes there and sometimes not, that is staffed by itinerant nuns, and it's a place that no-one in the village has a good word for. What kind of system allows that?"

"People always think that someone else will intervene. It's called the 'bystander effect'. Experiments show that if you put one person in a room and pump some smoke under the door to simulate fire, they act immediately. Put two people in and repeat the experiment and they both do something immediately. Put fifty people in the room and they don't act. They stand around, like sheep looking to see if anyone else does something first. There is always a delay before somebody does something that is logical and appropriate. We saw the people yesterday doing the bull running. Would you deliberately allow a bull to charge at you? An individual wouldn't do that on their own, but if they see other people doing it they join in the 'sport' . . ."

"Well, we're just passing through," said Lynch. "It's not something we can do anything about. We can't stop a whole country from bull fighting. We can't investigate some strange institution in a foreign country. We are meant to be on holiday." Lynch signed to another waitress that they wanted the bill, which duly arrived and which Lynch paid using several thousand-peseta banknotes.

The cobbled road out of the village took them back over the bridge and though a forest of oak back onto the Camino. Several rocks painted with yellow arrows helpfully showed them the direction towards Santiago.

The going under the afternoon sun was harder with full bellies and both Power and Lynch were tempted to lie down under a tree and snooze the afternoon away. The thought of a comfortable bed and lodgings in Astorga, a bathroom and 'proper tea' made them press on though.

The road carried on through the trees until; in a vast clearing in the forest, they saw a tumbledown shack.

"Ah," said Lynch. "This is the free bar that Mr Delgado mentioned."

"A free bar?" said Power, perking up at the thought.

"As you can see," said Lynch. "Free alcohol is probably not being served." Lynch pointed to a small cluster of wheeled carts sitting in the sun in front of a concrete shack. The ensemble was painted green and on top of this background were graffiti-style slogans and flowers painted in white and yellow. The phrase 'La llave de la Esencia es presencia' was written beneath a tableau of love-hearts. The bar area was topped with red watermelon under plastic domes, bananas in their skins, a thermos of coffee and a range of fruit juices in dumpy glass bottles. Nearby there was a fire where a kettle of fresh water was being boiled. The shack was largely open to the elements and adorned with purple tie-dye drapes and mandalas. The outside walls of the shack were daubed with peace signs and nearby, a set of wooden benches sat near a notice board, with a small roof to keep any rain off. The board was covered with photos of people who had visited, and their postcards and messages.

Nearby, standing tall in a pair of bathing trunks and a t-shirt was a tanned, long-legged, fair-haired man in sandals. He had matted dreadlocks and the widest grin that Power had ever seen. He looked calm, relaxed and beatifically happy. He carried an acoustic guitar, but never played a note.

"Welcome friends!" he shouted to Lynch and Power. "My name is Pieter, come and have some refreshment. It's free. Some coffee? Juice? Something to eat? It's free. The Way will provide. That's the key."

Power came close and noted the swarms of flies orbiting the bottle of juice. He felt it would be rude to refuse, however, and asked if he could have a black coffee and a banana. He had judged these the least risky of all the offerings.

Lynch seemed unduly relaxed and poured himself a glass of orange juice, waving the flies away.

"Are you pilgrims then?" asked Pieter.

"Erm, yes," said Power, munching on a banana. He took a seat by the notice board and felt a little uncomfortable as the be-trunked Pieter came close.

"I've been here six years," said Pieter. "No electricity. No water. No car. No bike. I came here as a pilgrim and I stayed. The Way provides me with everything I need. I have nothing. I am happy. Last year my partner, Sue, joined me. She was a walker too. She teaches people relaxation."

"Oh," said Power, finishing his banana and wondering if he should make a donation, but Pieter didn't seem to mind whether he did or not. There was a dish for donations, but Pieter couldn't seem to care less. Power felt he had to ask a question.

Lynch interrupted. "If you have no car, how do you get the supplies for your bar?"

"People donate as they pass by, or I ask a friend from Astorga to drive stuff up. I meet him in the morning by the crossroads up ahead. Since I've been here I've never had a day's sickness and I've never gone hungry. I keep a fire going and make coffee all day long. I watch the sun go up and down. I play my guitar as the sun sets. I make love." He beamed, and Power could see he was absolutely sincere. Perhaps the happiest and most contented person he had ever met.

"Don't you miss your family?" asked Lynch.

"I come from South Africa. It's a long way, and I haven't got a passport any more, but I write. Sure, I write. They could join me. No-one understands. But I am happy."

"You remind me of someone," said Power. "Although you don't talk in riddles so much as him. I am just wondering whether you have met him."

"I meet everybody on the Way," said Pieter. "They all have to pass the Free Bar if they are going to Santiago."

"I can imagine him here," said Power. "He is the Piper. Have you met anyone called the Piper?"

Pieter drummed the soundboard of the guitar with his fingers. His smile never left his face. "There are many pipers round here. Bagpipers. It's a thing."

"Not a bagpipe," said Power. "A flute or a tin whistle sometimes. He has a beard. He seems wise, distant, removed from this world. He travels a lot."

Lynch interrupted. "Come on, Carl. It would be unlikely for Pieter to know him . . ."

"But, I think I do," said Pieter, beckoning Power to the noticeboard. "Is this the man?" He pointed directly at a colour photograph of a group of musicians all playing in the vicinity of the shack. The Piper was sitting cross-legged in the centre of their circle.

"That's him," breathed Power. "Yes. That's him exactly."

Lynch peered over Power's shoulder but said nothing. He didn't particularly like being wrong, but it was more the case that over the last few days he had been irritated by the psychiatrist's intuitive thing and didn't want any hunches being rewarded.

Pieter nodded. "Every year or so he turns up. Sometimes on his own; sometimes with a group of friends. He stays a day or so. We play music and sing. I haven't seen him for over a year now. He had father trouble. He said his father understood him even less than mine understands me."

"Do you know how to contact him?"

"He's like life," said Pieter. "You just have to let it flow. He turns up when he wants to."

Power took another look at the heat-curled, light-faded photo of The Piper and filled his paper coffee cup again. Power put a donation of coins in Pieter's bowl and sat down again. Power was thinking, and went into a kind of reverie. Lynch poured himself some more juice and chatted to Pieter about his future plans, but could find no sense of any concern in Pieter for the future. Lynch wondered what he would do if his girlfriend fell pregnant or if he fell ill.

Dr Power was suddenly conscious of a set of eyes looking at him from somewhere in the trees.

Lucia saw a tall man with soulful eyes sitting on a bench in the clearing. He had dark eyes and hair, and looked kind and handsome. He was sipping coffee and seemed to be dreaming. At any rate, he looked a thoughtful man and someone who could possibly be trusted. He suddenly looked at her, and instinctively she ducked back into shadow. He gave her a smile and gave her a gentle wave with his hand.

She waved back reflexively, and felt a pang of regret at having done so. Her heart was beating so fast. She could only just swallow down her fear. Could she trust him?

All of a sudden the man stood and very slowly walked towards her. He took just a few steps, then he paused, as if seeking her permission to step any closer. Dr Power nodded at her and smiled again.

Lucia smiled back and he came a little closer and knelt down. She knew that he couldn't chase her so easily if he was kneeling.

"Hello," he said. "Or should I say 'hola'?" He was English and she thought the accent of his Spanish was difficult to understand. He probably knew how bad it was, as he asked if she spoke English. "Habla Inglés?"

"Yes," she said softly, and stepped out into the sun. It seemed very bright after the shade of the trees and she sneezed. A reflex. "The nuns taught me English. They are good on languages. They don't teach much else. They say that speaking a language will be good when our husband takes us away." She paused, wondering if she had said a bit too much. But the man nodded, as if she had said something perfectly reasonable, and she felt a little more confident.

Dr Power's mind was turning her words over, however, and his apparent bland acceptance was in reality a mask behind which there was a deeper concern.

"The nuns, yes," he said. "I see. Are you hungry? I could fetch you something? A banana maybe? Some water?" She nodded agreement, and Power got up and went over to where Lynch was talking to Pieter. Power selected a banana and poured out what he hoped was clean water.

Lynch had noticed. "Have you made a friend?"

Power grunted assent. "Try not to stare at her. Carry on talking, please." He asked Pieter, "Do you know her?"

"No," said Pieter. "She is very pale, don't you think?"

"And thin," said Lynch.

"I don't think she gets out much," said Power. "Stay here, both of you, please. I need to talk to her for a bit. She is frightened. If we crowd her she will run." He looked at Lynch. "She mentioned nuns."

"That orphanage?" asked Lynch.

"That's what I think," said Power. He turned to take the food and drink back. The girl had retreated into the shade, ready to take flight. Lynch chose to fill a mug with coffee and sat down to wait. Pieter went to tend the fire. Lynch felt sweat prickling on his brow at the edge of his hair. He had the most uncomfortable feeling that his holiday was suddenly over.

Power knelt in the sun a few yards from the girl. He judged her to be about twelve or thirteen. Lynch was right; she was very thin. Although the day was hot she shivered a bit. From experience he guessed she had a BMI of fourteen or fifteen. He thought she ate the banana hungrily. "Would you like another?" he asked.

"Maybe in a bit," she smiled. "I will have another in a bit. I haven't eaten since yesterday."

"Your last meal? The nuns made that?" She nodded and Power tried to glean a bit more information. "At the orphanage?" Another nod. "Did you run away?"

"And I don't want to go back; I won't go back."

"The gate was unlocked?" She nodded, but frowned.

"How did you know?"

"I guessed." Power knew because when he had been at the orphanage the gate had been tightly locked. He thought it was probably locked after Lucia's escape.

"Can I trust you, then?"

"My name is Carl," said Power. "I am a doctor, and I mean you no harm."

And in that moment when likings are made, she knew she could trust Dr Power. He reached across to her and shook her hand in a formal and respectful way. His palm was warm, dry and infinitely reassuring. Not like the men who came to the orphanage. Their hands were always damp, as if their guilt sweated through every pore.

He said, "It must be a bad place, to run away from like you have done?"

"Who are you with?" she asked. "You walked here with him?" Power looked back at Lynch who was sitting by the drinks cart. He was on the phone. Pieter was, by now, attending to other pilgrims who had walked up.

"He's a friend, yes. A good man." said Power. "We work together. He's a policeman."

She nodded. "How long have you known him?"

Power thought. "Seven years or more, I think."

She nodded and Power went on. "Can you talk about the place you have come from?"

She frowned at him. "You ask lots of questions. The nuns always said to me: 'Take care. Not every good question has a good answer.' And they also said 'The more you know, the sooner you grow old'."

"They didn't like questions? But that's how a child learns best, by asking questions."

"Well," said Lucia. "Questions would lead to a night in the cellar or a visit to the Father. And so I was careful what I asked and who I asked."

"The Father?" said Power. "It wasn't just nuns looking after you, then?"

"Father Bruce came and went. He had rooms at the top of the stairs. He is in charge of everyone and everything. Mind, soul and body."

"Is he the main thing you are running away from?"

Lucia nodded. "I hate him. Hate him."

Dr Power had decided this some time ago, but he thought he should say it now. "I won't take you back there."

She was defiant. "I could run off now, and you couldn't stop me."

"You could," said Power. "Or you could also let us help you. You have a choice. It's up to you."

"Yesterday, when I got up I saw that the front door was open.

And I saw that the gate in the yard was open too. They are never both open. Never. And so I made the choice then."

"Tell me about the priest, please."

"He is so blonde. His eyebrows and his hair are so pale. He stays out of the sun because he burns. His hands are always wet." She shuddered involuntarily. "And he smells and tastes of pepper. He has jars of pills in his desk, like a doctor."

"He touches you?" She nodded. Power thought about this for a moment and then asked, "What did the nuns say when you asked about that?"

"They told me I was covered in sin, to be quiet and go and have a bath. Then when I complained about having to visit him like the other girls had to, they slapped my face and pushed me down in the dark amongst the potatoes and onions."

Power tried not to show his anger.

"There are others?"

"There are always about ten girls in the dormitory. We have a few lessons in the morning – languages, like English and French – we mainly help the nuns with the housework; cleaning, washing and cooking. A few boys downstairs sleep on camp beds and are made to help with the gardens. When you get too old a man usually comes to marry you and you go away."

"Nobody is adopted or goes away to a mother and father?" asked Power. Lucia shook her head. "And how old is 'too old'?" he asked, trying not to show any agitation, but she saw his hand shaking in annoyance. She was finely tuned to this kind of signal.

"I told you that good questions don't always have good answers. Are you cross with me?"

Power shook his head. "I am not angry with you. I am only angry with the people who kept you there. I am sorry if that anger worries you. It's not you that makes me angry."

She nodded thoughtfully, and Power pressed on. "So girls stay in the orphanage until they are how old?"

"My friend Maria left last month when she was fifteen. Father Bruce took her on a plane."

"Would you like to put a stop to all this?" asked Power.

"I would," said Lucia. "But I don't think anyone can do it."

"We could try," said Power. "Together?"

"Maybe."

"Come and meet my friend, Andrew," said Power. "We are walking into Astorga. He will know what to do."

"Are you pilgrims?" she asked. Power nodded. "Well, I don't believe in God. He never helped when I prayed to Him. I told the nuns I didn't believe in God and they beat me. Who can beat God into someone?"

Power stood and offered his hand to her.

There was some hesitation on her part and Power wondered if he had done the right thing, but eventually she reached out and took his hand. They walked over to where Lynch was. He stood up. Lynch was a tall man and was conscious that he dwarfed the slight young girl.

He essayed a gruff kind of smile. "Hello."

"This is Lucia," said Dr Power. "She's from . . ."

". . . the orphanage?" guessed Lynch.

"How did you know?"

"Some policemen can use their brains," said Lynch. "Not all, I grant you that. Hello, Lucia." Lynch gave her a curt nod. "I guess Lucia has run away and is coming with us?"

"Yes," said Power.

"I told Pieter, here, that I thought this would happen when you started talking to Lucia. You're not the kind of person to leave a child in trouble. Duty calls, I guess."

"Yes," said Power. "We need to walk into Astorga town and think what to do next."

Lynch hefted his rucksack onto his back and picked up his pilgrim's staff. "I thought you would say that. So, I have phoned ahead. Mr Delgado was going to meet us in town, but I've asked him to get the driver to pick us up. Pieter says that there is a crossroads nearby. I have also taken the liberty of reserving a room for her at the hotel. We can work out what to do there."

"Okay," said Power. "It seems that the orphanage is a very bad place."

"I know," said Lynch, who had watched the difficult interview carefully and read the signs. "You can tell me more later. Let's get Lucia away and safe."

Chapter Six

Astorga

*I wanted real adventures to happen to myself.
But real adventures, I reflected,
do not happen to people who remain at home:
they must be sought abroad.*

James Joyce, Dubliners

Casa de la Caballeros was the name of their hotel, but it was also the home of a Count. At least this is what Dr Power gleaned from Mr Delgado the guide. A real-life Count and friend of the King. Dr Power could not be sure of this, but the Count did have exceedingly good manners and a white moustache that might have taken decades to cultivate. He shook Dr Power's hand and showed him the signed photograph of an audience he had had with the King. The Count was a head shorter than Dr Power, with a leonine white mane of hair, slightly hooded eyes and the most solemn manner. He took their passports, as hotel owners were required so to do for the local police, and took them on a tour of the ground floor, explaining, via Mr Delgado, the portrait of his seventeenth century ancestor who had founded the hotel as a charitable hospital for pilgrims that were travelling the Way. He showed them the salon, the gaming tables of yesteryear, the dining room and a splendid courtyard and fountain in the middle of the hotel. Here they were served a glass of champagne by the Count himself. The Count dispensed a chilled orange juice to Lucia. He might have commented on her unwashed and unkempt appearance, but he was too much of a gentleman. Mr

Delgado fielded the Count's enquiries regarding his two male guests. He seemed as interested in Dr Power and Superintendent Lynch as anyone could be. He greeted the young girl in their care with a degree of restrained chivalry and said that the Countess, *la Condesa*, would show the girl to her room. It was not courteous for a man to do this, he insisted.

When the Countess had whisked Lucia off to show her to a single room, and the four men stood alone in the courtyard, the early evening sunlight sparkling within their glasses and the fountain gently chuckling nearby, Lynch asked the Count for his assistance. The appearance of the girl on their pilgrimage was something of a surprise, an emergency even, and they could not ignore her plight.

The Count said that he would have thought less of them had they not responded to the need of a child in distress. He could see that they had rescued the girl. It was a tradition of the building and the family to offer help; after all, he said, he was a Knight himself. How could he help?

Lynch announced that they needed to speak to the Spanish police that very night. Power looked somewhat alarmed. "Don't we need to discuss that with Lucia?"

"If you think about it, Carl, it is the only logical thing for us to do, we would have to enlist their aid eventually and the longer we leave it, the more our actions could be, well, misconstrued by the authorities."

"But…" Power struggled to think of an alternative. He saw how they themselves might be thought of as abductors if they did not follow the path of Lynch's counsel. "I suppose you are right, but she has trusted us. Trusted me particularly – to help her. She can't go back."

"There is no question of her returning there," said Lynch. "But the Spanish authorities will want to regularize her position, enlist their social services, get emergency foster care sorted, whilst a thorough police investigation of the orphanage is made."

"What orphanage is this?" asked the Count. Power and Lynch described their arrival at the locked gates of the place and their mutual foreboding. They went on to tell the Count about the appearance of the girl in the clearing where the free bar had stood. The Count's frown was deep enough before Power had described the blonde priest who preyed on the girls. And after hearing, the Count shook his head and growled. "A wolf," he said. "In priest's clothing."

"Matthew Chapter Seven, of course" said Lynch. "Exactly. So if you can help me phone the police, Count, I would be very grateful."

The Count led the Superintendent away to the phone in his small office at the entrance. Power was left with Mr Delgado, their guide.

"I had such things planned," said Mr Delgado. "A fine restaurant for tonight, a special tour of the The Bishop's Palace by candlelight . . . it is one of Gaudi's few buildings outside Barcelona, the Cathedral, the museum . . ."

"Life cannot always be predictable," said Power. "Maybe we can do some of this tomorrow? We may need to spend a few days in Astorga to sort things out properly for Lucia."

"Yes," said Mr Delgado. "I will try and adapt your itinerary. Tonight, though . . . I had made a reservation for us at a very fine restaurant. And she is not dressed . . . well . . . I do not like to be unkind . . ."

Power understood. "Cancel the fancy restaurant. Find us somewhere that will have food she might like." He reached into his pocket for some money. "And please, would you mind? Can you buy her some new clothes? Blouses, t-shirts, underwear, some trainers and jeans?" He pressed the money into Mr Delgado's hands. "She needs some new clothes and you will know where to go."

Mr Delgado smiled a winning smile. "Of course, I know just the places. I will go now."

*   *   *

Dr Power sat on a cushioned bench under the colonnade in Casa de la Caballeros and supped at a glass of cold Mahou beer. While the fountain still splashed and played in the courtyard he could hear people walking along the glazed first floor verandah above, but otherwise he was at relative peace.

Lynch returned and sank into a wicker armchair at Power's side. The Count followed him with two further glasses of beer and gave one to Lynch. "If you will permit me," he said. "I will join you for a moment. The Countess is seeing to our small guest; she has given her the new clothes you bought her and has made sure she has drinks, has rested, showered and so forth. But I wanted to talk to you. It is upsetting for you that your holiday be interrupted I am sure, but it is upsetting for me that my town and my country should see such things to children in a place nearby.

"My ancestors were noblemen before me, and most of them were Knights of the Order of St James. Since the twelfth century. The twelfth century! The King himself restored the order and made me a Knight in honour of my ancestors. Now, I am an old man, one of only thirty-five Knights, I know it is nowadays only a ceremonial thing. A quaint thing. Is that the word? Quaint? Something not relevant to today perhaps?

"It was relevant in past times. When men were real. When Knights protected the people. Physically protected them. It is not so now, of course. But my ancestors fought the Moslems. The Moslems owned this country once, and then Christianity returned, bit-by-bit, regaining ground. And we, the Knights, had to fight along this

Pilgrim's Way to keep it safe. The pilgrims would be killed or robbed. The Knights kept the pilgrims safe. We sustained them with food along the way, cared for their wounds. We fought for Christianity here on the land, and at sea." Lynch listened and his eyes gleamed. "And now, here I am, old and with a title that is meaningless, because on my very doorstep these things happen to children. In a so-called Christian orphanage with nuns and priests?"

Power let out a sigh. "I don't think you should take it personally in any way," he said. "It seems to be a problem elsewhere too. I see survivors of such abuse in my clinic all the time. People who have been in children's homes run by county councils, or in schools run by Holy Orders in Ireland. The problem is everywhere. Don't misunderstand me, Count, but the problem is not confined to here."

Lynch looked at the beer standing on the table in front of him. Somehow he had lost his enthusiasm for it.

"Well, I have liaised with the local police," Lynch said. "With the Count's assistance. I think it would have been easier in medieval times, in the days of the Knights. We would have ridden to the orphanage and sorted matters directly with the priest – physically – summary justice perhaps, but possibly more effective. The local police say we must take Lucia to them late tomorrow afternoon to be interviewed. They mentioned emergency foster care. I guess you won't be keen on letting her out of our care?"

"No," said Power. "Not at all. She trusted us."

"I can sympathise with you there," said Lynch. "I think we must respect the local systems though. This is not our country."

Power said nothing, because he knew that Lynch shared his apprehensions.

"If I was a younger man," said the Count. "I would ride with you, Mr Lynch, to the orphanage. And we would dispense justice."

"Forgive me," said Lynch. "I respect the Law. I always have, but recently it seems the wrong people are benefiting from the Law and its protection. Criminals are hiding beneath the skirts of Lady Justice. I've never felt so justified in being cynical . . ."

"Lucia said it was the blonde priest," said Power. "I feel sure we have seen him, Andrew. We saw him in Leon. You know the one I mean."

"Not again, please," said Lynch. "There could be any number of blonde priests."

"A blonde priest?" said the Count. "I've never seen a blonde priest, ever. And I've been going to Mass for over sixty years." Lynch thought this comment most unhelpful, as it would only encourage Power's intuitive guesswork, and he didn't want this fuelled. Lynch preferred a degree of logic and certainty.

The Countess appeared at the doorway to the courtyard. She had come down from the girl's room and beckoned her husband over. She whispered to him discreetly then left. The Count relayed her message to Power and Lynch.

"My wife tells me that the girl drank a glass of warm milk, ate some ham and soft bread rolls and then fell fast asleep. The Countess will keep an eye on her. And I will guard the front office till late if you would like to go and get something to eat yourselves. The town square has an event on, and the bars there are quite good."

Lynch looked at Power. "I am hungry," said Power.

"As ever," said Lynch, conjuring up a smile from the depths that his heart had fallen into. "I think Mr Delgado wanted to meet us anyway, to brief us on our itinerary tomorrow. Perhaps Lucia can join us tomorrow as we look round the town."

They took leave of the Count and his prim little wife, the Countess, who both promised to do their very best to look after Lucia that evening as she slept. Power said that they wouldn't be long, just enough time to eat. Lynch phoned Mr Delgado. He and Patxi were already in the Town Square. As they walked down the narrow winding streets of Astorga together, Power and Lynch were silent.

"Dr Power! Señor Lynch!" Mr Delgado greeted them, as they entered the square. The square was full of people all clustered around a makeshift arena of metal railings.

"What's going on?" asked Lynch, taking in two hastily built stages at either end of the traditional Spanish square. Lighting engineers were even now only just hoisting lighting rigs into place above the stage by the seventeenth century stone Town Hall. In the centre of the square were parked a minibus and a coach. Several people in garish white leotards were strutting about laughing and barking at the crowd, which was composed mainly of families.

Mr Delgado and Patxi pressed a couple of bottles of pale beer into each of Power and Lynch's hands. "It is an annual festival in the town. First a show of strength and then a rock concert. You have arrived just in time!" Lynch looked rather uncertain about this. Mr Delgado pointed at the sequined figures, "Actually they are a gypsy family. The father there is the strongest man in the whole of Spain." He pointed out a barrel-chested man in his fifties with long grey hair in a pony tail. "He can carry two men on a bench and pull a truck with his teeth."

Just then Spain's Strongest Man lay down on the stone flags of the square and his henchmen placed first one, then two, then three paving slabs on his rib cage. With a roar, a vast turtle of a woman wielded a great sledge hammer in an arc to bring it smashing down on her husband's chest. The slabs cracked and fell to each side of the prone figure. He bounced to his feet, grinning, and let out a mighty roar. The crowd screamed in joy.

"They are waiting for him to be crushed!" grinned Mr Delgado.

Next the son of the family stepped forward. His thick, brown mane of hair was gathered into a ponytail by his sister and attached to a rope. Then the son pulled and strained at the rope, which by now had been attached to the van. No matter how hard he tried, the van would not budge.

"I think the handbrake is still on," muttered Power.

True enough, someone was dispatched to check and the handbrake was released. After much groaning and sighing the son managed to inch the van forwards by several feet.

Then the Spanish Strongman offered to push the same van using a pole with a dagger at one end.

The crowd cheered in anticipation. They had seen this done in previous years and it was a favourite. According to Mr Delgado, Spain's Strongest Man would place the dagger against his throat and push the van using his windpipe.

"Surely not!" said Lynch. He was keeping his hand on his wallet in his pocket, mindful of the crowd about him. Lynch moved forward slightly to peer across the crowded square at the Strong Man who brandished a six foot wooden pole with a broad, shining metal dagger at one end. The blunt end of the pole was slotted into a fixing on the back of the van by a helper. The Strong Man made a show of pressing a large grapefruit against the side of the knife. It sliced easily through the fruit and the two yellow halves fell to the floor. He picked them up and threw them into the crowd.

"It is a real knife!" Lynch shouted back to Power. Power hung back, sceptical of the performance.

The Strong Man, with much coughing and mock trepidation, placed the tip of the knife against his neck and bowed his head forward. He angled his body so his entire weight was thrust forward. His legs strained against the stone of the square. The wooden pole that the knife was mounted on began to bend.

"He's putting real pressure on," shouted Lynch. "You can see. How *is* he doing this?"

Steadily the big, white van moved forward under the pressure applied by the Strong Man. Suddenly the pole snapped with a loud crack and the Strong Man fell forward. He crashed to the floor. You could see that this was not part of the act because his family rushed forward. The Strong Man lay gasping on the floor. Power began to wonder if he was all right and for the first time edged forward to see.

"That is not right," said Mr Delgado. "They didn't expect the pole to snap. His neck is bleeding."

Power could see the Strong Man was holding a silk handkerchief to his neck. The crowd had fallen silent. Eventually the Strong Man stood, with his son's assistance, putting on a smiling face. The smile was false – the silk cloth of the handkerchief was stained red. He gathered himself up to his full height to save face and roared defiantly, waving the handkerchief. The crowd roared back, cheering his courage. Power could see a cut on the man's neck.

"He's all right," said Mr Delgado, as the gypsies gathered their leader into a van out of sight and started clearing away. The van sped off. "I think the performance is over," said Delgado. "Let's go to the bar over there, their tapas are good." He drew Lynch and Power over to a small, modern, brightly lit bar with some free tables and said he would organize some food and drink. Power insisted he bring some vegetarian food.

"Why did the Strong Man do that?" asked Lynch, as Mr Delgado wended his way to the bar . . . "He could have been killed."

"Only if the trick went badly wrong," said Power. "And I suppose it did go wrong. He was cut and he didn't expect that."

"But pushing a van with a knife, using your throat. I saw it with my own eyes. The knife was real. It was no trick."

"Do you want me to tell you?" asked Power. Lynch nodded. "The knife blade was wide, wasn't it?" Lynch nodded in assented. The blade had looked a few inches wide.

"But I saw it cut the fruit easily. It was sharp."

"It was sharp at either edge," said Power. "But the tip was broad and shallow. The two shoulders of the tip would fit snugly into the sternal notch."

"What's that?" asked Lynch.

"Feel along your collar bones. Towards the middle there is like a downward semicircle of bone, a notch. That's the sternal notch. The tip of the blade was fitted in there. So the top of the blade fitted snugly against bone. Two surfaces . . . bone and metal . . . two surfaces good and hard . . . good enough to push the van with force. And the tip was shallow, so the soft tissues of the throat were never at risk. And the other important thing he did was to put his head, his chin, forward and down to grip and fix the blade in place. That way the blade was wedged in place and fixed solid in the bony notch. No risk, except . . . except the pole snapped. Then he was in real danger."

"Ah", said Lynch. I understand the trick, but it was a good one wasn't it?" Power nodded. And at this, the food started arriving. Roasted vegetables, bread, tortilla and golden risotto for Power. Beef, tuna and prawns for Lynch. And Patxi and Delgado brought numerous bottles of Estrella Galicia clutched in their arms.

As they ate, Delgado outlined the day ahead, "Tomorrow we explore Astorga, this Roman city, formed on the Roman roads that conveyed gold and copper to the centre of the Empire. There is the Bishop's Palace built by Gaudi to see, and chocolate factories and the Cathedral . . . so much to do!"

The feast was progressing well and the holiday seemed suddenly back in full swing to Lynch, when he suddenly noticed the Countess had appeared at his elbow; silent and her face streaked with tears.

"The Count . . . my husband . . . asks that you come back to the hotel. The girl . . . the police have arrived and he asks that you come back as soon as you can."

They left immediately, leaving money with Delgado to cover the food and drink bill. Most of their supper lay untouched. Dr Power ran up the mild gradient of the cobbled streets towards the hotel. The Countess followed at a distance, along with Lynch who had taken her arm. She seemed unsteady in her emotional state, and he felt her leaning on him.

The Count was standing in the arch at the entrance to the hotel. His white hair and moustache were bathed in light from the lamp on the stonework overhead. He was wringing his hands.

"Doctor!" he cried, as he espied Power running round the bend of the narrow street.

"What is it?" asked Power, breathlessly. "Where is Lucia?"

"Gone, gone! They wouldn't wait. I told them . . ." he clutched at Power's hands and held them in his, and looked up into the doctor's eyes. "I told them not to disturb the child. She was sleeping peacefully, after all, like an angel."

Lynch had caught up with Power. "What's happened, Carl?"

"The police, they've come and taken her from her bed."

The Count dropped Power's hands and spread a caring arm around the shoulders of his wife. "I went and found them as quickly as I could. I have failed," she said.

"No, no," said the Count. "They weren't prepared to wait like decent folk. Let us go in. Passers-by should not hear our business." The Count drew them all indoors into a lounge and poured four glasses of Brandy de Jerez. He gulped at his and slumped into a high-backed chair. "I will tell you, I will tell you." He seemed to be finding it difficult to compose himself. "They were two. A man and a woman. The man was a Municipal Inspector, he said. In blue and white. The woman was a social worker. A hard, grey woman. A big nose and even bigger jaw. She had a barking voice, like a vixen. She went upstairs to get Lucia. She came down, rubbing her eyes, wrapped in a blanket. I said that I could not let the girl go; that she was under the protection of a doctor and a policeman from England. I said he should wait and talk it through with you. He said he wouldn't be kept waiting by foreigners and what was it to you to poke your noses in to the Country's affairs? He was rude. He called me an old man." The Count stared down at the floor. "He reminded me of the bad times, you know?" He looked at his wife and she reached over and patted his arm.

"You did what you could," she said.

"I am not a young man any more," he sighed. "They had a van waiting to take her into 'protection', they said. I said that we had agreed to take her into Astorga tomorrow and what was the sense of disturbing her sleep? But they were people with no heart."

"What did the inspector look like?" asked Lynch.

"A short man. Potbellied, but very smart. Very officious. Black hair with pomade. Tiny little moustache."

"What was he called?"

"He did say," said the old man, looking worried. "He showed me his warrant card and I checked the name. I made sure I checked it . . . but it seems my mind is going too. I have forgotten it."

"Never mind," said Lynch. "We will take it up with the authorities tomorrow. We had an appointment in the evening tomorrow, and I intend to keep that."

"I don't know how you can be so calm," said Power, upset. "We need to do something, right now."

"I am as upset as you. But if we go to the police station now, do you think they will reverse their decision and hand Lucia back to us?"

"We can't let her go, just like that!" said Power. "She trusted us."

Lynch bowed his head. "I know she did, Carl. The Spanish police do seem a little unpredictable, I grant you. But think about it. They have clearly changed their mind. Going and arguing with them about it in the night time will do no good."

"We didn't even get to say goodbye," said Power.

"I am so sorry," said the Count. "I only wanted to do the right thing."

Power took notice of the old man's guilty posture. 'I'm sorry, Count. I know that you did everything you could. Perhaps we should leave it till tomorrow, like my friend Mr Lynch suggests. We can't take on the world . . ."

"I am a Knight of the Order of St James, an Order that protected millions Christians on the Camino for hundreds of years," said the Count bitterly. "And of all those Knights, the Order is reduced to me, an old man who can't even control what goes on under my own roof, in my own hotel." His wife moved closer to him and hugged him. He whispered to her, "They won't do this me. I have to stand up." She hushed him tenderly and stroked his hair. He buried his face in her neck.

Throughout the past few minutes, Lynch had been increasingly agitated, tapping his hand on the arm of the chair. Lynch stood up now, muttering. "No peace at work. No peace when I'm at play. What more is it you want of me, Lord?" His brow was furrowed and his expression grim. He strode over to the door of the salon and wrenched it open.

"Where are you going?" asked Power, concerned for his friend. He stood up.

"I am going out to try and clear my head. I am *trying* to relax." He sounded anything but relaxed, more irritated to point of violence. "I just wanted a few peaceful days. Was it too bloody much to ask? I am going for a drink."

"I'll come with you," Power made a move towards his friend.

"No," said Lynch. "I want to be on my own. Why did you have to get us involved? I can't take it any more!" And with that he was gone. The door slammed behind him in his wake.

Power stood there perplexed. In all the time he had known his friend, Lynch had never snarled him in quite this way. Lynch's wife had warned him at the airport. Perhaps this anger had been simmering there throughout the first leg of their walk and masked by a thin veneer of enthusiasm for their pilgrimage. And all the time the rage had been bubbling away beneath.

Power didn't know what he should do. The Count was still being comforted by the Countess and looked up at him with watery eyes.

He spoke, but it wasn't clear whether he was speaking to Power, his wife or himself. "Maybe we never have the luxury of standing still, or growing old. Maybe we are required to use what strength we have left to fight for what we believe is right. Well then, I will fight." He looked at the Countess apologetically. "We cannot just stand by."

"Excuse me, I must go and find my friend," said Power. "He needs me."

"When you come back, we will help you. Whatever you need," said the Count.

Power hurried out of the archway at the front of the hotel and onto the Astorga streets. He and Lynch had always turned left. He looked up the road to the right and wondered if Lynch would have done anything different this evening. He reasoned that Lynch would probably have done exactly as before and so Power headed back towards the town square.

The Square was now full of people. The strongman show had been cleared away and a throng of locals was crowded expectantly in front of the stage. A glittering swirl of green and blue spotlights played over their upturned faces and bathed the ancient buildings around the square in a very different flickering light to earlier in the evening. On stage the band were just now picking up their instruments and waving to the crowd. Around the edge of the crowd there was still a movement of people walking happily through the colonnades by the bright lights of the bars and restaurants on the edge of the square.

All of a sudden the band struck a heavy chord and the drums began. The crowd roared.

In the middle of the milling swarm of people, Power thought he saw Lynch's broad back moving towards the corner of the square. Power pushed ahead, muttering excuses to the people he jostled, as he half-walked and half-ran. As he got closer to the corner of the square, he realised he had lost sight of the figure. He wondered if Lynch had ducked into the nearest bar and, breathless from his run, Power dived into the beery warmth of the bar. Eyes swivelled to look at Power; at the tall dark-eyed stranger who stood panting before them, scanning the bar for his friend. They thought he looked panicked, not a person like them, out for a good time. Just as suddenly, they saw him dive out of the bar and their interest returned to their beer and their friends.

Power systematically tried bar after bar along all four lengths of the square. As far as he could tell, Lynch was in none of them. Power wondered how many bars there were in Astorga and came to the conclusion that his quest was probably fruitless.

In the very last bar of the square he decided to rest and think. He ordered an Estrella Galicia for himself and sank into a seat fashioned out of a large wine barrel. He sipped beer and tried to think. He hadn't eaten much all day and the alcohol made him feel slightly light headed and rash. He thought of Lucia and what she had implied she suffered at the hands of the blonde priest and his nuns. Observers would have noted a dark mood settle over the doctor and how his mouth took on an increasingly grim and determined look. By the end of a second glass of beer, Power had abandoned any notion of caution and had formulated a plan which was sixty per cent bravado, thirty per cent disinhibition, and only ten per cent common sense.

He marched out of the bar to find a taxi. He located a small cobbled waiting area behind the northern end of the square and opened the door of the first taxi waiting at the taxi stand.

Power tried his Spanish. Alcohol did not grant him the fluency he imagined. "*Un orfanato. Cerca del camino . Al este de la ciudad. Llévame allí.*"

The taxi driver took pity on him and his accent. "An orphanage near the Camino. I don't know any . . ."

"Run by the Church – a priest and some nuns. I was there today. Past the hippy bar on the Camino. A big place in the hills, surrounded by iron railings."

The driver thought for a bit. "I think I know. You want to go there? It is late. It is . . . not a good place."

"I know that," said Power. "I think it is a very bad place, but I must go. I need to speak to the priest there. I have something I want to tell him."

"Okay," said the driver. "But just one way, from here to there. I am not waiting there for you. I cannot wait there. You understand?"

Power checked in his pocket for his phone. "If I phone you, would you come and pick me up?"

"Just one way. You can ask the other drivers. They will all say the same. They will take you, but they won't wait and they won't go there to pick anybody up."

"It sounds as if the place is well known and the reputation is bad?"

The driver affected not to understand. "You want to go, or stay safe in town. The fiesta is more fun, I think."

"I'm not in a mood for fun," said Power, musing on how he and

Lynch would have been enjoying the celebrations right now if he hadn't spied the girl earlier that day. "Okay, take me there. If it's got to be just one way, it's one way."

The driver angrily gunned the engine into life and they roared away from the town square area and up into the side streets that led out of town. Soon they were on a broad, unlit, grey road that wound its way up into the hills. On either side the moonlit land seemed bare or dotted with shadowy scrub. "Nothing grows here," said the driver. "The land is forgotten by God, barren."

When they were still some way off from the orphanage, the driver stopped the taxi and asked Power if he wanted to go back to the town now, and if not he wanted his money now. Power paid him and got out of the car.

Power watched the taxi speeding off into the darkness of the night. He watched the red tail-lights dwindling into nothingness. He realised then what danger he had put himself in. He was alone. He scrabbled in his pocket for his mobile phone and looked at the screen. The screen was glaringly bright, but Power could see that there was no reception whatsoever. He could not call for help even if he needed it.

The darkness was only relieved by the stars in the sky. Around him nearly all the ground seemed to slope upwards to the sky, as if he was in a crater. The orphanage buildings seemed to be composed of solid black squares and triangles against the silvery-blue gravel of the hills. Power imagined that he was an astronaut looking down on an alien base built on the surface of the moon. The base was deserted, as if the vacuum of space had broken in and stolen every life. There was no light on in the windows either and the silence was complete. He looked up at the sky and wondered that the same stars that looked down on the grey surface of the moon were looking down on him now. He recalled the communal bliss of watching the stars with Ramon and Lynch only a few nights before. Where was Ramon now? Many miles ahead on the Way? And where was Lynch drinking in the town below?

The orphanage buildings were surrounded by black iron railings. The paint on the railings glistened under the starlight. Power found his way to the gate which had been locked with chain and padlock. There was a small bell with bell pull hung on the right-hand pillar. It was not Power's intention to arrive unannounced, and his purpose, ill formed and ill conceived as it was, had been to confront the blonde priest and his nuns. On impulse, he reached up to the bell pull and tugged. The bell rang, shattering the oppressive blanket of silence that cloaked the orphanage.

There was no response. The quietness descended again on the group of buildings and the declivity they sat on.

Power stood alone in the darkness, and he was perplexed. He had arrived in anger and his anger had been met with a solid wall of silence, as obdurate as a stone sea wall that took all the energy of the waves that crashed against the sculpted rock, which survived against the odds, against the waves' watery fury. The darkness was implacable. Power stood and waited, and thought, and the sky above seemed to whirl about his head. He wondered if there was a God above his head. Schrödinger's God: there or not there?

"Are you there?" he asked, into the silence. "Or are you not there?" He remembered what Ramon had said when he had scoffed, 'He can't be here at one instant and light years away at another instant? How would He travel between?'

The old man, Ramon, had said something like, 'Embrace the paradoxes, Dr Power.' Power looked up at the stars above and remembered the Constellation's names: Perseus, Ursa Major, Andromeda, Cassiopoeia.

Power felt frustrated he could no longer remember which was

which. The huge sweep of the Starscape above, dwarfed him and his tiny hopes and fears.

He rang the bell one last time and the chime echoed across the crater. The windows of the orphanage showed not even the slightest glimmering chink of light to suggest that anyone had heard and was responding. Power was utterly alone.

In the distance he heard a howl. The sound was low and strangely protracted. He identified the sound as an Iberian wolf; probably miles away, thought Power, as he tried to reassure himself.

Power made his mind up to scale the railings. He climbed up on the stone wall that supported the iron railings' base and with infinite care braced his arms up on the top railing and swung his right leg over the arrow heads that topped the pickets of the railing. With his right foot he sought a purchase on the horizontal railing, twisting his body round to shift his weight to the right leg and moving his hands so that he angled his body over the railings. He did all this slowly and with intense concentration, fearful that any slip might render his ambition of having children with Laura only a remote possibility. With both feet finally secured on the inner side of the railings, Power took care to step carefully down onto the ground. A broken ankle here would be disastrous. The only benefit of falling here inside the railings would be that, although he couldn't summon help using his mobile, he was the right side of any railings from any wolf.

Power crunched his way across the dirt of the yard around the orphanage buildings. In the silence of the night the noises of that scrunching and even his breathing were almost deafening. He made a rough circuit of the buildings and could detect no sign of life. No lights, no noises, nothing.

He approached the oppressively dark shadow of the front porch and, turning the handles, pushed against the high wooden doors which remained impassively and obdurately shut. He pounded at one of the doors and heard the echo of his fists within the sounding box of the hall beyond.

Power made a second tour of the exterior main house checking each elevation for a possible way in to the hidden depths of the orphanage.

Every window downstairs seemed either shuttered or barred. On the wall opposite the long barn-like building there was, however, a plate-glass window into a large room that looked, in the starlight, to be an empty library. Power tapped at the glass, but he knew that no-one would answer.

Across the void, the howl of a wolf sounded again and Power fancied that the sound was, if anything, closer now than before. He shivered and was momentarily glad that he was behind the railings.

Then, spurred by frustration and a burgeoning anger about Lucia's story of defilement, Power marched across to the place where earlier he had seen the sombre boy and girl sitting in the sun. He wrenched the long wooden seat from the ground. It was decidedly heavy, but in his state of mind he hardly felt the weight. With singular determination and controlled rage, Power ran with the bench towards the single uncovered window and with a roar launched the wooden seat lengthways at the glass.

The glass shattered inwards with a splintered explosion and the bench banged down upon the parquet floor inside, and rolling, clattered over into an unseen wall.

Using a short plank of wood he found nearby, Power pushed at some of the jagged shards of glass that still stuck up in the window frame, to make a safe way in for him. As they fell tinkling to the ground, each fragment of glass reflected the last quarter moon that had risen in the sky behind him.

When the edge of the window looked safe, Power crunched and

slipped his way over the glass and climbed in through the open casement.

Glass on the parquet floor crackled underfoot as Power looked around his new surroundings. He had always considered himself a relatively meek person, but the anger that had spurred him on to break the window surprised him. It seemed to burn deep within, fuelled by a sense of great injustice vicariously derived from the cumulative experiences of hundreds of Power's patients over the years: the bullied subordinates, the beaten wives, and all the grown up abused children he had ministered to. Did their anger live, and grow, and fester, and bubble, and seethe inside him? If he let his guard down, did the anger issue forth in a Vulcanic stream? Or if the anger grew too much, did it rise like a tidal wave over the sea defences?

The room had once been a lofty nineteenth-century drawing room. It still had its original elegant wooden panelling, but other than the fallen bench there was no furniture and Power's footsteps echoed as he stepped over the bench and opened the door into the hall beyond. Light from the night sky filtered dimly into the hall from the long window on the stair well. Power decided to explore the downstairs rooms one by one. A dining room next to the kitchen had a long and roughly hewn wooden table, with two long benches either side for the children to sit at. This room was shuttered and dark, and Power could only glimpse the interior, but it sounded empty and deserted.

The kitchen had some small sacks of white beans and some old tins in the cupboards. It had been cleared of fresh groceries and milk that might spoil. In their haste to depart as quickly as possible, someone had knocked over a kitchen chair.

Power made his way to what seemed to be a study near the front door. There was a battered desk, two chairs, an old armchair with its stuffing leaking out and an empty bookcase. A filing cabinet stood empty with drawers wide open. There hadn't been enough time to close them to. A few scraps of paper lay in a sporadic trail across the floor from the cabinet to the door. Power picked them up. They looked like invoices, with descriptions of things bought, and a column of figures, but it was too dark to read them. He stuffed them in an inside pocket of his jacket. He was making a mental note to look at them later, when he froze in his tracks. His chest felt suddenly arrested in its breathing movements, as he heard the distinct and indisputable sound of the floorboards overhead, creaking. Power felt unable to breathe as he listened with infinite focus to the sound of heavy, purposeful footsteps on the floor above. There was no denying what the sound was as the footsteps moved away towards the back of the property towards the stairwell.

He felt somehow removed from himself, dissociated, and felt as if he was a distant observer noting the effect of panic on his thought processes. There was a thought, an impulse to run, to escape out of the house. But his confusion meant that he didn't seem to be able to progress the thought. He was unable to put the plan into action. Something inside him protested that he couldn't vault the railings – he would have to climb them as carefully as he had done before, and that would take time. The alternative idea, generated through a sticky and acid morass of fear, was to hide. But Power seemed unable to do anything but stand stock still in the middle of a room, where he would be obviously caught.

The footsteps were now descending the wooden staircase. As the only sound in the house they were as loud as could be, and each one resonated in Power's frozen heart. He couldn't leave the room now and dash to the drawing room where he had broken in, for he would be immediately visible to the other person as they came down the stairs. He would be caught like a rabbit as he ran past.

Without any hesitation the footsteps came closer across the ground floor hallway outside. The other person was not wasting time searching other rooms downstairs. They knew exactly where Power was.

Power looked round the barren room for a weapon.

The door slowly opened.

Chapter Seven

For my part I know nothing with certainty,
but the sight of the stars makes me dream.

Vincent Van Gogh

Dr Power had taken up a position by the wall near the door, which he had closed to in preparedness. He held a wooden chair aloft and was ready to bring it crashing down on the head of the person who had been treading the floor above and who was about to walk through the door to confront him. Power stood stock still, apart from a slight tremor in his limbs arising from a mixture of tension and fear. He was trying not to make a sound and his breathing was rapid and shallow.

The door slowly swung open and Power came face to face with his adversary.

He gasped. To avoid bringing the chair down on anyone, Power dropped the chair behind himself. It slammed onto the bare floor and clattered to rest.

Power looked into the eyes of a singular figure dressed in a black overall and wearing a blue plastic hair net, plastic gloves and plastic overshoes.

"You!" shouted Power, half in anger and half in relief. "I thought you were going for a bloody drink! I thought you were sitting in some bar in the town, drinking to numb your anger."

Lynch shrugged. "I thought it was you, but I wasn't sure. Ringing the bell, for goodness sake! Smashing the window with a bench! Clattering about down here. You could have woken the dead, man!"

"I thought you were going for a drink," Power righted the chair. "I could have killed you. Why didn't you tell me you were coming here? And what *are* you wearing? Where did you get that?"

"I am trying not to leave any traces of my being inside the building. I didn't bring you along, because I reasoned that if I was going to break the law I shouldn't involve you and get you into trouble in a foreign country. I thought I would be as discreet as possible and just see if I could talk to someone if they were here, but when I found the place empty I thought I'd have a convenient look around inside. And as you can see, they have left in very much of a hurry. So I thought I'd see if I could find out a trail, find evidence as to where they've gone."

"You came prepared," said Power, pointing at the gloves.

"Yes," said Lynch. "I stopped off on the way at a supermarket and got these. *I* didn't want to leave any evidence that *I'd* been here . . . I didn't smash the place up, unlike *somebody else* . . ." Lynch glared at Power. "You've left a trail of evidence just as clearly as if you'd written your name on the walls in letters ten foot high. Fingerprints, hair and goodness knows what else. You could have cut yourself on the glass. Left blood there . . ."

"I didn't though," said Power, feeling akin to a sulky child being chastised by his parent. "There was no other way in."

"Did you try the door?" asked Lynch.

"The front doors were locked," said Power.

"If you had been systematic you would have found I'd left the back door open."

"They left the back door open?"

"No," said Lynch. "I picked it. It's an easy skill that an old customer once taught me."

"By customer I presume you mean villain or criminal."

Lynch nodded. "Well, it's hard not to get to like some of them.

They are just people like you or I. And it's useful to learn to see things from another person's point of view."

"I guess," said Power. "And here we are on the wrong side of the law ourselves. Did you find anything upstairs?"

Lynch sat down on the very chair that had nearly been used to stun him. He was marshalling his thoughts. The house was silent in the night. "The house and the annexes are empty. The electricity is off. There are some beds upstairs. The nuns shared some rooms on the east side of the house. The priest, if he is indeed a priest, had several rooms on the west side; a flat, with a lockable door. The beds still have sheets and covers on. There are some old books, pictures and crucifixes on the walls. But nothing personal. No clothes. No photos of people. No personal papers. Not so much as a rosary! As if they lived in a way that meant they could run, and run quickly, travelling light. Like they lived as if they were always prepared to leave at any moment. Sling everything in a suitcase and go. Did you find any clues?"

"Nothing," said Power. "The rooms seem empty. Whatever files were in this filing cabinet have been bundled up and spirited away in haste. Maybe they had some vans on site ready at any time to move them somewhere."

"Maybe," said Lynch. "And if they were so prepared to leave in an instant, then they will have had a place, or places, prepared for them to run to. You know, I think we may have stumbled on something rather bigger than it first appears. Like a nest of some creatures, and we've disturbed them, and they've been sent off, scurrying and scuttling . . . like cockroaches racing for the shadows when you switch the light on."

"It takes some forethought, some organisation to have this place, and escape lines to other places," said Power. "What now?"

"There's nothing for us here," said Lynch. "No point in staying.

We cover our tracks here. We make our way back to Astorga; back to the hotel. We can ask the Count for his advice. We can do some sightseeing with our guide in the morning, as arranged. And then we are due to see the Spanish police tomorrow afternoon, also as arranged." Lynch stood and stretched. "Have you touched anything in the house? Door handles, for instance?"

"Hmm, I guess so. What are you proposing to do? Wipe things down?"

"Exactly," said Lynch. "We work our way backwards through the house, out of the back door and home."

"And what do we do? Walk home? There is no signal here to summon a taxi."

"We walk," said Lynch. "Walk along St James's Way like we walked earlier in the day, only now at night, following the Milky Way."

"Didn't you hear the wolves howling?" Power pointed vaguely in the general direction of outside. "You want to walk through the woods at night?"

"Miles away," said Lynch, trying to sound confident. "And they wouldn't attack two people. They are more interested in deer and wild boar I think."

Power grumbled about the danger as they set about erasing any traces of their visit. Eliminating Power's tracks was difficult. There was little light to see by, and although they took the bench outside again the smashed glass was impossible to repair.

"That's as much as we can do, I think," said Lynch eventually. The night was still and in the early hours of the morning they climbed the railings and began their night walk to Astorga. They found the path of St James's Way and began the journey of a few miles into town by the light of the stars. At one point they went through the woods, and Power strained his ears to hear the approach of any wild animals, but the Way was silent apart from the clacking and rustling of the branches of holm oak trees moving against each other in the soft breeze. In the darkness they passed a field of abandoned vines, sprawling, tumbling and crawling over one another. At the end of the field was a wine cellar burrowed deep into the earth. The door yawned open – an echoing shadowy mouth. Lynch looked at it and imagined Lazarus leaving his tomb. They passed rolling fields of beans and corn, and a field of aromatic hops fringed by black poplar trees.

"The thing I will never understand about your God," said Power. "Is how He allows such bad things to happen in his world. I once asked a vicar and he told me the answer was to be found in the Book of Job. I read it and afterwards I understood even less than I did before."

"The Problem of Evil," said Lynch. "Don't you think my work brings me in touch with this question every day? The things I see . . . I have no easy answer to explain why my God allows any of it to happen. I can only say that God gave man free will, and that evil was bred into our hearts from the Fall; when Cain put his mark on mankind. I pray that there is some purpose to everything, that some day all will be made true and clean of sin. That wrongs and injustices will be made right by the Lord. But man's justice is incomplete and sometimes horribly flawed. I can only pray that the Lord is all seeing, and that His justice is infallible and the ultimate in fair play. Until the Day of the Lord's Justice we are continually tested, and can only meet evil with our imperfect, human version of justice. As we have been walking on this Journey I am reminded of that saying; 'Life is the Journey, God plans the Itinerary.'"

Power looked at his watch. "Well, I hope the next thing on our itinerary is some sleep." It was long after one a.m. They had emerged from the wood onto a hillside and the lights of the town of Astorga were displayed below. "And after some sleep, a breakfast of some considerable size."

Power was so tired after the walk from the orphanage, that after he had found his room in the hotel, he was asleep within seconds of his head touching the pillow. He woke with the sun streaming into his room and onto the portion of his naked body that lay uncovered by the crisp white sheets. His stomach was rumbling with hunger. He showered under fizzing hot needles of water and put on espadrilles, soft fawn chinos and a white linen shirt.

Power breakfasted on slices of quince jelly, sourdough bread and butter, slices of fat, fresh oranges and drank his way through two pots of thick, black coffee. Lynch joined him at his table at eight thirty.

"Having a lie-in?" asked Power. "Not like you?"

"I've already breakfasted," said Lynch, proudly. "And I've taken a walk around the square with the Count. An interesting man. He would like to see the return of the Knights of St James. See things back to how it was in the olden days. He lent me a book on chivalry by someone called Llull." Lynch poured himself a fresh cup of tea. "I gather that the Knights owed loyalty to their Order, but they were often a law unto themselves."

"Like our friend Don Quixote," said Power. "He was definitely on his own as a knight, and he also went a bit mad . . ."

"I know you are a doctor and a psychiatrist, Carl, but do you like psychiatrists as a group?" asked Lynch.

"Not really," said Power. "To be honest I feel uncomfortable amongst them."

"It is the same for me, in a way," said Lynch. "The TV police soaps make us look dedicated, hard-working, resourceful and invincible," said Lynch. "I am afraid the truth is rather different. I despair of my colleagues who are, for the most part, a dull and supremely self-serving group, intent on feathering their own nests with overtime and pensions. They see the public as a nuisance and the public's concerns as an impediment to an easy life. The concept of duty, of service, probably died sometime in the nineteen-fifties, if it ever really existed. Sometimes somebody pulls their finger out and does some real detective work that encompasses some real thinking and skill; but only when the case is high profile and the police want to be seen to be 'doing their duty'. Like that poor little girl Sarah who disappeared in Surrey last month. They were all over that. Any other successes are based on the bumbling incompetence of criminals who happen to have made mistakes that even the police couldn't ignore."

"Are you not being a bit hard on your own profession?" asked Power. "You don't usually say things like this?"

"I don't know," said Lynch. "Sometimes I have distinct . . . doubts about my colleagues and my superiors. It was easier seeing the good in my colleagues when I set out as a young policeman. As you get older everything seems less clear-cut, and ethically more blurred."

The Count appeared at their table. "Any more coffee or tea gentleman? Can I get you anything?"

"No more coffee for me," said Power. "I won't sleep for a week if I do."

"I'll take some more tea," said Lynch. The Count gave a little bow and turned to get a fresh teapot, but hesitated.

"You are going to the police station later," the Count said. "May I accompany you? It may help to have a local with you."

"You would be more than welcome," said Lynch. "Thank you for the offer."

The streets of Astorga were flooded with morning sunlight and heat. Their guide, Mr Delgado, expertly shepherded Power and Lynch to the Bishop's Palace. They stood by the cavernous, mouth-like entrance and Mr Delgado held forth. "This is one of only three buildings by Gaudi that lie outside Barcelona. The Bishop lured Gaudi and his masons up here, but when he died the new Bishop wanted to use local craftsmen. Gaudi and his men left, and the Palace was finished by others. Only the genuine work in the building overseen by Gaudi himself is of any good." Power and Lynch explored the vaulted cellars and were then swept up the graceful spiral staircase. "I love spiral staircases," said Power.

There was a small museum of episcopal art on the first floor and Power burst into laughter at a primitive carving of the Madonna, which made the infant Christ look deformed. He tried to stifle his laughter before anyone noticed and took offence, but Mr Delgado and Lynch were both already frowning at him. A sight of three carved wooden priests with white wings, singing like so many cupids sent Power into another fit of the giggles and, knowing that he had drawn the further disapproval of both of his companions, left Power unable to muffle his laughter. He virtually ran away from their stern faces and hurried down the staircase and first hid on the ground floor and then exited the Palace. His companions emerged to find Power looking round the gift shop. No-one mentioned his bad behaviour and they marched in silence into the Cathedral. Lynch paused at the entrance to pray in silence. Power prayed less reverently that there was no more bad religious art inside.

The Cathedral was virtually empty and silent, as if disused except by a few tourists like themselves. Lynch noted that even the wall niche where Holy Water should have been, (the Sacrarium), had run dry.

The museum contained breathtakingly coloured vellum manuscripts, acres of golden copes and vestments, and a range of medieval paintings that were both gory and truly horrific in contrast to the primitive carvings that had amused Dr Power so in the Palace. Here lurid depictions of hideous red and blue demons tortured saints

– jabbing them with tridents, roasting them over hot coals, flaying them alive and unravelling their guts from their abdomens on rollers which they turned with maniacal glee. Power shuddered.

Lunch was at a small bar opposite the Bishop's Palace. The bar's frontage was adorned with baskets of greenery and flowers. The walls were festooned with the frames and wheels of old black bicycles. Power and Lynch sat quietly at a table laden with glasses of Estrella Galicia and plates of viridian Padron peppers, roasted in olive oil and glittering with grains of rock salt. The guide, Mr Delgado, warned them that every so often they would encounter a really hot pepper. There were plates of succulent white hake dressed in oil and capers and a deep dish of crisp slices of waxy fried potato crowned with fried eggs that the guide cut into again and again to distribute the whites and the yolks evenly. But despite the exercise of a morning's sightseeing neither Power nor Lynch were greatly hungry.

Power toyed with a plate of glistening yellow potatoes. Lynch tried a pepper, which turned out to be an example of the rare hot variety. He drowned the heat with a gulp of beer.

"I'm sorry," said Power. "I know that you needed this holiday, as a break from your work. And I seem to have found us another problem to solve."

"It's all right." said Lynch. "As I said last night, the Lord plans our itinerary. I am resigned to His will. You didn't go out of your way to find the girl. The Lord arranged for the meeting. And the problem you mention? It is the problem of evil, which we must all face and fight in our own way. This is just the way we are called to serve, Carl. If the Lord feels that we are somehow strong enough to serve, who are we to argue? I thought that all I was meant to do was to follow His will, just be a pilgrim and walk straight to Santiago. That our quest would finish there in seven days' time. But a detour has been planned for us, Carl. And there's no point in falling out over it."

"Good," said Power. "Because I was just going to say . . ."

". . . that you don't want to wait till this evening. That you want to go to the police straight after lunch?"

"Exactly," said Power. "You know me so well."

Lynch turned to Mr Delgado, who was looking up to the ceiling, rolling his eyes and shrugging all in one deeply expressive movement. "Mr Delgado. I'm sorry, but whatever you had planned for us this afternoon? We need to cancel. A little girl is at risk, and we cannot relax, we cannot go on until we sort things out for her."

"But you are due to walk this evening to your next stop," said Mr Delgado. "It is all booked."

"Don't worry, we will cover all the costs," said Lynch. "But we simply cannot walk away from this girl without seeing things resolved for her. You do understand?"

"Si, si, of course, of course," said Mr Delgado.

And with that, Lynch and Power left money for their half-eaten meal and started their way back to the hotel to pick up the Count.

The police station in Astorga was a grubby, classically-fronted building down a side street. Power and Lynch followed the Count as he boldly strode through the columns of the portico and into the entrance hall. A bored looking policeman, armed to the hilt, sat alone in the entrance hall, at a bare desk adorned by only a red telephone. He nodded to the trio as they entered.

"Buenas tardes," he said.

The Count drew himself up to his full and distinguished height and launched forth on an explanation of their mission. The Count was voluble. His moustache fairly bristled with indignation as he described the rescue of the girl by the two Englishmen, the hospitality he and his wife had offered, their concern for the girl, their contacting the police station the previous night, arrangements to bring the girl here, the sudden arrival of two state officials and the removal of the girl from the safety of his hotel – which was to the Count's evident great displeasure.

The police constable at the desk listened to all of this in polite silence and waited a moment or two at the end of the Count's tirade, just to ensure that the flow of opprobrium had truly ceased.

The police officer gave an appeasing smile and reached for his phone. Lynch looked at Power; Lynch's face was suddenly full of doubt.

The police constable spoke rapidly, but discreetly. The Count could not make out a word. Eventually, he replaced the receiver and holding his head slantways on one side, gave a diplomatic smile and spoke to the Count.

The Count listened to the short speech and when it finished turned to Power and Lynch. His face had grown ashen white.

"The constable says that there is no record of us having an appointment here tonight. I said we had phoned together, you and I, Senôr Lynch. There is no record. None. And worse still . . ."

"We were going to talk to someone about the girl and the orphanage. And no-one is available. How can it be worse?" asked Power.

"Oh, but it is," said the Count. He looked imploringly at Lynch and Lynch could see tears in the old man's eyes. "The constable says that no-one . . . no-one came to the hotel last night. No police officer picked any girl up. They have no record of any policeman or social worker attending last night. No one. Where is she?"

Lynch fished into his pocket and took a Constabulary Warrant Card from his wallet. He asked the Count to interpret and gestured to the Spanish police officer. "Tell him, tell him something for me. Tell him that I am a senior detective from England. Tell him I am not happy and that I want to talk to the most senior officer on duty in this Godforsaken place."

Dr Power did not get back to the hotel until late evening. He had watched Lynch systematically and firmly interrogate the senior officer on duty, a Lieutenant. Lieutenant Arquila had initially alternated between pomposity and disdain, but after a few minutes with Lynch had decided that no matter what Lynch's nationality, Lynch was not someone to be mollified, patronized, or otherwise fobbed off. Lynch was physically imposing, impressive, relentless in his pursuit of right and distinctly determined. And after half an hour or so of his questioning Lynch believed Arquila. Arquila had no idea that Power and Lynch would attend the police station that night. There was no record of any conversation that the Count and he had had the previous night. Lynch cursed himself for not taking the details of the officer he thought he had been speaking to. He blamed his inefficiency on the fact he had been speaking through an interpreter. Efforts to trace who he might have spoken to had come to naught. No one admitted taking the call the previous night. And there genuinely seemed to be no police officer of any kind who fitted the Count's description of the officer who had seemingly attended the hotel the previous night. None. The town's social services had no record of sending out a children's social worker with the police, nor of receiving any girl into care in the previous twenty-four hours, nor even at any time in the last month. Power could see how the old man, the Count, had felt when asked for the name of the people who had attended. He seemed to diminish in size and Lynch offered him some comfort.

"You forgot, Count, but don't worry yourself about forgetting. Do not reproach yourself for a minute," said Lynch.

"But I do," said the Count. "Very much so. She was under my roof, my care."

"I will tell you why you shouldn't worry, Count. The people that came to your hotel were impostors and deceivers. Any name they gave you and that you remembered would have been a false name. A false name would get us nowhere." At this realization the Count brightened, but only a little.

"I will find them," said the Count. "If the police don't care to do their jobs, if they don't succeed . . . then I will find them. I am not a Knight for nothing."

* * *

The chef in the hotel kitchens made Power and Lynch a light supper, which they had in the upstairs salon, surrounded by family ornaments and pictures of the Count's children playing happily with their presents at Epiphany; children long since grown up. On one shelf of the bookcase Power noticed a black and white picture of a much younger Count in dinner jacket paired with a laughing, slim young woman with black bouffant hair by his side. She carried a bouquet of roses. They were standing by the side of a Ferrari. It was difficult to settle to eat, but they were somehow famished at the same time. There was bread and wine, of course, and a rich cabbage and bean soup. A sweet of baked peaches with roast almonds and thick cream. Power looked up from his bowl, seeking absolution. "I feel guilty for eating." he said.

"We must eat," said Lynch. "And sleep. But then what? We have no leads. We have no resources. I am a police officer without a team, and in a foreign land. What do we do? Walk on? Walk on by?" He shook his head. "Can you think of anything else we can do?"

Power didn't know. "I am trying to understand what is happening to us. Last night I broke into a children's home. I hadn't planned on that. I can't believe I did that. Did I do that? Everything suddenly seems unreal to me. Unfamiliar. I want to run back home to something familiar. I am . . . unhomed."

Lynch was thinking out loud. "The girl, Lucia. She is kept in a home with other children, by nuns and a priest. They are complicit in her abuse. She runs away. We take her into our protection. The people who know she is with us . . . include the guide, the driver, the hotel staff . . . and we contact the police. I am sure it was the police we spoke to, but there is no record. Or a record is erased. Unexpectedly, whilst we are out in the company of the guide, two people, a man and a woman, turn up. The man is not described by the Count as being like the priest. He doesn't have blonde hair, you will note. He is older too, maybe? It doesn't sound as if Lucia recognised either of them. So the woman was not a nun at the home. Perhaps I am making too many assumptions. They say they are taking Lucia in to the care of the social services. In fact they are impostors and they are abducting her. Where do they take her? Not back to the home, because the home is bare. When was it evacuated? When they found Lucia had gone, or when they were tipped off that we had Lucia? When the risk of being exposed was real? And we have no leads. Like they were all acting together, all acting like an animal or a beast with a wound and they have acted to close the wound up to heal themselves."

"So they couldn't have known she was sleeping upstairs here . . . unless they were told. Who tipped them off," said Power. "Who betrayed us, and Lucia?"

"Who knew?" said Lynch, ticking people off on his hands. "Mr Delgado, the guide, our driver who ferried us here, the Count, the Countess? Do you suspect any of them?"

"No," said Power. "Actually, I don't."

"The hippy at the free bar? She turned up in the clearing where he lives. He watched us walk away and take her with us."

'Maybe," said Power. "He sees everything. He pretends to be a child of nature, living off the grid. But he could pass a message through friend or he could have a mobile phone and be as in touch with the world as you or I. Or it could be a maid here, or a kitchen worker, or the police in Astorga."

"Unlikely to be the police," said Lynch. "I thought Lieutenant Arquila was genuine enough."

Power thought to remind Lynch of the harsh words he had spoken earlier about his police colleagues, but bit his tongue. He too had thought Arquila harmless enough. "But someone knew where she was, and that we intended to take her to the police the next day and must somehow have alerted or co-ordinated the impostors."

"True," said Lynch. "And where is Lucia?"

Chapter Eight

From Astorga Westwards

O dark dark dark. They all go into the dark,
The vacant interstellar spaces, the vacant into the vacant,
The captains, merchant bankers, eminent men of letters,
The generous patrons of art, the statesmen and the rulers,
Distinguished civil servants, chairmen of many committees,
Industrial lords and petty contractors, all go into the dark
TS Eliot – The Four Quartets

Patxi drove the white Mercedes van at great speed up the winding road that led westwards out of Astorga. The song 'Freestyler' by Bomfunk MC's was playing on the radio in the front of the van, and the roads were blissfully empty at this early hour. In the middle of the van Lynch and Power were quiet and looking out of the windows at the countryside as it rolled past them downhill. Lynch was thinking back to their leave-taking from the Count and Countess outside the hotel. The old man, proudly resplendent in smart blue striped shirt and cravat, had stood by the photographs taken of King Juan Carlos when he had stayed at the hotel. As Lynch had admired a black and white photograph of the Count as a young man wearing goggles and standing by a racing car, the Count had smiled proudly beneath his white moustache, basked in Lynch's attention towards his past life in photos, and sipped strong coffee. And later, with his arm around his wife, the Count had waved Power and Lynch both a fond goodbye. He had expressed a hope that they would return one day and said they would always be welcome in his home. He

SCHRÖDINGER'S GOD

apologised for any troubles during their stay, and he looked solemnly into Lynch's eyes as he shook his hand and promised that, as a Knight, he would continue seek justice for the loss of the girl. The Count said that it was his quest now.

The van roared on up into the hills, and still Lynch could not shake off the guilty feeling that he should be doing something to find the girl, rather than continuing his pilgrimage. But, as he had said to Power before, what could they do in a foreign land, with no resources? He could not help but feel that he was pitted against something shrouded, something deeply malign and also something unexpectedly complex. And he was troubled by the suspicion that someone, somewhere, had betrayed them and the girl, Lucia. He looked at the van driver, Patxi, who was humming happily to himself. Lynch looked at Mr Delgado, and wondered. He suddenly felt an unexpected wave of panic, a feeling that was alien to him, born out of a realization that he was not in control of events, and maybe never had been. He was vaguely aware that the guide, Mr Delgado, had turned round in his front seat and was talking. Whatever Delgado was saying did not seem to be registering with him or sinking into his memory. Lynch felt split and he struggled to understand what Delgado had been saying for the last few minutes. From remembered fragments, Lynch tried to piece together what the guide had been telling them about the next leg of their pilgrimage, a twenty kilometre trek across the mountains to Rabanal del Camino and a continuation of their journey to Santiago de Compostela. Lynch nodded to signal he had understood, but he was quietly swallowing down a sensation of panic in his throat.

After some time, Patxi slowed the van beside a small roadside church and Mr Delgado turned round and smiled broadly. He asked them if they had packed cagoules in their packs as some light rain had been promised on the radio. Dr Power looked in his rucksack.

125

Beneath the water bottle, a paperback and his camera was a red cagoule.

Patxi had clambered out of the driver's side and was standing waiting as Power and Lynch climbed out. Patxi had retrieved three walking staffs from the back of the van and handed them, smiling, to the two walkers and their guide. Lynch nodded back at him, unsmiling, still nursing the unusual feeling of panic.

"The Pilgrim's Way is over on the other side of that hill," said Delgado, pointing over to their right. "Patxi will drive our stuff over to Rabanal and meet us there. But don't worry, I can summon him at any time, if need be." Delgado chuckled to himself. As they crossed the road to the foot of the hill Patxi got back in the van and gunned the engine into life. The van sped off, and disappeared behind grey-black trees as the road wound through a distant fir plantation. They crossed the road towards a slope covered with broom and oak trees.

They climbed an overgrown path upwards through a tangle of undergrowth. "It's okay," said Mr Delgado. "This was a farm once." Power looked around at the young oak saplings that lined the narrow path and the tumbled, winding plants that crawled over the earth. "Vines," said Mr Delgado. "Once upon a time, they were well tended and trained in rows, now they wander wherever they want, wherever they choose. The vineyards became . . . uneconomic. The children of this area, they are drawn to the cities. The old ones cannot manage." By the path was the ruin of a farmhouse – the remains of stuccoed stone walls stood jagged and silent, like so many rotten teeth in an ancient skull. Vegetation burst out of a doorway and spilled onto the doorstep. The slate-covered roof was punctured here and there by etiolated trees searching for the light. The farmhouse windows had been punched out by their branches. Near the house were some gnarled pear trees. Some pears were shining yellow in the sun. A half-forgotten line of old poetry came into Power's mind: 'For the sun has stippled the pear & polished the apple.'

They passed the old farmyard and Delgado pointed out a narrow structure resting on stone stilts or pillars. It was a small building that was tall, long and narrow. A tiny pitched roof covered the length of the building. "This is a hórreo. It is typical of this area of Spain. There have been hórreos here for centuries. Maybe they are of Roman design." He pointed at either end of the roof. "At one end there is a stone crucifix, to guarantee the blessing of the Christian God, but at the other there is a . . . Phallus," he pronounced it phalloos. "It is to please the pagan gods that were here before the Christian god. A fertility symbol from more ancient times. They saw no reason to bring on the disapproval of any deity, so they dedicated the hórreo to all their gods."

"What is the building for?" asked Power. "Is it a temple or something?"

"It's a granary. It is set up on legs to stop vermin and damp getting in. It is vital to the working of the farm; it keeps the grain safe over the winter. And of course they invoked all the gods in the grain's safekeeping. A fine insurance policy."

Power looked at the rotten wooden sides of the hórreo. Nearby there was a long earth-barrow, with a door set into the ground. This Power knew, from earlier in their journey, was a wine cellar. Power looked away from the barrow-like earthwork, shuddering at a sudden memory. All around this place there was a sense of order being displaced by nature, of the earth reaching upwards and grabbing at the heart of the farm, wresting it from man, and pulling it down, deep into its soil.

The trio walked on and, cresting the top of the hill, saw the path of the Camino on the other side, as promised by Mr Delgado. The

Camino was empty of any other pilgrims for it was still very early in the day. Power looked up at the sky and felt the warmth of the morning sun on his face, and smiled, welcoming its heat. The vast sweep of the sky was deep blue and devoid of any cloud. Power looked up at the great bowl of azure sky above him and thought that bringing his red cagoule along would undoubtedly prove to be a pointless exercise.

They joined the Camino. The stone path crunched beneath their boots and the dust kicked up by their feet tingled inside Power's nose as they marched west towards Rabanal.

"If you look at the stones," said Delgado. "The stones on the path round here, whether they are small like this or big slabs like paving stones in the towns, they all glitter." Power looked at the grey stone and discerned that Delgado was right, the stone glinted, reflecting and twinkling in the sun. "This is another reason they call the Way the path of stars. Because there are stars above your head in the Milky Way and there are stars at your feet in the stone you walk upon." He chuckled again.

"I suppose you're right," said Power. Lynch was deep in thought and did not seem to have registered Delgado's latest observation at all.

After half an hour or so of walking they paused to take some water. As Power glugged mouthfuls of cold water, Delgado rested, chin propped on both his hands at the top of his staff. He waited until Lynch and Power had finished drinking, then pointed to an array of what seemed to be small stone buildings with peaked roofs, over on the left of the Camino, a few hundred yards ahead. A low stone wall circuited the buildings. "What do you think they are?"

"I don't know," said Power. "It looks like a collection of those granary things; hórreos."

"No," said Delgado. "They are graves. They survive even after the church has gone." He gestured towards a mound of rubble and slate nearby, which was all that remained of a wayside chapel. "The graves survive after all the people have left the land behind. The dead can't leave."

The Way passed right by the graveyard and as they walked Lynch shrugged off his troubled silence and began to talk to Delgado about Catholicism in Spain.

Power looked at the tall grave-houses they were passing. The grave-houses were clustered close together within the low periphery wall so it was impossible to see inside the graveyard. There were some shadowy cracks between the monuments, and through these Power caught glimpses of a possible sunlit, grassy courtyard or space beyond. In the sunlight above the grey stone grave-houses were clouds of tiny insects, gossamer wings glinting as they floated in the warm, moist air.

"I think I will take a photograph inside," Power called out to his companions as they wandered ahead of him, deep in muttered conversation. They waved to him, absently, to show they had heard. Power shouted to them, "I will catch you up."

Power squeezed through the shade of a narrow chasm between two grave-houses and found himself on a sunny path covered in deep moss at the edge of a square of overgrown lawn. Aromatic clover and couch grass were delightfully springy beneath his feet. The internal tombs in the graveyard were organised into squares around three or four such lawns, like small cottages around a village green. Power looked around for some secluded place. He had no intention of taking a photograph. He was merely seeking some privacy to make water.

Now he was here, he wondered about the moral dimensions of relieving himself in such a place. Maybe he had judged poorly, he thought. The graveyard was so silent that it was oppressively forbidding. Power saw an old oak tree and a bush that might afford him some cover and hid himself between them. He tried to pass water there, but somehow in this place, deserted of any living eyes, he felt that he was still under scrutiny and being judged wanting. After some initial frustration he let forth a stream of urine and it pattered against the tree and ran down and into the ground.

Relieved, Power made his way from the tree through the graveyard intending to rejoin his companions.

All at once he was arrested by the sight of one grave-house in particular. There was a tall pedimented back wall and before it a wide ledge or altar. And on that there was something pink, or even flesh-coloured, displayed or draped on the ledge. He blinked twice, as if this would remove the image that was now engraved in his eyes. But the image would not disappear now it had been perceived, and his wishing the image away would never change the reality of the tiny, naked form, lying on its back, upon the altar stone.

He moved closer to the grave-house and when he was nearer he could see, without any doubt, the head of the girl with her neck thrown back over the edge of the altar stone. Her long brown hair hung downwards towards the gravel of the path, and moved gently, chillingly and silently in the breeze.

Power reacted physically, before he had full comprehension of what he was looking at. His legs gave way, just as if a giant had scythed Power through the thighs. He crumpled heavily down onto his knees with a thud. The shock of what he saw was met with a vasovagal response. The circulation to his legs seemed to have failed and for a moment his vision was narrowed to a tunnel. The outside world seemed to diminish and recede. In the heat of the day the dried and sunken eyes of the girl were open and had seemingly locked their gaze reproachfully on to Power's own eyes.

Power's throat, unbeknownst to him let forth a kind of low moan of sorrow that somehow softly blended itself into the silence of the graveyard and died away into nothing.

Power didn't know how long he knelt there. It might have been many minutes or just a few seconds. Eventually he rose on staggering feet and made his way to do what he had been trained to do as a doctor. He checked Lucia's body for signs of life, but this was just a routine he ran through automatically. There was no carotid pulse, and there clearly hadn't been for some hours. The body was cool beneath his touch. The skin was a greyish pink, devoid of life and more akin to the rough grey stone on which her body had been draped. There were purple areas of lividity, pooled blood on the lowest edges of her body, round her shoulders and scalp. He scanned the rest of her body, grimly noting what had been done to the child before her death. Power felt sick. He took a close look at a needle sharp line that ran right around the girl's pale throat where she had finally been garrotted. Power opened his rucksack and ferreted inside. He retrieved his cagoule and laid it over Lucia. She was so small, his man-size coat covered most of her body, except for her ankles and feet.

With that accomplished Power was promptly violently sick, and once done he slumped, shaking uncontrollably, down onto the ground.

PART TWO

Chapter Nine

Time present and time past
Are both perhaps present in time future
And time future contained in time past.
If all time is eternally present
All time is unredeemable.

TS Eliot – The Four Quartets

"Are you listening, Doctor?"

Dr Power had been gazing out of the patient's front window at the puddles on the drive. The puddles simultaneously reflected the white clouds of the English sky and were stippled by falling raindrops. Power looked at his old Saab as it shouldered the downpour; all of its tyres were standing in a vast pool of water at the edge of the carriageway. Dr Power had been back in England for a week and it seemed as if it had never stopped raining. Somewhere in the house, maybe in the kitchen, a radio was playing. It was faint, but Power recognized the beat of the song, 'Blue Monday'. Dr Power turned his attention back to the man that the family doctor had asked him to see on a domiciliary visit. Power nodded, "Of course I'm listening. Tell me where you grew up."

Paul Driffield was a slight man, rendered as thin as a lath by lack of appetite and depression. He had untidy hair, which had been unwashed for days and which was slicked down to his forehead by a combination of sweat and grease. His eyes were pale blue and he looked as if he had not been out into the sunlight for weeks. The family doctor had been concerned by Driffield's lack of progress on fluoxetine, and alarmed by his ominous murmurings about suicide and had asked Power for a consultant psychiatric opinion. Dr Power had elicited a history of redundancy from a local firm of surveyors, a decline into torpor and irritability, the departure of wife and daughter for the in-laws, and Driffield's complaints of poor sleep and weight loss.

"I grew up in North Wales, near the sea. A catholic family in a protestant town. My father left when I was two. He died when I was five and my mother spent no time hanging about. My stepfather arrived suddenly one day a couple of years later like she'd ordered him through the post, from a catalogue. He was just sitting there in the lounge when I got back from school. And within two months I'd got sent to a private boarding school, not a million miles from Chester. In the countryside."

Power calculated the boy's probable age at the time. "You were sent away that young?" asked Power. The room was stuffy. Driffield had the heating on even though it was still August. The windows were closed. The house smelled of Driffield's sweat and self-pity. Power acknowledged a feeling inside himself. He recognised that he didn't like Mr Driffield much and wondered if this was how other people also reacted to this man. Power countered the feeling and struggled to listen to what Driffield was saying behind the words he mumbled.

"That young. He sent me away. He wanted my mother to himself. Not that it was a marriage of bliss. He was a jealous man, he liked a drink, neat whisky – by the bottle, and he beat her on a Saturday night."

"Did you ever see that?" asked Power.

"I saw him put her through a plate-glass window in the dining room door," said Driffield. "I said to her, when I could get her on her own, 'why don't you leave him Mum?' But she just shook her head and looked wide-eyed and frightened and said nothing. I suppose by then she had had two little ones by him. He refused to let her work, so she was financially dependent on him you see. She had nowhere to go. He was a wealthy man, with a factory that made engine filters for cars, you know? All he cared about was money, which he wore on his fingers as gold sovereign rings. He flaunted a ghastly gold-coloured Rolls Royce too. Dreadful taste."

"What was the school like? The boarding school?" asked Power.

"I had one good friend. Jacob. He stayed with me until the second year of the seniors. Otherwise, I was either ignored or bullied for being a swot. Can I tell you something?" Power paused, and then nodded. "This is something I've never told anyone, not even my wife. Can you keep it confidential?"

"I have a duty of confidentiality," said Power, and thought in the moment, that those words sounded unduly priggish. "But unless a third party is at risk, I won't be telling anyone else."

"That depends then," said Driffield. "On whether people are still alive. I hope one person in particular isn't to be honest."

"Someone at the school?" Power hazarded a guess.

"Yes," said Driffield. He looked at Power again. He was checking him again; his first impression of the doctor had led him to decide Power could be trusted. Mr Driffield seldom trusted anyone, but he felt comfortable with Dr Power even though he did keep staring out of the window at the rain. "It was somebody at the school. He chose me for the rugby team. I wasn't the type. I wasn't powerful enough and I wasn't fast enough. But he said it would make a man of me . . . Mr Cooper. He used to be a priest I think, but he said the calling wasn't for him. The whole place was run by an offshoot of the Catholic Church. Cooper chose me and Jacob for the first team. And he said we'd both need extra tuition, after hours, in the gym. Looking back at what he said, maybe you can hear the alarm bells. But when you are twelve and with no-one to guide you, you believe these people. You trust them. You don't hear the warning bells." He looked at Power. "You are frowning. Have I upset you or something?"

Power shook his head. He made an open-handed gesture. "I'm not upset at you," he said, trying to choose his words as carefully as he could. "I . . . think that I am becoming annoyed, but on your behalf. I am cross at what I think happened to you next. Not at you."

"Then you have probably guessed. He robbed me, Dr Power. He robbed me of everything, I think. There was rough and tumble in the gym in the evenings, and gradually the touchings got worse. More intrusive. He'd insist on us wearing fewer clothes. He'd insist on privacy, that things were secret, that we were his special pupils. First of all he saw Jacob and me together, then he started tutoring us alone. I was confused. Afterwards I was puzzled. The only person I could ask was Jacob. Was the same thing happening to him? I asked Jacob what happened in his sessions, but he wouldn't say. It was a secret, he said. I didn't know whether I liked what was happening to me. Cooper said the way my body reacted was normal, a part of growing up, special. My body's reaction to his . . . touching . . . meant that I was that way. I felt hugely embarrassed. And ashamed too. He said he wouldn't tell anyone that I was gay. Of course, I know now that I wasn't gay at all. It took me years to get everything right in my mind. For years after school, like at University, I wouldn't go near a girl. I'd go out maybe with a girl as a friend, but if things got sexual I'd practically run away. There was the unbelieving it was happening. I'd just sort of go elsewhere in my head when it happened to me. When he touched me and pulled my clothes off, I'd just go somewhere else in my head while it was happening. And afterwards I'd lie there not sleeping, wondering if what had happened, really happened. The next day Mr Cooper would act as if nothing had happened. So I'd ask myself, did what I thought had happened to me the day before really happen? It felt unreal. And I've come to realise, over the years, that when you get that feeling of puzzlement, or perplexity over whether some thing has happened – that's when you've just been deceived or abused."

"Do you dream about those times?" asked Power. Driffield nodded. "Nightmares?" asked Power.

"I wake in a cold sweat."

"And do you find yourself thinking about those times, even though you don't want to; see images in your mind's eye? Experience the old sounds? Smells?"

"I remember his smell," said Driffield. "A kind of sickly men's cologne. It makes me want to vomit when I smell that aftershave on someone now. I can't talk to them and I have to leave the room. But to be honest I try my best not to think about it, and if someone ever talks about abuse in conversation I just go."

"And are you very protective of your child and others you care about?" asked Power.

"Yes, how did you know?"

Power couldn't help looking out at the leaden sky as he tried to manage his own feelings.

He kept thinking about Lucia and what she had suffered. Driffield's history was bringing everything crashing back on him, like a solid grey wave in heavy seas. Events from the past and the present seemed to be merging together in his mind and it was a struggle to keep things separate.

"Is it difficult to be close with your wife now? Do you feel, detached? Is it difficult to trust anyone?"

"I am a jealous man. I recognize that. Strange that as you grow you start to behave in ways you deplored and hated in others. I sometimes feel as jealous and angry as my stepfather would have been. I have never hit my wife, but it would be so easy to pull on my stepfather's shadow, like putting on a glove or something. And I don't trust anybody nowadays. Nobody in a position of authority."

"It must be difficult to trust me," said Power, and wondered whether he should have said that. Driffield just looked at him.

"I think every man is evil. Fundamentally evil. All men are. All men have darkness at their heart like a shadow and I believe that they cast this shadow behind them through life. All we can do as men is to try and make this shadow smaller. That's the measure of a man. To make his shadow small enough that it doesn't touch those around him." He stared into Power's eyes, trying to fathom the doctor.

"What happened?" asked Power. "Did you try and tell someone?"

"I ran away from the boarding school one night. I walked and hitched lifts all the way back home. I turned up on my mother's doorstep the next morning. And my stepfather got his fucking gold Rolls Royce out of the garage and drove me straight back to the school, except for a short stop on the way at a service station where he beat me black and blue. So I didn't try to leave again after that."

"And Jacob," asked Power, with sudden resurgence of the feeling that all his worlds, past and present, were colliding together at once. "What happened to Jacob?"

"Jacob stopped walking. Whether he was putting it on or not I never knew. One day he just fell to the ground, while we were playing rugby. He just keeled over in front of Mr Cooper and he said his back hurt and that he couldn't move. Of course Cooper was scared shitless that Jacob had broken his spine or something. But it wasn't as if there'd been a scrum or anything. The paramedics arrived, put him on a stretcher, and took Jacob away in an ambulance. He was his parents' worry again. I think he spent months in a hospital. I never heard from him again."

"And his name," said Power suddenly gathering old unwanted memories together like Autumn leaves. "Was it Tuke? Jacob Tuke?"

Driffield frowned. His expression then seemed to betray a mixture of fear and anger. "How did you know that? Know that his name was Tuke. How do you know that Dr Power?"

"I think I met him once," said Power slightly unconvincingly, cursing himself for mentioning the name. Power realised he had put his need to know ahead of the patient's feelings. Now Driffield might feel that Power knew rather too much, and so Power had jeopardised Driffield's trust in him. And Power couldn't reveal how he had once treated Jacob Tuke, or indeed what he knew had happened to Tuke. He tried to cover up his mistake. "It isn't a name you forget."

Driffield glared at him. "I suppose Jacob is an unusual name, but . . . you won't contact Jacob will you? You wont tell him will you? I don't want to get involved in all that again. Too painful."

"I won't be contacting him," said Power, knowing rather uncomfortably that he could never contact Tuke as he was long dead, and that he couldn't reveal any more about Tuke for fear of losing Driffield altogether. Power felt doubly, trebly awkward and now he was battling with memories that flocked around him like unbidden demons.

"And there is one more thing I want to tell you about the school, before we move on." Driffield's voice had diminished to something just above a whisper. "There were visitors to the school. People I didn't know. They were never introduced. Some of them looked a bit like they were off the television, or something. One might be there one week, and another the next. They seemed friendly with Cooper. They came in to my 'tutorials', and . . ." his voice broke off. He looked imploringly at Power, willing him to understand.

"I see," said Power. "I think I understand."

"One man," said Driffield. "He was a priest. An old priest who smelt of pink soap and cigarettes and sherry. He pressed himself against me." Driffield shuddered visibly.

They spoke for maybe half an hour more. Power offered a longer appointment at his office. He knew there was no merit in pulling all the facts out of Driffield at once. That would be too intrusive and would damage everything. Power offered empathy, antidepressants, therapy and most importantly he offered hope that things could change. And with a comforting smile and a handshake, Power left for home in his rain-soaked old Saab.

Power's drive back along the winding Cheshire lanes was little more than a blur of green fields and hedges. At one point Power realised he couldn't remember the last five minutes of the drive, so busy were his thoughts about the patient he had seen and his mention of Jacob Tuke. Not only had the subject matter of organised abuse of Driffield as a young boy at boarding school been so disturbing, there had been the mention of an old patient, Tuke. Recognising that his mind was anywhere but his driving, Power turned off the road into a layby. The layby had been fashioned from a leftover bend in the old road when it had been straightened years before.

Power sat in the silence of the car. He contemplated the incessant drizzle accumulating on the windscreen and obscuring his vision of the outside world. His mind was full of thought. Part of him refused to accept that past and present had collided so hard across time and space. Echoes of the past abuse suffered by Tuke and Driffield had resurfaced and reverberated with the organised conspiracy that had led to the death of Lucia. Power felt dizzy and nauseated by the memories crashing about in his skull, and he opened the car door lest he be sick again as he had been in the graveyard.

He had not dreamed of Tuke for some years, but the discovery of Lucia's body had re-awakened this particular wound and in recent days he had been suffering from nightmares about Tuke's death. The mention of Tuke by the patient on today's domiciliary visit had somehow linked the day with night, muddling the reality of Power's day job with his dreamworld. And now Power felt unhinged, undone. Tuke had been a patient of his, and the work had not gone well. Power might have tried his best to help Tuke, but he had failed. Tuke had fallen too far. But perhaps the failure of others, years before Power had been involved, had damaged Tuke too much for anyone to heal. More than the failure of others, thought Power, it had been the deliberate actions of others that had destroyed Driffield, Tuke and now Lucia; deliberate actions that were cynical, self-obsessed and driven by overwhelming lust.

When he had calmed the competing demons of his thoughts as much as he could, Power decided he would go home and withdraw to the solidity of Alderley House and seek some comfort from its familiar old walls, and the words of his partner, Laura. He drove slowly, limpingly, back to Alderley Edge. The old Saab climbed the hill into the woods with growling steadiness. As Power drove through the village and passed the De Trafford Arms he looked for the Piper. The Piper had sometimes been seen in the Edge, and although Power had talked to him many times in the past there, the wandering Piper seemed to have disappeared for good, and this saddened the doctor.

Laura's white Mini was parked in the driveway and Power felt an immediate sense of relief that someone was at home. Power was planning a replacement for the rust-bedevilled old Mini and he had had thoughts of buying one of the new BMW Minis for Laura as a surprise.

He found Laura in the living room listening to music. "You're home early," she said, as she looked Power up and down. She thought he had a wild, panicky look in his eyes. He hadn't been quite the same since his return from Spain. He had talked about finding the girl, and she understood him well. "Would you like a cup of tea?"

"I definitely would," said Power.

"Well, sit down," she said, heading for the kitchen. "I've just been reading some poetry."

Power sank on to the sofa and picking up the book, which she had left behind, slumped back. There were some lines of Shelley on the open page which he was unfamiliar with:

> *Oppressive law no more shall power retain,*
> *Peace, Love, and concord once shall rule again,*
> *And heal the anguish of a suffering world;*
> *Then, then shall things, which now confusedly hurled,*
> *Seem Chaos, be resolved to order's sway,*
> *And errors night be turned to virtue's day.*

Laura returned with two freshly brewed mugs of tea and a plate of gooseberry pie. "You look as if you'd had a bit of a shock," she said. He nodded as she handed him the mug and smiled at the pie on the plate. Power looked more drawn and older than he had when he had left that misty morning at eight. "Do you want to talk about it?" she asked.

Power looked up from the pie he was already eating in a famished way. "Not yet," he said.

"Did you have an accident or something?" she asked.

"No," said Power. "Just troubled by some ghosts from the past. I'll talk about it when I've got my head straight. What are you listening to? It sounds a bit . . . rustic?"

"It's a folk band called Morris On – old songs."

Power listened to the track that was playing. A line in the song struck a chord with him: 'Two pairs to dance; one pair to play; and that's all we ever need to drive our cares away'. He put his plate down by the mug on the side table and stood up. As the phrase of music and lyric repeated itself he caught of Laura round her shapely waist. She felt warm through the thin cotton of her dress, and as the song suggested he began to dance with her, turning round and round the room. She giggled. They smiled, and somehow his cares receded a little as the tune had promised.

* * *

In those days the Chester Police Headquarters was in a concrete monolith of a building on Nuns Road in the city centre. Chester CID occupied two full floors of what Pevsner called 'this objectionably-sited, concrete monstrosity'. Superintendent Lynch's office was on the seventh storey. The best that could really be said of his office was that it boasted a superb view over the Roodee and racecourse towards Hawarden, where Gladstone the Prime Minister had once lived, and beyond that the Welsh Hills, green-blanketed and rolling.

Lynch sat at his desk surveying the remains of a plate of lunchtime egg sandwiches and an emptied cup of tea. Lynch had not found the return to work of any satisfaction. He was between cases, having returned from holiday early, to the surprise, if not consternation, of his superiors. They had been congratulating themselves on coaxing Lynch into taking his leave. Unlike almost every other employee in the Force, Lynch always took less than his allotted annual leave. Although he could be held up as an example of dedication to his juniors, he also unfortunately made his seniors look work-shy. Lynch had felt obliged to return to work. What else could he do in all conscience? He had taken leave to walk to Santiago. Since he and Power had felt unable to continue their pilgrimage in the circumstances surrounding Lucia's death they had flown home early. They had solemnly promised each other to finish their pilgrimage in a month or so, but Lynch was now keen to plunge himself back into work and he harboured some doubts that the pilgrimage would ever be finished.

By returning to his post on the seventh floor, Lynch had hoped to expunge the memories of Lucia's death by immersing himself in the detail of some new investigation. No case had been allotted to him, however, and he was dreading being sucked into the politics that had so worn him down before he had left on his journey.

By way of brief diversion his younger colleague and protégé, Sergeant Beresford, had ventured into Lynch's office with his news. Beresford had brought his old boss and himself two large takeaway cups of coffee from a new place on Eastgate Street.

Now they sat sipping the lattes. Beresford had always thought Lynch a buttoned-up, tight-lipped sort of man, but he had always respected and even liked him.

For his part Lynch regarded the younger man as his protégé and he tended to confide in him rather more than he would any other officer.

"You're back earlier than we thought," said Beresford. "Did you have enough of walking?"

"Something happened along the way," said Lynch. "Work happened to me, although I was trying to avoid it."

"You mean they contacted you? On your leave?"

"No," said Lynch, sadly. "There was a murder. A young girl was killed and Dr Power found the body. After we'd settled things with the local police, well, we didn't have the heart to continue really."

Beresford was taken aback at the news, "Well no, you don't expect anything like that on your holiday," he said. "Poor Dr Power."

"He was devastated," said Lynch. "I'd not seen him like that. Collapsed in shock. And the local police were . . . difficult. He'd put his coat over the body and they tore a strip off him for contaminating the crime scene with his DNA. Went on at him about prosecuting him for obstruction of the investigation. Threatened to hold on to him, onto us, because he might have been the murderer. They implied that he was a suspect. Nonsense of course; he was just doing the decent thing, covering her. She was naked."

"Distressing all round," said Beresford. "Had she been abused? Sexually assaulted?"

Lynch frowned. "I haven't seen any Post Mortem report, of course," he said. "But Carl saw the external surface of the body. He's a doctor, of course, and he doesn't miss anything. Power said she had been bruised. That is to say, he eventually told me, when he had calmed down later that day. He said there were very recent bruises around the genitals, as if she had been deliberately hurt there."

"Why was he so upset?"

Lynch nodded. He was admiring how his student had picked up on that. Beresford knew full well that Power would have seen many bodies in his work with the police, and had spotted a significant difference in this account. "We had found the girl running away. She was running from some kind of orphanage that wasn't what it seemed. We were in the process of finding some responsible person to look after her, when she was . . . abducted . . . this was not the chance discovery of a murdered stranger. We had known the girl for a day or so before she was taken from our care. So Dr Power and I must assume some responsibility, or even guilt, for letting the girl be taken. And that is a heavy burden, and one which I am not prepared to accept without question, without doing my very best to find out what really happened and visiting justice upon the evil creatures that did this."

"There were several perpetrators, then?" queried Beresford. "Not some lone pervert?"

"No, not just one person . . ." said Lynch. "This was a group, of men *and* women, which makes the crime against the girl infinitely worse in way. Because they probably all share the same twisted beliefs, and it's difficult enough to come to terms with the notion that even one man should hold such ideas, but a group of people?" Lynch shuddered. "We are dealing with evil here."

"You know the Payne case?"

"Sarah Payne? That was going on before we left for Spain," said Lynch.

"I was talking to colleague in Surrey. They think they've got the man in custody, Whiting. A known paedophile. They're holding him on a dangerous driving charge after he tried to get away at seventy miles per hour in a stolen car on normal roads. And they know his alibi was false; he said he was at a funfair, but they found a receipt at his house for petrol from a garage where they'd already found one of the little girl's shoes. They just don't have anything to link him to the killing for definite. At least not enough to convince a jury yet."

Lynch thought over what Beresford had said. "If Whiting was followed driving a stolen car . . . what vehicle was he driving when he was buying petrol in the garage? Tell your friends in Surrey to find that other vehicle. He probably used a van."

Beresford mulled this over, and made a mental note to do so. He put his empty coffee cup in the bin. "And so, what are you working on, now you're back?"

"I'd cleared my desk before I left. And I haven't picked up anything new yet. I might spend an hour or so making some enquiries about Lucia. That was the Spanish girl's name. Then I'll go looking for a new project here. Although to be honest, I am made to feel such a dinosaur these days." He chose not to mention a particularly upsetting meeting he'd had before his holiday with the ACC, where Lynch's own faith had become the topic of criticism. Lynch had been lectured for half an hour and told, in no uncertain terms, that it was apparently no longer acceptable to overtly 'proselytise or advertise your belief'. Younger colleagues had taken exception to Lynch having an open Bible on his office desk, even though he had never read to them from it. Lynch was not allowed to 'show any outward symbol of belief lest it offend.' Throughout the interview Lynch had stared at the ACC's masonic cufflinks in simmering disgust.

"I wanted to give you my news," said Beresford, wondering if now was the right time, as Lynch's mood seemed to have darkened. "And thank you for all your help."

"Help?" asked Lynch.

"Over the OSPRE exams," said Beresford. "I had the Part Two exam just before you went on holiday and got the results a couple of days ago."

"Of course," said Lynch. "Of course. I'm sorry. Rude of me. I should have asked." The OSPRE exams determined whether a sergeant like Beresford could be promoted to inspector rank. There was a multiple choice exam and then a role-playing assessment. Lynch had tutored Beresford through the latter. "How did it go?"

"I passed!" Beresford grinned. "You're looking at a new inspector."

Lynch stood up and shook Beresford's hand, grinning. He was genuinely pleased.

As he was sitting down, Beresford dropped his voice, "You know I was worried, I had heard the panel could be a bit . . . racist."

"I know," said Lynch. "Prejudices die hard, especially amongst our colleagues. But it is a done thing then? You have it all in writing?" Lynch was a firm believer in getting everything in writing. Beresford nodded and produced the letter for his superior's attention.

Lynch made to read it through, and indeed made a show of doing so, but somehow, deep inside, he was wondering about the probable fact that he would never himself receive any further promotion. He was simply too old, and possibly also too unpopular with his superiors now, it seemed.

At length he finished 'reading' and beamed at Beresford, who made his exit satisfied that he had dutifully thanked his old mentor for his help.

Lynch, alone once again, stared out of the window at the grey skies over the racecourse. His mind wandered back to the moment in Spain that he and Delgado had realised that something must have happened to Power, and their discovery of him in the graveyard slumped before a stone altar-piece on which the small body had been draped or displayed. Power had been insensible with grief and for a while no words could be coaxed from him. A glimpse under the red coat at the body on the altar had explained Power's mute dismay. The guide, Delgado, had summoned Patxi who parked as close as he could and, not knowing what else could possibly be appropriate, had brought some rugs and a flask of brandy for them. Delgado had alerted the police and when they eventually arrived, Power had surprised Lynch by suddenly breaking his silence and shouting at them angrily for their failure, as he saw it, to protect the girl. It was this anger of Power's that led the local police to respond with threats to arrest the doctor for 'contaminating' the crime scene with his red coat. Lynch attempted, via Delgado's translation, to pour oil on troubled waters but hurt professional pride had led to a defensive obstinacy amongst the police. There had followed an informal kind of arrest, where Power and Lynch were both bundled into a police van and spirited back into Astorga, for several hours of unpleasant questioning in separate rooms. The police had only reluctantly allowed them to leave after it had become obvious to all concerned that Power and Lynch were innocent of any crime. They were, however, obliged to give written assurances that they would return for any questioning on any matter deemed relevant, and of course, for the Inquest.

And at this, their involvement in the official police investigation had come to an end.

Lynch had asked Delgado and the driver Patxi to get them to the airport in Madrid immediately. He deemed this prudent lest the police create some charge or other complication to hold them with.

Power asked Lynch whether such a rapid departure was necessary, "We have to leave immediately; is it as bad as that?"

"Worse," said Lynch. "I have no confidence in them whatsoever. We have time to maybe see the Count before we go on our way, and break the news to him. We owe him that, but as soon as we can, we must go."

The holiday had been ruined beyond redemption. Lynch covered all Delgado's expenses and had promised faithfully that maybe he would return one day to complete the Pilgrimage.

On the sombre journey back to the airport, Lynch had coaxed details from Power about what he thought, as a doctor, had happened to Lucia. In the front seat of the van, Delgado and Patxi had grown pale.

Lynch, ever the professional, had made a few brief notes at the time in case Power should forget anything. Power had rambled about a thin ligature mark, from a garrot wire tightly wound into and around the girl's slim neck, and the suffused skin of her face, the small splinters of blood in the whites of her eyes – Power used the word *petechiae*, the generally thin nature of the cadaver, and the bruising around the vulva which, he insisted, were characteristic of sexual assault with some blunt object.

Lynch considered what size of organisation it would take to manage, or farm, children under the cover of an orphanage, hiding in full view within the propriety of trusted institutions such as the church and the police.

He considered how someone had tipped off this machine that they – Power and Lynch – weren't there at the hotel. Lynch factored in that maybe someone else had also arranged for the orphanage to be emptied. How someone arranged for two other people to risk themselves to abduct the girl in plain sight. How another person or persons had sadistically placed the dead girl in their path? How arrogant and audacious was that particular move? How much this taunting of them with the body of a child smacked of people who were supremely confident of their powers and seemed to be able to defy the law at will; people who maybe even controlled some of the police themselves.

This was no simple crime committed by an individual, and born of gratuitous impulse. This was a cynical, deep-rooted, long-standing conspiracy of many. All of this took planning, a network of people, great organisation and deep and highly motivated investment of time and energy. Motivated by what? Money, or sexual desire, or both? Lynch reached in his drawer and withdrew his well-thumbed Bible. He flicked to Chapter 7 of the Gospel of Matthew. He was reassured to find the apposite verse that he wanted exactly where he thought it was. He placed the Bible carefully back in the drawer.

He logged into the Web on his computer and searched for the hotel they had stayed at in Astorga. There was a rudimentary site in existence with a picture of the archway entrance framing the Count and his wife. Lynch dialled the international dialling code and the number for the hotel.

The Count answered after two rings. "Hello," said Lynch. "It's Superintendent Andrew Lynch. We stayed with you a few days back, do you remember?"

"How could I forget?" replied the Count, switching to English with consummate ease. "I am not senile yet, you know. How are you Superintendent?"

"I wanted to ask your advice," said Lynch.

"And I have been meaning to talk to you since yesterday morning, so this phone call is most opportune," said the Count. Lynch imagined the Count sitting in his stone-walled office, his moustache bristling. "You go ahead first with your question. Ask me whatever you need to."

"Well, Count, I am hoping to write an advertisement to put in your local and national newspapers. I want to see if we can fish for information about the activities of the orphanage and find out about the children – where they have come from and what happens to them? I will put in a safe way of getting information back to me confidentially. So we can break through any wall of silence. What do you think? Do you think that is a good idea?"

"It is an excellent idea," said the Count, with a decided firmness to his voice.

"Will you help me write the advertisement? If I fax you a draft?"

"Of course," said the Count. "I want to help in anyway I can. I will be your agent here, because I am afraid that there is no one else." It sounded as if the Count shared Lynch's guarded suspicion of the local police.

Lynch went on, "Can you give me your advice as to which newspapers we put the ad in? I need some local newspapers in your region and some national Spanish papers."

"No problem; let me have a think what is best and I will phone you back later on. Fax me through the advert you would like to publish and I will check over the language."

Lynch added one more request, "Count, I need Spanish newspapers that have on-line counterparts. I want to find young people and of course they will use the Internet these days. And maybe some of them will be abroad, and might just read the papers on-line to keep it touch."

"All right, I will see," said the Count. "I have written that all down. Now I have news for you, Superintendent Lynch. Are you ready?"

"I am," said Lynch.

"I told you that I would not let this matter rest, did I not?"

"You did."

"Well, I expected that the death of the girl would be the talk of the town, that it would be big news. That there would be, as you say, an outcry."

"Yes, I'd expect that too."

"Nothing," said the Count. "Nothing on the news. Nothing. I wait two or three days and there is nothing. She is forgotten. So I go to the local newspaper office, and I phone the regional papers. I ask the newspapers, what about this crime? They act as if I have lost my mind. What girl they ask me? What proof do you have of this dreadful thing? And of course, I have none." The Count coughed apologetically. "And so I go to the police. I go to the police station and I ask the officer on the door about the investigation. What is happening? They look at me as if I am a simpleton, or as if I am mad. Loco. You know?"

The Count continued, "They say there is no record. And they advise me that I would be well advised to drop what I am saying. That I am an old man, and that I should stop saying these things, because maybe someone will say that I am suffering with dementia. Is that the word?" The Count sounded justifiably angry. "And you know, all this is very puzzling. And I wonder if what happened was real? Did it really happen, or am I going mad? I saw the girl myself, but if they say these things, was the girl ever here? They tell you one thing is so and you know another thing is right and the two things cannot match. So are you going mad, you wonder? They say leave this thing, Count. You are a respectable man, forget these things. They never happened. And it reminds me of the bad times when I was a boy, and the Nationalists and the Fascists fought, and people disappeared overnight or ended up in prison for years without trial, without anyone knowing, no visitors, no lawyers. No-one heard from them again. I thought those days were over. But it has happened before in my lifetime, and it could all happen again. It is frightening for me, but I will not give up."

Lynch interrupted, to clarify what he had heard. "Count, listen to me. This thing happened. I saw the girl dead. Dr Power saw her. Delgado saw her, Patxi saw her. You and I saw the girl alive at the hotel. Your wife saw the girl alive at the hotel. We know that the girl existed. We know this. But it sounds as if someone just wants to erase her from the world, and thinks that they can. They think they have the power to just rub any record of a life out. You are saying that there is no record of her death, and that even the police deny that a murder happened?"

"Exactly, I . . . I feel so perplexed, because what I know to be true is being denied. That feeling twists you inside you know, so somehow you don't trust even yourself."

"It is real, Count."

"I know. It is horrible. But I tell you this; I will not give this up now. No matter what it takes. Even if it is the last thing I can do in my life. I will not be made to feel like this. They can't do this to me. I have my own networks," said the Count. "I have my own methods. I am a Knight after all, but I tell you this, Superintendent Lynch. We are surrounded by wolves. Can't you feel it? Something is very wrong."

Chapter Ten

He kept his tippet stuffed with pins for curls,
And pocket-knives, to give to pretty girls.
Geoffrey Chaucer, The Canterbury Tales

Power and Lynch were standing on the highest point inside the keep of Beeston Castle. Here they perched on a sandstone crag some three hundred and fifty feet above the Cheshire Plain. The Plain rolled out far below them like green baize undulating across a patchwork of fields. Today, the wind was strong in this corner of Northwest England and woven together with a driving drizzle. Although this was undoubtedly a most inspiring ruin from the thirteenth century, Power's notion that this walk might somehow recapture the lost feeling of the Santiago Way was falling far short of the mark. Power had wanted to banish the glumness that had descended on them both after their experience in Spain.

A few hardy families and sightseers had braved the elements atop the hill that Saturday. The families mooched in a rather subdued manner round the castle walls. Their brightly-coloured raincoats and wellingtons could not dispel the bad weather. Although both Mrs Lynch and Laura had been invited on the walk, both women had looked out of their respective windows at the grey skies and had made a polite excuse.

Lynch surveyed the distant horizon, beyond the Cheshire Plain, and seemed to be formulating what he wanted to say next. Power waited with bated breath. Eventually the words came. "I think," said Lynch. "If we take everything into consideration we have achieved our goal of going on a walk. I now propose that we adjourn to somewhere to eat and, because it is very much an English August, also somewhere to get warm."

"Agreed," said Dr Power, whose whole demeanour had brightened at the mention of food. "The Pheasant Inn is only a couple of miles away."

"A couple of miles. Are you proposing that we walk?"

"Goodness no," said Power. "We'll take the car."

"I was rather hoping that you would say that," said Lynch. And together the old friends left the windy and exposed summit and half-walked, half-slithered down the gleaming wet grass and mud that covered the hill to the car park. Against Lynch's better judgment they were in Power's old Saab. Lynch half expected the engine to fail to splutter into life. However, the classic car started first time in loyalty to the doctor and they were off down the winding country road to The Pheasant Inn in Burwardsley.

Despite it being a summer month, a comforting log fire was blazing in the central hearth-space. Lynch and Power acquired two pints of Badger Tanglefoot Ale and some bar menus and settled down in wingback armchairs across a table for two.

A bright little waitress appeared at Power's elbow. He was thinking she had a trim figure and lovely brown eyes, when he felt the almost physical force of Lynch's glare. Power coughed and ordered himself a roast nut wellington with roast potatoes. Lynch ordered a steak pie with chips.

"I didn't say anything before," said Lynch. "To tell you the truth, I didn't want to bring it up, but I have been making enquiries into what happened in Astorga to Lucia. I have placed adverts in Spanish papers to see what information we can flush out. That is, if anybody dares to speak."

"I don't know what you were worried about. Why didn't you say earlier? I don't mind that. I didn't expect that you would just let things go. I'd have been worried about you if you didn't do something."

"No," said Lynch. "It's not that doing something about Lucia concerns me. And you're right, I couldn't sit on my hands and do nothing. It's something more worrying still and I don't know what we can do about it. What can you do against a conspiracy of silence? I spoke to the Count a few days ago. He sounded well enough and he was full of fighting spirit, but all of a sudden I realise that he's a lone voice out there."

"What do you mean?" asked Power, after a gulp of Badger's.

"There has been no media interest in the murder. None. Nothing on the television news or the radio. Nothing in the papers. Isn't that remarkable? And when our friend went to the police to see how their investigation was progressing, they point blank denied there had been any murder. What you and I saw has not happened according to official records. It seems that in official circles there was no Lucia, dead or alive."

"What do you mean? No Lucia . . . dead or alive?" Power's voice was louder than it should have been in the public house and his face wore an expression of such perplexity that other diners stared momentarily before resuming their lunch.

Lynch's voice fell to a compensatory hush. "I mean this . . . that just as there is no official record of anybody being murdered, and no body, in fact there is also no record of Lucia's birth. Officially, all the records that should be there about a person are just not there; it is a vacuum. If you look in the records now – Lucia never even existed. I can think of no precedent for this. And I must confess my mind is greatly troubled. We are fighting smoke and shadows. We are dependent on someone talking and someone saying the truth. And unless they do, we are lost, for who will believe us?"

"But we all saw her," hissed Power. "You, me, Delgado, the police.

In broad daylight. That sort of thing cannot be denied." He sat there silent for a while, staring into space. "I can't believe it," he said. "This can't be happening. Am I going mad?"

"No," said Lynch. "You're not. I was there. It happened. I would get down on my knees and pray until the end of time that that child's murder did not happen, but it did. And now we must think of a way to make things right. Because it will keep on happening if we don't."

At this, their food arrived steaming hot from the kitchens and the waitress asked if more drinks were required. Power looked and saw he had somehow gulped down the whole pint. He was about to order another, when he saw Lynch frowning, because Power was meant to be driving later. They compromised with an order for lime and sodas, despite Power's feeling that alcohol was required.

"So what do we do?" asked Power.

"We must wait – for something will betray them, some truth will surface," said Lynch. "We will gather information. I have made some enquiries internationally and the Count, although clearly Quixotic to a degree, does have some genuine well-placed contacts as well."

"So the Count is *'Our Man in Havana'*, eh?" said Power. "It's all very well, but we are over a thousand miles away, which makes us of little help to him. And what is more, that distance makes him on his own. Apart from us. Isolated. These kind of people will have no remorse or compunction about finishing him off if he becomes even the remotest threat to them. They have the police in their pocket. If Lucia can disappear, then so can an old man."

"I wouldn't dismiss him on account of age," said Lynch defensively. "Old men like the Count are also more resilient, have more experience and have more resources than you might think."

Power nodded assent and focused his attention on the golden-brown roast potatoes sitting in front of him, which were rather fine. He had picked up on the personal element that might lie behind

Lynch's defence of the older man. He knew that Lynch was approaching an age when he would have completed thirty years' police service and could theoretically retire. Lynch didn't seem like a man who would be content with cardigans, morning coffee, jigsaws and pruning the roses. Power toyed with the idea of asking a question about what his friend's future plans might be, but couldn't think how to phrase it without potentially offending Lynch. For his own part, Power had felt his hospital work had a degree of repetitiveness and he, too, sought some extra challenge. He had started writing another book, entitled *Uncommon Psychiatric Symptoms.* Sometimes Power wondered if he would like a post that could let him spend a day or so a week teaching and researching at the University.

Power was re-formulating his question when Lynch interrupted his thoughts.

"When I joined the force as a young man there were older officers that told me that the job had changed around them, that I shouldn't stay in the new police force I was joining. And I didn't listen to the older men. I suppose for the most part I've enjoyed it. Some things you never forget; like the first time you're called to a sudden death. I can even remember the man's first name and the road he lived in. I remember his wife making me a cup of tea. It should have been other way round. It was the first time I'd seen a dead body. She'd been in the war – a civilian in the Blitz – and seen many."

"I suppose that's a significant event in anyone's life," said Power, thinking back to his first day in the dissection room as a first year medical student.

"And here I am, an older officer myself, and if I was with a young probationer, I'd probably tell him what they told me. That the job was not the same, that it had changed beyond all recognition and that I shouldn't stay."

Power chuckled. "When I told people that I was going to specialize in psychiatry they told me not to, that it was a Cinderella speciality. Underfunded. Poor reputation. That psychiatrists themselves went mad. And when I passed my Membership exams in psychiatry my mother asked me if I would now think about going back to real medicine. So maybe these anxieties are always there around professions?"

"You know how I function," said Lynch. "I cope with all the things I see with the help of my Faith. I pray. So when some cares that I face seem just too much for one man to bear, well I pray, and I leave all my cares in the Lord's hands. I let Him worry about them. I feel that that aspect of me is under attack. I know that colleagues see me as odd. Not just old-fashioned. I am become a relic myself; some relic from a time when Christianity mattered, when prayer was an ordinary, everyday thing. And I come from a time when a policeman didn't spend hours filling out forms, and preparing reams of documents for a prosecution service – just to see if, on the off chance, they would do anything about an offender. When I started police work, we wouldn't wait and do paperwork, we'd act ourselves. Now it's like trying to fight villains with both hands behind your back.

"The other day I was talking to Beresford. He'd been on overtime, waiting for a tip-off about a bank job to materialise. Officers waiting about in a few vans. A night-watchmen was reportedly going to let the thieves in to a regional cash centre according to intelligence gathered. Well the robbers arrived, parked up and went into the bank centre. Once they were inside, they became suspicious, somehow something was different and they made a break for it. And they started to run. At that point the dog handlers had arrived and after a warning they let the dogs off the leash. And they acted. The dogs acted. No pointless paper exercises. No havering about with the Police and Criminal Evidence Act. No solicitor putting his dead hand on proceedings. The dogs acted. Instinctively and decisively. And they brought the villains down, every one. With their teeth."

Power nodded because he thought he knew what Lynch meant. He toyed with the idea of putting forward a counter-argument, but decided against doing so. The look on Lynch's face was definite.

* * *

That night Laura had taken her temperature and decided that it was the right time of the month to begin to try for a baby again. For many years Dr Power had yearned for a child. He had long entertained thoughts of filling the vastness of Alderley House with the shrieks of children's laughter and the thump-thump-thumps of running feet on the landing and stairs.

Laura and Power had retired early to bed and the first floor of the house had resounded with their noisy and joyous lovemaking for a couple of hours, before they had both drifted into a tired and satisfied sleep.

At four he had woken suddenly after a vivid dream, replaying the morning he had found Lucia's body. Thrashing about in the sheets, Power had woken disorientated and panicky. The moon had been shining through the bedroom window. The stillness of the soft, blue light falling over the counterpane of their bed had somehow calmed and stabilised him. His breathing settled from short gasps into a more even pattern that matched his sleeping partner, Laura.

He looked down at her, fascinated suddenly by the curves contained in the nape of her neck. He liked how a curl of her blonde hair glowed in the moonlight.

Looking out at the night he saw stars twinkling faintly and Power thought how much clearer they had been in the sky over Northern Spain.

He recalled how they had lain on the earth looking up at the constellations as Ramon had explained them one by one.

The house was still and quiet. Power felt almost guilty to be awake, but he knew there was no chance of further sleep that night. He made his way down the deeply-carpeted stairs to the kitchen and brewed himself a coffee and made some slices of toast. He took a pot of damson jam from a cupboard. As he waited for the toaster to brown the bread, he glanced nervously over at the heavy, wide kitchen dresser. Once while decorating, Power had discovered a false wall behind the dresser. The wall had hidden an undiscovered room and a stone stairway down into the caves within the rock of the Edge. The sudden discovery of the tunnel down into the dark had frightened him and he had wasted no time in exploring the caves, but had urgently sealed the entrance up and slid the massive bulk of the dresser back to prevent any venture down into the caves for exploration, and also any access up the stairway into his house from the caves below.

Power buttered the toast and spread it thickly with damson jam. He carried the full plate and a mug of coffee and made his way into his study. He fired up the study's computer and opened the file of the latest chapter of his book. At his side he had a tall stack of photocopied scientific papers and he sifted through these to find the ones he wanted on *Capgras syndrome.*

He switched on the radio and listened to Radio 3 as he read through the papers and made some notes. Occasionally he paused to sip coffee or formulated a sentence to add with an associated reference to his text.

The sun was beginning to dilute the ink of night with daylight as Power added the last fact he had culled about *Capgras syndrome* from the papers he had collected. The radio was playing 'On Wenlock Edge' by Vaughan Williams. He was suddenly aware of a soft step behind him and, startled, he turned to see Laura behind him. She reached out a hand to stroke his hair. "You're up very early," she said. "Was it another dream?"

"It was," said Power, looking out at the dawn as it gathered pace.

"About the man who attacked you?"

"Ah," said Power. "And which man would that be?"

"Wasn't there a man called Tuke?" Laura had a good memory for names.

"Yes," said Power, looking out of the window at a squirrel running along a branch. "And his name came up again recently. I had bad dreams about him years ago. Nightmares actually. About him. He was the one who fell from a cliff in North Wales. Either he wanted to push me over and escape, or he wanted to take me with him. I thought he was fully gone, entirely in the past now. The dreams had all but gone. Only, his name cropped up again a few days ago when I saw a patient who was at the same school with him. It seems that he was abused by a master there – both of them in fact – Tuke and this other boy, the patient I saw. And that makes me feel a bit guilty, because I never appreciated what Tuke had been through in the past."

"Why would you feel guilty? If Tuke tried to kill you?"

Power sighed. "Because I should have known more. It makes me wonder. Maybe I could have helped him more if I'd known more about him, understood him better. Maybe if I'd done something differently."

Laura dealt with Power's mournfully reflective mood in a straightforward way, "'If wishes were horses, beggars would ride', as they say. Shall we have some breakfast, or in your case," she viewed the tell tale crumbs on the plate at Power's side. "Some more breakfast?"

Power followed her into the kitchen, where he put the kettle on.

Laura started poaching a couple of eggs in vinegared water and made some more toast.

"There's no point in dwelling on it, is there, Carl? We can't change the past."

He paused for a moment, and looked at Laura as she broke an egg into the swirling, boiling water to poach. "I wish I could. If I could have saved that girl in Spain . . ."

"Don't, Carl. Leave it."

Power wondered if he should broach the topic of the efforts that Lynch was making to investigate the murder, albeit at a distance. He thought, rather, that this was not the time. Laura watched the egg as it solidified, then retrieved it and placed it carefully on a fresh piece of buttered toast. She handed him the plate.

"Eat your egg and think of something positive to look forward to."

* * *

In Astorga, the Count had switched off the lights and closed the dining-room doors and windows. He was checking all the communal rooms, putting chairs and tables straight, tidying ready for the cleaners in the morning as he always did at this hour. The small family hotel seemed awash with sleep. All the Count's guests from scattered countries around the world had retired to the comfort of their rooms for the night and now it was his time to finish work and slumber.

He picked up a discarded German magazine, *Der Spiegel*, from a sofa in the lounge and brought it through to the office near the front door. He laid the well-thumbed magazine on his desk in the cone of light that fell from his desk lamp. Every room in the hotel was now in shadow. He picked up the keys to the heavy, wooden front door and the iron gate that doubled the protection at the front entrance.

165

As the Count moved to go to the entrance, he saw something out of the corner of his eye. Something peeled itself from the shadow. Something that was darker than the penumbra, gathered itself from a chair and moved towards him.

"What is that?" said the Count. "Who is it?" His voice was, by instinct, stern and strong, but there was a shake in it.

"Do not be alarmed, Count," a slippery voice, full of false reassurance. "I was waiting for you to finish your rounds."

The figure was wrapped in a cloak, and a hood obscured the wearer's identity.

"I can't see you," said the Count. "Show your face."

"Alas, I have a . . . disfigurement. I apologise to you for my sudden appearance, Count. I wanted your help."

"You are a pilgrim, maybe? You want a room for the night? The hotel is full I am afraid."

"You are lucky to have a flourishing business, Count."

"Who are you? What do you want?" The Count thought of shouting for help.

"Not very hospitable," said the visitor, softly and reproachfully. A hand reached into the folds of the cloak and withdrew a piece of paper, which was tossed onto the desk where it sat accusingly in the bright cocoon of light from the desk-lamp. "Did you help place this advertisement in the papers?"

The Count glanced briefly at the paper on the desk. He did not pick it up. It was Lynch's advertisement that the Count had advised upon. "I did not place this," said the Count. "My only advertisements are for the hotel."

"A flourishing business, as I have already said." The visitor's left hand darted into the light and the Count noticed a gold wedding band. The Count noted also that it was a young man's hand. Just as suddenly the hand snatched up the advertisement and buried it deep in the cloak's folds. "Businesses can wither on the vine though; if reputations are lost."

"Is that a threat?"

"If I wanted to threaten you, I'd threaten your life, or the life of your wife. I expect you wouldn't want to go on without your wife, would you?"

Although he was an old man, the Count could be fast when he wanted. He shot out a hand and caught hold of the visitor's arm. His grip was strong and his fingers dug into the visitor's forearm. His voice rose in volume. "No one threatens me or my wife! I will defend myself like an honourable man. I am not a snake that hides in the shadows, or kills little girls."

The shadow jerked his arm free and ran for the front entrance. As the figure passed the old man, the Count pushed him, and the cloaked figure staggered, but did not fall.

"Get out!" shouted the Count. "Get out!" He scooped up the keys and as the figure passed through the archway, the Count clanged the iron gate to and locked the bolts home. "And don't come back!" The Count closed and locked the sturdy front door and sank back against it with some relief. His heart was pounding. "*Cobarde*," he muttered. "*Cobarde*."

* * *

Lynch sat in his office in the police headquarters at Nuns Road, surrounded by the debris of a chicken sandwich lunch. He looked at the humming computer on his desk with some disdain. He had been trying to log-on it for twenty minutes, long enough to consume lunch. The server was slow.

He was finishing off a bag of crisps and washing this down with some hot tea when the phone rang.

Lynch reached over and picked up the receiver.

"Is that Mr Lynch?" The voice was young, feminine and accented. Lynch found the accent difficult to place.

"It is Superintendent Lynch," he said. "Who's calling please?"

"I can't say. I'm calling from Düsseldorf. You are a policeman?"

"I am," Lynch reached for some paper and a pen. The girl sounded nervous and frightened. "How can I help; are you all right?"

"I read your advertisement. I read the online papers. To keep in touch with home. You made a plea for information about a girl who was found in Spain."

"Yes," said Lynch. "The Spanish police didn't seem very . . . interested so I thought I would make my own enquiries. Do you know anything? Did you know her?"

"Is it . . . is it . . . Lucia?" There was genuine fear in her voice.

"You know a Lucia?" said Lynch. "What colour hair did Lucia have?"

"Brown," said the girl at the other end of the line.

"How old was she?"

"Thirteen, she had her birthday before I left. Is she dead then?"

Lynch was writing her comments and his own thoughts down. He was trying to get as much information out of a call he knew might end at any moment. He had verified that the person on the phone probably had known Lucia. "Did Lucia have a surname?"

"A what?"

"A second name?"

"The nuns gave us our names. She was Lucia. I don't know what you mean. She was my friend. You haven't told me. Please, is she dead?"

"What's your name?" asked Lynch. "We need to know more about Lucia, about where she came from. We need to know the name of the nuns who took care of you. And there was a priest. Lucia said there was a priest. We need the priest's name too if you can help us. We need your help. It's very important . . ."

"My name is Maria. I can't tell you much, because I don't know much, but there was always a priest there," the girl said. "I can't say much more. I live with a policeman now and he knows everything about me. He watches everything I do. He is my father now."

The girl could not see the expression of astonishment on Lynch's face at the other end of the phone line. "You say you are in Düsseldorf? Lucia was found in Spain."

"I was sent here by the priest. I survived that place, but Lucia always fought. And you can't fight them. You won't win. You can never win against them. There are too many of them. They are everywhere."

"The priest's name? Please help me."

"Stop fighting them, I told her. I tell you that too. They are everywhere – in plain sight. And you won't win. So don't even try."

"Please," said Lynch. "I can get you out of there. Get you safe. What is the policeman's name?"

"There is no safe for us. Anywhere. I only rang to see if it was Lucia. I wanted to know. That's *all* I wanted to know. To know what happened to her. That's all. You haven't told me so, but I know from your voice that she is dead."

The line itself now went dead.

Lynch replaced the receiver on the phone with a heavy heart. Then Lynch phoned the switchboard. "The last call," he said. "The last outside call that came through to me. Can you trace it please?"

"I will check, Superintendent," said the operator. There was a pause. "No, I'm sorry. All we have is that it was an International call, from Germany. The rest of the number was anonymised."

Lynch phoned Power later that afternoon. He was busy in clinic and returned Lynch's call between patients.

"Andrew? It's Carl. My secretary pushed a note under the door to say that there'd been a development?"

"Exactly – thanks for getting back to me, Carl. We have a lead. The advert on the Spanish website attracted a caller. A young girl phoned me from Düsseldorf. She said her name was Maria, which may or may not be true. She was a friend of Lucia's, but poor girl, she is in trouble. She was too frightened to give me anything much to go on. I wrote down everything she said. And it's pitifully thin stuff. She grew up with Lucia. In the same orphanage. She confirmed there was a priest and a set of nuns. She implied Lucia was something of a rebel against the system and that Lucia wouldn't conform."

"Düsseldorf? How did she get there?"

"We have stumbled on to something much bigger than we realised, Carl. I had maybe only a minute to talk with her, but I would guess that she has been trafficked by the priest from Spain to Germany. She lives with some man she calls her father, and what is more he is a policeman. A policeman, Carl."

* * *

The request for a face-to-face interview came through Lynch's superiors. The name of the officer who had requested Lynch's time was unknown to him. The venue was a small office in a grey city centre tower block in Manchester. Lynch had never been there before.

The unit he was summoned to was ostensibly a national police agency charged with 'Compliance and Governance'. Lynch had never heard of it in over thirty years of policing, but such units were everywhere these days.

He drove into Manchester and parked in a multi-storey car park. He half remembered a joke that he had heard and wondered about this as he tried to find the street where his appointment was. Finally, he remembered what he thought was the joke; 'Crime in multi-storey car parks, wrong on so many levels.' This memory afforded him a brief respite from stress as he anticipated the meeting. He found the building and a porter lazily took his details, made him a badge with his name on and sent him up to the fourth floor. Lynch was met at the lift door by a secretary who led him to a waiting area. A small and insubstantial sign, propped on the table, said 'Compliance and Governance Waiting Area'. He wasn't offered a cup of tea or coffee. The appointment was at ten a.m. and he was made to wait until ten fifteen.

"Inspector Lynch," an unsmiling man barked at him. He wore black trousers, a white shirt and a black tie. He had steely-grey hair above the darkest eyebrows Lynch had seen.

"*Superintendent*," corrected Lynch. "Superintendent Lynch."

The correction was not acknowledged. "In here please." A door was held wide open for him. There was no introduction. No handshake. Lynch observed that he was meant to feel uncomfortable and tried to counter this attempt to unsettle him by relaxing himself as best he could.

"The ACC asked me to come along today," said Lynch, in the silence that followed their entry into the room and closure of the door behind them both. As he wasn't asked to take a seat, Lynch took one himself. "To whom do I have the pleasure of speaking?" Lynch asked, as no introduction had been forthcoming.

"I am a representative of the National Police Compliance and Governance unit and the Independent Government Oversight team. My name is Collins, I am a police officer. My rank is senior to yours."

"Do I have the right to have a union representative here? This interview seems somewhat clandestine, and I would appreciate..."

"No." Collins glared at Lynch.

"I'm not sure of the status of this unit. I've never heard of . . ."

"You have been misusing your office and police funds."

"I have not, I really think that . . ."

"You can be summarily dismissed and your pension stripped from you."

"I have not misused any funds . . ." Lynch was boiling with anger and, of course, this had been the desired effect.

"Wasting police funds . . . your salary . . . your paid-for time on some sort of grudge against the Spanish police. Spending hours of taxpayers' time on following up a so-called crime in another country. Placing adverts asking for witnesses in a foreign country . . ."

"I paid for those press adverts myself. My own money."

"Phoning hotels in Spain. Taking phone calls from . . ." Collins held up a single piece of paper with a long number on it. "Is this familiar?"

"I don't know that number."

"You are denying the truth."

"No, I am not. I simply don't know that number."

Collins allowed himself a smile, as if of triumph. "The telephone number in Germany is of this phone call." He pulled out a small digital recorder and played the conversation Lynch had had with, Maria, the girl from Dusseldorf.

The recording ran:

"Is that Mr Lynch?"

"It is Superintendent Lynch, who's calling please?"

"I can't say. I'm calling from Dusseldorf. You are a policeman?"

Collins switched the recording off.

"You've been recording my calls at Headquarters?" Lynch was aghast.

"It was recorded elsewhere as a matter of fact. That doesn't really matter, though. Your fellow officers in Chester are as concerned about your unofficial activities as this unit is."

"What is this all about?"

"Compliance. You focus on the issues that you are given by your superiors to deal with. You DON'T waste taxpayers' money on extraneous matters. This is a warning. Your ONLY warning. Drop the enquiries you are making and focus on your legitimate work Inspector."

"*Superintendent,*" insisted Lynch.

"Or maybe not if you keep on the path you are walking down. And demotion is the very least of what we can do to you. Now, can I ask – have you got the message?"

"I'd have to be stupid not to have 'got the message'," said Lynch.

"As long as I made it loud and clear I am happy. Goodbye." Collins stood up and pointed to the door. Lynch glowered at him, but stood with as much dignity and reserve as he could, all the time suppressing the imperative urge to punch Collins. Lynch left the office, the unit, and the building and ran into the street as swiftly as he could.

Lynch was so angry and so upset he almost failed to see the lorry bearing down on him. The lorry swerved slightly and missed him by inches. It rumbled down the street, horn blaring. Lynch had felt the waft of the air turbulence as the lorry hurtled past. Passers-by stared at him, wondering if he was drunk, and Lynch crossed the now-empty road sheepishly and took refuge in a coffee shop. He ordered the first thing he saw on the menu: a filter coffee that was served in something approaching a bucket in size. He took a seat and munched sorrowfully on an overlarge biscuit. Lynch mulled over the conversation he had just had.

Coffee finished and, much calmer, he re-crossed the road and went back into the office building he had just been in. Lynch ignored the porter, who treated him similarly, and took the lift to the fourth floor. As he suspected, the secretary was gone. The table with its waiting sign was empty. Of Collins there was no sign.

The Compliance and Governance Unit had evaporated like a mirage, but the message 'Collins' had passed on to Lynch remained. And the disappearance of the Unit was of no consequence, nor was the discovery of it's fake nature. The message had been conveyed to Lynch and that was sufficient.

Lynch phoned Power on his way back to the car park and described his morning.

"Are you all right?" asked Power.

"I am now," said Lynch. "I'm annoyed that they fooled me and frustrated with myself that I let them get to me. But I don't really think that they intended to deceive me for long. They just wanted to impart the message that they could end my career if they wanted. They just want me to toe the line. So they can go on as they always have. But they also gave us two pieces of information. I know that HQ didn't have the number of the girl on the phone that rang me from Dusseldorf. But Collins showed me the actual number. And he had a tape of the conversation. And he said that wasn't taped at police HQ."

"And you believe him?"

"He could have been lying throughout, yes, but I don't think that Collins was lying then. The girl on the phone, Maria, said she was living with a policeman. In Düsseldorf. They know she talked to me. And I am very sorry to say that, as a result of that phone call, I think she has probably disappeared by now."

"Dead?"

"These people clearly have a network larger than we can imagine, and she may just disappear and be moved far away, or, as you say, be dead."

There was hushed silence at Power's end of the phone.

"Are you still there?" asked Lynch.

"I was just thinking. This network . . . the police and the church and God knows who else? This set up you faced this morning. It was all fairly elaborate."

"It was. These are clever, focused people with money. They must be for them to set this morning's charade up. I almost believed it too."

"It was designed to confuse you. You believed it because it was introduced as genuine by someone you trusted, Andrew. You said that it was the ACC himself who told you to attend. Is that person part of it?"

"I wouldn't have thought so," said Lynch. "The ACC might have been contacted and fooled just like me. How do we know who can be trusted? We are surrounded by wolves."

Chapter Eleven

People are not separate individuals as they think,
they are variations on themes outside themselves.
Lawrence Durrell
The Avignon Quintet (Constance)

D r Power's Friday morning clinic had been light. Of three new
patients, two had cancelled, and he was at an unaccustomed
loose end. He had driven the few miles from the hospital into the
City Centre. He was on a mission to investigate the building where
Lynch had been subjected to his interrogation by the imposter,
Collins. Power had agreed the expedition with Lynch, via mobile
phones. Lynch had become wary of the phones at the Police HQ.

It was not intended to be a controversial or dangerous mission.
Power was merely required to be someone other than Lynch, an
unfamiliar face, and to scout around the building and ask questions
about the tenure of the offices there. Power was reasonably good at
getting anyone talking and Lynch hoped he would persuade the
porter to divulge details of who had rented the offices on the fourth
floor that day.

A conversation between Lynch and the ACC who had sent him
the fake interview request had been necessary, but led to no
conclusion. The ACC said he was appalled that he had been misled
into passing on an order to Lynch to attend the interview. He
apologized profusely and mumbled something about a security
breach and how one of his officers – Lynch – might have been sent
unwittingly into danger. The ACC had forestalled any further protest

by Lynch of his insistence that an Inquiry should held. Lynch thought the ACC's effusive concerns appeared genuine, but he was no longer convinced.

Lynch had lost his faith in his employer.

And so Power found himself walking past the Manchester Central Library and Town Hall and into Mosley Street. He crossed the street, skipping over the tramlines. Power had fully intended to complete his mission and was even planning taking a 'business lunch' in Chinatown when he was stopped in his tracks by the sight of a person walking towards him on the pavement.

The man walked with all the striding self-confidence anyone could muster. His long face was serene and centred about a discreet smile of contentment. Against the grey Manchester pavement he was a tall column of black punctuated by the whiteness of a dog collar and topped by a shock of unruly, tufted blonde hair. Power was stunned into stillness by the shock of recognition. He was like a rabbit frozen in the glare of headlights. This was the priest he had seen in the Cathedral in Leon. The priest gave no sign of recognizing Power, however, and suddenly turned on his heel, ascended some stone steps on his left at a run and ducked into the City Art Gallery.

Without a further thought, Power jettisoned his original mission and scurried up the wide stone steps to follow the priest into the Gallery. The priest was striding ahead across the marble floor and into a gallery of paintings just as the doctor entered the main entrance hall. Power followed him, slowing as he entered the painting space, so as not to create a commotion that might attract the priest's attention. As the priest circled the walls, gazing at each painting in turn, he could be seen consulting a small catalogue that he had withdrawn from the black depths of his cassock. Power looked at the paintings too, but the priest was ever in the corner of his eye. Power noticed that the priest kept looking at his watch and assumed that he was waiting for someone. At length a slim, young woman entered the gallery. Her short hair was brunette and her eyes were a meld of turquoise and green. Her high heels click-clacked across the floor. She walked straight up to the priest, who made a show of being so engrossed in the art that he didn't appear to have noticed her arrival. Power ducked behind a column and watched them. The young woman offered a hand to the priest to shake. She did not embrace him and her body language suggested a slight distance between them. They spoke for a while, but Power was unable to discern their conversation beyond a few words; 'Gallery', 'Artist', 'Loan', and 'Insurance'. Then she pointed to an archway and the pair, the priest and the young woman, left the room. Power followed, keeping a certain distance behind the couple and discovered they were going to the Gallery café. Power queued directly behind them and watched the priest order tea, jam and scones for them both. They went to a small booth on the edge of the café, and were talking animatedly. Power carried a tray of coffee and dark chocolate cake over to a table near the door from which he could surreptitiously watch the pair and ensure they would not leave without passing him. He munched the cake fairly happily, it was moist and he was enjoying the buttercream. He liked to think he was a connoisseur of cafes and this one was, he thought, pretty good. Usually café cake had a tendency to be dried out. Occasionally, he would glance over at the table where the priest sat. From his table's vantage point Power admired the turquoise eyes of the priest's companion, and her curves. He could almost hear Lynch admonishing him for the sin of lust.

Power was almost considering a second round of coffee and cake when the priest stood up. He shook his companion's hand, bowed and started to march off alone, out of the café. Power scrambled to his feet and followed, catching up with the priest just as his quarry was rapidly disappearing through the main entrance hall and down the steps.

The priest hurried down the pavement outside the deep portico of the gallery and turned right, down Nicholas Street at the gallery's corner. It was fortuitous that Power had reacted so quickly and had sprinted after the black-cassocked figure as the priest's destination was not far from the gallery itself. Had Power been a second too slow, the priest would have scurried into a porchway unseen and lost the good doctor, and then Power might have assumed the priest had gone in any direction down any street. It is possible that if Dr Power had seen the priest enter Nicholas Street, however, he could have worked out that the priest had dived into the porch of this particular building as it was a small city-centre church.

The church was just opposite the Art Gallery. The arched entrance was recessed into what was a redbrick office building. A brass plaque said in *Times New Roman,* 'St Mary Magdalene's Catholic Church'. Of the building itself, architectural writer Pevsner had once written, 'The exterior could be mistaken for a Victorian mission house, but is graced by an ornate sawtooth arched doorway. The vestibule beyond has a statue of two angels kneeling before Christ. It opens on to a rich carved sandstone Victorian interior with heavy mahogany pews and a pulpit that overwhelmingly dominates the relatively small space. The high altar is made of travertine and has a tabernacle of Christ bearing the Sacred Heart. Rather unusual but fine drawings by illustrator Robert Fawcett depict the Stations of the Cross. A short corridor links the body of the church to the finely-panelled vestry and a suite of offices and retiring rooms for the priest.'

Power made his way into the body of the church through a small dark corridor. He moved into an open space, with wooden pews set on a glossy parquet floor. Strong sunlight shone in a diagonal beam down from a window high above the altar. The atmosphere was still and quiet and dust motes floated slowly about in the sunlight. Power felt quite alone. Of the priest, there was no sign. Power was faintly puzzled.

In the shadows beyond the shaft of sunlight he saw a figure move, which he initially assumed was the priest. He tried the name of the priest that Lucia had told him in conversation the day they had first met.

"Hello, Father Bruce?"

The shape of the figure resolved itself into a small feminine figure of advanced age. She moved swiftly through the bright sunlight to appear before Power. Janet was an older woman with such watery blue eyes, pale pink skin and titanium-white hair that they made the doctor in Power wonder about a diagnosis of anaemia. She seemed spry enough, though, and she afforded the doctor a wide smile. He noticed she was wearing a blue check, wrap-around coverall. "There's no Father of that name here," she said. "But welcome to St Mary Magdalene's. Can I help you?"

"I am sorry to disturb you," said Dr Power, wondering if he should leave.

"It's no bother," she said. "I was arranging some flowers." She pointed over towards a floral display. The sun had gone behind a cloud, and without the brilliance of the shaft of its light Power could see an array of flowers spread out ready on some flattened paper by the flower stand. He could smell the cut stems. The clouds passed and the brilliant sunlight tumbled into the church once again.

"I thought I saw a priest come in here," Power felt at a loss for words now.

"That would be Father Michael. He's gone through to his quarters. I tidy up after him through the week and look after the church. Did you want to speak with him?"

"Has he just joined this Church?" Power wondered if he should have used the word 'parish'. He was unfamiliar with the differences between the denominations and wondered whether parishes were only associated with Anglican churches.

"Father Michael has been with this particular church in the city centre for . . ." she raised her eyes to heaven and her lips mouthed through various numbers as she calculated, ". . . six years, or maybe seven."

"He's not been in Spain recently then?"

She frowned and regarded Power with some suspicion now. "He's not the holidaying type. I haven't known him take a holiday in all the time he's been here."

"Oh," said Power, confused. "He lives here then?"

"Sometimes," said the old woman. "There is a priest's house in Didsbury that goes with the church. The priest wouldn't want to live in the city centre. I look after that for him too." Power could hear her voice becoming more guarded with each response.

"I am sorry," said Power. "You must think me very nosey. I thought I recognised the Father. I've been abroad."

"He's never left the city in all the time I've known him," she said. "You can ask anybody at St Mary Magdalene's. I've never known him go anywhere apart from a day trip to York. And that was with the Elder Branch Summer Coach Trip."

Power felt tempted to remark on the excruciating dullness of such a life and was swallowing down these words when there was a noise from the passageway leading to the priest's office and quarters.

A tall, and black-shrouded figure emerged silently from a passageway on Power's right. The priest stood in the sunlight and his blonde hair glowed all at once, like a halo.

"Do I hear a priest's name being taken in vain?" said the priest.

He advanced upon the doctor with a perfunctory grin plastered on his face. He offered a hand to shake.

"This is Father Michael," said the old woman, Janet, to Power. She turned to the priest. "I was just welcoming this gentleman into our church, Father."

"Forgive me for overhearing," Father Michael said. "I think you were asking for a Father Bruce?"

Power wondered how long the priest had been in the shadows, listening. He was wondering whether to honestly introduce himself as Dr Power, as he was in a church, or to assume some other identity for the sake of convenience.

Power wondered for so long, that the pause in the conversation seemed awkward. He became aware that the priest was waiting for him to speak. "I'm sorry," said Power. "I must have confused you with someone else. I was on holiday in Leon and I saw a priest there in the Cathedral."

"As Janet said, I rarely even leave the Diocese. Can I help you in some other way, Mr . . . ?"

The priest was prompting Power for his name and, by some instinct, the doctor decided to assume a mask, one he had used once before. "My name is Dr Steingrimur. I am an art expert."

The priest arched an eyebrow. "An unusual name to choose or be given," he said. "An art expert. That must explain why you were in the Gallery just now?" Power swallowed. The priest had seemed completely oblivious of Power as he sat in the café with the woman. Although the doctor had chosen a distant table to sit at whilst guzzling coffee and cake, the priest had quite clearly observed Power.

"Would you like a cup of tea, Father?" the old woman asked.

"No, thank you, Janet. But would you like one, Dr . . . Steingrimur?"

"No, that's all right," said Power.

"We've both had something to drink, in the café just now, Janet," said the priest. "The doctor had chocolate cake, if I recall. I have an eidetic memory, you see. Never forget a face. Useful in this line of work. Let me show you something, then." He beckoned Power over to the passageway that led to his domain. Power caught a glimpse of an office beyond the passageway, with an ornate, carved wooden desk and armchairs set around an iron Victorian fireplace.

The priest took up a position before four framed tinted drawings on the wall of the passage. "Dr Steingrimur, an unusual name, where does it come from?"

Power was beginning to curse his assumption of a false identity. He had used the name once before in an investigation with Lynch. They had been confronting an art forger about a clutch of fake Lowry canvases. Now, here in the church, it was Power himself who was the fake.

"It's an Icelandic name," said Power. "Are these drawings what you wanted to show me?"

"Naturally," said the priest. "They are one of the features of this church. We keep them here in the shade. Too much light would fade the tinting. In fact, these are the drawings I was only now discussing with the conservator at the Gallery. We are loaning them for an exhibition there and we are taking the opportunity to have them properly assessed. So it's doubly fortunate you came here today. What do you think of them?"

Power looked at the drawings. They were of Biblical times. He could make out Jesus carrying the cross. He thought they were a bit gloomy and the colours didn't seem quite right. "Hmmmm," he murmured, trying to sound vaguely erudite. "Of course, I am more interested in oils. Degas, Valazquez, that sort of thing. These are fine, but not my thing."

The priest regarded Power with a guarded half-smile. "When do you think these were . . . er, drawn?"

"They appear to be late Victorian in origin," Power bluffed.

"Not bad," said Father Michael. "About twenty years out though. They are by an illustrator called Robert Fawcett. From North America. The subject matter is, of course, the Four Stations of the Cross, hence the four engravings. Fawcett did them whilst he was at the Slade School of Art in London. Whilst he still had some ambitions to be a fine artist. Later on he bowed to commercial forces and became an illustrator. He is famous, of course, for his illustrations of Sherlock Holmes and Dr Watson."

"Oh," said Dr Power. "Yes, I think I recognise his work now. This isn't my area of expertise, you know."

"Of course," said the priest. "The art world is a massive, and encompasses so many niche subjects. Anyway, Doctor, I am afraid that I have some letters to reply to and a phone call to make. I wonder if you would excuse me, please?" The priest stuck out his right hand to shake hands with Power.

"Nice to meet you," said Dr Power, as the priest shook his hand. The priest noted that Power's hand was slightly moist betraying anxiety. His eyes seemed to bore into Power.

"Goodbye," said the priest, and watched as Power walked hurriedly out of the church.

Power crossed the road, dived into a nearby public house and uncharacteristically ordered a whisky to steady his nerves. His heart was beating rapidly and he felt fear prickling upon his neck.

* * *

Power parked the old Saab by the riverside at Chester and walked along the banks of the Dee in the sun. He came to the gate in the walls that led up Lower Bridge Street into the ancient Roman city. Power climbed the steep slope past the timber-framed Bear and Billet pub and on up into the belly of the city. At the High Cross he stopped to hear the music of a ragged man playing shrill, keen notes on a tin whistle. The tune was bouncy and medieval. He moved closer to the player and listened. People rushed on past the musician and his audience of one. As the phrase he was playing ended, the musician's eyes met Power's. Power reached into his pocket and threw a few pounds into a woollen hat that lay upon the stone flags.

"Thanks. Do I know you?" the young man paused to ask Power.

"No," said Power. "But would you know a friend of mine? He used to play the flute and we called him the Piper. He was a traveller and his first name was Simon. I haven't seen him in a while, and I'm worried that . . ."

"I know him," said the musician, scooping up the money Power had given him. "He's doing well."

"Then, where is he?" asked Power.

"I wouldn't know, but I can send a word, if you're minded."

"Yes," said Power. "If you would." The musician nodded at the now empty hat, and taking the hint, Power threw a few more coins into the wool. "Can you tell him that Dr Power misses him and would he get in touch?"

"Is that all?"

"That's all," said Power. The musician nodded and, taking a breath, began to play again.

Power stuck his hands in his pockets and turned right into Eastgate Street. The city was full of tourists and shoppers today. They bustled past the doctor. Power climbed up some stone steps, which had been curved and worn by countless feet over the decades and ascended to the level of the Rows. The Rows ran either side of the city streets, a covered wooden arcade dating back to medieval times. Chester's guides boasted that they were unique. From the Rows there were entrances into shops, restaurants and pubs.

Power had arranged to meet Lynch in the Olde Boot Inn. A plaque on the wall near the front door informed him that the Inn had traded since sixteen forty-three. Power wondered about joking with Lynch that as it was now precisely five o'clock the pub had only been open for seventeen minutes, but he thought better of this and strode into the beery warmth of the tavern.

Lynch was at the first table near the door, slumped down, sombre and deep within himself. A half-finished pint stood on the table in front of him beside a pad of paper on which he had been writing. Lynch seemed preoccupied and had not yet seen Power. Power took a look round the darkness of the old pub. The light from the bar stood out like beacon in the gloom. All the tables were crowded with pints of beer in various stages of consumption and shades from gold to stout-darkness all guarded by men with white hair. They were smoking, reading newspapers or playing cards. The walls were rendered plaster over wattle and daub, slabs of nicotined whiteness between ancient dark oak beams. The interior had acquired a distinct patina of age.

"Hello, Andrew!" Power announced himself. Lynch looked up. His eyes looked red-rimmed through tiredness.

"Hello, you," said Lynch, standing up and shaking Power's hand. "What are you having?"

"I'll get these," said Power. He pointed at Lynch's half-empty glass. "Do you want another? Bitter?" Lynch nodded and Power went over to the bar. The young woman behind the bar had shaved peroxide hair and a piercing through her nose. She was possibly the youngest person in the pub other than Power himself, and she was younger than him by twenty years at least. Power asked for two pints of Weetwood Bitter. As she was drawing the pints of ale, a small, stocky customer sidled up to the bar and interrupted her to ask if his friend Henry had been seen in the bar since Thursday. The girl shrugged. The old man wondered out loud if his friend was all right and went off to sit down.

Power was pleased by the unexpectedly low price for the beer, but as he sat down on a low bar stool opposite his friend he questioned the choice of venue. He said as quietly as he could; "The beer's fine, but the pub seems to be full of old men."

"That's what I feel like," said Lynch. "It matches my mood. Although to be fair it is also quiet and so I can think and write."

Power wondered if Lynch was depressed. "Are you sleeping all right?"

"Fine," said Lynch, sipping at one of his glasses of beer. "You?"

"So-so," said Power. The discovery of the girl's body had restarted his nightmares, but Power did not want to disclose that.

"I could have done with a trouble-free holiday. Somehow not finishing the journey – not getting all the way to Santiago – well, somehow it's thrown me. My life is somehow interrupted. Do you think we could go back some day and finish the pilgrimage?"

"I know what you mean. The unfinished journey is something nagging away at me. A feeling that you've left something important undone."

"I think I need to do this soon, Carl. I feel like I have no choice. It is something I must do, within weeks."

"I can make some time, if you can." said Power. "I still have time owing from the hospital and Laura would be fine about it, I'm sure."

Lynch nodded. "I will look into it then," he said.

"I was looking at the plaque outside the door. This place has been here over three hundred years. Can you feel the ghosts all around you?" Lynch rolled his eyes. "Oh, I'm sorry Christians don't believe in ghosts, do they?"

"On the contrary," said Lynch. "Each to his own, of course. There is the Holy Spirit or Holy Ghost for a start, and there is the account of Jesus who meets a man who seems to be possessed. Christ exorcises him and drives out a cluster of spirits called Legion. That is in three of the Gospels, Matthew, Mark and of course, Luke – the doctor."

"And here we are ourselves, taking refuge in spirits now, well beer at least." said Power.

Lynch frowned at the levity. "These days I only take refuge in the Lord," said Lynch. "And I need Him more and more these days. I was in the Cathedral praying for an hour before I wandered in here."

"Are you really sleeping okay?" asked Power, wondering again whether Lynch might actually be depressed.

"Like a log," said Lynch. "I leave all my worries with the Lord. He will not test me more than I can bear, although sometimes I do wonder about how much I can withstand. Hence my suggestion we restart our quest."

"Could we restart at the Casa de la Caballeros and see the Count again? Then walk to Santiago de Compostela from there?"

"Indeed," said Lynch. "And on that point we need to talk about the Count and safety."

"And I need to update you on a priest I met."

Lynch raised an eyebrow. "Why don't you start then, what have you been up to? You were meant to be checking on the building I went to in Manchester."

Power coughed, nervously clearing his throat for the confession. "Forgive me," he said. "I was distracted for a good reason. I saw the priest. And I was sure he was the priest we saw at the Cathedral in Leon. The blonde-haired priest who ran the orphanage."

Lynch tried not to groan or look unduly sceptical.

"I was sure it was him," said Power. "Walking down the street in Manchester by the tram tracks, as large as life. The priest went into the Art Gallery and I followed him there, and then afterwards when he left I followed him across the road and into a small church hidden in the city centre."

"Did he see you?"

"Erm … yes. I went into the church. There was an old lady there, a kind of caretaker who looks after him."

"Did you ask her about him? Did you find out a name, Carl?"

"It wasn't Father Bruce. She said he was Father Michael. And then he came out of his office and made a beeline for me. I am afraid I panicked and I pretended to be someone else?"

Lynch could not suppress a groan of disapproval any longer. "Who?"

"That art dealer's identity – the one I once used. Dr Steingrimur."

"Did he believe it?"

"No, not for a moment," said Dr Power. "I think he probably suspected me in the Art Gallery. This wasn't my finest work, I have to say."

"Did you get a surname?" asked Lynch, pen poised over the pad of paper he had been writing on.

"It doesn't matter, I suppose. The caretaker said he'd not been abroad in years. A day trip to York was the limit of this priest's travelling."

Lynch was impassive, and persistent. "I can exclude him from the frame if you give me his surname, Carl."

"Doyle, Michael Doyle," said Dr Power, as he drained his pint. "I looked it up afterwards on the Church website. Are you annoyed with me?"

Lynch wrote the name down. "In this particular case, I'm worried, because you strayed off your mission."

"But if I hadn't followed the priest we would never know his name or where he works."

"Well, using a false name is hardly the living embodiment of the word or spirit of the Police and Criminal Evidence Act 1984, is it, Carl?"

"I'm not a police officer," said Power. "I was convinced I had recognised the priest."

Lynch looked down at the name again and shook his head. "Although someone is clearly keeping an eye on everything we do, I will look into this priest. I may need to use some indirect means. It is difficult knowing who I can trust anymore." He looked up at his friend. "This isn't some cozy detective story about somebody else, something remote. This isn't even a case we are observing and trying to solve. We are involved directly inside this one. This is a real life struggle between good and evil – real as can be – and it has become a test of my Faith. You talked about history and the present all collapsing together – well this is about everything I hold close to my heart – about right and wrong, about innocence and guilt, and it will be a struggle to the death.

"The Count phoned me the other day. He had had a visitor, late at night. There was a direct confrontation. He was locking the hotel up and suddenly this man was there in the hotel office with him, you know, the office at the front of the building? He threatened the Count. A clear threat. Well this man was in shadow so the Count couldn't see his face, but the Count described his voice as urbane and cultured and he saw the man's hand as it came into the light. I suspect it was the priest you were actually searching for. His hand was young, tanned, smooth. The nails were well-manicured and trim. There was a wedding ring on the left hand."

"So *not* a priest then?"

"I don't know," said Lynch. "Because some priests in orders do wear wedding rings as a symbol of their marriage to the Church. Not as a ring to indicate they have a human partner. Anyway, this hand was smooth, a hand that did no manual work, according to the Count.

The hand of man that writes sermons, reads books and pushes his greedy fingers up little girl's skirts." Lynch spat these last words out disdainfully.

Power looked thoughtfully at his friend and colleague. There was anger burning like a red-hot coal inside him.

"And one more thing," said Lynch. "The Count assumed that the intruder was there to threaten him, that he was seeking to frighten the Count so that he would leave them all alone – so they could go on doing what they have been doing, hidden in plain sight, for years."

"That wasn't the purpose?"

"No," said Lynch. "I asked the Count to remember to check his files after he phoned me. A few minutes later he phoned back to say that his files of guest names and addresses for the last few months had gone. The intruder had taken them from the office before the Count discovered him. You remember the forms that we signed for the Count when we arrived at the hotel? The intruder, or priest, or whoever he was wanted our names and addresses. Frightening the Count was just camouflage for what he really needed."

Power felt his stomach sinking, like it had suddenly acquired a lead weight inside.

"Whoever these people are, wherever their network runs, they intend to bring the fight to our own doorsteps. And that's why I was concerned to hear you'd followed this priest. Although he has a clear enough alibi. It's not him. But from now on we must be so careful, we must assume they know everything about us – our identities, what we've done and what we're doing. We are operating in a goldfish bowl.

"All the traces we leave in modern life are being used against us here – phone conversations that can be monitored or tapped and emails that can be read without our consent or knowledge. They are turning our own tactics against us. We are being tracked. The wolves are sniffing their way right to our front door. So maybe we need to follow the old ways. Trusting no-one with our thoughts. Talking face to face together. Or else they will use our tactics for good, against us. As they say, even 'The devil can cite Scripture for his purpose.'" Lynch stood, pocketed his note pad, and left a thoughtful Dr Power alone at his table in the Olde Boot Inn.

* * *

Power attempted to comfort himself with the thought that he would have discussed what he was thinking of doing with Lynch had he only stayed in the pub a little longer. As Lynch had left somewhat peremptorily Power felt he really could not be blamed for his actions. And Lynch had virtually forbidden telephone communication. So how could Power have forewarned Lynch he had acquired the address of the Church house that Father Michael Doyle occupied?

The internet search engine, Alta Vista, had supplied a poorly designed webpage about the city centre church and given the priest's full name and house address.

Power had been parked in his Saab on leafy Palatine Road for maybe an hour. The summer evening was blending into night. The road was in suburban Didsbury, an affluent area of the city. Power could see the house between the gateposts. An Edwardian double-fronted redbrick villa with deep sash windows. There were cellar gratings on both sides of the property. Downstairs the light was on in a living room. The curtains were drawn in a room upstairs and a blue glow emanated from the window. Around the villa, where once had been gardens, was a sea of tarmac now.

Power had waited patiently, but he hadn't yet seen any human being. Neither Father Michael, nor his housekeeper had shown themselves.

Dr Power was just thinking about setting off when a police car slowed and swung in front of Power's Saab, coming to rest.

The officer got out and walked slowly and deliberately to Power's car and gestured to him to get out.

Power climbed out and joined the officer on the pavement. "Good evening, Constable. Is there something wrong?"

"Dr Power, I believe?"

"Er . . . yes, that's right. How did you know?"

"Number plate check. But the owner of the house you are sitting outside also made a specific complaint naming you. So, two pieces of information told me you were probably Dr Power. Now can I ask why you are outside this property. I am assuming that you are not here on professional business . . . as a doctor."

"No, no . . ." said Dr Power, who was at a loss for words. He felt that he had been thoroughly outsmarted.

"The owner of the house says you have been following him. Pretending to be someone else. And I find you here, right outside his house. Confirming his account."

"I haven't done anything," Dr Power blabbered, off guard. "I haven't broken any laws. I am just minding my own business, sitting in my car."

"The occupants of the house have made a complaint, sir. I must ask you to move along. And to be frank with you there is a law now, which covers harassment. It's called the Protection from Harassment Act 1997. And it comes into play when someone feels distress at unwanted contact. If the occupant of the house was to press the point, you see, I'd have to bring you in and maybe charge you. And as you know, Doctor, the General Medical Council would have to be involved if you were convicted. They would take a dim view of a conviction, wouldn't they?"

Power said nothing. He nodded. He made a mental note of the

number on the officer's epaulette. He felt too intimidated to ask for sight of the officer's warrant card.

"Am I free to go, then?" asked Power.

"This time, Dr Power. This time. But make sure you steer clear of this house and its occupants in future, will you sir?"

Power hurried into his car and drove off, almost without checking his rear view mirror. Lynch's words were playing over in his head: 'They are turning our own tactics against us. We are being tracked. The wolves are sniffing their way right to our front door.'

Chapter Twelve

It is a good life.
Though you will not know how good
until you come to the end.

T S Eliot - The Cocktail Party

T he evening sun had faded and shadows were closing in on the day. The priest had sat in his study at the front of the house and watched the police officer stop his car by the battered old Saab. Father Michael Doyle had watched the conversation between the officer and Dr Power. A half-smile had flickered on his lips as he saw the doctor's expression of surprise at the arrival of the police. The priest had especially enjoyed the evolution of Power's emotions from alarm into fear.

The priest kept staring out into the road long after the doctor and the policeman had gone. He was thinking things through, back and forth, trying to eliminate any mistakes in his plan. His hands were rested flat on the red-leather desktop. Eventually, he picked up the pay-as-you-go Nokia mobile phone that was sitting beside the land-line on his desk. He dredged his memory and punched in the remembered number of another mobile. There was the briefest of pauses before a familiar voice answered.

In the gathering shadows of the suburban summer evening, the priest spoke, "Michael here, can you talk? Are you alone? Yes, I involved the police. I thought it was for the best." He listened to the voice at the other end, and then laughed.

Outside the door, his housekeeper paused. Janet was carrying a tray which had a cup of tea and a plateful of bourbon biscuits on it that she was ostensibly bringing the priest. She could hear the priest was talking on the phone, though, and hesitated, not wanting to interrupt and curtail the conversation. She moved from one foot to the other in ambitendence. On the one hand she wanted to listen to the priest's conversation and on the other she did not want to be discovered. She could sometimes listen in to conversations if the priest used the land-line. The extension in the hall near the kitchen was good for this. The light would come on the other extension phone when the priest was using it. She would pick it up breathlessly, put her palm over the mouthpiece and listen in. She suspected that the priest had bought a mobile phone just to thwart her.

Janet had found the new priest something of an enigma (he was new in her eyes even though Father Michael had been there for seven or more years). He was always aloof. He would never tell her anything. He did not 'chat' like the other priests she had known. Most of them were inveterate gossips, and to be fair, that was one of the perks of the job for Janet.

Father Doyle would only allow her the run of the ground floor, and specifically the kitchen, the living room and his study. Those were the 'public' places he allowed her. He managed his own bedroom and bathroom and, to be frank, he considered the rest of the house, both upstairs and in the cellars, off limits for her. He would chastise her if he noticed a thing out of place.

She looked at the cup of tea on the tray she was holding. It would be getting cold. She noticed how the surface rippled as her hand trembled. Was it old age or nerves? If he burst through the door now she would claim she was just bringing the tea to him. On the other hand, though, the tea would be getting cold, and she worried that might be a clue that she had loitered here in the corridor rather longer than she claimed. She wondered about Father Doyle. He had always seemed distant, asexual even. And for a young man he could be very forgetful at times, and vague about things he had said maybe. Occasionally, he seemed so preoccupied he forgot entire conversations, which she thought unusual for someone of his age. She estimated he was in his early thirties. He had ignored any of her well-meant probes about his birthday. Not like the last Father who had celebrated with a meal out for all his friends in the church, including her. He had been a better man, she thought.

Janet strained her ears to hear Father Michael's words. Was he arguing? His voice seemed raised with whoever was at the other end of the conversation.

She heard: ". . . to be honest, it's overdue. I feel the need. You know what I mean. A change is long overdue here. Can I expect you then? Good . . . yes . . . I will send her off on holiday . . . She's due some leave . . . always hanging around, yes . . . best you do it . . . I would love to see the fear on his face again."

Janet sensed that this part of the conversation might be about her and felt her face grow hot with a mixture of embarrassment and annoyance. She had never heard him speak like this on the telephone before. His voice sounded deliberately and joyously cruel. All of a sudden, Janet realised that she knew him not at all. She balanced the tray of tea and biscuits on one hand and rapped at the door. More than anything she wanted to interrupt the conversation and remind the priest that she was there and that she mattered.

At Janet's rapping on the door the conversation seemed to end. The priest called her in. By the time she had pushed the door open he was replacing the receiver on the land-line, as if he had just finished a conversation on that phone. A pretence, she concluded. She placed the tray beside him on the desk, but she couldn't bring herself to smile or say anything. Janet was hurting, even though she knew that there was a possibility the priest had not been referring to her at all. There was another puzzle too. What was Father Michael trying to do, acting as if he'd been using the land-line; putting the receiver down on a phone she knew he had not been using. She knew because she had passed the extension phone earlier, and there had been no light on. She managed a nod, a brief inclination of the head and she scurried off out of the study, closing the door softly behind her.

The priest opened the desk drawer and took out the mobile phone and spoke softly so that his voice would not carry. "Are you still there? Good . . . Yes . . . I think she was listening at the door, yes . . ." He went on speaking for some time and made a few notes on a piece of paper. After the call was finished the priest tried the tea. It was stone cold. He spat it back into the cup and, disgusted, poured the cold tea into the soft earth of a houseplant.

* * *

A large yellow sticky-note had been left on his computer screen. It was a record of a telephone call, with date, time and duration. Lynch had missed the caller by only a few minutes. He had been talking with Beresford in his office one floor down. The call had lasted only a minute. The message read: 'Young female called asking for you by name, in relation to a previous conversation with you and advertisement in a paper. Asking for help, but would not specify what kind or where she was. Call recorded for security purposes.'

Lynch hurried down to the communications room in the basement and sought out the author of the message.

"Good afternoon, Superintendent. I ran the message up to your office myself. I thought you would want it straightaway, sir."

"Yes, yes," said Lynch, impatiently. "Thank you. It was important. Can I hear it? You said you recorded it."

"Just a moment, sir. Let me find the file log. Here it is." The officer handed over a pair of headphones which Lynch put on. "Shall I play it now?" she asked.

Lynch nodded, and the nervous young girl began speaking. In her panic her Spanish accent was somehow clearer. The call was as the duty officer had described it. The description had not, however, caught the level of fear that was in the young girl's voice. Lynch silently formed the name of the girl, Maria, with his own mouth. The note had also not mentioned the background noise. There were passing voices, the sounds of bustle and business. An announcement in the distance? Maybe a train station?

"Play it back again," Lynch ordered. He listened intently. He caught only fragments of the announcement in the background. Enough to make out that the speaker was using English. There was something about London. "Play it back again," Lynch said, grimly. He heard Maria's fearful voice again. Somehow it tore at him and made him feel guilty for missing the call. There was something about 'leaving for London.' Was it a train? Or a plane, or a bus? What form of transport was heading for London.

"Can you trace the call?" asked Lynch.

"I didn't know it was this level of importance, sir. I can see if anything can be done, but the call volume means that . . ."

"Try your best," said Lynch. "Her life might depend on it. I'll be in my office."

Lynch hurried out of the communications room, but he did not go directly to his office. He chose another route, to call on another old friend. Someone he thought he could trust, and who might do work in secret without divulging Lynch's name. Lynch knew that all the favours he was asking all over Headquarters and elsewhere would soon dry up. He could not ask too many times. He could not ask anyone to do too much. He decided to limit his attack now and focus the favour he was asking on the airport. He wanted the passenger lists of all flights in to Manchester that day from Düsseldorf. And if there was CCTV footage of the arriving passengers walking down the purple-carpeted corridors towards passport control, he would do anything for that. As he hurried back to his office he wondered whether his attack was too narrow, too limited. His investigation was predicated on the flight being direct and to Manchester. He was making an intuitive leap that defied logic. What if the girl had been flown in via another airport such as Schiphol? What if the girl hadn't been at any airport, but had been at a train station anywhere in the United Kingdom and the announcement Lynch had heard was for the express train to London? And Lynch could not call on a team as usual. He could not afford to show his hand. Lynch felt incredibly alone.

* * *

Dr Power stopped writing on the crisp white pages and looked more closely at his patient. Mr Gerrard was a rotund man who seemed to be perspiring more than the temperature in the clinic warranted. He was crying silently. Power pushed a box of tissues towards him, but he waved them away and wrapped his arms around himself. His torso shook with sobbing.

Eventually, he brought the emotion under some limited control and continued talking. "It's just I have never told anyone that before, Doctor," he said. "Not even my wife, in twenty years of marriage." He reached into a pocket and pulled out a handkerchief to dry his eyes and wipe his nose.

"It's all right," said Dr Power. "Tell me as much as you need."

"It's not just the church, though, it's everywhere nowadays. But I see them in the street and I feel bad. I drive a bus, and a priest tried to get on. I shut the doors and I drove off. I was on an escalator in the shopping centre going down and there were nuns on the other side coming up. I felt sick, panicky. It never goes away." He had been talking earlier about being beaten in a boarding school run by the church in Ireland. Mr Gerrard had watched a documentary about others in Ireland and had broken down. Hence, his referral to the psychiatrist. "I try to make it go away," he said. "I try not to think about it. If somebody talks about child abuse at work, I walk away. I watch my own children like a hawk. They resent it. But I have to know they are safe. And I'd kill any man who touched them. I'd kill them!" The last sentence was spoken loudly and with anger. "I've never been back to Ireland. I don't know what I'd do if I did. I once got on a ferry at Liverpool. I had a plan to find the house where one of them lived. One of the brothers who ran the school lived in Artane. That's where he was. I remember he always smelled of pipe smoke and urine. I planned to knock on his door. He'd answer and I'd punch him. Straight in the face. And while he was lying there unconscious, I'd rip his belly open with a carving knife and leave him to wake with his entrails on the floor. I've thought about that, for years. I mean . . . don't think I'm a violent man." Power raised an eyebrow. "I'd not hurt a fly nowadays. But in the day, when I was growing up, I'd drink. To forget. And I'd pick a fight. It made me feel better, somehow. To get rid of the anger inside. Do you know?"

"Would you go and attack the priest now?"

Mr Gerrard corrected Power. "He was a Brother, not a priest. It was just an idea I had."

"A fantasy?" Power suggested.

Mr Gerrard nodded. "But it was a powerful good fantasy. I loved the idea of hurting him, like he hurt me and countless others. But I wouldn't do it, I don't think. I mean I got off the ship before it left the dock in Liverpool. But I got that far. I knew where he lived. He might be dead now, though. I wouldn't really do it, probably. But it would be no loss if people like him were erased from the earth, would it?"

Power made a note in the patient records that Mr Gerrard had no definite plans to harm anyone. He looked at the patient again. Mr Gerrard was objectively only a few years older than Power, but he looked as if there might have been decades between them. Somehow, Power felt unutterably sad that all this badness had been unnoticed by him. It had been happening all around him and he hadn't suspected a thing. These people were contemporaries. He had grown up assuming that bad things only happened to the fictional children in Victorian settings, like Dickens's *Oliver Twist*. Such horrors were somehow possible to think of when they were in the past. You assumed that things had improved and that society had moved on from times when scrawny waifs were doled out gruel in cold workhouses.

It had come as a shock to Power to find his cosy assumptions were plain wrong. A shock, that he had been unaware of the reality unfolding to others around him and blind to the suffering of his contemporaries.

"I'm sorry this happened to you," Power said, but it sounded a feeble thing to say and of little comfort.

"You believe me?"

"Of course," said Power, puzzled as the patient collapsed into another bout of shuddering tears.

"You don't know what that means to me, Dr Power. To be listened to and understood."

"I am sorry," said Power. "Because it feels like I've been stumbling around for so many years. Not seeing. Like when an old girlfriend said she hated her grandfather. And I thought that was odd. To hate your grandfather? What did that say about someone, that they harboured such feelings? Well, now I can guess why she hated him. And another time when I was a student doctor and the sister on one of the wards said something about a celebrity visitor. A famous man who did marathons for charity. And she said that it was well known amongst nurses that you never left him alone with patients or children. And I thought, that's an odd thing to say. What did she mean? Well now, knowing what I know now, well, I can guess what she really meant."

Gerrard nodded, but he too was not really able to hear. Power checked what plans Gerrard had for the next week, to reassure himself that the patient was safe, and made another appointment.

At the end of the session, and before the next patient, he ducked out into the clinic's kitchen and made himself a cup of coffee. He stood staring out into the untended and bleak hospital garden trying to gather his thoughts after the last patient. He was swigging coffee and snaffling a piece of chocolate cake that Laura had put in silver foil for him, when the kitchen door opened.

"They said you'd be in here." It was Lynch. He had taken to appearing in person now, rather than phoning. "Can we talk?"

Power led the Superintendent back to his office and checked to see if the next patient had arrived yet. "She's not here yet, we have a few minutes. What's happening?"

"Two things I want to talk about," said Lynch. "Is there anything you want to tell me?"

Power felt his face reddening. "I may have been indiscreet."

"I rather think so," said Lynch. "You were lurking outside the priest's house, I gather."

Power nodded shamefacedly.

"Tut-tut," said Lynch. "I heard through my Manchester colleagues. You can't go round doing this for one thing. And for another thing that wreck of a car of yours could not be more conspicuous. What *were* you thinking?"

"It's him," said Power, defensively. "I'm sure it's him. I wouldn't forget a man like that."

Lynch practically growled at Power, "You can be as convinced, or rather as deluded as you like, Carl. It is not him. Please leave him alone, you're confusing things."

"I . . ." Power stopped. He could see that Lynch was in earnest and that they would fall out if he continued. "Is there something else I don't know?"

"I asked Beresford to make enquiries. I asked him as a favour and to keep my name out of it. He checked with the Home Office and Passport Office about Father Michael Doyle. To see when he'd last been in Spain. Well, you said the old lady in the church said he never went on holiday. It seems she was right. Firstly, there's no record of him travelling abroad this year. Indeed the last time he travelled out of the UK was seven years ago. And, in fact, his passport ran out three years ago. I'm sorry, Carl, but he is definitely not our man. Most definitely not our man. So, I'm asking you to stand down on this one. Okay?"

Power slumped in his chair. He had never felt so wrong or so foolish and it hurt somewhat. He looked away at the sky outside his consulting room window and nodded glumly. Eventually, when he thought he could stomach it, Power asked, ". . . and the second thing you wanted me to talk about?"

"The girl called Maria. The girl from Düsseldorf. She phoned me again." Power looked back at Lynch, making eye contact for the first time in a few minutes. "She phoned from a payphone somewhere. I'm afraid that I wasn't in the office so I missed her call, and for that I feel very bad, but at least there was a recording. She was frightened." Lynch took a sip from the mug of tea that Power had made him. "And I have no way of contacting her back. The thing is, Carl, that I think she may be in this country now. There were sounds of a station or an airport behind her. An announcement. In English, not German. Something about London. Not much help, because we don't know whether she was there or just somewhere that had transport to London. And a lot of places connect to London. So nothing definite for us to go on, really. Although I have asked about a hunch I had. We will have to wait and see." He stood up, leaving his tea unfinished. "Sorry, this is a flying visit . . ."

"I've got patients to see, anyway," said Power. He was still smarting a bit after being reproved by Lynch.

"Don't take it badly," said Lynch. "Not all our intuitions can turn out correct." Lynch paused. "On a positive note, I've booked leave, so I think we can book our flight to Spain to finish our journey. That's something to look forward to." And with that, Lynch was gone. Power sat thinking for quite some time before the clinic receptionist eventually rang to ask when he was going to see the next patient, who had been waiting too long.

* * *

Early on a Saturday morning the priest accompanied the old woman to the bus station in Altrincham. They went by black cab. Janet felt inhibited by the driver's presence, even though there was a glass divider between driver and passengers. The cab's diesel engine rattled and rumbled along at a pace. Her luggage, such as it was, a small battered leather suitcase, sat on the taxi floor between her and Father Doyle. She hadn't enjoyed packing. She wasn't used to it and too many questions had assailed her. How many nighties should she take? Should she pack soap and towels or would these be provided? Would they dress for dinner, or be slovenly and eat dinner in the clothes they'd travelled in all day? She looked over at the priest. He sat with his back to the driver. She had asked him to take that seat because she couldn't bear to travel facing backwards. It didn't seem natural not to see where you were going. He smiled at her. Or at least his lips curled into a smile, but his eyes remained flinty and watchful as if he expected she might make a bid for escape. She had noticed that the taxi driver had locked all the doors automatically, but she assumed this was some automatic precaution to prevent fare dodgers leaping from the cab on arrival at their destination. The locking of the doors had not reassured her uneasy mind one bit, though.

Janet overcame her natural inhibitions as the cab sat idling at some lights to ask the priest a question. "We couldn't turn back, could we? I think I've left something turned on?" Her voice sounded wheedling as if she was begging for mercy.

"Not at all," said Father Michael. "It will be perfectly safe. You deserve a holiday and you will take one." The fake smile blossomed on his face again, and she resisted an urge to shudder. Why had she started to feel this way about him?

He went on to describe the holiday he had booked for her. "You're lucky to be able to join this tour. Yours was the last seat left on the coach."

"I suppose they are a big group and everyone will know each other, except me."

"Not at all," said the priest. "You will fit in sooner than you know. Don't be scared. The eight days will go by in a flash, just you wait and see. You'll go south by one route taking in some lovely stately homes and gardens. I think there's a stop at the great glass house of Kew. Then you'll visit Canterbury. You're to meditate on the fact that when it was built it was a Catholic place, of course. So, you can reclaim it for us." He laughed a little at his own witticism. She did not. "And then a different route back north and some different country houses. Ah, you will enjoy it. I wish I was going with you."

She felt like offering him her seat on the coach in that case, but stifled the ungrateful thought.

"Who was that you were speaking to on the phone the other night?" The words were hardly out of her mouth, before she regretted them. It was unnatural for her to be so blunt. Even the priest looked mildly shocked at the temerity of her question.

"Which evening would that be, Janet? So many people call me."

"The evening after the police were talking to that man on the road outside."

"I'm not sure," he said. "As I said, there are so many people who phone."

Janet fell silent. If he wouldn't tell her there was no purpose in her pointing out that she recalled perfectly well that no person had phoned in to the house that night.

The taxi remained idling, waiting for the priest to return after he had put Janet on the coach. As they walked together over to the bus Janet noticed the coach had a painted name on the driver's door; "Nemesis". It didn't sound very leisure orientated. She climbed on board in silence, clasping a paperback by Agatha Christie and a bag of knitting. She hoped there might be a cup of tea at some point. Janet was preoccupied and forgot to say goodbye to the priest who had bought her the holiday. Again, later, she thought how ungracious she must have seemed, but she was certain that both of them knew she didn't want to go. She settled herself down on the bench seat.

"She's a bit nervous," said the priest to the driver. "Can you look after her please? Make sure she doesn't wander off?"

"She's not got Alzheimer's has she?" asked the driver. "I'm not a nursemaid." The priest tutted at the thought and said Janet was wholly fit. The driver went on, "Only one time this family loaded an old lady on board and she was, I'm sorry to say, completely gaga. They expected us to be some sort of cheap respite care for a week."

"Not at all," said the priest, taking a twenty pound note from a purse. He proffered it to the driver, who accepted with alacrity. "Just take good care of her and make sure you keep her on board." The buxom tour guide who was accompanying the driver came to the front of the coach, she'd counted up the passengers, having ticked off all their names. "Are you ready to go?" asked the priest.

"Yes," she said. "Thirty-two for Canterbury. Unless you intend to stay on board and make it thirty-three?"

"Oh, no," said the priest, climbing down the steps to the waiting taxi. "I've got places to go and people to meet." He stood by the taxi and waved the coach off, smiling his special smile. Janet did not wave back.

* * *

The Count had been scouring the countryside. He had driven back and forth along the country roads around Astorga in a borrowed silver-blue Seat Alhambra. He reasoned that it was not easy to move the occupants and contents of an orphanage very far. His logic was not perfect, but he was of course, unable to conduct any kind of national search. He was just doing what he could. As he drove he listened to guitar music of Montoya, and mused how, once upon a time, there would have been many Knights ranging across the countryside, assigned to the task of keeping pilgrims safe on the road to Santiago. And although he contemplated how much faster he could travel with an engine harnessing the power equivalent of one hundred and twenty horses, he was but one man. Where could the priest and nuns have hidden themselves and a clutch of ten or so children? So here he was, looking for another big house or farm in the hill country around the town. He was devoting more and more time to his quest, to the anxiety of his wife who chided him about his age and consequent lack of fitness for the role of a hero. This merely spurred the Count on to greater endeavour. And early in the morning he would set off, with binoculars, a range of maps, and a big basket packed by his wife with bread, ham, cheese and wine from the Albariño grape.

After a few days, he realised that one man could not accomplish the task and that he needed many eyes to help him. He had quite given up on the agents of the State and asked the people he met in the area around the deserted orphanage if they knew anything about a move, or had seen the direction any vehicles had taken from the empty buildings. The locals had listened to his enquiries with some patience, but they thought his quest outlandish and laughed behind his back about the crazy, old man. His questions had taken the Count down on to the Pilgrim's Way itself and he had spent several hours quizzing walkers about whether they had noticed anything on their travels. He judged this a waste of time after a while and bemoaned his lack of progress to Pieter, the hippy, who ran the free bar where Power and Lynch had first encountered the runaway, Lucia.

Pieter had offered to ask his own contacts about any movements of children into vacant properties in the area, but he gave the Count an idea to widen his network of eyes and this had led the Count into the forests around the Rio Turienzo. There amongst the oak and chestnut trees the Count had found an encampment of the *mercheros* folk. These were Romani folk who had somehow survived in Spain since before medieval times. There he met the head man, Señor Salazar, a mountain of a man with a bushy beard, who greeted him stiffly and warily. The dapper Count offered him some bottles of wine. "What brings you here?" Salazar asked the Count bluntly, although he accepted the gift quickly enough.

"I must be honest, I ask a big favour of you?"

"And why do you, a big man, a rich man, arrive in this place?"

The Count looked around at the dilapidated lean-to shelters of the *mercheros* encampment on public land. "You have eyes that see things that other people miss." said the Count, and he introduced himself and outlined his problem. The missing children. The murder of Lucia. The apparent corruption of the police. A network of those who would exploit children.

"You criticise our church, Count" said Salazar. "People may not welcome us, we may be seen as the lowest, but we are Catholics and we are proud of our Faith. And you tell us our priests do this?"

"These are not Christian men and women like you, Señor. They hide behind religion, because they reason who would challenge a holy man? This is not about the church. It is about men and women who defile our Faith."

Salazar thought this over for a good while, and poured them both some coffee that he had been brewing over a log fire. The Count grasped the enamel mug of coffee as he might a lifeline. The sharing of drink between them was important, he knew. It could be a symbol of joint enterprise. Salazar was silent for a long while, however. He was watching the children in the encampment.

"Our people. My people. We have been outsiders. Forever outsiders. We live apart to stay together, and because we are not understood, and not wanted. We are called gypsies and we are seen as thieves. They forbade us marriage within our people. In olden times they sent villagers with fire against us. To burn out the plague, or burn out the devil. We came from the east, from India once. We took up new beliefs, became Christians. But we still did not belong. Franco broke up our camps with the Guardia Civil, yes? We didn't belong. We will never belong. Today we are supposed to be drug dealers and the police come and search for heroin. We are always outside society, but we are not stupid and we are not blind. We are not child stealers, like many say. The reverse. Because we, too, have lost children over the years. Maybe these people you speak of, the wolves inside priests and nuns. Maybe they stole them all along? Do you think maybe?"

"Maybe," said the Count. "You say that you have lost children from here? Did you tell the police?"

Salazar laughed, but there was no joy in his laughter. "Tell the police? What for? They only help if they want to help, and they don't want to help us. Yes, we have lost children. Two or three boys and girls have disappeared from our tribes over the decades. And more than that if you add in other families and tribes in the North. Do you know where they take the children?"

"My friend, Lynch, says one girl was sent to Germany. Paid for probably. Bought by a policeman."

Salazar grunted. "Well, we have a network of people, too. You are not like us, Count. But you seem a good man and we will help you look if you want. Tell me what you are looking for?"

"A house or farm that was empty. And where suddenly one day, a few weeks ago, some vehicles arrived. Big vans carrying furniture – beds, desks, chairs. Ten or more children, boys and girls. Some nuns. And a young priest, a blonde man."

*   *   *

After clinic, Dr Power had hurried into Manchester for a meeting. He had been surprised to receive an invitation to tea at the renowned Indulgence Café, just off St Ann's square. The elegant banking hall was now host to a Swiss-style tea room. Dr Power had felt honoured and also slightly daunted. He had never spoken to a Vice-Chancellor before, and here he was, summoned to afternoon tea.

There had been some difficulty finding a space to park and, consequently, he was a few minutes late. He looked at his watch as he hurried, and flustered into the baroque gold and white entrance hall. He was perhaps three minutes overdue, but Professor Armitage had taken his seat at a food-laden table in the corner, having already taken the opportunity to order. The Vice-Chancellor was not a tall man, and seated at the marble-topped table behind a pile of sandwiches and a triple-tiered stand of cream cakes, he was almost hidden from view.

"Carl!" he called across the café, oblivious to other diners. "Over here!" Dr Power approached nervously. The VC proffered a plump palm and shook the doctor's hand. "Sit down, sit down, we meet at last."

Power surveyed the feast and wondered if all this was really meant for just two men. There were cheese scones with butter; sandwiches with fillings of cucumber and mint, smoked salmon, egg and cress, and ham and tomato; scones with clotted cream and jam; the most chocolatey chocolate cake, Victoria sponge oozing fresh cream and jam, ginger and orange cake, and rich fruit cake. The VC picked up a large oval gold and white teapot and poured steaming tea into china cups. He offered a cup to Dr Power.

"Fill up a plate," he said. "Then we can talk."

Power chose some egg and cress sandwiches. The bread was soft and white. The VC piled his plate high and began to eat, not greedily, but almost daintily. His cherubic face was shiny and mottled with red. Power felt like he wanted to check his blood pressure. The VC munched in silence, but for an occasional broadcast of a sighing murmur of gustatory appreciation. He had moved onto a raisin-crammed cream scone when he paused to wipe a smear of red jam from his cheek. The pause seemed to focus him on the real reason for his tea with the doctor.

"Maybe to business," he said. "I wanted to talk to you about Medicine, as a subject. The University in Allminster doesn't have a medical school. We have nursing, of course. Of course we have nursing. But nursing is just nursing, after all. And other decent Universities; Manchester, Liverpool, Sheffield, they have all had Medicine for quite some time. I won't be happy until Allminster has Medicine too. We have a considerable reputation for subjects like theology, of course. Of course we have theology; we were set up by Gladstone and the Church of England. I am a Canon myself. The VC of Allminster must always be a practicing Christian." He folded his hands on his stomach and looked directly and appraisingly at Power for the first time. "I have had good reports about you. I had a letter a few weeks ago, that prompted me to ask to meet you. Do you know Professor Anastasi?"

Power did. It would be fair to say that he loathed him. They had sparred for years over various cases. They could never see eye to eye. Anastasi would always take the opposing view. If Power appeared for the defence, Anastasi would be there for the claimant. If Power appeared with a report for the claimant, Anastasi would be sniping for the defence. He seemed to have written to the Vice-Chancellor Armitage, however. Power couldn't imagine that he had said anything good.

"I know Professor Anastasi, of course," said Dr Power. "I don't think he works at Allminster, does he?"

"No, in point of fact, we don't have any doctors working at Allminster." The VC was still looking unrelentingly at Power. "Professor Anastasi wrote kindly about you. He described your research and your papers on psychopathology, PTSD, and your specific emphases on the importance of diagnosis and psychopharmacology." He paused, gauging Power's nonverbal response. "He recommended you for a chair."

"A chair!" Power exclaimed.

The VC smiled at his surprise. "Yes, as a matter of fact, having looked at your *curriculum vitae* I'm inclined to think that Professor Anastasi is right."

Power didn't know what to say. The recommendation by Anastasi was not something he would ever have imagined possible.

"We are a small University, despite our long history as a college. I am expanding the student numbers and our breadth of subjects. I think we should work towards Medicine. The subject would give us more . . . credibility. Nursing is all very well, but, nursing's never going to develop a cure for cancer. Speaking of cures – I know we all owe you a huge debt over the malaria crisis a few years ago. I know it wasn't your discovery – it was Dr McAdams's team that got the posthumous Nobel. But you played your part brilliantly, so I am told . . . and that's the kind of initiative we need at Allminster." Power could not help but smile, the Vice-Chancellor had done his research assiduously and was stroking his ego. "Will you join us? Help us secure Medicine as a new subject? It will be a bit of a battle. With other Universities. And the other Deans in the existing Faculties of our University are likely to resist, mainly because they find it difficult to see beyond their narrow self-interest. I have to look at the bigger picture, you see."

"What exactly would I have to do?"

"Start with us. Just a few days a week. A toe in the door. Help us get things off the ground for Medicine. What do you say?"

"Well, yes, probably, yes. It's a bit of a surprise. A welcome surprise." Power thought he should check. He couldn't quite believe his fortune. "You do mean you want me as a Professor?" The VC smiled.

"We are a small University, It's difficult for us to compete with the big boys, but we could probably offer you work for a day or two a week. At academic rates. We can't afford the same rates as the NHS." Power frowned, the wily VC was negotiating so very cunningly.

The 'promotion' to professor would necessarily entail a small reduction in his income and he hurriedly tried to weigh up the benefits to his self-esteem against the deficits to his salary and pension. The VC waited patiently to see if he had hooked the doctor and whether he could now reel him in. In the pause, the VC reached for some fruitcake and signalled to a slim, prim, lace-bedecked waitress that he wanted another pot of tea. "So, Dr Power, shall I set things in motion with the Senate for your appointment? Or would you prefer some more time to consider? You might need to consult your hospital's Chief Executive perhaps? Or maybe the academic life does not attract you?"

Power had never imagined the possibility that one day he might be offered a chair. The thought of the offer disappearing again, galvanized him into an impulsive acceptance without perhaps full deliberation. He did not, for instance, have any idea of what an academic earned. "No," he said. "I'm very grateful for the offer. I'd be only too grateful to accept."

"Good," said the Canon Armitage. "That's settled then. I will prod the Senate into action and you will hear from Human Resources in due course."

Business settled, the VC returned his loving gaze to the residual food items on the table. "Now, if we can just finish this off, I can get back to Allminster before six."

* * *

In the bathroom at Alderley House, Laura was sitting on the edge of the deep Victorian bath looking at the white plastic stick of a pregnancy test. She was stubbornly waiting, and willing the lines on the test she wanted to see appear. Laura re-read the leaflet to see if she had made a mistake. Disheartened, she threw the plastic stick at the mirror on the wall, and wondered at the angry glare that the young woman in the mirror was giving her.

She picked up the pregnancy test, its box and leaflet and made her way downstairs to dispose of the evidence in the main bin. She didn't want Carl to know. Her period must just be late; there was no baby.

* * *

Dr Power was not a vain man. Non-one who drove the car he did, by choice, could be accused of excessive pride. Nevertheless, after his meeting with the Vice-Chancellor, Dr Power drove back home to Alderley Edge as if he were riding high on a cloud in a brilliant blue sky. He kept imagining his name with the title Professor instead of Doctor and amused himself with self-congratulatory thoughts. Up until the meeting with the VC he had been overwhelmed with a sense of perplexity. The unrefutable intelligence that the priest hadn't been abroad in years and didn't even have passport had shaken him. Power had been so convinced he was right, and to be proved so wrong by Lynch had filled him with a cloud of self doubt. Meeting the Vice-Chancellor and hearing his kind words had dispelled the gloom entirely.

As he motored along the back roads of the Cheshire countryside in a haze of self-congratulation Power signally failed to notice four police cars in a National Trust layby near the Edge, or officers standing about drinking tea from an incident support van.

Had he recognised the unusual appearance of such a cluster of police, then his mind might have wandered back through the past seven years to a time when a similar gaggle of police had taken over the Edge and the events that led to the crossing of his life path with Superintendent Lynch's.

As it was, Power was too bound up with his own hubris to detect the oncoming storm.

He barrelled out of the Saab and ran into the house to see Laura. She was sitting quietly in the kitchen with a pot of coffee and eating a *pain-au-chocolat*. Normally, Power would have noticed she looked distracted, but he was full of himself and blurted out his news as she poured him his own mug of tea. He waved aside her offer of the remaining *pain-au-chocolat*. He was anything but hungry. He babbled about his meeting with the Vice-Chancellor and the offer of a professorial title. Laura was pleased. She smiled. She said all the right things. But, psychiatrist as he was, he did not pick up on her inner pain.

There was a knock at the door and a call: "Hello?" Power had left the front door open in his haste, and as he and Laura made their way into the hall, a tall police officer in fluorescent, yellow jacket was waiting there in the doorway, a shadow against the sunlight of early evening.

"Hello?" The officer repeated himself. "Are you Dr Power? Dr Carl Power?"

"Yes," said Power. "Can I help you?"

"I hope so, you may have seen that we are in the area." Power hadn't noticed. "My name is Sergeant Collins. There's been a body found on the Edge and we are asking local residents if they have seen anything."

"Oh, no," said Laura. She was standing behind Carl. "Has somebody fallen?" There were steep drops around the escarpment and mine workings.

"No, madam. This is a murder we believe."

Power felt a sudden sense of misgiving. A sinking in the pit of his stomach.

"A murder? Who?"

"Well, Doctor. We want to ask you some questions."

"That's all right, I normally help the police; I have a role with Superintendent Lynch."

"We know. He isn't involved in this investigation, though. Now will you come with me, please? Best if we do this in a more formal setting."

"Oh," said Power, feeling the evening was taking on a more ominous hue. Laura was pale and shaking at his side. "Are you arresting me?"

"Not if you come and assist us voluntarily, sir. But I must tell you that we may be interviewing you under caution."

Power touched Laura's hand silently and gave it a squeeze, he noticed his mouth had gone dry. He picked up his red cagoule off the coat-rack, and followed the officer to the police car that had been waiting at the gates all along.

Chapter Thirteen

The truth may be stretched thin, but it never breaks,
and it always surfaces above lies, as oil floats on water.
Cervantes, Don Quixote

Superintendent Lynch had left the Police Headquarters in Chester at eleven o'clock that morning for an appointment. His journey did not take him very far as the solicitor he was to see worked in White Friars, an ancient street in Chester that had once housed a Carmelite Friary. The solicitors were close by a dental practice. As Lynch passed by, a patient emerged holding their jaw. The patient was so preoccupied by pain that he didn't see Lynch striding towards him and Lynch had to step into the cobbled street to avoid collision.

The appointment had been set up at the solicitor's behest and the purpose was something of a mystery to him. Mrs Lynch, on hearing of the mystery appointment, had wondered out loud whether a sizeable bequest from a long lost relative was in the offing. Lynch warily considered any possible link to the meeting he had had in Manchester with an impostor, and so he was entering the meeting with high levels of curiosity, suspicion and caution.

The solicitors' office building, a brick-faced, Georgian terraced house was reassuringly old. Preliminary enquiries had confirmed that the firm had been trading since the nineteenth century. This was, therefore, no pop-up office in an anonymous concrete office block. A pale blue Georgian door opened from the street on to a small, dark waiting-room. Lynch gave his name in to a bespectacled receptionist behind a tall desk and then sank into a very low and squidgy leather sofa opposite. As he sat down his view of the receptionist was obliterated, but she kept speaking to him. "Mr Berckley is just finishing off a telephone call," said the disembodied voice. "Would you like a coffee? Or tea?"

"No, thank you," said Lynch, into the air above his head. "I've only just had a cup."

"Well, he won't be long then."

Mr Berckley was long however, and Lynch was looking at his watch and considering leaving to get some sandwiches and go back to work when Berckley appeared. He was a small man with neat white hair and gold-rimmed spectacles. He smelled of sandalwood, and smiled most apologetically. "I am so sorry," he shook Lynch's hand. "I just wanted to confer with my client about our meeting today. To clarify one or two matters, and at first he could not be found by his secretary, and then once located seemed to want to chat away. I hate being late for an appointment, I do apologise again, come in."

Lynch followed the solicitor into his office on the first floor up some rickety stairs. The office was a wood-panelled affair at the back of the building with a view out towards the Castle.

"I am so sorry to be mysterious, Superintendent Lynch, and I thank you for coming along under the circumstances."

"It wasn't far to travel," said Lynch. "I work about three hundred yards away. But I was a bit wary about attending, as I do like things to be straightforward. I can't imagine what this is about."

"I will tell you what I can," said Berckley. "It is an offer, a generous one. And you can go away and think about it. There is no pressure."

"An offer of what?" asked Lynch. Police officers are always wary of being bribed. "And what is required of me?"

"The offer comes from someone who perceives a need to right certain wrongs, to deliver justice as it were. From someone who perceives that the agents of justice cannot always do what they would like, fettered by process and politics and so on. He is a strong believer in justice, but not necessarily a believer in the state mechanisms for delivering this. He would like to see some organisation that is morally and ethically founded. That rights wrongs for people who do not traditionally have a voice in our society; the outsiders, the infirm, the disabled, the disadvantaged, the young and old who are victims of abuse."

"What is the name of this 'foundation'?" asked Lynch. "I've not heard of anything like this."

"No," said Berckley. "You wouldn't have, because the offer is to give you the funds to set such an organisation up. To design it, to name it, to direct it. A sort of charity, I suppose, funded by my client, but at arm's length from him, with an ethical constitution and mission that you choose, and your own strategy and tactics. You could set up something that you have dreamed of."

Lynch was silent for a while, mulling over possibilities.

"Why is your client doing this?" asked Lynch. "What wrong has he done?"

"I don't think my client has ever done wrong, rather that he has suddenly come into great wealth and is trying to direct it towards a decent end through honest and worthwhile means. He is offering the organisation a million pounds a year for the first five years of its life, so that it can set itself up. And more thereafter if it is seen to be working well. In perpetuity. The costs that he would bear would necessarily cover your salary and the setting up of such an organisation, which would need to be independently audited of course, and to ideally work within the confines of the laws of the various lands in which it operated."

"Like a private police force?" asked Lynch, with some concern in his voice.

Berckley laughed, "That's not for me to say. I am not intending to direct you, merely to announce the offer and leave you to consider how best the aims can be achieved."

"I would need to talk to your client," said Lynch. "How can I know what he or she wants without communication?"

"My client has the utmost faith in you," said Berckley. "He met you once upon a time and has known of you for years. But I must be the conduit. This is, as I have said, at arm's length. I am offering you the resources to do what you need to do."

Lynch thought of all the frustrations he had endured in recent months and wondered if his struggles were known to this mythical benefactor. Part of him wondered whether the difficulties had been engineered, as he had been hardened and rendered most suspicious by his recent experiences. Lynch could not bring himself to believe the extent of the offer or the purity of its provenance. His voice was unnaturally harsh as he asked, "Is this benefactor some crook, like Magwitch the convict in Dickens's book?"

Lynch's attitude mildly appalled the lawyer. He had been warned Lynch might be difficult to convince. His pale white cheeks were tinged with some colour as he spoke, "I am not in the habit of knowingly representing criminal clients, Mr Lynch. My client is eminently well-placed, having come into his inheritance as it were, to make this significant and entirely legitimate philanthropic gesture. I am instructed to make you the offer, in good faith, in the earnest hope you will take it up. As a gesture of goodwill and knowing that you would be cautious in this respect, the offer will remain open to you for a year and a day."

Lynch had clammed up and said nothing. He was perplexed as to how he should respond more than anything else. He thought of the Count in Spain and how he was a Knight, the last remnant of some greater force for good. Was there a model there? On the other hand, who was this mystery funding from? He wondered how could be asked to trust someone he didn't know, couldn't see or talk to.

Berckley spoke into the silent gulf between them. "I have described the general intent of my client, and the extent of his financial commitment to the project. It is a most generous and noble offer. I think it is such a noble offer, that even you, whom I know to be a man of strong Faith, would have difficulty believing in this particular day and age. I am asking you to trust me when I say that my client can afford every penny of this offer and more. The offer remains open to you. You have a very long time to think it over. If you can sign a non-disclosure agreement I will write you a letter confirming what I can. This letter would be absolutely confidential. If you wish to discuss the letter further, to agree terms, a memorandum of understanding would follow and we could negotiate the minutiae. All I am asking is that you set any world-weary cynicism to one side and consider this noble act of generosity with an open mind."

Lynch stood. "I can't think what to say at present. I will need time to think and pray about everything you have said. Prayer will set it straight for me." He reached across the table, shook the lawyer's hand and left.

* * *

The runner, sheathed in black and turquoise lycra pounded along the track. His feet thumped on the springy forest ground. The track ran along the foot of the escarpment and began to climb up through the trees. He paused a moment to rehydrate and sucked on a bottle of water. He looked at his watch and calculated that he had taken slightly less time to get here than the day before. Stowing the water bottle back in the small back pack he began to climb the hill again. He was probably a mile or so from his car. He could be back in Wilmslow to have a shower fifteen minutes before his first appointment of the afternoon. He jumped up the rocks that made up the approach to the high viewpoint on the top of the escarpment, Stormy Point.

For a late summer day there were remarkably few people about. He had found the Edge wreathed in mist only half an hour before. He supposed that had deterred the usual walkers. He had run between the trees, through moist air, enjoying the solitude. Now sun had dispelled the morning mist and the day was gathering in heat.

He felt a surge of might as he reached the flat rocks that paved the surface of the Point. He did not stop to look at the view over the countryside. The view was commonplace to him now. His mind was focused on the time. He was urging his muscles on, but still mindful of where he placed his feet. The Edge could be a treacherous place and he didn't fancy breaking a leg in an unseen cleft or chasm. The Edge's surface was pocked with natural ravines and the mine workings of Romans and Victorians. He took a path that would lead him to the Beacon and then to his parked car. His speed would be a record if he could just keep up this pace.

He stopped.

He had reached the Druid's Circle. A circle of flat-topped sandstone rocks that had been put together a few hundred years before to simulate some antiquity. It was not the sight of the stones which halted his progress, for he had passed them many times, rather what someone had left draped across the largest stone.

At first he thought it might be a side of meat such as a butcher might have hanging in a shop. He was puzzled by this. Why would someone leave meat up here?

He edged closer, fearing there might be a smell. There were one or two flies gathering.

His overwhelming feeling was one of disbelief. He couldn't process what he was seeing or make out what it was. There were bare arms and legs, draped over the edge of the stone. A naked girl's body, pale in the open air. Splayed wide open to the skies above. He half expected the girl to get up, maybe to laugh at him. But this girl would never laugh or move again. He edged still closer. He could not bring himself to touch her and see if there was a pulse. He hovered nearby, watching to see if her bare chest moved with the breath of life. It did not.

He looked around. Could anybody else see her, see him? He unslung the back pack from his shoulders and retrieved a mobile phone. There was barely a signal up here, but it was enough to make the call he wanted. He noticed that as he spoke his voice sounded distant as if it was someone else speaking to the emergency service.

* * *

The police station in nearby Wilmslow was a low, redbrick pavilion surrounded by ornamental cherry trees. Dr Power thought it resembled a school pavilion such as might house changing rooms and a kitchen with polished silver urns to make half-time tea of the weak, milky variety, inevitably dispensed in white polystyrene cups.

As he walked to the police station door he was vaguely aware of Sergeant Collins's hand on his right upper arm, just above the elbow. He felt the warm grip through his red jacket. The hand was guiding him, even propelling him into the police station. Power was irritated and wanted to shrug it off.

The doors opened automatically in front of them and they were suddenly inside a tiny, grey-painted foyer. There were some plastic chairs welded to a metal frame that was fixed deep into the concrete below the green linoleum floor. There was a noticeboard with some posters about the crime of harassment and another about a so-called 'PCSO surgery'. A list of new station opening times apologised for a reduced service out of hours. Power and Sergeant Collins stood at the hermetically sealed counter, which was unmanned. Collins pressed a button. In the distance a bell rang in a muffled fashion. After a few minutes a young constable peered around the corner of a wall. "Can I help, Sergeant?"

"Yes you can," said Collins. "I haven't got all day. The inspector asked me to bring this doctor here in for questioning."

"Which inspector do you mean, Sergeant?"

"Don't play games, Constable. I haven't got all day. I know for a fact there's only the one inspector here today and he's here for the murder. Inspector Boardman. He's taken over one of the offices here for the day. Do you recall him now?" The constable nodded quickly. 'Then fetch him here, please? He hasn't got time to waste either." The constable disappeared into the recesses of the station.

Seconds later, he reappeared in the presence of an older colleague in a silver-grey suit and a silk paisley-patterned tie. He had tightly curled brown hair flecked with grey at the temples. Dr Power noticed a lack of any smile and grey-green eyes devoid of any warmth.

"Good evening, Sergeant, whom have we got here?"

"A Dr Power, sir," said Collins.

"Dr Power as in the email?"

"The very same, sir," said Collins.

"Is he under caution?"

"I cautioned him in the car, sir."

"Very good, Sergeant. Buzz them in, Constable, and show Dr Power into the interview suite."

Dr Power listened to the exchange and his stomach curled and coiled within his belly, twisting itself into a knot of anxiety. He wanted to shout out and protest, but there were no lines for him in this script between the police officers and he felt confused and belittled in their presence. He was escorted, again with the unwelcome grip around his arm, through a glass side-door which buzzed all the time until they were beyond, and into the working area of the police station.

The doctor had been in many police stations over the years in the course of his work with Superintendent Lynch, but until now he had always had the option to leave whenever he chose. The pressure on his arm was an unsubtle reminder that he had no option but to comply with a police agenda of which he had no inkling. He began to wonder at what point he should insist on summoning a solicitor. He held off, still wondering how bad this was going to get and somehow hoping that things weren't so serious that he needed a solicitor by his side.

Power felt hot and his forehead was suddenly a sheen of sweat. He fought a temptation to ask numerous questions. The world around him suddenly felt like some oneiroid state, a Kafkaesque waking dream.

He was led into an interview room. They were deep in the belly of the station and there was no window. The furnishing was minimal and bleak. A shiny, black-topped table, with mahogany edging. He found himself focusing irrelevantly on the minute swirling scratches on the black surface. There were four chairs, two on each side. Inspector Boardman sat down and began unwrapping a cassette tape. Power was wondering at the use of semi-obsolete technology, and he realised that somehow his thoughts had decayed into trivial meaninglessness, such must be his anxiety. Collins manoeuvered him into a chair and sat down by the inspector. Both police officers opposed Power.

Inspector Boardman started the tape, listed the occupants of the room, repeated the caution in full. "You do not have to say anything. But it may harm your defence if you do not mention, when questioned, something which you later rely on in court. Anything you do say may be given in evidence." Then he asked if Dr Power understood the caution.

"I understand the caution, yes," said Dr Power. "But I don't understand why I am here. Am I under arrest for something?"

"No, no, you're not being charged for anything yet. Not under arrest. Just being questioned. Under caution."

"What for?" said Power. The doctor was aware of a note of desperation in his own voice.

"Do you know a young girl, called Maria?"

Power thought, "No one comes to mind. I may have known a Maria at some point, but . . ."

"So it's possible you do know a Maria?"

"I can't think of anyone called Maria that I know nowadays."

"I see. That doesn't seem to be a yes or a no, does it?"

"I'm not sure what the context is. No one called Maria springs to mind. I can't rule out having met someone years ago. I see many people in clinic every week. Over the year I've seen thousands of different people all with different names."

Boardman smiled. It seemed to him that Dr Power had just given a very clever answer to get himself out of difficulty. "We were called to a body high up on the Edge, near Stormy Point. We have reason to believe that she was a young girl called Maria. Does that jog your memory, Dr Power?"

"No, it doesn't," said Power, his mind racing now. "Today?"

"Today."

"I've been in clinic all day, practically."

"Oh, really? All day?"

"Most of the day."

"That's right, we phoned your hospital, and you weren't there when we phoned."

"I was in town, meeting the Vice-Chancellor." But Boardman did not look as if he believed Dr Power.

"You said under caution that you were in clinic all day, and then you admit that you weren't. Isn't that right?"

"I was in clinic, then I went straight into the city and had tea at the Indulgence Café."

"I see," said Boardman. "She was found naked, sprawled on a stone. Like some kind of sacrifice. Are you sure you don't know someone about fourteen or fifteen, we think. Dark hair, brown eyes. Dead, garrotted."

"I don't know any girl. I don't know anything about this." Power's mind cast back through the years to a time when another body had been found on the Edge. How the police had taken over the driveway outside his home. He recalled how he had first met Superintendent Lynch and how they had become colleagues and firm friends. "Can't you call Superintendent Lynch? I'm sure he can sort this out."

"It would be convenient if your friend could 'sort this out', for you, wouldn't it? But some might see that as an abuse of process, or an exercise of privilege. It's odd you should mention my colleague, Superintendent Lynch, don't you think? Doesn't it remind you of something?"

"I don't know what you mean," said Power.

Boardman turned to Collins. "Do you remember old Superintendent Lynch, Sergeant?"

Collins nodded. "He used to teach us in training, sir. His old cases."

"Yes," said Boardman. "His old cases. I remember, too. There was the Ley Man, do you remember? There was a body found on the Edge in that case wasn't there?" Collins nodded. "A young female?" Collins nodded more vigorously. Power despised him angrily. He looked like some kind of nodding dog in the doctor's eyes. "Young and naked. A bit like the girl found today."

"Had she been abused?" asked Power. "Was she abused? Was there any semen?" He was trying to distinguish the cases between then and now.

"I'm afraid you don't get to ask the questions here, Dr Power. It's not your consultancy we want. It's not your professional advice we are seeking, you see. You are, I am afraid, a suspect."

Power's mouth dropped open. He couldn't help it. His stomach seemed to plummet like lead falling down inside his belly. "What?"

"There are quite a lot of us who don't rate Superintendent Lynch. His holier than thou attitude and working outside the protocols. I never thought his analysis of those Ley Man murders held water. Unconvincing. I never thought he'd got the right man you see."

"I was there," said Power. "I can tell you they got the right man. He was trying to kill my partner. Trying to kill me."

"So you would say, Dr Power. And of course the Ley Man was convicted. He is in prison. And yet here we are discussing another young woman's body found on the Edge. And from where I am sitting, Dr Power," Boardman shifted his chair and leaned so far forward he was only inches from Power's face. "From where I am sitting, the Ley Man, locked up safe in his prison cell, well, he has a better alibi than you, doesn't he?"

"It's preposterous," said Power. "He was caught red-handed."

"But what if he was innocent? Then you have to admit that the only common denominator is you, living up there on the Edge in your big house, thinking you're all safe and above the law."

"I've been out all day, I have nothing to do with this. Please believe me," Power was almost begging. He stopped in mid-speech. A thought had occurred to him that chilled him even on this summer evening. "I don't suppose the Ley Man has been released, has he?" It had been seven years; maybe it was possible? He thought of Laura up on the hill at the Edge, alone, and colour drained from his face.

"We're not amateurs," said Collins. "The inspector asked me to ring the Ashworth and he's still locked up safe and sound, Doctor." The Ashworth Hospital was a high security hospital. "He's not been released. He's not escaped. And he's going nowhere. He hasn't killed the girl up on the Edge today. So the only common factor *is* you." Collins challenged him further. "Have you been emailing Maria?"

"No!" said Power. "I told you. I don't know anybody called Maria."

Boardman pulled a photocopied piece of paper from a blue opaque plastic folder. "This is a printout of an email from you to Maria, dated a week ago. You made arrangements to meet her at the airport and take her home – to bed her there." He pushed the copy over to Power. "It's an enlarged copy, it focuses on the details."

Power looked at the page. It was dated a few days earlier. Her address was mariam@yahoo.de and the email did indeed appear to come from his own account. The email ran:

> Very much looking forward to seeing you in the flesh at last. All this time we've been chatting online and now we are finally going to meet. I will pick you up from your flight at Manchester Airport at 2 p.m. Thursday. I hope you are ready to go straight to bed when we get back to mine! Carl.

He pushed the photocopy back towards Boardman, his lips curled in disdain and anger.

"Listen," said Power. "All my life I have done my best to help people, and in the last few years I've done everything I can to help the catch the most dangerous criminals. Someone is trying to cause trouble for me. Look beyond the obvious. Do you really, really think I'd do this?

"For this police force I have tried, at four o'clock in the morning, to calm a psychotic, naked, heavily pregnant woman attempting to throw herself off a bridge.

"I've tried to talk through the cell doors of psychotic prisoners, to be hit in the face by spit, and endured the stench of their faeces and stale urine, and done my best to keep them alive when they tried to kill themselves. I have assessed another victim of some dreadful violent relationship in one of your cells, and got them to hand over to me the shard of glass she has been cutting herself with.

"I've written countless court reports for you.

"I've sat through hours and hours of murder trials to give expert witness to the Court.

"I have been to murder scenes and waded through the blood and vomit of victims, and de-escalated their violent murderers who were crying in self-pity.

"I have talked to a survivor of child abuse I did not know would jump off a motorway bridge a few hours later, after he made up a story of how he was feeling better with the medicine I gave him to save my feelings.

"I have sat on gravel by the railway and listened to the last words of a man who was dying after being bound to a railway line; and interviewed psychotic souls who confessed to murders they could never have committed because they were told to by voices who endlessly mock them from the shadows, and I have tried with every inch of my heart to help the law, and I have done this at every hour of the day and night for you, because illness does not rest.

"The police often look to me for answers, I am not perfect, but I do the best I can. And all I ask back from the police is your faith that I am doing good, and here I am – with you sitting there and seriously considering that I have abused and killed someone."

Boardman pushed the piece of paper back at Power across the desk. "A pretty little speech, Doctor, but too full of self-pity. You really think a lot of yourself. However, as you are aware, being a doctor or some high-flying politician doesn't make you a god, it doesn't make you infallible. And you are as likely as any other man to have sexual feelings. I think this email is good enough proof to arrest you."

"Where did you find it? You implied she was naked."

"Under her body."

"Doesn't that strike you as unusual," said Power. "To leave such a conspicuous clue?" He wondered whether to talk to them about the girl's body he had found in Spain. They hadn't mentioned Lucia. He rather thought that disclosing this event would not help him in any way. It would merely confirm Boardman's rabid suspicions.

"Leaving the email was a huge mistake. Criminals make mistakes. That's how we catch them, Dr Power."

"I never sent any email to this girl," said Power. Boardman stayed silent and merely pointed to the email. Power felt like hitting him. "You said it's just a section of the email. What else was on the paper? What other details were there?"

"Boring internet stuff," said Boardman. "Gobbledegook. The message is what's important."

"Can I see?" asked Power. "It would have to be disclosed in any case."

Boardman fished in his folder again and retrieved a copy of the full message. Power pored over it. Boardman was perturbed to see him beginning to smile. Eventually, Power gave it back to the two officers.

"The gobbledegook at the head of the email is important. The email is supposed to be to a girl with a German email account. Anyone can set that account up. And yes, someone knows what my real email address is, that's for sure. They've manipulated the server to send this email out as a proxy. The first lines suggest it's from me using a UK server, but if you look deeper in the 'boring internet stuff' in the header you'll see the email, bouncing between servers, was originally from a server in Germany. It's gone through six servers, you can see the route it took – these long server numbers each with four components – each one is a computer server or node that the email has passed through. And they are all in Germany. It's just that they made it look as if it was from my email address. The proof is there. Whoever faked this was in Germany, using German servers. They owned both the address it came from and the address that appears to be Maria's. If she is actually someone called Maria."

Boardman was silent. Collins asked, "Do you know much about the internet then?"

"Not very much," said Power. "But more than you apparently. Enough to know that you need to look below the surface. No court would accept this as evidence."

"I . . . I . . . I am not so sure," said Boardman. "You might be able to pull the wool over that credulous old man, Superintendent Lynch, with all your psychobabble. Not me. The modern police force has no room for dinosaurs like him. He once had the audacity to talk to me about the power of prayer – how it helped him reflect and solve cases."

"And yet," said Power, sticking up for his friend despite the dangers of doing so in his present position. "Dinosaur or not, he'd have spotted the problem with the header of this email. He'd have seen it was a fake."

Collins and Boardman both stared at Power in a silence that ran uncomfortably on.

There was a knock at the door, which then opened slowly.

The familiar face of Inspector Beresford looked round the door. "I am so sorry, Inspector Boardman and Sergeant Collins." He nodded to Dr Power. "I have something that I think you will need to see."

"Can't it wait?" snapped Boardman. "Inspector Beresford has entered the room," he said into the tape machine. "Can't you see we are interviewing Dr Power, under caution?"

Beresford smiled as benignly as he could manage. "You will wish to suspend the interview, I am sure. Once you take account of what I have brought over from HQ."

"I am interviewing a suspect about a murder, what could be more important?" asked Boardman.

"To you? Your professional reputation, maybe?" said Beresford. There was an edge of irritation in his voice. The newly appointed inspector pushed his way into the room and pulled over a TV and DVD player that was on a stand. "You will want to see this, Inspector Boardman." Without asking for permission Beresford switched the machine on and took a shiny silver DVD out of an envelope.

"Interview suspended at twenty-ten," Boardman said into the tape machine and clicked it off. "This had better be worth it, Beresford," he snarled.

"It is," said Beresford. "We scanned the arrivals at Manchester for the last few days and found one fifteen year old girl. First name Maria. We have footage of her in baggage reclaim and in the arrivals hall."

The four men watched the edited CCTV footage. The video pictures were from three locked off cameras in the baggage hall and arrivals hall. The images were in colour. The slight brown-haired girl walked slowly, as if in some pain. Her face was motionless, like a mask, and her arm was linked with a tall man who dwarfed her slim figure. Power watched as the man picked a suitcase off the baggage carousel. Just one bag. He took Maria by the elbow and steered her off screen and out though customs. The cameras next picked up the two in the arrivals hall where they headed towards the taxi rank. Maria walked slowly as if she was unwell, or unwilling.

Her eyes stared ahead. Power wondered if she was perhaps drugged as well as in pain.

"I think we are agreed that Maria was not picked up by Dr Power," said Beresford. "You can see that the man on the screen is clearly someone else, entirely."

"Someone's been busy," said Boardman. "You don't just come across evidence like this by chance. Especially when it's not even your case. Who . . ."

"Are we agreed that this is not Dr Power?" said Beresford.

Boardman nodded silently.

"And you have no evidence, real evidence, to link him to this crime. No reason to interview him under caution, do you?"

"Not now," said Boardman.

"I suggest," said Beresford. "I respectfully suggest that you concentrate your attentions on finding this man." He had paused the video and it was frozen at a point where the girl and her escort were just passing out of the camera's view. "Can Dr Power go, please? There's no reason for you to detain him any longer."

"No, well, no there's no evidence to justify further questioning, I suppose."

"I'll just take Dr Power out, then if I can have a quick word with you, Inspector?" Boardman nodded in a subdued and chastened manner.

Power stood up and left the room. Nothing was said.

Outside, Beresford closed the door to gently and whispered. "Hope you're okay, Carl. That must have been . . . unpleasant. I came as quick as I could. Some traffic between Chester and here. It was Lynch who got that footage and he sent me over with it. I'm glad I could help."

"Thank you," said Dr Power.

"The video footage of the girl . . . do you know who the man accompanying the girl is?"

"No idea," said Dr Power, looking away down the corridor towards the promising light at the end where the police station exit was.

"And if we leave the investigation to Inspector Plod there, we'll never know," said Beresford. "I'm sorry you had to encounter him."

"It's okay," said Power distantly. "I've met the type."

"Are you really all right?" asked Beresford. "These things can shake you up. Where are you going now?"

"Home," said Power, and more bitterly, "to reassure my partner that I'm not a child murderer. Thank you for your help. I'm sorry I am not quite myself. I will see you soon."

And Power left the police station, but his steps were angry ones. He phoned Laura as he walked and told her the news. She was relieved. He said he would not be back straight away, though. He said he loved her. After he ended the call he realised that his angry steps were taking him nowhere. As he had been taken to the police station, he had no car. He walked to the railway station to find a taxi, swearing under his breath as he went.

He found a black cab with an orange 'for hire' light on and got in. he gave an address to the driver, but it was not his home in Alderley Edge.

Although, in the police station, Power had said he didn't know the man who had brought Maria from Germany; Power had recognised him for sure. A tall, blond man; young and blue-eyed. In a travelling suit, not a cassock, but still the same man.

Chapter Fourteen

Forbid Us Something and That Thing we Desire
Geoffrey Chaucer

For most people the evening had been languorous and warm, and the day was still filled with sunlight. There was perhaps an hour or so of daylight left as Power's taxi drew up at his destination. In contrast to most people's experience of that Summer's day, Dr Power's evening had been a stressful one, filled with a degree of fear and anxiety that had sweat prickling all over his forehead and neck. Power had survived an interrogation that he had never expected to get and he was now struggling to contain an overwhelming rage within. He had disliked the two police officers who had tortured him with bitter questions and twisted suspicion, having an aversion to Boardman the most. He suspected that if any credible shred of evidence had remained after Beresford's timely intervention, he would be in a police cell by now. And he would be sitting on the coarse grey blanket on the bench-like bed and cudgeling his brains to form some kind of defence against the most grave of crimes, a child murder.

In the end, Power had decided against making any mention of the Spanish child murder to Boardman. The similarity would no doubt have been twisted by him. An instinct for self-preservation had, for once, outweighed any notion of duty that he might have. Instead of treating the information calmly and logically Boardman would merely have used the information against him, of that Carl Power was sure.

"That'll be twenty pounds, sir," said the cabbie, for the second time. His passenger had seemed very preoccupied throughout the journey. Power had been oblivious to any attempt at conversation, and even now was staring out of the cab window at the leafy villas of the road they had stopped on. "Are you all right, sir?"

"What? Oh, I'm sorry," said Dr Power. "How much do I owe you?"

"That'll be twenty pounds, please."

Power fished around in his wallet and took out a note. He looked briefly at the picture of Michael Faraday on it as he handed it over. Faraday's hair was all over the place as if he'd had a shock from the electricity he was trying to tame as a scientist. He followed it up with a couple of pound coins and got out. The taxi roared off, and Power took stock of the house in front of him.

He had put his red cagoule on. The gathering shadows of the night were putting a chill into the air. He put his hands in his pockets and wondered what to do next. He felt something – a folded piece of paper – against his right hand and pulled it out to see what it was. It seemed to be some kind of scribbled invoice. It was in Spanish. He made out several scrawls of blue biro and these few words described quantities of food: arozz, tomates, patatas, pescado, aceite de olive, but all in considerable quantities. Too large an amount for a household, more like . . . an institution. Then Power remembered the origin of the piece of paper. He'd fished it up off the floor on the night that he and Lynch had paid their visit to the empty orphanage. He had not chanced to look at it then or since, and here he was wearing the same jacket that he had worn then, and the paper had chosen to wait till now to present itself to him?

He looked at the head of the invoice for the organisation that the bill was made out to. The address didn't mean much to him, but it did include the town; Astorga. There was also a name: Padre Doyle.

This final clue, the name Doyle, seemed to reinforce all Dr

Power's reasons for coming to this urbane villa in Didsbury; and the name of the priest, Padre Doyle, had distilled his grief at the girls' deaths into an pure blaze of anger that he could now focus on a known individual.

The doctor paused, and tried to gather his reserves. The evening was cooling now, and the leaves of the shrubs were rustling in the gently moving air. In the distance somebody must have been having a barbecue as there was a trace of the smell of smoke and cooking on the air. Suddenly, he became aware that someone was looking at him.

The priest stood on the hallway front-step and looked down at him from the open front doorway. He had opened the door slowly and silently without Power noticing. Father Doyle smiled benignly and innocently at the doctor, "Yes?"

"I thought we should have a talk," said Power.

"Quite," said the priest. "Of course. Would you like to come in?" He opened the door wide and beckoned Power into the hallway. This deferential and smiling politeness was somewhat unexpected and Power found himself nodding and even thanking the priest. He caught himself doing so, and felt puzzled both at his reception and at the automatic courtesy of his response.

The priest closed the front door and bestowed another smile on the doctor. "Can I perhaps ask you for a proper introduction? Your name maybe?"

"Dr Power," said Dr Power, uneasily. "We met before."

"Quite," said the priest. "Of course. Forgive my memory. I meet so many people in the course of a normal week."

"You called the police on me when I was sitting peacefully in my car on the road outside?"

"Did I?" The priest seemed surprised. "Maybe that was someone else. My housekeeper perhaps. She's out at the moment. A much needed holiday. Can I show you into my study perhaps and then we can have that little talk you wanted."

Dr Power was guided, a gentle hand on his arm, into the priest's study which was at the front of the house. He was offered a leather wingback chair and the priest sat in a chair opposite, steepling his fingers. At a small table by Power's right hand was a selection of prayer books, the musical score of a hymn and a mobile phone.

"How can I help you, Dr Power? Fire away!"

"I think you know very well what I want to talk about."

The priest raised an eyebrow and silently shook his head. "Forgive me, Doctor, I'm no mind reader."

"About your involvement with two young girls," said Power. "And what happened to them."

"And what did happen to them, Dr Power? I'm afraid I'm no wiser about this matter."

"They are both dead."

"Oh dear," said the priest. "I'm so very sorry to hear that, but what brings you to *my* door in particular?"

"You knew both girls," said Power.

A smile from Doyle. "People say these things about the Church. About single priests. None of it is true. You must know that people have fantasies and make things up. Like patients who think they're having an affair with their doctor, and they tell people and people gossip, and before you know it the whole village knows and the doctor is the last to know. The last to know, because none of it is true. I think you are familiar with the problem, it's called *de Clerambault's* syndrome by psychiatrists. I'm sure that this matter is something like that. A misunderstanding."

"Except that I've seen the body of one of the two girls, and this is nothing to do with anyone's delusion."

"Where was that, Doctor? Where were these bodies?"

"I think you know where," said Power. He felt the priest was toying with him, and was determined not to unleash his temper too early. He tried to remain calm. "Spain, for one."

"Except the record proves I've never been there. So heaven knows why you turn up unannounced laying these accusations at my door."

"I saw you there, in the Cathedral in Leon."

"I have witnesses that will swear I have never left my parish. May I ask, what kind of doctor are you?"

"A psychiatrist," said Power. "I think you know that too."

"And there was I talking about *de Clerambault's* syndrome to a real psychiatrist. I must have sensed it. Maybe you have been working with the deluded a little too closely, Dr Power. You are projecting things onto me that are simply absurd, and demonstrably so."

"The CCTV records from Manchester Airport show that you were there with the latest dead girl. I've seen the video with my own eyes."

There was the briefest of pauses. Power was sure that the mention of CCTV footage had hit home. "I assure you that was probably somebody else; I haven't been to an airport in many years." He stood up, and Power thought he was about to be asked to leave. Instead the priest said, "I think we need a longer talk to set matters quite straight. You, of all people, must be aware that the public tends to project all manner of things on to people like us; people in authority. Let's try and calm things down. I will go and make us a cup of tea. Is that an idea? What would you like?"

"Anything," said Power. "Tea will do."

"Sugar? Milk?" The priest strode past Power's chair. "I'll just be a moment in the kitchen."

"Just milk," said Power, puzzled by the offer of hospitality in the middle of this particular conversation. "But don't bother . . ." Doyle didn't hear him. The priest had gone, Power had heard the door opening and closing. He looked around the wingback chair with difficulty, in case the priest was hiding. The room really was empty. He wondered about the priest in the kitchen and all the knives that would be to hand. The thought of the sharp steel edges and points made him wonder about leaving.

The mobile on the table suddenly shook and buzzed about, vibrating its way across the table, startling the doctor. It moved as it buzzed and seemed to be heading lemming-like towards the table edge. He caught it as it dropped and got a glimpse of the screen, which was flashing the number '2'. He replaced the phone on the table but it distracted Power as it jiggled excitedly about.

Power managed to hear the door opening behind him above the buzzing of the phone. The priest seemed to be back with his tray of tea before a kettle had practically time to boil. He could hear what he took to be the clink of cups and saucers and teapot on the tray as the priest carried it in.

"Oh, I don't want to miss that call," said Father Doyle. "While I set this down do you think you could answer for me?"

Power picked the mobile up and pressed the green answer button. He was vaguely aware of the priest scuffling about behind his leather chair, ostensibly putting the rattling tray on a table near the window. He put the phone to his ear. "Hello?" he asked.

"Is that Dr Power?" The voice at the other end was quiet, distant and sounded a bit like Father Doyle, having a slight Irish burr to it.

"Yes," said Power. "Who is this? How did you know my name."

At this point an arm wrapped round his neck from behind, and the body of the priest was on him from above the back of his chair, pinning him back and down into the leather. Power dropped the phone and cried out. He struggled to move forwards but the priest was younger than him, heavy, and his left arm had a grip like iron.

The priest's right hand carried a vast swathe of cotton wool, balled up in his fist. The wool stank of pungently sweet desflurane as it was clamped to Power's mouth and nose.

The priest held his face away from the fumes as best he could. Power, eyes wide and bulging in fear, inhaled desflurane deeply into his lungs in his panic and was suddenly lost to the world of consciousness. The priest held him for a few long moments until Power's muscle tone disappeared and he slumped like a rag doll. Doyle stood up and threw the cotton wool aside. He had been holding his breath as best he could, but his eyes were running and he felt mildly dizzy. He went near the window and lifted the sash and gulped in fresh air. He looked at Power and wondered if he was still alive. It was always tricky getting the balance between unconsciousness and death right.

Power didn't look as if he was breathing. Maybe Doyle had held him a minute or two too long? If so, it didn't really matter in the scheme of things. He might go back and check and see if Power's pulse was absent when his own head cleared.

* * *

"How was Carl?" asked Lynch. He was speaking to Beresford on his home telephone. It was late and darkness had fallen. He was sitting agitatedly on the edge of an armchair. His wife had put a milky cup of coffee by his side, but it had grown cold some time ago.

"I didn't get much chance to talk to him," said Inspector Beresford. "I rescued him from their clutches and then he was off from the police station like a rocket. He must have got a taxi or something. I was left talking to Boardman and Collins."

"I expect he raced home to Laura," said Lynch. "She's a sensible person, and of course she'd trust Carl with her life, but she will have seen him arrested and she will have wondered . . . inevitably. He will want to reassure her . . ."

"He spotted that the email was fake before Boardman and Collins, I don't think that they liked that. To have been fooled into accusing Dr Power by planted evidence."

"You think that they didn't know the email was planted evidence?" asked Lynch. "There wasn't a stitch on the girl except for the printed email. It was the only item left on her. It was an obvious move, to manipulate the credulous and implicate Carl. I can't believe they didn't see it."

"Maybe they only saw what they wanted to see," suggested Beresford. "And they still don't know about the girl in Spain, is it right to withhold that information from them?"

"Do you trust them?" asked Lynch.

"We have to trust our colleagues. How can they solve this without all the facts?"

"But would you trust Boardman with your life?"

There was a long pause.

"No," said Beresford.

"And neither would I," said Lynch.

"Then we'll let them work with the video we sent them," said Beresford. "Let them try and identify her full identity and the man who brought her here."

"I wonder whether I should go to Alderley Edge and see Carl?" wondered Lynch.

"As you said earlier, he'll be in some pretty intense conversations with his partner, wont he? She'll have some questions . . ."

"Poor Carl. Perhaps I'll wait till tomorrow before I contact them both. I thought I might just pour oil on troubled waters."

* * *

Power woke gradually from a vivid dream in red and orange; coloured shapes that wriggled and writhed on his retinas. He opened his eyes and felt sure that he had gone deaf and blind. All about him was silent darkness, like thick, lush, suffocating, inky velvet. His instinct was to shout out, but he stilled this drive and tried to take stock in spite of the panicky feeling in his throat.

His mouth felt dry and thick. He remembered the pungent aromatic smell of the cotton wool that had been clamped to his face. His throat felt ragged and hurt. He remembered up to the struggle, with the fabric clamped over his face. The priest had diverted him with the phone and that must have been when he poured the anaesthetic agent onto the cotton and quickly jammed it against Power's mouth and nose. He remembered the fear of not being able to breathe, and the invading organic solvent smell. It had been over so quick. One minute he was there in the study talking into the mobile phone and the next? Nothingness.

And now here he was in total blackness. No electric light. No candlelight. Not even a silvery finger of moonlight illuminated Power's fearful new world. An absence of light. Utter darkness. He remembered a previous immersion in this dark, and the associated all-encompassing fear. He had found a way out of the darkness then; surely he could again?

Power tried to orientate himself. He was lying on a cold concrete floor, where he had been dumped in a heap. The rough concrete was harsh against his cheek and hurt where his head had fallen onto the floor. Sensations from his arms and legs seemed to be altogether new to him, as if he'd never experienced this particular body before. Power struggled to lift his dull head from the floor and sit up. His hands felt full of pins and needles. His skull was almost too heavy to lift up from the ground, it nodded leadenly as he heaved it up.

His sense of hearing seemed muffled as if there was a mile

between his ears and reality. He supposed the solvent was taking time to wear off. The scrape of the soles of his shoes on the stone floor as he tried to prop himself up into a sitting position sounded as if it came from a few rooms away. He turned about and about, to try and see anything. But there was nothing. He was surprised most of all by the loudness of his own breathing, and his own heart beating fast, in fright and panic.

Power wondered how long he had been unconscious? Hours? Days? And what had happened to him in the meantime. Had the priest dragged him down to the cellar of the parish house, or was he somewhere else entirely. This could be his tomb.

The darkness seemed pressingly permanent and he doubted that the sun would ever penetrate here. It could be day or night.

He had climbed to his feet in the last few minutes. His legs felt shaky and he wondered if he would fall. Without his sight he had no cue as to his orientation in the space around him. There existed a floor and darkness. That was all. That was his world. If he walked forward would he encounter a wall or open space? If there was a door, where was it?

"God help me," he whispered, and stretched his arms out.

'Why didn't I take more care?' Power scolded himself. 'Why didn't I wait till I was prepared to confront him?' Now he was alone, in the dark, with what else? It is easy in the daylight sun to shrug off any fears of the unknown and the supernatural, but alone in the absolute dark, and cold fear grips one's soul absolutely.

Power shouted out, but heard his cry fading into space like water disappearing in black sand. His voice surprised him because it sounded like someone else's voice, hacked with fear.

The open space all around him was disorienting. He walked forward and reached out his hands and touched the walls, planting his palms open wide, feeling the solidity for reassurance that he still existed. He must move. 'Left or right? The answer matters so much,' he thought. 'The floor seems solid, but there might be a pit sunk into it, or a flight of stairs.' He might move the wrong way, fall down a shaft and break a leg. No one knew he was here, but the priest. No one would rescue him. No one would find him until it was too late.

He decided. He would move to the right, round the walls. Inch by inch, feeling his way gradually, testing each and every footstep to avoid any sudden fall down a shaft or stair well.

He still felt dizzy. There was a ringing in his ears and his knees felt as if they would give way. Power was suddenly beset by the idea that the priest might be watching him through night lenses and might come at him in the dark. He wondered what the priest had used to anaesthetize him. Had it damaged his sight maybe? Was there a light on that he couldn't see?

He moved forward and touched the cold wall in front of him. It was uneven brickwork, but it felt greasy, maybe thickly painted with gloss paint. He wondered what colour it could be. Power moved to the right and the wall continued. He reached up. Just within reach there was a ceiling at right angles, again covered with the same glossy paint. He moved on, skirting the walls of the space: four. There was one door with a flat, smooth surface. To Power's tapping fingers the door felt cold; metallic. There was no handle on the inside.

He estimated the room was only about eight foot square. Perhaps eight foot tall too? A square box of a room: but where was it?

In his mole-like traverse of the room he had encountered only two objects, which he had nearly tripped over. One felt like an ancient knife polisher; round, wooden and box-like with a bone-handled knife still stuck deep in the box unto its hilt. Power pulled the bony handle and a flat, spatula-like knife came out. The edge was blunt and rusty. The next object was a dusty cardboard box filled with china cups and saucers. He wondered about shattering one and using its sharp edge against the priest should he ever enter the room. Power's mind flashed back to a hospital patient he had been called to as an emergency. He had been a registrar dragged from his bed in the middle of the night. The patient, a young woman, had been found lying in a pool of blood in the seclusion room, her ulnar artery slashed by a shard of crockery that she had carefully secreted in her vagina to avoid discovery. Once secluded in the locked room she had set to ripping at her own flesh. Power shuddered at the memory, but he hadn't forgotten how sharp the edge of crockery could be. He remembered paddling through the sticky blood as it darkened, to save the girl's life.

His exploration of the room at an end, and with no discernible means of escape, he began to beat his fists upon the metal door, and shout.

After an age, the priest arrived in the corridor outside. He switched on a light and Power could hear a chair scraping on the floor beyond the door as the priest sat down. Inside the room a thin rim of light glimmered around the edge of the door. Power could smell cigar smoke too and imagine Doyle seated outside, smoking. But after he sat down there was nothing but silence from the priest. The minutes seemed like hours.

Power could not bear the wait, "Are you there?" he asked.

"I am," said Doyle, speaking slowly and with a studied nonchalance. "Summoned here by your infernal racket."

"Where am I?" asked Power.

"I will only give you information that I want to give you; I don't really want to help you, or incriminate myself, so I will please myself what I say."

"What did you use on me?" asked Power. "Chloroform?"

"No – I've tried using that," said the priest. "Chloroform takes too long. I tried it once. There was a long struggle and I had to end it with the edge of a brick." He laughed. "I used desflurane on you. It's quicker."

"Where do you get a drug like that?" asked Power. "It's not something you just go and get down the chemist's."

"Friends," said the priest. "We friends work as a team and we watch out for one another."

"Did your friends arrange for the police to interrogate me about the girl's murder? Did they incriminate me?"

The priest chuckled. "I said I wouldn't incriminate myself. Although, I suppose it wouldn't matter if I told you everything now. Still, why should I confess to anything?"

"Isn't confession good for the Catholic soul?" suggested Power.

"You sound like a bitter Protestant to me," laughed the priest. "Shall I make a confession, then? Would you like that? Maybe I shall while an hour or so away with you. Why not? I will stay until you bore me, or annoy me too much. Then I'll let you be."

"Did you kill Lucia in Spain? You can confess that if you like. And did you kill the girl here? Maria was it?"

"Ah-ah," said Doyle. Power could imagine him wagging his finger at him through the door. "I'm not going to incriminate myself. But what if I said that I didn't do those things? Would that make any difference to your last few hours? After all, logically, I couldn't have killed the girl in Spain. No Father Doyle has ever left the country, or even left the parish! You know that for a fact. No. Let me tell you of my time in the seminary instead, now that would be a confession for you. Shall I tell you, my confessor, of those first few days away from home? Do you know how much I wanted the Church to heal me? That I thought my future lay with the Church when I realised that I wasn't developing the same way as other young men. When I realised that I wasn't attracted to women? Can you imagine the leaving of home and this new world you go into with such hope. A bright serene world of vaulted ceilings, high and white above your head. Everything tall, and spacious, and quiet – the slightest whisper echoing. And you have to be silent, and it makes you wonder what people are thinking of you. And you wonder whether they can hear your thoughts. The listening to interminable lectures about sin, and the long hours of reading in the silent library. A feeling of being judged. A feeling that your simple enjoyment of food, of warmth, or comfort, is somehow indulgent." The priest paused to light another cigar. Power could hear the rasp of the matchhead on the sandpaper at the side of the box. "And you're a young man, with urges, and the nights are so long, and you know it's a sin to touch yourself. Sometimes they advise you to sleep with your hands tied behind you. Have you ever tried sleeping like that? I expect not. Well, those urges aren't easily suppressed, even by the interminable boredom of studying incessant commentaries on prayer and the Saints. And they know you're young. They know you have these urges, because the ancient paper dry fossils in their perfumed cassocks, remember a time when they must have been young. And they wheedle and connive to hear your lusts and your torment, because they somehow enjoy the memory of once being alive themselves. Anyway, they harp on and on and on at you. They will not leave you be, trying to get inside your head. And you feel you're going to be rejected if you tell them that your real desires, your inner wants, are not normal ones. But they keep on going, and your anxiety levels rise, and you stutter and sweat in that confession box as you try to avoid saying the truth. For fear of being, I don't know, expelled, or damned for having these lusts. And the more you resist the ideas, the stronger they somehow get. You know?" Power said nothing, because he knew there was no stopping the priest. "And they wheedle it out of you, some months in, when you're terrified of being sent home, terrified of what kind of demon they will say you are – and that they'll treat you like you're some abomination, and at the same time equally terrified of not getting it all off your chest. You crave their forgiveness. The process is mental torture. They really do a job on you, you know. So you don't know your own self, or what's best for you. And you have to trust someone, and they've cut you off from everything that went before, your home and your family, so you feel so alone, and you are desperate for their, I don't know, absolution? And in the end they break you. And you shake as you confess your weakness, your penchant for younger girls. Women are not your thing. They look wrong, these women, frightening somehow, but the young and innocent . . . And to your shock and also your horrified guilty pleasure they actually welcome you. I mean welcome your confession. They forgive you and they welcome your sin. They indulge it and even tell you that it's all right. That that kind of pleasure is, like a perk of the job. If I remember correctly that's exactly the word that some of them said. And you don't know what a guilty relief that was. To have those desires entertained and, well, fostered by my colleagues and superiors. It no longer seemed something to be guilty about any more. It was a relief. And in fact they introduce you to others, like an enlightened brotherhood. There are friends we have – police, councillors . . . and the bottom line, Dr Power, is that we've always been there, for years and years, a network. We're more powerful than you could ever imagine, and so powerful that really you never could have won against us, in any case."

Power felt sick to his belly. He hurled himself at the vast expanse of the wooden door. He crashed against it in rage, but it did not yield and he bounced back with an ineffective crash. On the other side the priest laughed at him.

"You'll only dislocate your shoulder," said Doyle. "Just then it sounded like I had some wild animal caged in there. A monster in the dark."

"You're the only monster here," said Power.

"Be careful," said Doyle. "I'm only here while you interest me. Once you start being boring or offensive I'm easily as happy to leave you here in the dark. I haven't got to be anywhere else, just yet."

Power decided to try it. He'd been right in his intuition about the priest all along. Maybe he was right about other things, too. Like the first night in Spain when he'd seen the dark priest with an eye patch.

He asked through the door – "Do you know a man called Cousins? Is he involved?"

Doyle laughed unkindly, sneeringly. "There are no cousins involved."

"You said you would leave me here. Where are you going?" asked Power.

"Why should I tell you that?"

"It's not as if I can tell anybody; stuck in here," said Power.

"And it's not as if you will be getting out alive," said the priest. "But still, I was taught to be cautious in the seminary, and you stick to the old training drills. So, I won't be telling you my plans like some madman in a film. Except to say, I always had a contingency plan. And a backup for that, too, in case that fell through."

"When I was growing up I trusted people," said Power. "I was taught that people in authority were good. The police. They were good people. They upheld the law, were honest and punished villains. The judges told the truth and always found the villains guilty. The vicars and the priests represented God and were good at heart. God's representatives on earth – a symbol of heaven. And then you grow up and you realise that men like you are nothing more than men of straw. No better than anyone else and just hiding behind their power and abusing your faith; using your credulous innocence against you. Using your own faith, your naiveté and your ignorance of their evil hearts as a shield for the bad deeds they do. And then you realise that the only monsters in this world are human. And you get angry and you want to destroy them and their works."

"You've nailed every profession there except doctors," said Doyle. "Are you really so pure? Earning money through human sickness? Would you have your big house in Alderley, Dr Power, if it wasn't through other people's fears and depression? Your wealth is just the other side of the coin of human suffering. And have you forgotten the prodigal doctor, Harold Shipman? How many did he slaughter? Or would you conveniently airbrush him out of recent history to salve your conscience?"

"We're human, all of us," said Power. "We're all potential monsters; we can all use our skills to kill and harm others. But we don't have to do any of it. We all have shadows. A patient told me the trick to being a good person is to keep your shadow small."

"You sound a very worthy, prudish and dull man, Dr Power."

"I am just a normal person," said Power. "No-one special."

"Then you have normal wants and needs and desires and lusts," said the priest. "You like your food no doubt. Are you hungry?"

"I could do with a little something," said Power. "But I will survive without I dare say."

"Will you survive, indeed?" laughed the priest. "And no doubt you are a red-blooded individual with a sexual drive?"

"I am human," said Power.

"You must have been tempted over the years? To sleep with a patient, maybe?"

"No," said Power. "I don't see people in that way when I'm working."

"Very virtuous, very dull" said the priest. "But you paused, and to be honest you sound a little too good to be true. The thought must have crossed your mind. A flirtatious young patient with a good body maybe?"

"Maybe you find it reassuring to think that everybody is the same as you?" Power suggested.

"We could be a team, if you unburdened yourself of your true desires. We could have it all. I could unlock everything for you. You could indulge every desire."

"Or you could just let me out," said Power. "And take responsibility for what you have done to others."

"Haven't you ever, ever, looked at a young girl and wanted her," whispered the priest. "Be honest. Confess that you have. Maybe a girl you looked at and wanted and she was seventeen?" The priest's voice sounded thick with his own lust. Power stayed silent in his darkness, conscious that anything he said could represent a wrong move. On the whole, he preferred to maintain silence. "Or maybe you were attracted to a girl and found she was fifteen? What could you do with your desires then? You couldn't put those feelings away in a box and pretend you hadn't had them, could you? Your attraction was there when you saw her. What did it matter whether you knew her age. The attraction was there, to how she was, her shape, her body, as she was in front of your gaze; not what you knew about her. You couldn't deny the desire, or could you? To deny the attraction would be . . . hypocrisy at best."

Silence from the doctor.

The priest yawned. "Somehow I can tell you aren't going to play along. You're too closed and too damn boring to admit your own desires. You don't know when opportunity is knocking at the door." He knocked on the metal door to illustrate his point. "When you only have to say, tell me what you desire and you could have everything. Freedom from your prison; life to live in a group that understands you and fulfilment of any fantasy you want."

"But I'd lose myself," said Power. "Whatever a soul is, whatever I am; that would be gone."

"You understand nothing," said the priest, suddenly feeling achingly bored. "You have a closed mind. You are unenlightened about the possibilities of life here on earth and certainly don't understand what happens after you die." The priest's thoughts turned to cruelty. "Tell me, now, does anyone know you're here?"

Power lied. "I came here ahead of my friend, Superintendent Lynch. He won't be far behind me."

"Well, he's more than several hours late, then," said the priest. "You know what? I don't think he's coming to save you. And to be frank, Dr Power. I've met so many people in my life, that I know perfectly well when people are lying to me. You paused to think, Doctor . . . and that means that no-one knows you're here. You were acting in haste coming here. My friends would have warned me if you'd officially told the policeman."

The priest stood up. Power heard a scraping of the chair on the floor just beyond the door. Outside in the corridor, Doyle took his cigar out of his mouth, threw it on the floor and stamped its life out, then fished in his pocket.

There was a screeching, scrawping sound.

"Do you know what this is?"

"I've no idea," said Power. "But I feel sure that you will probably tell me."

Doyle unwound some more duct tape from the roll. "It's your nemesis. Can you see any light in there, beside the crack of light around the door?

"No," said Power.

"That's because the cellar has no windows. I had them bricked up. And the walls are painted with thick, impervious paint. And that means the air you're breathing, the only air, is coming in to the cellar through that little crack around the door. And in my hand I have a roll of thick tape, to seal up the crack. Do you know how long the air supply in there will last you? Being a doctor, I am sure that you can work it out." Power could hear the priest pulling a length of tape off the roll. Inside the cellar he could see the light at the top of the door disappearing as the priest pressed the tape firmly against the crack.

"Are you scared of the dark, Doctor?"

Power's mind flashed back to his medical school days and a lecture on physiology. The thin old man at the lectern, voice quavering, said, 'A man can survive around forty days without food before he descends into hallucinations and coma from ketosis. Without water he can last maybe two or three days before his kidneys fail, toxins accumulate and his blood pressure drops too low for his brain to survive. Of course only a couple of minutes or so without oxygen ...'

Power wondered how big the cellar was. When he had moved around it he had assumed it was a box of only eight foot cubed. Around five hundred cubic feet; a very finite amount.

The priest was pulling another length of tape from the roll with a screeching sound. The crack of light on the left-hand side of the door went dark.

The atmosphere is about 20% oxygen. People breathe this in, and breathe out air that is 15% oxygen, so oxygen in a closed space will drop gradually, but Power knew that it was the accumulation of carbon dioxide that would kill him. First he would feel breathless and then his heart would start adding beats. His muscles would twitch and his hands flap. His pulse would feel full as his blood pressure rose and he would have headaches and then, in the darkness, he would lapse into coma, his heart might fibrillate, and he might convulse. Death would follow soon after that.

Usually inhaled air has carbon dioxide at a proportion of 0.04% by volume, and when exhaled the proportion rises to a bit over 4%. The carbon dioxide in the room would therefore rapidly accumulate.

A person breathes about 300 cubic feet per day. A man's breathing would decrease the cellar's oxygen by 18 cubic feet per day. His breathing would increase the cellar's carbon dioxide by 12 cubic feet per day. Fatal carbon dioxide levels are just above 3% of room air. Power calculated he had about a day, or less.

The priest ripped another length of tape from the roll and sealed the vertical right-hand crack. The darkness was almost absolute again.

"I'll be off after this last piece," said the priest. "No sense in hanging about. I am not coming back here myself. Time to move on, I think. I don't expect anybody will check on the house for weeks. Whoever does might find you. The cleaner is on her holidays. And she's forbidden to go anywhere but the ground floor, really. The gardener, of course, never comes in the house and he comes once a fortnight. He was here last week."

Power shouted out, "Nothing will stop me coming after you!"

But the priest merely laughed at the doctor's muffled voice, locked and sealed within his tomb. "You're a joke," said Doyle. "You're sealed in a box. It's a big box, but it's just a coffin, all the same."

And with that, the priest sealed the last edge of the door, pressing the tape firmly into the corner between door and floor.

The darkness was total.

The doctor listened to the retreating steps of the priest down the corridor. He imagined, but could not hear, the priest ascending some stairs. And the house went silent, all except for Power's breathing.

Power mused for a second on the irony of being killed by your own breathing. Feelings of panic, gave way to some kind of plan. He knelt and felt about on the floor for the oddments that he had stumbled on earlier. He pulled out the rusty old, bone-handled knife and crouched down by the door. He pushed the blunt blade through the crack at one of the vertical edges, but the door jamb prevented him from touching the tape and thwarted him from thus piercing the seal. Only at the very bottom of the door could he push the blade sufficiently far enough to touch and push at the tape. Here he could effect some improvement in his parlous state. The tape yielded and fell away, breaking the total seal. Power ran the flat blade along the length of the bottom of the door, releasing the tape at the bottom of the door, restoring some kind of gap. He put his mouth near the crack and felt the most minuscule amount of fresh air trickling over his face. This would not change the air in the sealed room anything like as much as he needed, but it had bought him some time. He sucked at the fresh air as best he could and blew his exhaled air in the hope that this carbon dioxide rich air would not accumulate, for this was the main threat to his life.

Occasionally, he would reach up and beat and thrash at the metal door in the vain hope that someone would hear and come to his aid. But no-one came. Power wondered where everyone was. Had the priest left the house now and was he, even now, beginning his new life? Where was Lynch, what was he doing? Was Laura still asleep, or wakened and worried about him? He lay there for hours, the hard floor grating against his hip and shoulder. He should have felt cold, but he was starting to feel hot and flushed as the carbon dioxide accumulated. Eventually, as he had himself foretold from his knowledge of physiology, Dr Power lapsed into unconsciousness . . .

Chapter Fifteen

For if a priest be foul, on whom we trust,
No wonder is a common man should rust

The Prologue of Chaucer's Canterbury Tales
Geoffrey Chaucer

The coach trip had not been to Janet's liking, not at all. She did not like being forced to make polite conversation with a group of old people, even if they were her peers. The moving from hotel bed to hotel bed had destroyed her sleep pattern and she had felt irritable walking round a succession of mausoleum-like stately homes. There was only so much tea and scones that a soul could endure. After Castle Howard at York, she had made a run for it and scurried with her bag to the rail station. She had taken the first express train to Manchester Piccadilly. She had splashed out on a taxi, but she was desperate to get back to her routine. And for Janet that meant her work, from which she had not been separated for many years.

She castigated herself for ever having agreed to go on holiday, and was so pleased to draw up outside the parish house that she did not even question the taxi driver's extortionate fare.

The house was empty and chill when she pushed her way in through the front door.

She sensed that the priest's presence was not there, but she also sensed that something was wrong. There were signs of a struggle in the study. A table knocked over and some books and cushions spilled onto the floor. A pungent smelling pad of cotton wool was discarded in the corner of the room. There was a bottle of some chemical on a tray near the window.

She decided to explore. She went places she had never been allowed before. Upstairs there were some disgusting photographs in a bedside bureau. After she had seen them she realised with a cold feeling in her stomach that she couldn't work there any more. This was another unpleasant shock for her after the holiday, but she realised now that she had instinctually known something was wrong with this priest for some time. The wardrobe and chest of drawers had been left open, and there were signs of some rapid packing. There were signs too that the upstairs bedrooms had been in use by more than one person. At least two of the beds looked used.

She made her way down into the cellar. There was a smell of fresh cigar smoke. The priest didn't usually smoke. She disapproved of smoking. 'While the cat's away, the mice will play,' she thought. She noticed that the cellars had been freshly painted since she had last been allowed down here. New electric lights had been put in and the large space that she remembered had been divided up by brick walls into several small rooms with doors, like dungeons. A stout green metal door at the end of a whitewashed corridor took her attention. This had ugly silver duct tape over the edges of the doors, sealing them. She was half-tempted to go and make herself a cup of tea at this point, but something, providence perhaps, made her explore a bit more.

Janet pulled the strips of tape away. She disliked the very sticky substance on the tapes. It clung to her fingers. There was a round brass handle and a lock with a heavy key in it. She felt a little uneasy, wondering what might be behind the door. She felt frightened. The unsavoury photos upstairs looked as if they might have been taken in one of these downstairs rooms.

She turned the key. The lock was well lubricated and it glided open. Janet turned the brass knob and pushed the door in. It was bit difficult to open the door, as if something was lying behind the door. Undaunted, she pushed with all her might and the thing shifted enough for the door to open a crack. Enough, at least, for her to put her head in and peer round into the gloom. It was too dark to see. She found a light switch in the corridor and flicked it on. Bright light streamed out of the room beyond and she put her head in again.

There was a body on the floor. It was quite, quite still. A young man. She thought he must have been quite handsome with his dark hair. Now he lay there unshaven and pale. He was so still, that she took him for dead. He looked very peaceful.

Power groaned suddenly and rolled onto his back. Janet jumped.

His almond brown eyes opened and Power stared fuzzily up at the old woman. "Hello? Can you call the police," he asked. "Superintendent Lynch, please."

"Oh, dear," said Janet, looking at Power's pallid face. "Shouldn't I call a doctor first?"

"I am a doctor," said Power. "Call the police, they may be able to catch him."

Janet knew exactly whom Power was referring to.

"All right," said Janet. "Maybe you're right. But come upstairs, and while we phone, I will make you a hot cup of tea. I need one myself . . ."

PART THREE

Chapter Sixteen

*The most perceptive character in a play is the fool,
because the man who wishes to seem simple
cannot possibly be a simpleton.*

Cervantes, Don Quixote

Dr Power picked up a sharp knife from the crisp white tablecloth and deftly quartered the soft purple fig on a wooden platter. He scattered the quarters on to the yoghurt in his bowl along with the others he had already cut and drizzled some golden-yellow honey over them. The honey glinted and sparkled in the morning sun as it drooled its way down onto the white yoghurt from Power's silver spoon.

He made his way from the heavy dark sideboard, laden with breakfast things and sat down at the table where Lynch was already wolfing down sourdough bread and ham. The Count himself brought them a heavy silver pot of freshly brewed coffee. Steam wafted gently from the spout as the Count set it down.

"And you set forth today?" asked the Count.

"Yes," said Lynch. "This time we walk alone. No guide. No van, just our own legs. No phone. No interruptions; just the old-fashioned way. We walk until we arrive, weary but physically and spiritually fitter in Santiago de Compostela, in approximately ten days' time."

"I see," the Count took it upon himself to pour their coffee, he raised the pot highly as he did so. The coffee swooped out of the pot in a steaming arc of dark liquid. "Perhaps we could have a talk, in private, before you depart? Maybe, after breakfast in the garden?"

"Of course," said Lynch, although he was eager to get away and walk without too much distraction. He keenly needed a complete break and talk of the murders might be more than he could bear.

The Count nodded, smiled, and seemed to stand to attention before he left to look after another table.

"I guess he wants to make a report to you, before we go," said Power.

"Mmm, yes," said Lynch. "But I want to focus on our walk this time."

Power understood his friend, but even as he himself was spooning up his first mouthful of the figs, he caught sight of a new arrival in the dining room mirror. He turned round in his chair to greet the pilgrim they had met during their first few days on the Camino.

Power stood and hailed him and offered him a seat at their table, "Hello, Ramon?"

The old man beamed at Dr Power. "Hello!" He looked at Power and Lynch and drew a triangle between them. "We three lay on the ground and looked at the stars. We talked of entangled electrons and my friend Schrödinger whom I once met in Dublin. Am I right?"

"You are right," said Power, smiling at him. "Will you join us for breakfast?"

"By all means," said Ramon, and accepting the cup of coffee that Power offered him sat down opposite Lynch.

"You haven't got very far along the Way, have you?" said Power. "I expected you to have got to Santiago weeks ago."

"And indeed, you are right," said Ramon, with a twinkle in his eye. "I reached Santiago de Compostela a fortnight after we last met. I am now on my way home. Unlike most, I always walk there, *and* I also walk all the way back. There is always a journey out into the world, and a journey back home. Until the last journey, of course."

"And where do you come from?" asked Power. "Where is home?"

"I live in Valetta and work at the University of Malta. I listen to the stars from there. And tell me, critic, why have you not got any farther than Astorga? This is a lovely hotel, to be sure. And I always like to stay here with the Count when I walk on my way home. I treat myself on the way back. I do penance on the way to Santiago, and reward myself on the way back. On my return leg I stay in nice hotels, and eat like a king. So, what misfortune prevented you reaching the pilgrim city?"

"It's a long story," said Lynch.

Ramon could tell that neither Lynch nor Power wanted to talk about their experiences. "No matter," he said. "Are you both well, though?"

"Yes," said Power. "Never better."

"I can see you both have been through something difficult," said Ramon. "But I won't probe, except to say that you are like an entangled pair of particles, what has happened to one seems to have happened to the other."

"That's a bit deep for breakfast time," said Power. "But I did listen carefully to what you said under the stars, you know. When I got back home I tried to read up about what you told me. And I came upon a passage where Schrödinger predicted that some changes might occur *before* a particle interaction. That effects of the interaction could, as it were, travel backwards in time."

"Ah yes, I think I know what you mean," said Ramon. 'There is a symmetricality of time to equations like the Maxwell Equation and people like Feynman and Schrödinger found a similar symmetricality of time in other places too. What I think you are talking about, is how when a charged particle is agitated, that somehow, waves from that can radiate both into the future and into the past. And those waves can interact with other particles and they too can radiate waves into the future and into the past. Mostly, of course, you understand they cancel out . . ."

"Waves go into the future and the past," sighed Power blissfully at the thought. "How mind blowing! So maybe everything happens at once, collapses together?" Lynch frowned at the further mention of things collapsing together; a return of an idea he had heard from Power before.

"These are big ideas for breakfast time, you are right, and maybe somewhere, in some universe or dimension, you are correct," said Ramon, smiling. "But we are talking at a quantum level here, Maxwell was not, I think, putting forward a basis for prophecy or foreknowledge. The rules that seem to apply at the quantum level, that very, very small level, don't necessarily translate to Newtonian physics. Or else clever Isaac would have found them first. Don't you wonder what these people from the past would have dreamed up if they had access to our resources now? We always seem to think that our ancestors were stupid and that intelligence has risen exponentially in recent times. We imagine Neanderthals and even people from a few hundred years ago to be stupid. And yet on Malta, where I live, you will find complex stone temples from thousands of years before your Stonehenge. It is not our ancestors who were stupid, it is our new generation that is becoming stupid and stupider. Relying on the internet and inanimate computers for social interaction and information, when people, miracles of life and love are right in front of them. All of them dying of thirst whilst standing in a river. Pardon me, I am reminded that I must get some food and drink myself."

He stood up and made his way to the sideboard of breakfast dishes.

"You didn't want to talk to him?" Power asked Lynch in a whisper.

"I don't particularly want to talk to anyone about what happened before," said Lynch. "But doesn't it strike you as odd, that he should re-appear here and now at this place and time, when we are here?"

"Maybe," said Power. "And maybe it's just synchronicity."

Lynch coughed, disapprovingly, "All this irrelevant stuff about entangled twin particles and time." He put his knife and fork down on his plate. He seemed much more irritable than usual. "I'll go and bring down our packs and check the room. Shall I meet you outside in the garden and debrief the Count before we go?"

"Okay," said Power, nodding. "Then we can be off, and get away from everything." Power watched as Lynch strode from the dining room and into the lobby outside. He hoped that Lynch would relax once they were back on the Camino.

"I am sorry if I disturbed your friend's peace of mind and breakfast," said Ramon, as he resumed his seat. His plate was piled with slices of cheese, Serrano ham, quince jelly, sliced pear and bread. "Walking the Way always involves some kind of spiritual challenge, you know. The challenge can't be escaped, just as in life really. But your friend, his mind is not easy, you know."

"No," said Power. "He has a stressful job, and he wanted some peace away from everything. Then we encountered this orphan girl, who had been looked after by some religious order, apparently. She'd run away. So we altered our plans to fit her and brought her here to this hotel, as a matter of fact. Perhaps we should have chosen another hotel to begin our walk again, I don't know. Then she was taken from here by some people pretending to be officials. Then we found her on the Way itself. She'd been killed."

"No, no!" Ramon seemed genuinely shocked. "I never heard anything. There was nothing about this in the newspapers."

"It is true, I saw her," said Power, softly.

"And now you are attempting to re-write the past," said Ramon. "And your friend hopes to complete your journey in peace, without further incident?" Power nodded. "When you see an interaction between particles in a cloud chamber. When particles collide suddenly . . . well, there is an element of chaos that you can't predict or control. The results of the collision; subparticles fly everywhere. You can see these paths, curving and sparking all over the place! They follow rules, of course, but you can't know that things will go a certain way. And life is like that too. It's difficult to control, and we mustn't be too disappointed when things don't fit. Because our human belief is that we can control things; well of course, that's an illusion. Maybe we can only observe the show and enjoy it while we can. Is that too passive a philosophy, do you think?"

"Or maybe," said Power, "we should try and give things a nudge in the positive direction every now and then?"

"Of course," said Ramon. "Let's abide with that."

"Do you like working in a University?" asked Power, who had been thinking about the Vice-Chancellor's offer in Allminster ever since he had finally had time to discuss it with Laura. "Are you a Professor then?"

"Maybe, and yes," said Ramon. "I am a very old Professor, though, and I have seen many Faculties over the years. You would think a University was a quiet and considerate place, where thinking and research are at the fore. This is anything but true. As you may well find out yourself."

"How did you know I might find out?" asked Power.

"It is no spooky, quantum foreknowledge on my part," said Ramon. "Just that maybe your asking of the question implies that you are thinking of a University role." He laughed, and looked at his empty plate. "I think you will enjoy the fray. I must leave you now; I must get to San Martin by the afternoon. One thing. It is good you are together on the Way. I was alone in the hills in a tent, as you know, and one night the wolves seemed to chance to come very close to me. They will tackle a deer, you know, and that is not much smaller than a man, and for some reason the pack were hungry; well, I don't know, they sounded hungry. So be careful in the hills. Try and stay at the Auberges." He stood up at last and shook Power's hand and wished him, "Buen Camino!"

"Buena vida," said Power.

When Ramon had left to pay his dues to the Count, Power wandered into the garden and sat under an oleander tree.

In due course, the Count and Lynch wandered into the garden and Power joined them on a set of white armchairs on the verandah where there was a small bar.

The Count poured them all a small Fino sherry. The morning shone within the Fino just as it had lived and sparkled in the breakfast honey.

"It is a great pleasure to me that you have returned to the Casa de la Caballeros. The Countess and I had hoped that you would return and we wish you a happy pilgrimage. I wished also to advise you of my endeavours and to ask if you have any news for me."

"Thank you for your hospitality, Count," said Lynch. "I am grateful for your continued help, but would ask that you do not, under any circumstances put yourself at any further risk."

Power sipped his sherry, thoughtfully.

"Pah," said the Count, with a frown. "I am more than cautious enough. I am not too old and where I lack for physical vigour I make up for this in wisdom. Do not worry, I will not go tilting at windmills. But I have little to report since we last spoke. There have been no more night-time intruders at the Casa. And the network of spies that I set up across the region, well they have been silent. So just maybe our birds have flown? Maybe we chased them off?"

"Or maybe they've just gone to earth," said Lynch. He fished in his pocket and brought out a photo. It was a still from the airport footage. And this Lynch supplemented by another still photo supplied by Janet, of the priest taken at a Church fete.

"This is the man we wish to interview. His name is Doyle. Father Michael Doyle. He was in England, certainly, until recently. His passport has not been used, we know that, so maybe he is still there. He admitted to Dr Power that he was a paedophile – we know that as he confessed voluntarily. And there was a child murder, which he did not confess to. He has no convictions and despite our enquiries seems to have led a life without scandal, without charges, and without convictions. Carl thinks he recognised him from our first trip to Leon, though."

"I am certain now," said Power.

"Do you recognise him?" asked Lynch.

The Count reached into his pockets for his reading glasses and peered at the grainy pictures. After a minute or so he shook his head sadly, "I have never seen this man." He looked up over the top of his spectacles. "Can I keep the photographs? In case I need to show them – to see if others can identify him?"

"Of course," said Lynch.

"But all those facts you said before. They don't fit do they? They can't all be true."

"Maybe not," said Lynch. "That's real life for you. Life is not some contrived jigsaw puzzle where everything fits and you have exactly the right number of pieces. If this is a five hundred piece puzzle we might have five hundred and fifty pieces. Maybe we have to discard some ideas. But there are links between the crimes in England and Spain . . . and Germany. The girl who was killed in England was flown in from Germany. I believe that she had tried to make contact with me, and that she may have come from the original 'orphanage' in Spain. Although the place seems to be less a Catholic orphanage than a criminal centre where these poor children were groomed by people who might have been religious at one point, but fell into darkness long ago. In the group they work together, reinforcing each other's beliefs, protecting each other. Once enmeshed within their group, either as a perpetrator or a victim, I suspect you are unable to leave. Poor Maria was a victim, and when she tried to leave she was killed. The same fate might befall a perpetrator who tried to leave the group. I don't know. Anyway, the murders of the girls in England and here were similar. The bodies were displayed naked, and there had been cruel use of a ligature and other instruments." Lynch downed his sherry in one gulp, not for enjoyment, but to try and dull any pain. "Both children had been beaten about the vulva. Penetrated and beaten. But there was no DNA evidence. It was all very calculated, and cruel. And it . . . it . . . makes me more angry than I can tell.

"Every offender has a signature. And this offender's hallmark is cold and cruel. My friend here, Carl, was left to die in a sealed room. The planning that went into that attempted murder was similarly calculated and bore the cold signature of cruelty. We must find that man, Doyle." Lynch pointed at the photographs in the Count's hand.

The Count turned to Power, "You found him, and you confronted him? That is so brave!"

"Maybe," interrupted Lynch. "But also perhaps it was foolish."

"I know it was foolish," said Power, looking out at the fountain the garden rather than meet Lynch's gaze. "Laura told me it was foolish. You both berated me. At the time, though, at that moment . . . I couldn't stop myself."

"Good for you!" The Count leant over and shook Power's hand.

"Carl was on his own. The priest drugged him, and whilst he was unconscious, locked him up and left him to die. He was fortuitous that the priest's housekeeper returned early from her holiday. No-one knew where he was. And so I am asking you again, Count, not to intervene yourself."

"Do not worry, Andrew Lynch, I know the odds."

Lynch grunted. The Count was clearly not promising anything. Lynch didn't feel he could say much more. "If you hear anything, Count, wait until we contact you again. We will phone you from Santiago de Compostela."

"And you be careful too," warned the Count. "I ask you, who knows you are walking the Way?"

Lynch pondered the Count's implicit warning. "Only those close to us. Our wives . . . close colleagues, yourself."

"Colleagues? Are they close friends with closed mouths too?" Lynch shrugged. The Count poured another Fino despite their protests. "We drink to your walk. You can afford a little alcohol. It is not as hot as before, you don't need to drink quite as much water. The Autumn is coming. In a few weeks the Chestnut Season. A toast to your trip." The trio raised their glasses and drank to a successful Camino. Moments later Power and Lynch had said their farewells to the Count and the Countess and were walking down the cobbled streets of Astorga, boots clumping on the ground and the metal spikes of their staffs clanging on the stones.

The Way took them through the town and out onto dusty paths that led into the countryside between chestnut and holm oak trees. The morning sun warmed their bones and they marched silently, but happily, up into the foothills of the mountains. They passed through small villages, with low, stone buildings, such as Murias de Rechivaldo, where they topped up their water bottles and rested, sitting on a wall. At Elganso, Power mused on the diminished nature of the village. A handful of people lived there now, in some stone houses with thatch or clay-tiled roofs, whereas in the twelfth century there had been a bustling small town with a hospital for the pilgrims.

As the path climbed into the mountains the temperature cooled, especially in the shade of the pine trees that lined the mountain slopes. Here, Power and Lynch even took light jumpers out of their packs and put them on as they admired some gathering cloud in the valley below them. From above, the cloud looked like a white wad of thick, cotton wool.

"There were Roman mines around here," said Lynch. "For copper and gold, mined with labour drawn from the ancient tribes and slaves the Romans brought. And all that precious metal got put in carts that rattled and rolled back down the hill on Roman roads, through Astorga to Rome, like a surge of blood pumped back through the veins to the heart of empire."

Power thought of the Roman mine workings in the sandstone around his own home in Alderley Edge. He wondered at the size and the organization of the Roman Empire and its enduring presence over hundreds of years. Then he recalled the dark tunnels that ran underneath the rock his house was built on and shuddered at his memories of the darkness there.

"Cold?" asked Lynch, noticing Power's shiver. "We'll move into the sunlight and have a sit down and something to eat. There don't seem to be many cafés round here."

"No," said Power. 'There wasn't much in the last village."

"We might have to wait until Rabanal," said Lynch.

In a few minutes, they munched chocolate that Power had hidden in the cooler depths of his rucksack. They were sitting in the sun on a way marker stone which was the size of a coffee table. Power's thighs and calves were aching from the climb, but he reasoned that the strain would get better day by day, and that this was one of the steeper ascents of the Way.

After a few moments rest, Power voiced a fear that had been troubling him since before they left Astorga. "Last time when we left Astorga, we were walking towards Rabanal. Patxi had just left us and we were walking past the graveyard . . ."

"I know," said Lynch. "I took us on a detour a few miles back, to avoid the spot. Do you mind that I did that?"

"No, no," said Power, who was more than a little relieved. "I didn't want to retrace those steps." An image of the child Lucia, atop the gravestone, absorbed his mind for a while.

"I didn't think it would be good for either of us, so this is a slightly different route to Rabanal. There's more than one route to Santiago," said Lynch, standing and patting his old friend on the shoulder. "Come on, let's get to Rabanal for some proper food."

"Are we cowards for not going there?" asked Power.

"You're anything but a coward," said Lynch, thinking of Power's journey to confront the priest, Doyle. "The problem comes when the Count takes you as his example. He's too old for all this, we should never have involved him."

They shouldered their packs and started to move off again on the Way. "You know," said Power. "When you say that he's too old, isn't that a bit how your younger colleagues in the Force treat you?"

"Touché – the biter bit." Power smiled – it seemed as if Lynch was beginning to able to laugh at himself again.

Rabanal was a small town built astride the Way itself. Stone houses clustered along the narrow cobbled path as it climbed. St Mary's, an old church with a rounded apse, sat midway up the town. Lynch pointed at some building works. "They are re-opening a Benedictine monastery here."

"Churchianity," said Power. "Is your faith not diminished by the priest, by the things we have seen these last few weeks?"

"It's not just a priest though, is it?" said Lynch, peering into a shop window along the way. He was looking for a sign to the Alberge, but distracted by the sight of food. Power peered into the shop from the doorway. Lynch continued, "There's at least one police officer involved, amongst others. Do we blame an orchard for one bad apple in a barrel? Are all sheep to bear the burden of the wolf that hides in one sheep's fleece?"

Power ducked inside the shop and emerged, after some conversation with the shopkeeper, carrying some custard tarts. "These are more like the Portuguese *pasteis de nata*," he said, offering one to Lynch. "The shopkeeper said his father was a Maragato, but his mother was Portuguese and she made these."

"We're not far from Portugal, really," said Lynch, as Power started munching the golden custard pastry. "We go through the Bierzo region, then Galicia, and both are only just a bit north of Portugal. Now, have you got your *Credencial*?" Power looked blank. Lynch was referring to the card Pilgrim's Passport they had been given many weeks before. "We need it to stay at the Alberge." Power looked crestfallen and rather pale.

"It's all right," said Lynch. "You see, I can tease you as well. I brought them along for us both."

"You had them?" asked Power.

"All along," said Lynch. "And I even got the Count to stamp both before we left."

They continued up the road to the Refugio Gaucelmo, the place they hoped to stay. Only pilgrims on foot were allowed, and for one night only. As luck would have it, the hostel was nearly empty and a room for two was available, otherwise Power and Lynch would have had to sleep in a barn dormitory with fourteen others. There was a separate bathroom, which Power commandeered almost immediately for his aching leg muscles. He soaked himself in a bath of deep hot water for a good half an hour.

"My legs feel a bit better for that," he said, as Lynch passed by to do the same.

Lynch looked at the steamed up walls and window. "I hear that a cold bath is the best for aches and pains."

"Are you going to have an ice cold bath then?"

"Er no . . ." said Lynch, as he closed the door to.

There was some approximation to afternoon tea put on at precisely five o'clock in the garden behind the Alberge. There was hot sweet tea, freshly baked scones, butter and fresh figs harvested from the trees that surrounded the lawn. Power tucked in with an appetite and chatted to a schoolteacher from Milan, who had started in Southern France and been walking alone for twenty days. She was in her late fifties and said the walking got easier day-by-day, but that the last few days had been particularly difficult with the climb into the mountains. She explained that nearly all routes converged upon the pass at Rabanal. Power asked whether the climb was now over as he hoped that his aching muscles would not be prevailed upon to ascend any further the next day. "Oh no," she said. "Tomorrow we must all tackle Monte Irago and Montes de León." Power groaned internally and smiled the best social smile he could fake.

The small village, at the turn of the century, had only forty or so inhabitants. There was no pub, or restaurant, and at the close of afternoon tea the pilgrims at the Refugio were shown the kitchen and advised they could use this to cook whatever they could buy from the village shop where Power had bought his Portuguese custard tarts.

That night Power cooked herb and cheese omelettes for six. The residents ate these with relish at a large table outdoors on the patio. After, they had bowls of strawberries and honey, the whole being washed down by four bottles of local Crianza. Lynch brewed coffee. Power phoned Laura from the payphone inside the Refugio front entrance. By ten o'clock Power and Lynch were both fast asleep and dead to the world till the sun stole into their room at six a.m.

People tend to start their journeys at different times in the morning and, of course, they progress at their own pace, and so it was that Power and Lynch were the first to leave the Refugio that day. Lynch had been first up, showered and breakfasted and was saying his morning prayers at the old church while, at a more sedate pace, Power ate bread, drank strong coffee and filled up his water bottles for the day ahead. Lynch joined him at the door to the church, "Eleventh century," said Lynch. "Possibly a Templar church."

Power nodded and asked, "Do we really need to be up this early? It's not a race."

"If we climb our way up the mountains in the cool of the morning it will be better for us both," said Lynch. The morning sun, at an angle, was merely warm on their skin. They began their walk out of the cobbled street of Rabanal del Camino and into a country lane. They passed an Alberge and four kilometres later they came to the village of Foncebadón. Hot, dry and thirsty, they stopped at a small bar that pressed apples immediately in front of them into cold, cloudy green juice. They drank two glasses each. Outside, Power dunked his white cloth hat into a horse trough of water and clamped it streaming wet and cold onto his head At around eleven o'clock they achieved the summit of Monte Irago. By the side of the broad road Lynch pointed out a vast pile of stones. Set in the midst of this hill of stones was a sturdy red-black column topped with a thin cross, the Cruz de Ferro (The Iron Cross). "There used to be a Roman altar to Mercury here a thousand years ago. It has been transformed into the Cross."

Lynch paused by the slopes of the pile. "The stones aren't from round here," he said. 'They are brought here by pilgrims from their homeland. He bent down to pick a small pebble up. It had something written on it, which he read out. "Sara, Argentina, a prayer for my mother." He placed it carefully back amongst the jumble of rocks.

Lynch opened his rucksack.

"You didn't bring one from home too, did you?" Power sounded incredulous.

"I brought two," said Lynch. "One from outside my home, and one that Laura chose from outside yours."

Power raised an eyebrow at the news. He was pleased to see that the red sandstones Lynch had retrieved were not too big, if nothing else, for the sake of Lynch's back. "Well, I must thank you then," said Power. "I would have carried my own, if I had known."

"Well, these stones are meant to symbolize your spiritual burden, and you have been carrying that all along the journey in any case. I shouldn't think your burden's that heavy?"

Power looked into Lynch's gaze for a moment, head on one side. "Actually, I had a dream about this last night. I dreamed I was talking to an Irish girl. I think I was treating her, psychotherapy or the like. And I remember feeling that I found her attractive. And I felt guilty at that feeling. And all of a sudden she vanished, and there was a small boy in her place. He had my eyes. And that was the end of the dream. Guilt and a sudden change. I don't know what it means."

"Well, you're the psychiatrist," said Lynch. "Anyway, here's the symbol of your guilt, or spiritual burden. Shall we go and place them?"

The pair walked up a gravelled path that had been placed in the midst of the mound of stones and approached the iron cross, where a small party of fellow pilgrims were placing their stones. As Power and Lynch approached, they seemed to have their heads bowed in silent prayer. Lynch did likewise, kneeling to place his own stone, and bowing his head in a minute's prayer. Dr Power felt very much the observer of other people's beliefs, but he too placed the burdensome stone that Lynch had shouldered for him in deference to his friend's faith.

They walked down the path from the Iron Cross towards the main road to resume their journey.

Lynch confided, "You know, sometimes I wish that an angel would swoop down from the sky and transform my life for the better.

Like the sudden appearance of angel of the annunciation. But such things don't happen to me."

From this point the Way started to descend and for the first time Power felt a steady pull in his calf muscles on the slope down. After two kilometres or so they reached the village of Manjarín. At a ramshackle shelter, a signpost with numerous name boards nailed to it announced that Santiago de Compostela was two hundred and twenty-two kilometres away. Another of the boards announced that Jerusalem was five thousand kilometres away.

Most of the houses seemed deserted. "This village only existed because of the Way," said Lynch. "It lived and died with the popularity. Once it had a small hospital for pilgrims too. Now there are only a few inhabitants."

"I can't see anyone," said Power, looking around the ruins of old homesteads. "It seems deserted."

"The Way has only become a bit more popular in recent years," said Lynch. "It is odd to think that this was a bustling place a thousand years ago." Manjarín was so small that just as they arrived at the village they were leaving. "All of Europe once walked this Way. It could be that a previous generation of our families once walked these hills."

"Not in my family, at least not in recent generations," said Power.

The day was past noon now, and over twenty-five degrees celsius. Power could feel the September sun beating down upon his hat. A mile or so further on Lynch announced that according to his maps they were at the highest point of the entire Camino de Santiago at one thousand five hundred and fifteen metres above sea level. They paused and breathed in the clearest mountain air and looked across green fields and forests and over to blue hills in the distance.

"From here, we descend and we head into the El Bierzo valley. Next stop, Acebo. And after that, we will soon be in Galicia, if you think of Spain as a square the top left-hand corner is Galicia. And Galicia is a Celtic kingdom, with the same ancient people as Brittany, Wales or Cornwall. They even have bagpipes."

"Good grief, no," said Power. "Do they speak Gaelic?"

"No," said Lynch. "There's been nothing like that since the Middle Ages. They speak Galician, obviously . . . which is a bit like Portuguese, I think."

The road wended down a steep hillside, covered by brown scrub at times, roasted by the sun over Summer. In the distance were rolling hillsides, turning to blue on the horizon. And then they came round a bend and into a clutter of inhabited houses falling away down the hill in a cascade, with stone walls, wooden balconies in the mountain style and grey slate roofs. "The village of El Acebo," said Lynch, as they walked down the central main street. A bar was open and they went in; ordering beer and a repast of bean stew for Power and ham and chips for Lynch. Fortified, they climbed down the hill and towards a small town set by the river. They crossed the Puente de los Peregrinos, a narrow stone bridge with semicircular arches, and walked past the church and into the town of Molinaseca. Lynch had booked them rooms at a hostel called 'The Oven', where Power fell, shuddering with physical tiredness, into a warm bath, where he sat drinking glass after glass from a jug of iced water. He did not emerge from his room until early evening, and it was really only hunger that could motivate him to get up from his bed. He was wondering whether he could go on. The second day seemed to have taken more from him than the first.

They had an evening meal at a small restaurant that overlooked the bridge. They could see locals jumping into the Meruelo River from the Roman bridge to cool themselves. Their laughter filled the warm evening air. Lynch and Power ate in companionable silence through the meal of pesto, mushrooms and pimentos. Nourished by the food and drink, and with coffee and almond cake in front of him, Power found his voice restored.

"Perhaps we should try not to speak of such things, but it has been going round and round in my head all day. The Count pointed out that there were such inconsistences in the case of the two girls."

"There are always facts that don't fit in real life," said Lynch. "In my experience, it's usually because witnesses see even the same events very differently, and so give different accounts. Or sometimes it's because the offender lays a path of lies to draw you into the wrong conclusions. You shouldn't let the discrepancies worry you, not here and now, anyway."

There was a pause during which Power felt guilty for having brought the topic up. Eventually Lynch could not resist a question. "What inconsistencies do you mean?"

"The priest I confronted, Doyle, acts as if guilty. He drugged me and imprisoned me and taunted me, and then ran away. That is guilty behaviour if ever there was. He was in England. We have footage of him and the girl. He had the opportunity to kill her in England. But he says he did not."

"He's lying," said Lynch.

"I sort of believed him," said Power.

Lynch chuckled. "Maybe you were a bit groggy after being unconscious. And surely it's a bit difficult to tell anything through a steel door. You couldn't see his face to tell anything."

"No, perhaps you're right" said Power, conceding the point. "But then, if he killed Maria in England the chances are he killed Lucia in Spain. The injuries were very similar. The choice of victim . . . and yet his passport details say he's never left the UK."

"A fake identity with a fake passport," said Lynch confidently. "It's still fairly easy to get one done."

"And his housekeeper, even after all that she found out about him and his desires. After she found me nearly dead in his dungeon, she still swore he'd never left the parish."

"Then you have to look at the assertions you've made," said Lynch. "One or two must be incorrect. A fake passport and an old cleaner's fading memory could explain everything. It's clear she never really knew what made him tick. He kept so much hidden from her."

"She was as bright as a button," said Power. "She saved my life. She was also clearly shocked by the pornographic material the priest left behind. I think she is telling the truth, too. I just can't reconcile it all – the invoice we found in Spain with the surname Doyle, for instance. And where have the nuns disappeared to? Where is the priest himself?"

"He could be anywhere," said Lynch, looking into the sunset. "With friends such as he has, undoubtedly they will shield him, not least because it is in their best interests. If he falls then they might fall, so then everyone works to keep everyone safe." Lynch picked up some crumbs from his dessert plate with a moistened finger and ate them thoughtfully. "I'm sorry not to have any answers, Carl; he might have escaped into Germany, or France or Portugal. Who knows? We would need to root them out one by one. That would be a long fight, and not one that any state agency has picked up – to date. And if no state agency has the appetite to fight these people, then who will? We would then probably need outside help . . . who will fund this? And I ask you, who actually has the courage and the resources to do that?"

". . . And another thing," said Power. "Where are the children that were still with the nuns? According to Lucia there had been a whole house full before she ran away." The pair fell silent for a while. "Maybe I shouldn't have mentioned any of this," said Power, as he looked at Lynch's frown of concentration. There were the sounds of birds settling for the night; the distant sound of drunken men singing in the streets of the town near a tavern; the sound of running river water sluicing and foaming past the stone piers of the bridge; and in the forest, miles distant, Power heard the faint sound of a lonely wolf's cry.

"I know," said Lynch. "Don't apologise. I can't stop the puzzles going through my mind, either. I try to, but they keep coming back. I pray that a solution will present itself. What more can we do? Lay your troubles at the Lord's door, and rest. That's what I will be doing. And given our walking today, I expect to sleep soundly. That is another benefit of physical exertion. Sound sleep. And tomorrow we follow the yellow markers to Villafranca. Thirty kilometres. So we need our rest." He stood up from the table, yawning. "Are you coming?"

"In a bit," said Power. "I'll phone Laura from reception first."

Lynch wandered off to his bed and Power looked into the gathering dusk. He wondered whether he done the wrong thing in raising the subject of the anomalies with Lynch.

* * *

In the Casa de la Caballeros the Count was fast asleep and gently snoring. It was past midnight. His wife, the Countess, an inveterate insomniac, was reading in the bed by his, using the light of a small bedside lamp. The window was open and the light of the Milky Way shone in the night sky above. A cool, nocturnal zephyr played over their beds. All was still and peaceful.

Suddenly there was a jumping, buzzing sound as the Count's mobile phone began hopping around the wooden top of his bedside table. The Countess was startled, and the Count jumped bolt upright in mid-snore. "What? What's that?"

"The phone," she cried out. "The one that never rings, is ringing now. In the middle of the night! Answer it before it disturbs our guests."

The Count fumbled about on the bedside table. He had it upside down and could not see what button to press. The phone leapt from his hands and fell on the floor, buzzing there on the floorboards and circling like a demented bee. His wife picked it up, and in her hands the vibrating phone felt like a frog about to leap. She was quicker at finding the 'answer' button and clamped it to her ear.

"Hello, who is it?" She looked at her husband. "You want to speak to the Count?" She handed it over to the Count, who was looking a little more awake and less groggy. With a dismissive shrug she lay down again and turned her back on the old man.

"Hello, it is the Count. What do you want?" He listened for a few minutes. "Where is the farm, please?" he asked. "How do I get there? Can it wait till dawn? I will be there then." He peered at the phone and switched the call off.

"Well?" said the Countess. "What was it?" She turned round and sat up. To her alarm she saw the Count was up and gathering some clothes from a set of drawers, to put on. "What do you think you're doing? It's one a.m!"

"It was the gypsies. One has sighted the priest. It sounds like the gypsy was poaching. Touring round his traps for rabbits or something. He saw a light on at a farm, and some car he hadn't seen earlier on. He'd seen this car only a few times before, but it'd always gone by dawn. And when he looked in the window he saw him. He saw that the man, the priest, had arrived. The one we have been looking for."

"I know," said the Countess. "The evil one who sleeps with children and kills them. And what do you plan to do about it? Call the police and let them do their business."

"I am a Knight of St James. It is *my* business."

"You are a foolish, foolish old man who should just stop what he is doing right now and get back into bed."

He looked defiantly at her, and drew himself to full height. In his eyes she thought she suddenly saw a hint of a much younger soul, not the fumbling old man who was unable to manage a mobile phone.

"This I must do."

"What will you do? What can you do? I cannot understand why you are so angry, so invested in all of this."

"Enough," said the Count. "I can't say quite why this matters so much. But I will find him and I will stop him."

"Please, please don't," she said. She implored him to stay, but by now he was dressed.

"I have the car stocked, ready for this. I was waiting for this call." He bent over her bed and kissed her with an unaccustomed passion. "If I don't go now, he will have fled by dawn. He only seems to go there under cover of dark. Don't worry, I have the advantage of surprise. And a certain charm, even if I say so myself."

She chuckled, despite her underlying concern. But as her amusement waned she tilted her head to look at him and frowned. She said one last time, "Don't go." He shook his head. She sighed, "then I wish you good luck in your hunting. Avenge the girl."

Chapter Seventeen

The dance along the artery
The circulation of the lymph
Are figured in the drift of stars
TS Eliot - The Four Quartets

Drawn thin against a pale moon, wisps of early morning mist lay across the heavens, grainy and ethereal. The headlights of the borrowed Seat Alhambra were on full beam as the Count hurried along the country roads. The light picked out the curving trunks and branches of holm oaks that overarched and framed the lanes. The roads at this early hour were devoid of any other traffic and the automatic Alhambra purred along, its two litre engine untroubled even by the swift pace. Beside him on the passenger seat was a knapsack packed with a blindingly bright torch, maps and compass, a flask of hot coffee, bottles of water and packets of sandwiches. The Count was well prepared.

He was heading into the hills of the Bierzo region, almost a hundred kilometres from home. A region famed for wines from the Mencia and Godello grapes grown here since the times of Pliny the Elder. He had been driving quickly for over an hour. He knew that he should have felt tired, but the Count was energized. The winding roads had reminded him of decades past ,when, for a few years as a younger man, he had raced for a living. Although he told everyone of his lineage, before assuming the mantle of Count and his rights as inheritor of the family estates, he had been something of a playboy.

The nineteen-sixties had seen the young man as a tall, raffish individual with swept-back, wavy black hair and moustache, surrounded by dark-eyed sixties groupies. For Angel Moreno had been a highly sought after bachelor. For two brief years he had driven the hawk-like red Ferrari 250 GTO in the Spanish Grand Prix. The great win of his career had been in the Spanish Grand Tourer Race on the Jarama course (north of Madrid) in nineteen sixty-seven. The course has a short straight and is notorious for its tricky, tight twisty corners – eleven in all, over a treacherous course of nearly four kilometres. That year Moreno had achieved the lap record at Jarama, which he had held until nineteen seventy-nine when he lost it to Villeneuve. Nineteen sixty-eight by turn had been a decisive year for Moreno. He had survived a potentially fatal crash in September on the ninety-ninth lap at Le Mans, breaking his right collarbone and femur. In November, Moreno grew up over night when his father died and he, in his turn, became the Count.

At last the Count took a right turn onto the Carucedo Road and slowed. He was looking for a sign towards a turning on the left, for a farm, La Finca Ladera, and moved gingerly through the night under the canopy of the trees. Suddenly there was a movement on his left and the Count jumped. It had looked as if one of the trees had moved a few feet to the right. But it was man. A giant of a man was now standing in the road in his path. The Count reacted quickly and braked hard. The front of the car came to a swift halt within a few feet of Salazar, the bearded *mercheros* leader. Salazar put a finger to his lips and gestured to the Count to switch off the engine and exit his vehicle.

"Salazar!" whispered the Count. "What are you doing here? This is my mission alone."

"I came here as soon as I put the phone down," said Salazar. "I wanted to make sure you found the priest."

"Is he still at the farm?" Salazar nodded. "Where is it?"

"There," Salazar pointed to a turning, partially hidden in a gap within a series of huge bushes. "The poacher and I didn't want you to miss the turn. It's easy to miss at night. If you follow the track, there, for about a quarter of a mile through the woods, you will find the old farmhouse. He has chosen a good place to hide the children and the nuns away. It took a man of the woods to find it."

"How did he find the place?"

"The poacher was surprised to find the place inhabited. It has been empty for years. One night he was on his rounds, checking his traps in the forest, and he found the women and children there, which he knew was odd. And he knew we also wanted the priest and that he might be with the children. We had your photos of him. But there was no sign of any man with them. So the poacher leaves, and returns another night to check his traps. They are empty. No *ciervo*, *jabali* or *macho montes* these days. He is a poor man, and hungry too nowadays. The game has all but vanished."

The Count reached in his pocket and detached some notes from a roll and passed them to Salazar. 'For the poacher's trouble,' offered the Count.

"For the poacher then," nodded Salazar. "But we have our own reasons to help you, Count. We will be interested in the place ourselves – after you have the priest. I told you that we have lost children, as well. We want to see these children ourselves, before any authorities spirit them away."

"You were telling me about the poacher and the place," said the Count. "Go on."

"Well, that night, on his return, the poacher sees a car there, and he looks in at the window and he sees the man in the photo. The priest. And by day, he sees his car is gone. A few nights later, the car is back, and gone at first light. And so that is when he told me, and I said, 'When the priest returns tell me immediately', and that was tonight, when I phoned you." Salazar looked intently at the Count. Around them the woods were still. In the distance a small branch fell, clattering quietly against other branches as it fell to the forest floor. The air was mild, damp and smelled of leaf mould. The Count looked small and pale in the night. He was looking at his feet and Salazar wondered if the Count was having second thoughts about confronting the priest in his lair. "Would you like me to come with you? I can phone some other men to hold him to account. No-one will see or complain or call the police if we take him away."

The Count seemed to come to, as he realised what Salazar was saying. He shook his head. "No, this is my mission, Salazar. You can go back to bed. Leave it to me. I can handle this."

"You have your phone, then, if you need help? You will phone me?" asked Salazar. The Count nodded. "Then let me tell you where the farmhouse is. Follow the track for about four hundred yards. There is a wooden barn on the right, falling down with age. The priest has parked his car, a white Golf, in that space. Block it in with your car. The farmhouse is just a few yards beyond. Three women or nuns live there. The poacher has counted six children; five girls, one boy. The track is downhill all the way. For the last few hundred yards – you can turn off the engine and coast to a halt. No headlights. Then you will have the element of surprise. It may be crucial you have that. He is a younger man after all . . ."

"And I have right on my side," said the Count. "That is where I draw my strength. All right, I will go now and I will drive the car exactly as you said. That seems wise."

"Well," said Salazar. "There are people on the priest's side, but there are many on our side, and I have yet to tell you – I have news for you of another who will help us. But that will wait, go alone, if you must."

Salazar watched impassively as the Count climbed back into the Alhambra and switched the ignition on. Salazar merely stepped aside and faded into the undergrowth as the Count passed him by.

The Count turned left onto the farm track and, as Salazar had suggested, almost immediately switched the lights and engine off. He peered into the gloom to try and fathom his way. Salazar had told him the track was straight downhill and the slope was such that the car was able to roll gently and silently forwards into the dark. The Count's eyes gradually accustomed themselves to night in the forest without the headlights and he found that he could see around twelve feet ahead. The experience was new to him and he crept into the darkness like a drowning man drifting down through the silent ocean's watery depths. All at once, he saw a gabled wooden barn/garage on his right standing up out of the undergrowth, and there, as Salazar had promised, was the priest's white car. The Count pressed gently on the brake and came to a halt in a turning space in front of the garage, with his own car's bonnet just sticking out in front of the Golf to prevent escape. The Count still had plenty of room to open his driver's door as quietly as he could manage. He climbed out and carefully set the door just to, without closing it shut. He did not want the bang of a car door alerting the priest to his presence early.

The moonlight, filtering through the branches of the trees, was just sufficient for the Count to make out the white walls and black windows of the farmhouse. On his right was the front elevation of the farmhouse. In front, the L-shaped building had spawned a ground floor extension. The Count made his way over the mossy, cobbled courtyard to peer in firstly at the kitchen window, where all was still, and then over to the sturdy wooden front door, which was firmly locked. He saw a faint glow coming from the side of the extension and this sparked his curiosity. The Count trod carefully across the farmyard, placing his feet firmly and deliberately on the ground to make no noise.

The Count reached the end of the farmhouse extension and stood outside the window of a ground-floor bedroom. A warm, yellow glow flickered within and flowed out onto the stony path outside. There were no curtains, for none had been deemed necessary in such a remote place. The window was slightly ajar due to the warmth of the night. The Count peered in the window to see a scene lit by a flame within a small lantern, like a light and shadow tableau by the painter Caravaggio.

The priest lay within, naked to the waist, a young man with a muscled torso and short blonde hair shaved at the side to golden bristles. He was sated, and sleeping deeply, sprawled in a deeply relaxed state with an arm draped around the youngest of the girls. Her brown eyes were wide open and she seemed transfixed like a rabbit caught in a snare. All of a sudden her eyes swivelled round to the window and saw the old man standing outside in the shadows. She started to scream.

The priest woke with a start. Although the girl's scream had not been foreseen by the Count, he decided to further disorientate the priest by shouting at him as loudly as he could.

"Priest! Come outside and meet your fate!"

Doyle did not know where to look – at the screaming girl or at the stentorian-voiced Count. The priest scrabbled around on the floor for some clothes and shrugged on some black trousers and an overlarge shirt. As Doyle struggled to put on his clothes he surveyed the figure outside the bedroom window. With a glare of absolute hatred towards the silver-haired Count, the priest shot out of the bedroom. The girl pulled a sheet around her and made her way to her own room shivering in fear.

The front door of the farmhouse exploded open and the priest sprinted over the farmyard to the Count. By now, the Count was standing by an empty stone trough in the centre of the farmyard, arms loose by his sides, fingers curled into fists and feet wide apart to give him greater stability. He drew himself up to his full height and shouted at the priest to disconcert him. "You killed the girl! And you laid her out like a trophy on the Camino. You disgust me. You are covered in sin and you will pay." His voice dropped to an icy quiet, but he remained sternly firm. "You are coming with me now, so you can be tried by the Law."

"Who are you?" asked the priest. "Who are you to come here and make these accusations to a priest in the middle of the night?"

"I am a Knight of St James," said the Count. "And I claim the right to make the Holy Way safe, as my forefathers did before me. You defiled the Way. And you are no priest. God would have none of your sins."

The priest slapped the Count hard across the face with the back of his arm, and the old man staggered.

"You are alone, and old," said the priest. "And an ancient fool at that." He slapped the Count again and pushed him back. The Count felt the cold stone of the trough behind his thighs. "You make these accusations, but no court in the world would ever convict me. I swear to you by God, hand on my heart, that I did not kill the girl. Now get going."

"You came to my home in the middle of the night. Hiding in the shadows in my office. You threatened me. I recognize your voice. And I saw you just now, in there with a child in your arms," the Count snarled. "I know in my heart that you are guilty."

The priest slapped the old man again, across the other side of his face. And with his next words the Count confused the priest, for they were unexpected. "You work with others to hide your sin. But I work with others too. Your name is Doyle. There is Dr Power, whom you tried to kill. And Superintendent Lynch. And a whole network of people who have been watching you. Watching you here at this very place. I am NOT alone." The priest paused, took a step back and checked to see if he could hear anyone in the woods. "I've hunted you here," said the Count. "And Dr Power and Lynch will be here within minutes."

The priest sneered at the Count. "Why are *you* involved in all this when you are so old and weak? Why, you know I could snap you like a twig."

"I tell you this, so you know. I am doing this because one such as you abused *me* when I was a boy, an altar boy. Over the years I have tried to forget, but it is always with me. And I have never been able to tell anybody except for now – and now I damn you – I damn you all to hell. And that's what I've wanted to say every day for sixty-five years. It's taken me all this time to find my voice, because your kind thrives on the silence of your victims. And so that – that's why I am here, to tell you that you are damned."

The priest shrugged and pretended he did not care, but he looked somehow shaken, and at the back of his mind lurked the idea that it was possible that the Superintendent might even now be driving down the track towards the farm. "You can threaten me with jail, and you can say what you like," said the priest. "But I tell you that no court in the world will convict me. For which of us is innocent and which guilty?"

With this last defiance the priest turned on his heel and walked quickly away towards the wooden canopy that housed his car. The Count hurried after him. "Stop! I am arresting you for your sins."

"I am not sure what strange time or dimension you come from," said the priest. "But I am not about to submit to you. Did you seriously think I would?" The priest fished the Golf's ignition key out of his pocket and opened the car door.

"You can't leave," protested the Count, plaintively. "I've blocked you in." Even as the Count reached the garage, the priest was inside the Golf, had locked the door, and had started the engine. He revved the engine and the car suddenly surged forward barging the corner of Count's Alhambra. The Alhambra moved several feet to the left and the priest reversed the Golf for a second attempt. There was a second crash and a splintering of headlight glass as the priest rammed forward again. This time the Alhambra shifted on the slimy cobbles and the priest squeezed the Golf through, scraping the side of his vehicle on the battered bumper of the Alhambra. The sound was of a grating and scraping nature that set the Count's teeth on edge. The Count had to jump backward as the Golf surged forward, spinning around the yard and heading off up the dark track like a rocket.

For a split second only, the Count was flummoxed. He had not quite foreseen this turn of events. Nevertheless, he was not about to let his quarry escape that easily and he hurried to the Alhambra and scrabbled at the door handle. He dropped the keys on the cobbles and cursed softly as he retrieved them, joints protesting as he bent to do so. He pulled the door open. The Count made his own turnaround in the yard. By now there were lights showing in various windows as the children and the women of the house peered out into the night. Then the Count, too, squeezed the accelerator and shot off up the track, the light from the single remaining headlight blazing into the early morning darkness. As the Count hurtled through the undergrowth and trees that lined the track he wondered which way the priest would turn at the end of the track. The slight delay in starting off after the priest could be vital if he could not follow the Golf and make up lost time. He hoped that he might see the red glow of the Golf's rear lights as he hurried up the track, but there was no sign. The Count was calculating the relative size of the engines in the two vehicles and whether he could ever catch the priest up. He reckoned that the Alhambra's engine was around two times the size of the Golf, but the Alhambra was a heavier vehicle altogether. It would be close. As he neared the end of the track the Count again wondered whether to turn left or right. The priest was gone, but Salazar had not listened to the Count's advice to return home and he had returned. He stood at the side of the road, opposite the track, and he was pointing the way for the Count. He indicated the priest had swerved his car left to *Las Medulas*. As the Count took advantage of the signal and passed Salazar, he looked in the mirror and saw the big man waving a long farewell in the rosy glow of the vehicle's rear lights.

The Count drove with controlled speed and determination, sitting close to the steering wheel, hands at a three and nine o'clock position for better manoeuvering and mastery over the steering. In the distance he caught a glimpse of the priest's car straight ahead, and he squeezed the accelerator and smiled as the engine acceded to his will, and delivered more power and speed. The gap between the two vehicles diminished. The Alhambra was an automatic and the Golf a geared car, thinking ahead, the Count reckoned this would give him an advantage. He knew there were twists in the road ahead. He moved his left leg to just hover near the brake. If need be he could switch between his left foot on the brake and his right foot on the accelerator. Another advantage.

The landscape changed from the forest to a more ancient landscape; the Romans had transformed this land from a range of red stone mountains to a craggy, industrial landscape that looked like the red rock of Mars. This was the relatively small area of land that had yielded twenty per cent of the income of the entire, vast Roman Empire; *Las Medulas*. The countryside was either barren, dusty, red cliffs and spires of stone, or thick oily bushes and chestnut trees the Romans had planted to supplement the diet of the slaves and tribal workers. There was a small village that sat at the entry to the higher roads through the hills. The road twisted tortuously through the village, another advantage for the Count, as the priest would have to slow and use three pedals for clutch, brake and acceleration. The Count pressed harder on the accelerator. As the priest turned sharply left into Carucedo village the road rose sharply between the high yellow angles of the walls of houses and barns. The priest simply had to slow.

The Count accelerated suddenly, deliberately and violently slamming into the rear of the priest's Golf. The Count watched the priest's head whiplash in the impact and could not suppress a smile of satisfaction. The priest accelerated away, engine whining horribly, but he was not wholly in control after the impact and the front of his bonnet gouged a long groove in the soft wall of someone's house, and nearly cannoned into a wall at seeming right angles as the road deviated sharply right and away up the hill past a tourist centre. The early morning peace of the sleeping village was shattered as the two vehicles duelled for supremacy through the twists and turns. The skills that the Count had thought long gone returned to his hands and feet, as he braked and accelerated his way with alacrity through the maze of walls that enclosed the village roads.

The priest hurtled out of the village and was nearly away up onto the mountain road, just as the Count gained on him again and thumped into the hatchback rear bumper. The Golf hiccupped forward under the impact, and to escape, the priest pressed the accelerator close to its very limit, exceeding any safe speed by double or more.

There was a long upward sweeping curve on the road ahead; the Count knew this. In the Count's mind, somehow, Doyle had become the man who had abused him in the vestry so many years ago. The refusal of Doyle to acknowledge his own guilt and make any kind of confession had hardened the Count's heart.

The Count readied himself, pressed the accelerator to the floor and the Alhambra launched itself at the rear of the Golf again, slamming into the back. The priest reacted by pushing his accelerator all the way down, just as the Count was braking in wariness of the long bend ahead. And as the Count was slowing and preparing to take evasive action or stop, the priest had unwisely pushed his protesting and whining engine to its absolute limit on a bend that would tolerate no excess.

The Count gradually slowed to a standstill and watched the priest attempt to slow and steer the Golf too late. The car wobbled and started to rotate as the wheels lost traction. At a speed of over seventy miles an hour the Golf hit the verge at the side of the road. Two of its wheels left the ground and it started to turn around its axis, describing a screw-like motion as it became airborne and crashed down to the surface of the road on its roof, slithering and sliding across the carriageway to slam into the verge on the opposite side of the road.

The Count opened his door and got out, surveying the wreck some seventy metres away. Where just seconds before there had been noise, and the hideous scrape of metal against asphalt, now there was silence apart from the hiss of steam escaping from a ruptured radiator. There was the smell of burned rubber and vaguely that of spilled petrol, too. The darkness of the night was still upon the earth. All the lights in the priest's car had gone off and the headlights of the Count's vehicle showed no movement. The cubes of shattered glass from the windscreen and windows glinted on the road. The Count wondered then whether he had caused the priest's death and he felt the smallest pang of guilt. Then, suddenly, he saw movement within the wreck. A hand emerged from the upside-down

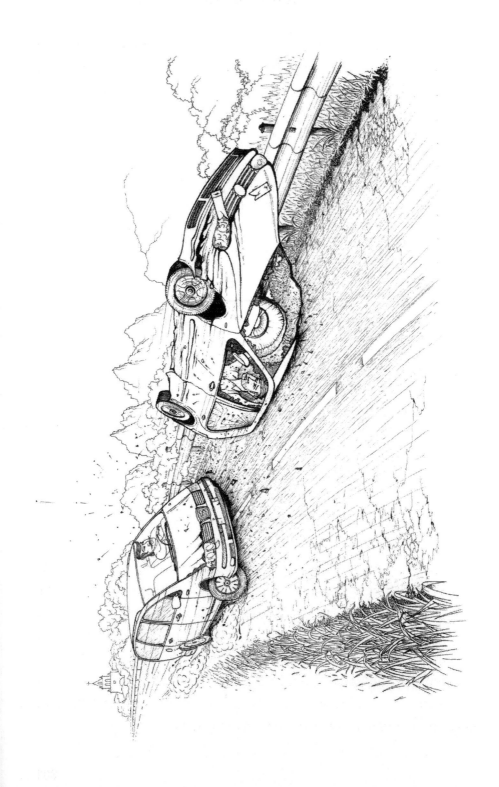

window and placed its palm upon the road. Doyle was crawling out of the twisted wreckage of the car. Amazingly, he began to stand up. For a moment the priest seemed disorientated, and then he looked directly at the Count and began to stagger his way towards him. The Count observed that all four limbs seemed unbroken, and that from an initial stagger the priest was picking up his walk remarkably well and even hurrying towards him and he thought he could see a graze on the man's forehead, or maybe a burn from the airbag. Whatever it was, the priest now seemed undaunted by the accident.

The Count thought of getting in the car and locking the doors, but he stood his ground. "Now," he shouted. "Will you surrender yourself, come with me and make your confession?"

The priest said nothing, but began to run and cannoned into the Count at full tilt. The Count fell backwards, half onto the cold, damp verge and half onto the road. The impact and fall had winded him, and he was not physically able to rebound quickly to his feet to meet the challenge and fight back.

The priest looked down at the old man as he lay winded on the floor by the Alhambra. "Give me the keys."

The old man shook his head.

"Then I'll take them when you're dead." And he took a length of cord from his pocket to strangle the old man with.

The Count reached in his pocket and retrieved the keys. He dangled them in front of the priest. "Here they are," he said. And as the priest made to grab them the Count flung them into the scrub that covered the slope beyond the safety barrier. They fell into the darkness. "Now there's no vehicle that can help you escape what you have done," said the Count. "You can't keep running."

The priest was enraged. He looked at the Count as he lay half slumped and half sitting-up. Deliberately, he chose the Count's right leg and raising his foot stamped upon his shin.

Bone mineral density declines from the age of thirty. Cross linking collagen fibres disappear and elderly bone can shatter like brittle glass. The tibia and fibula in the Count's right leg snapped under the priest's boot as it stamped upon them. The priest laughed as he felt the Count's leg crunch under his heel. The Count gasped and shut his eyes momentarily, in pain. He drew a breath into his lungs and it hissed out between his teeth. Then he looked into the woods on the other side of the road behind the priest and tried to steady himself for what was to come.

"Only one of us can escape now," Doyle said. "You know, I think we're alone now. I don't think that anybody is going to get here to save you. There's nobody on the way."

But the Count was looking into the forest behind. "I'm not sure we are alone. I can see eyes in there, in the woods, they are reflecting the headlights."

The priest looked behind him, but could see nothing.

He looked back at the Count. In the seconds it had taken the priest to look into the wood and check out the Count's words, the Count had reached into his jacket.

The priest was now looking into the muzzle of a pistol, a Gabilondo Omni III, which the Count had owned for decades. It was a 9mm parabellum pistole with a thirteen round magazine.

"You expect to just take my life like that, do you?" asked the Count. "That I'd let you go and strangle me?"

"You distracted me," the priest said.

"Not really," said the Count. "We are being watched. But not by humans."

"I don't believe you," said the priest, sneering.

The Count shot him in the shoulder. At the sound of the shot and the simultaneous priest's scream, the eyes in the forest disappeared.

"You shot me!" Doyle said, astonished. He clutched his right shoulder where his clothes were already soaked with blood. Warm red blood splashed on to the ground. In the darkness it looked black, like oil.

"It was the logical next thing to do," said the Count, still aiming at the priest. "So you can know now that I am not afraid to shoot you. So you know I can fire a gun and that I can hit any part of your body – wherever I want to. I can shoot you in the head or in the heart, whichever I choose. And you have two seconds to start running." The priest wavered one second too long and the Count shot near his foot. The bullet grazed Doyle's foot, exactly as intended, and the priest, heart in his mouth and loose-bowelled with fear, turned and ran.

The Count watched Doyle disappear up the road into the gloom. He did not regret throwing the keys into the bush. He could no longer drive himself, and the thought of the priest making any kind of escape by car had been more than he could bear.

He shivered suddenly. Maybe a loss of blood in his leg was causing a degree of shock. He must get in the car. There was shelter there, food and drink. And he could see now, that some of the hungry eyes in the wood had returned. The silvery retinas of the eyes glinted in the light from the Alhambra's headlights.

The Count shifted his weight onto the side opposite his broken leg and, using both arms and flexing his unbroken leg, he began to half-crawl, half-drag himself towards the open door of the car. His breath hissed between his gritted teeth as he suffered the pain, and his head felt light as if he might collapse, but he knew that passing out would be fatal. There was an unearthly sound, somewhere between a bark and a cough, from the woods.

The Count was trying not to cry out in his agony as he dragged himself over to the sill of the Alhambra's door. He wanted to give no audible sign of his distress, but his breathing was both laboured and sizzling with pain. He levered his torso up onto the edge of the car seat and reached forward to the handbrake and pulled himself up on his left leg. His right foot dangled uselessly, like a piece of meat. He could already hear a clattering of claws on the road as he pulled his right leg up and into the footwell and, reaching out to the interior door handle pulled the door too with a slam. As he did so the first wolf jumped against the car door, claws skittering over the glass of the driver's window. Mouth open wide, canine teeth clashing against the window, snarling and growling. Strings of saliva splattered against the glass as the wolf's head collided with it. A second wolf jumped onto the Alhambra's bonnet and the Count glimpsed yellow-brown eyes staring hungrily at him, devouring him visually, before sliding off the angled bonnet. A third from the pack snarled at him through the passenger side window.

"Oh, dear God," said the Count. He locked the door and felt instantly safer. Then he wound the car window down a crack. This took a great degree of courage, for the first animal, the pack leader, was still at the window and its hooked claws could now scrabble at the edge of the glass. He could even feel the heat of its breath as it growled and snapped at him.

The Count felt shaky now, partly from blood loss and partly as a reaction to the latest attack. Nevertheless, he pulled the pistol again from its holster under his left arm and taking the safety lock off, angled the muzzle a bit through the gap. The gap was as wide as the Count could bear. The wolf's snarling mouth was now spattering his face with foul-smelling, hot saliva.

He steadied his hand and pulled the trigger. The bullet was deliberately aimed away into the night and it disappeared harmlessly into the dark blue sky. The gun's report was deafening in the confines of the Alhambra, but the sound was enough to disperse the wolves one more time. They scattered at the shot and retreated to a safe distance. The pack leader watched the Count warily.

In evolutionary terms, wolves separated from dogs some thirty thousand years ago. Wolves have larger brains than dogs, and although dogs are more adept at attuning themselves to human emotional expressions, wolves are more intelligent and have a better grasp of logic than dogs. Problem solving is easier for the wolf. The Count was vulnerable but in a place they could not reach, and besides it was not the Count who smelled of the blood. The scent of the Count and the scent from the blood on the road were different.

The Count watched as the pack paced warily about in the distance. Eyes glinting in the headlights. All at once, the leader of the pack made his decision, and turned tail and started to run away up the hill past the wreck of Doyle's car and away along the spotted trail of blood.

The Count sighed in relief. However, he still felt as if he was just about to pass out. He reached into his jacket pocket and retrieved his mobile phone and dialled a number.

"Salazar? Salazar, I need your help, please. I'm sorry to have to ask, but . . . I'm in my car on the road above Las Medulas. Please come quickly."

Chapter Eighteen

Between un-being and being.
Sudden in a shaft of sunlight
Even while the dust moves
There rises the hidden laughter
Of children in the foliage

TS Eliot – The Four Quartets

D oyle was running into the darkness, away from the lights of the Alhambra on the mountain road. The heavens above his head were a Prussian blue, and the moon a golden yellow. He decided to get off the road. If he was on the road he could be spotted and picked up.

He clambered over a roadside barrier and onto a steep slope of dust and scrub. He was moving into an ancient landscape that had not changed since the Roman occupation. Under the hot daytime sun the land was usually a deep rusty red, that contrasted with the deepest, lustrous green leaves of chestnut, yew, holm oak, field maple, walnut, and pine trees. In the darkness, the priest could feel the shrubs brushing past his arms and face as he ran and stumbled forwards. Even in the hours before dawn the air was heady with the scent of myrrh and camphor and Cistaceae plants.

The Romans had planted chestnuts to feed their slaves, and gum trees for the sticky gum that was used in filtering out the gold from the hills. Some of the chestnut trees were four or five hundred years old, with thick gnarled trunks and twisted branches.

The valley that Doyle was climbing down into might, he thought, afford him somewhere to rest and recuperate, and most of all consider his next move. There could be no going back to the farmhouse.

Between the shrubs, the slopes were covered in dry red soil, and the dust from it billowed up around the priest in a cloud as he descended into the valley. Tall jagged rock pillars, like turrets, stood around him. While others, like broad, decayed carnassial teeth stuck out of the red gums of the earth. Once, all the valleys round Las Médulas had been mountains themselves, convex shapes many hundreds of metres high, rather than the eroded valleys they were now. The landscape had forever been changed by the Roman Empire's greed for gold. Mining had been set up here on a truly modern industrial scale using thousands of men, woman and children. Inside the mountains thousands of miners had worked for months at a time without seeing daylight. Many had died inside the tunnels. The Romans had ordered two hundred and forty million cubic metres of rock to be carved from the landscape and broken down smaller and smaller to ferret every lump of gold from it. Ingenious minds had engineered an ambitious scheme to harness the hydraulic power of millions of gallons of water from the Aquilano mountains, more than fifteen kilometres away. Pliny the Elder called the process *ruina montium*, the collapse of the mountains.

They built channels to divert water from mountain streams and rivers along aqueducts into vast holding areas that could be emptied suddenly, and skillfully directed into tunnels burrowed into the rock. Under such enormous pressure the water in these tunnels and galleries would explode the mountains from within and a cascade of rock, water and gold would be channelled for further examination and filtration. Rome got rich on eight hundred thousand kilograms of gold, while the mountains of Spain exploded into dust. Where proud mountains had once stood there were now eroded valleys, with huge deserted caverns, galleries caves and tunnels.

From nests high up on the vertical sandstone walls, hundreds of birds were waking with the approaching dawn. They streamed and whirled above the priest's head as he scoured through the valley looking for some shelter.

He had lost blood. His shoulder was a bloodied mass of torn skin and muscle, and shards of shattered white bone. He felt faint, confused and frightened, which was unusual for him. He saw his role as being to inflict pain, not to suffer it personally. He felt so tired, but he knew he could rest only a short while, to think, and then he really must find a sympathetic doctor.

He was standing amidst myrrh plants. The smell reminded him of incense in the church and death.

It was the first time he had stood still. He was aware of blood running down his arm from his shoulder. He was cradling one arm with the other. The pain was really becoming excruciating now the shock of being shot was wearing off. He looked down and saw a drop fall from his elbow to the dust below. His blood. Disappearing into the dust.

He looked around and saw a vast chasm opening up ahead in the cliffs on the left, perhaps forty metres wide, with an over-riding arch of rock as a roof sixty metres above.

All at once he realised that he was not alone. He turned and saw eyes glinting higher up on the slope. Low grey bodies were loping casually down the hillside towards him. They did not seem in a hurry for some reason. Maybe they had no need.

The priest observed himself as if from a point outside his body – as though from the point of view of a bird high in an oak tree, looking down on a silent, still, black figure being gradually approached on all sides, by wolves moving with the assured and measured steps of a predator group in overwhelming numbers approaching a defenceless, weakened prey.

The priest suddenly realised that he did not have the benefit of a distant vantage point and that the wolves had fixed him with their eyes. They were so close now, he could see the white of their teeth, hear the growl of their throats, and smell the rank stench of their coats. He glared at them and shouted as loud as he could. "Get Away!" His voice echoed as it bounced off the valley's rock walls. The wolves halted. A few faltered and stole back a few steps, but the leader of the pack snarled at him in defiance.

The priest turned and ran for the cavern mouth, sprinting as fast as his broken body and blood loss would allow him. He pelted down the tourist footpath and into the gloom of the cavern.

The wolves advanced steadily behind their leader.

The priest ran to the back of the cavern where a huge pile of scree and broken rock had been left from the last Roman mining. The pile of scree seemed to go up and up. He craned his neck to see. The pile went up towards some galleries near the roof of the cavern that might offer some protection if he could just climb and gain enough distance . . .

Gasping in pain the priest scrabbled and stumbled and staggered up the shifting pebbles and dust. Dust covered his knees and hands, and ascended in a cloud to be inhaled by his lungs and clog his nose. The wolves waited at the foot of the scree pile and watched him climb maybe sixty metres up into the highest reaches of the cavern. Here the priest saw tunnels burrowed into the higher gallery. He fantasised that the tunnels, made by human hands with hammer and pick, might lead up and out onto the broad top of the mountain, where he might escape. He realised he had not heard the animals climbing up the shifting scree beside or behind him and looked back down the slope to see the wolves waiting patiently side by side on the cavern floor. He was so far ahead of them now, he felt he could afford to laugh out loud at them. His laughter boomed in the cavern and in the distance a few pebbles fell from the roof and trickled down the slope in response to the vibrations in the air caused by his voice.

With that, the wolf pack, all as one, leapt onto the slope and, their feet flailing in the dirt, began to scramble upwards towards the meal at the top of the cavern.

The priest, pulse pounding and chest pained and breathless in alarm, fought his way to the very top of the scree, and hedging his bets, dived rightwards into the nearest circular tunnel. He could manage to almost stand up in the rock-hewn tube and, clutching his shattered arm tightly, he made his way along as fast as he could. The tunnel turned gradually leftwards and angling down, narrowed deliberately to increase the pressure should any water be pumped through it. Doyle smelled fresh air and there was light ahead which spoke of a potential opening, where he might climb up to the sky, and in his fantasy, escape.

He could hear the wolves' claws clattering along the rock floor of the tunnel as they hunted him down. They started their strange cough-like barking in excitement of the chase.

The priest stopped.

Ahead, there was fresh air and the prospect of a lightening sky. His fantasy escape had involved a climb up into the air, but the opening was not above him. The sun was rising in the sky and he could see the valley floor in the distance below. Wolves are most active at dusk and dawn.

The opening to the tunnel had been the place where hundreds of years before, a thick, almost solid column of high pressure river water had been guided. It had exploded the cliff face outwards at the end of the tunnel, spewing thousands of tonnes of gold-rich rock into the valley and leaving a gaping maw out of which the priest now looked. Around the face of the red rock outside, birds were whirling like flies. Their nests were burrowed into the rock. There was only the prospect of a fall to the valley floor some sixty metres below, or the teeth of the wolf. It was a choice he hesitated to make, and in his hesitation the wolves decided his end as they fell upon him with jaws and teeth and claws.

Chapter Nineteen

Villafranca del Bierzo to Paradela

Sometime she driveth o'er a soldier's neck,
And then dreams he of cutting foreign throats,
Of breaches, ambuscadoes, Spanish blades,
Of healths five-fathom deep; and then anon
Drums in his ear, at which he starts and wakes.

Mercutio, speaking of Queen Mab,
In Shakespeare's Romeo and Juliet

The path ahead of them wound upward into the mountains. The air felt fresher and was scented with pine. They were marching westward towards Galicia, and now the path wound through the Bierzo region. As they rested in the shade, Power and Lynch put their walking staffs aside and ferreted in their rucksacks for cans of drink they had bought at the last village. Wrapped in their clothes in the dark of the sacks, the cans of Kas Limon were still cool, tart and refreshing. Dr Power stood swigging his can and took in the mountain air, breathing deeply. He felt that day-by-day his legs were getting stronger and he felt less out of breath on exertion.

The hills around them were covered with an assortment of trees, their slopes dotted with cherry and fig trees, chestnuts and poplars. Here and there, were small farmhouses built of stone and slate. In the distance they could see the Ancares mountains of Galicia.

Power and Lynch finished their drinks and walked on over the hills and down into the small town of Villafranca del Bierzo. They passed a castle with vast rounded towers at either end, each topped with conical slate roofs surrounded by crenellations. And at that moment there sounded a swirling, wailing sound, not unlike bagpipes, and on hearing this noise they paused.

"There's your piper!" shouted Lynch over the din and pointed at a solitary figure nursing a bagpipe. "Playing Galician pipes."

Power looked. It wasn't *his* piper. "I didn't imagine Scottish people here," said Power, frowning.

"He's probably a local," tutted Lynch. "Galicia is a Celtic kingdom, like Wales and Scotland. Probably all the Celts migrated north from here by sea. You can see the links in words like Gaelic . . . Galicia, you know?"

"Couldn't they have left the bagpipes here in Galicia then?" asked Power, peering at the piper dressed in traditional clothes with a tall, curved hat that Power imagined to be ancient. He recalled school Classics lessons from long ago and pictures of Medeans with tall, pointed hats.

"If you listen carefully, I think it's a more complex sound than our bagpipes," said Lynch.

Power was looking at the piper himself. "It's not him, you know," he was disappointed.

"You could ask him if he knew the Piper," suggested Lynch.

"Maybe later, if he's still about," said Power, who had left messages for the Piper everywhere and was feeling dispirited. "I'm not sure I'll ever see him again. Can we find our lodgings? We are staying the night here, I take it?"

"Are you tired, then?"

Power nodded.

"Then you might like the place I booked," said Lynch. "It's a new hotel, a parador, with a pool." A smile spread over Power's face at the idea of plunging deep into cool, sparkling water.

They turned left by the tower at the far end of the castle and went down a winding road to find the parador. Paradors are luxurious hotels in historic buildings. Power's room was spacious and calm compared to some of the auberges they had had to sleep in along the Camino. He showered in sweet-smelling foam, and in a deeply-soft white robe he made his way down to an outdoor pool, whose water shimmered and glistened in the afternoon sun. Lynch was already there, ploughing his way forcefully up and down the pool. Power sank into the cool water and luxuriated as the aches in his muscles were soothed away. The mountain air was clean, scented with fresh pine and the sun on his back was bright and warm.

In the evening they wended their way down steep stairways and winding narrow streets to a restaurant, to dine. The dusk was gathering. As they walked, Lynch pointed out a townhouse with jutting balconies and a watchtower that lowered threateningly above them, a shadow against the sky. "The Palace de Torquemada," he whispered.

"Why are you whispering?" asked Power.

"It's named after Torquemada, who began the Inquisition."

"It's okay, Andrew, I don't think he's listening and if his family live here, well, they've probably learned the error of their ancestor's ways. Now, where is this restaurant?" Power's stomach rumbled.

"Down here," said Lynch, navigating them using a guidebook. He steered them to a small green painted door, with buckets of flowers in perfusion on either side. A small hand-painted sign announced the name of the restaurant, La Pedrera. A young waiter showed them to a table out in the garden in the dusk. They were ushered over the lush grass to a single table covered in pure white, heavy damask. There they sat under crisscrossing strings of small white light bulbs. Somewhere in the undergrowth and hedges surrounding the garden there chirruped a *grillo*. One by one the crickets added to form an orchestra. "It's like something out of *Midsummer Night's Dream*," said

Power. "The place is magical, but empty. I expect some kind of enchantment, maybe. To see Puck or some wood nymphs."

"The guidebook says the food is very good," said Lynch. "A good vegetarian range for you, Dr Power." The waiter was hovering with menus and asked them in English what they would drink.

"Some mineral water," said Power. "And can you recommend a good wine – a red wine from somewhere nearby?"

The waiter nodded, and returned as they were surveying the menu. He poured ice pure Fontecelta water into blue glasses and uncorked a bottle of Altos de Losada wine for Power to taste. Power was in mid-anecdote about a patient. The doctor paused in his tale, to sniff and sip the plush red wine. He approved the wine with a smile and a nod to the waiter. As he poured two glasses for them both the young man asked Power, "You are a doctor then?"

"Yes," said Power. "A doctor of the mind."

The waiter nodded. "I am a medical student from the University in Santiago."

"How many years have you completed?" asked Power.

"Three," said the waiter. "Tell me, have you chosen something to eat?"

"Not yet," said Power.

"Then let me and the chef choose for you. I will ask him to make something special for you."

Power looked at Lynch who shrugged with a smile. "Why not?"

"All right," said Power. "Let us see what the Way brings us. But I am vegetarian."

"And I am certainly *not* vegetarian," said Lynch.

The waiter nodded happily and wandered off to the kitchens.

Lynch mused. "The guidebook says there has been a University in Santiago de Compostela since the fifteenth century. In England, only Oxford and Cambridge are older. There was a college for the

Irish . . . for priests . . ." Lynch paused. His face seemed to fall ever so slightly. He took a sip of wine and looked into the night sky. "I told you about my boy, didn't I? My son?"

"A long time ago," said Power. Lynch's son had died in childhood.

"He's been very much on my mind this last year. I don't know why. I feel I am getting old. And a man must have a son, or at least it feels that way. And quite suddenly it has hit me that I will never have one. And that has been the case for years. That I'd never have a son. But it hit me, suddenly. That was that. The chance really had passed." Power felt uneasy. For he wanted a child too. He and Laura had been trying. "Looking at that student. The waiter I mean," said Lynch. "Well, the student waiter would be the right age. If my son had lived he would be finishing university now. That boy could be my son, grown up." Power could see tears welling up in his friend's eyes and he himself felt desolate and somehow afraid of Lynch's grief. Lynch never lost control. Power realised he feared his friend losing control. He knew what he would say and do for a patient, but what could he do for his friend?

"Has this been the matter – troubling you all along? I thought it was the job maybe . . ."

"That hasn't helped," said Lynch, struggling to regain his composure. "Being made to feel that you're somewhere near the end of your career. A feeling that things are drawing to a close."

"But they're not," said Power. "There's so much more to be done. Both of us have new offers to think about. New opportunities."

"I think I rather threw myself into my work after he died. It swallowed my feelings." Lynch looked away from his friend. He took a long drink of water. "Better now. I'm not sure where that came from."

"It's okay," said Power, watching his friend and wondering whether everything was indeed okay. 'There's no one watching but the stars and no one listening apart from the crickets."

"They say that all your stresses and emotional baggage come out on the Way," said Lynch. "Maybe they're right." And with that the summer evening returned to a tranquil calm. Lynch's emotions disappeared beneath the surface like a smooth grey stone sinking slowly into the dark liquid depths of a lake.

Just then a small dish of locally grown soft chickpeas arrived. Lynch and Power focused on their dining in the garden. The chickpeas had been flash fried with garlic so that their brown exterior was crisp. Their insides, though, were soft and buttery and the crisp chickpeas burst in their mouths as they ate them.

After the chickpeas Lynch took comfort in a plate of hake with figs, and Power ate garden vegetables roasted to perfection with a pilaff of rice. A dessert of glazed chestnuts on cheesecakes finished their repast. They finished one bottle, then two, and the tone of the evening evolved from regret into a night of laughter under the starry sky. The Milky Way looked down on Power and Lynch as they left the restaurant with smiles and waves to the assembled waiting and kitchen staff and wove their way happily back to the parador through deserted streets. Many of the houses seemed abandoned. On Agua Street some buildings looked as if they were slumping to the ground, with crumbling brickwork and rot splintered wood, doors fallen off their rusted hinges and massive cobwebs stretching across from jamb to jamb.

The town they walked through was still and silent. "Maybe only the pilgrims keep this place alive," said Lynch. "Maybe all the young people leave for the city as soon as they can."

At the parador, Lynch excused himself saying he was tired and made his way to his room. Power ordered a gin and tonic and sat down in the hotel garden to look at the stars. He was sucking on a slice of lemon when the tall and thin receptionist Miguel appeared at his side. "Excuse me, Dr Power. There is a telephone call from someone asking for you. Someone who says he is from Astorga and is checking if you are here. I said I would go and see if we had a guest of that name. I haven't confirmed you are here. What would you like me to say? Will you take the call?"

"Who is it? Did they say?"

"I didn't ask the name, I am sorry. My mistake. It is from someone with a local accent. An old man."

"I think I know who that will be," said Power. He drained his glass and stood up. He followed the receptionist to the front desk and picked up the receiver that Miguel pointed out. "Hello, is that the Count?"

"It is," said a distant, frail voice. "I am glad to hear you, Dr Power. This is the seventh hotel I have tried tonight."

"Is everything all right?"

"Yes, and no," said the Count. "I got out of hospital this morning. I have a sort of plastic boot thing on my leg. I broke my tibia and fibula and it needed some pins. But when I say I broke my leg it was more of the case that my leg was broken for me."

"Are you at home?"

"I am back at our family home, yes."

"Who did this to you?"

"The priest."

"Did he come to the office again and attack you?"

"No," the Count seemed reluctant to say. He had been scolded enough by the Countess. "My friends told me where the priest was. He had set up another den in Bierzo. He had merely moved his quarters and was carrying on as before. He was in bed with a child when I found him. I hunted him down. He would not confess. He showed no remorse. He despised us and all that is good. He believed he and his kind can go on doing whatever they like. Taking what they want from children. Feeding off others."

Power could hear the Count was growing angry again. "What happened next?"

"I gave chase, through the village and up into the mountains, towards the ancient mines. And there he lost control of the car. I am not sure how he survived that. The car rolled over, but he walked away. They make cars safer now, I suppose. He came over and fought me. I gave him the chance to come with me. I am a Christian – I still believe in my God – I gave him the chance to repent, but he was too far gone and he stamped upon my leg. His eyes were cruel. I suppose your bones grow brittle with age. I almost fainted with the pain, but I knew I would be dead if I lost consciousness." There was a pause while the Count wondered if he really could trust Power. He looked around for his wife to see if she was in earshot and whispered into the receiver. "I shot him. Don't tell anyone. But it was my only defence, forgive me. It was him or me. It was only a flesh wound; if I had wanted to kill him, I would have."

"Good God," said Power. "You took a gun?"

"It seemed reasonable. He killed the girls. He was a killer. It would have been foolish to go unprepared. I am not proud of what I did, but it gave me time to get in the car. And I watched him run off into the dark. He was still alive when I last saw him."

"And is he still alive?" asked Power.

"You won't have listened to the local radio," said the Count. "Why would you? It is pop drivel mostly. But the news carries reports of a body found in the caves in Las Medulas. A man half-eaten by wolves. Head with no skin left, the muscles on his shoulders and legs torn and eaten by savage teeth. Hungry mouths. This year the wolves have grown in number and have eaten all the game. You knew there were wolves?"

"I heard them," said Power, shuddering at the image of the gnawed and dismembered priest in his mind. "I haven't seen them."

"They wouldn't approach a fit man, and certainly not the two of you," said the Count. "But this man was weak, and bleeding heavily. And they hunted him down. They looked at me too, but I was safe in my car, protected by hard glass and metal." The Count sighed. "So I needed to tell you that the priest is gone and it is over."

"Yes," said Power, still taking the news in. "I suppose that it is . . . Do you think the radio story is true? That it is him?"

"I do," said the Count. "Because someone I know and trust went looking and found the body."

"Who?"

"You haven't met him yet," said the Count. "But I am tired now, Dr Power. I am tired with the painkillers, and now I have told you that the priest is dead, I think maybe I can rest. Do you think it is over?"

"It must be," said Power. "Don't you think it is?"

"In my bones, in my broken bones, I don't feel sure, and I don't know why."

"Well, you lock all your doors, Count, and sleep well. Make sure you get rest tonight, but try and keep mobilising as best you can through the day. You don't want to seize up. I will tell Andrew in the morning and we will come and see you as soon as we can."

"After you reach the end in Santiago come and see me, all right? Make sure you both get to Santiago de Compostela and finish it. You are not far now. Everything will be right after you have done that," said the Count. "I will say good night now?"

"Good night, we will be thinking of you."

Power retired for the night thinking admiringly of the courage that the Count had shown.

The Count nestled down in his bed as best he could with the orthopaedic boot on his foot. His wife sat up by his side, reading under a night light.

Occasionally she would reach over to stroke his thin, white hair as he slept.

* * *

Dr Power woke early, or rather at a time which was early for him. The sun was streaming through his bedroom window. He rose, took a swim in the pool, showered and dressed, and packed his rucksack. At eight o'clock the doctor was ready to take breakfast with Lynch and start their walk again. Only Lynch was not in his room.

Power went down to the reception. He asked if anyone knew his friend's whereabouts, to be told that Lynch had awoken long before Power and had left a message that he was going to the Church of St James. Dr Power begged a map and followed the receptionist's directions up the road and past the Castle to the Church, which in Spanish was Iglesia de Santiago, that he had circled in blue biro on the map.

Lynch was sitting on the stone steps outside the North Door, a gothic arched door with columns, in the middle of a twelfth century church stone wall. Lynch was reading but looked up with a smile as Power approached.

"Good morning, what are you reading?" asked Power.

"The Book of Job. It is always a puzzle to me."

"Couldn't you get in?" Power nodded to the fast shut door.

"This door rarely opens," said Lynch. "And the church seems closed anyway. So I sat here and prayed and read on my own. This door is where believers could get an Indulgence, a relief from the punishment they'd have to serve in returned for their sins on earth. You walked the Way and if you were too ill to carry on to Santiago you could come here to this particular church, and visit the Door of Forgiveness, and get part of the Indulgence." Power was looking at the carvings. "All about the three wise men," said Lynch. "Astronomers from the East." Lynch got to his feet. "Are we ready to walk?"

"After breakfast?" said Power, hopefully. "Presumably there's breakfast paid for at the parador?"

"Well, let's indulge in breakfast then," said Lynch, and they started back down the hill towards the hotel and a certain breakfast.

"After all we've seen together, the things you see everyday in your job, can I ask you – why do you still believe in religion?" asked Power.

"I don't believe in religion. I believe in God. Nothing changes my personal relationship with Him. And as far as religions go, all have their fair share of twisted fanatics. They all have a clique of fundamentalists quibbling and scribbling and squabbling. And as for the Catholic Church it doesn't seem to have cottoned on to how our world has changed; we've grown up and the scales have fallen from our eyes. I don't think the Church has ever done enough over the years to root out the paedophile priests and now they have an infestation that will damage people's faith in the church, if not God. It makes me angry, bitterly angry; because I think that Jesus was fully aware of the special nature of children and how they must be nourished and protected. He said 'Suffer little children to come unto me, and forbid them not: for of such is the kingdom of God.' And as for how God will treat these animals? The Bible says 'It were better for him that a millstone were hanged about his neck, and he cast into the sea, than that he should offend one of these little ones.' And it feels to me that the very people who should have listened to his words have done just the opposite." Lynch stood up. "Do you know what I have been praying about?"

"No," said Power. "Praying for good weather?"

"Not at all," said Lynch. "Although I believe it does tend to be more rainy in Galicia, where we will be walking later. No, I've been praying for understanding. Ever since we met Ramon again. I couldn't work out quite why he upset me. I thought it was because he wanted to talk about the murder, but it wasn't that. It was because he made me think. About quantum physics of all things. He was talking about science, which had always seemed so cut and dried to me. So definite and predictable. And I suppose I'm used to people using science to belittle my faith. But there he was, talking about mysteries. Twinned particles being linked over space and time. Electrons being either particles or waves. Waves going backwards and forwards in time. And there was mystery there, and I have been thinking about all that, and praying. Because it seems to me, that suddenly science can't be used to prove God doesn't exist. Because suddenly anything in an infinite universe could be possible. And God could be here or there, nowhere and everywhere. He might even exist and not exist, and it's only our faith or observation that makes him exist. And after my prayer, I think maybe I was a bit rude to poor old Ramon last time. Maybe I owe him an apology."

"So," said Power. "It was like God talked to you, in prayer?"

"Not like a hallucination, *Dr* Power! But if you listen, really listen, you can understand Him."

"Hmm," said Power, as they walked through the hotel's main entrance and tried to work out where the breakfast room was. "Sometimes I am frightened that God might be speaking to me," said Power.

Lynch pointed the way to the dining room. "Frightened. Why?"

"Because if He spoke, then I might have to listen to what He said. And I might not like it," said Power.

"Ah, Carl, God knows that you are a better man than you know."

They were being seated at their table and being offered tea or coffee when Power was reminded of the phone call he had the night before. Coffee arrived in heavy silver pots. "I was phoned last night by the Count," said Power. "I should have said straight away." And over butter and bread, and figs and eggs, Dr Power revisited the conversation he had had with the Count.

"So," said Lynch. "The priest, Doyle, is dead. The Count is certain it was him?"

"The Count had the photograph. He talked to the priest himself. The body could be no-one else's."

Lynch nodded thoughtfully. "And so the perpetrator is dead. And do you think it's over?" asked Lynch.

"I don't think so," said Power.

"But the abuser and murderer of the girls, the man who tried to kill you is found and dead. Is that not an end to the matter?"

"I don't know," said Power.

"A feeling you have? An intuition?" asked Lynch. Power nodded. "May the Lord preserve us then," said Lynch. He downed his coffee and surveyed the clutter of empty plates around Dr Power. "I'll just say that this world is probably well rid of Father Doyle and now thankfully he's the Lord's problem. Well, if you've finished are we ready for the road?"

The brief hinterland of suburbs around Villafranca soon dwindled into farms and countryside. The Camino path was fringed with oak trees. Every now and then was a garden with lemon and fig trees or an orchard of apples and pears.

They walked quickly now. Days of exercise had rendered them slimmer and fitter. Even the packs they carried seemed lighter. The miles flew past under their feet as they ventured deeper into Galicia. They had entered an entirely different countryside, more akin to the leafy lanes of England than Spain. The Camino was fringed with hawthorn hedges and the fields on either side were full of lush, deep-green grass. At times the dusty mud of the path was replaced by a road or pavement of carefully crafted grey stone from Roman times. The stone road with ancient cart ruts reminded Power of the roads in Pompeii. The grey sun had flecks, which twinkled in the sun. "A road of stars below the feet," Lynch called it, referring again to his guidebook. "A road of stars to match the Milky Way above the pilgrim's heads."

As they were passing a vast field of sunflowers Power gasped. "Look," he said. "Standing stones. Like Avebury."

Lynch and he left the path and passing down a narrow track between the jostling sunflower heads walked up to three vast standing stones with a lintel stone balanced carefully atop them. Power patted the rough surface, warm from bathing in the rays of the sun. He laughed. "Just like at home!"

Lynch nodded. "They were built by the same people."

By the evening, they had reached a cluster of buildings in the Sarria region of Galicia, known as the town of Paradela. A sign announced they had one hundred and eight kilometres to walk to Santiago de Compostela.

Power's legs were aching as they clumped their way in walking boots through a narrow archway into Case Grande – a farmhouse on the hill that offered beds to pilgrims. They each went to their own rooms and showered, and then together on a terrace under the trees drank local cider as they watched the sun go down. A pattering of rain on the leaves prompted them to go in to supper. "It rains more in Galicia," said Lynch, as they settled at a wooden table in the farm kitchen. He looked out of the window as torrents of rain began to pour out of the sky.

"The rain will all be over by tomorrow morning," said the farmer's wife.

She set platters and bowls of food before them with salads and bread. There was a thick tortilla in an earthenware dish, smothered in fiery red tomatoes for Dr Power. Crispy succulent pork with apples arrived for Lynch and for them both numerous flagons of cider.

The rain had stopped and they had moved outside again and were sipping hot coffee under the black velvet sky. Different coloured stars from distant galaxies looked down upon them.

"The end of a perfect day," said Lynch, yawning all of a sudden. "And tell me, Carl, are you any more reassured now, that things are resolved? Now you've lived all day with the fact that the priest is dead?"

"You would think so, wouldn't you, but I'm not. I am still puzzled."

"Then maybe after a long day of walking, a night of good sleep will take your worries away? And if not, then maybe you can lay your puzzles at the door of Queen Mab."

"Queen Mab?"

"You don't know your Shakespeare, Carl. I remember reading about her at school. Queen Mab looks after your dreams. Gives you the ones you want or need, or more likely what she wants you to have. She can be a tad tricky, Queen Mab can."

"As long as it's not a nightmare," said Power, as they climbed the stone staircase to their rooms.

"I'm sure you will sleep well enough," said Lynch, yawning again at the entrance to his room. "After walking all those miles, Good night, Carl."

"Good night," said Dr Power.

* * *

The dream was about particles.

And when it was over the meaning was very clear to Dr Power. He lay in his bed astonished at his own conclusion. He switched the light on and looked at his watch. Three a.m. Shaking with the sudden awakening he pulled on a shirt and struggled into trousers, stumbling around the bedroom as he did so. He picked up his keycard and hurried out of the door and down the corridor to Lynch's room.

It took a long time for Lynch to respond and Power was worried about waking the entire establishment. Lynch's door eventually opened and he stood there groggy. He sniffed the air, "Is there a fire or something?"

"No," said Power. "But I had the dream. About particles."

"Particles?" asked Lynch, bemusedly.

"The answer was there all along. I was so puzzled and the answer came in a dream, like you said."

Lynch waved Power into his room and switched the lights on. He dimmed the light to a tolerable level. He was struggling with being awake. He shut his eyes and swayed a bit then pointed Power towards a chair. "I need coffee first. Don't say any more. Sit down in that chair while I make coffee." And Lynch turned his back on Power and fumbled with the kettle, half-asleep. At one point he seemed to have gone back to sleep he was so still, but suddenly he started emptying sachets of Lavazza coffee into two mugs. He stood swaying slightly, back to his friend, as the kettle boiled. Then with a supreme effort he poured the boiling water and turned to Power with two steaming mugs of coffee.

He placed both coffee mugs on the bedroom table between them and slumped into the armchair opposite Power.

He fixed Power with bloodshot eyes. "I think I'm awake," he said. He sipped a bit of coffee. "Goodness that's hot." He put it back on the table. He spoke blearily. "You mentioned you were puzzled just now. Let's start with the puzzle. What's the puzzle?"

"I first saw the priest, Doyle, in the Cathedral in Leon, here in Spain."

"You're certain?"

"I'm certain."

"Because you know the passport office said Doyle had never left England."

"I'm certain and I'm right."

Lynch raised his eyes to heaven, opened his palms and sighed.

"I'm certain," said Power. "The priest was in Spain, and then the killing of the girl was in Spain. He did that."

"You can't be certain he did that. You know your own mind, and if you saw him in Leon, you can be certain you saw him. But no one saw the murder of the girl."

Power smiled. "Bear with me. Let's assume it was him." Lynch shrugged and motioned his friend to continue. "And then we travel home, and I see the priest again in the Gallery, and in his church in the city centre. And yes, I'm certain it was Doyle. And I track him to his lair in the Parish House, and he calls the police on me. So in calling them he is sending me a warning, because he knows exactly who I am, and why he should be frightened of being exposed by me. He is a guilty man. For what? It could only be the murder in Spain, I thought. But no-one believes me." There was the slightest glimmer of an accusatory glare at his friend. "Then another girl dies, in our country. The same style of murder. A young girl, ligatured, displayed in the open air in broad daylight, injuries to her vulva. No semen. Murdered and displayed near my house, and a clumsy attempt to frame me with a forged email. And I take the bait and I go to the monster's den. And he's ready for me. I sit in the wingback chair thinking he's making a pot of tea in the kitchen, and all the time he's preparing a bottle of anaesthetic liquid. And the phone goes. And it's his voice. It's *his* voice at the end of the line, Doyle's voice talking to me and distracting me. And at the same time Doyle is reaching around behind me with both arms, pinning me down and clamping that foul, stinking pad over my face. You see, I remember his voice clearly on the phone, and at the same time *two* arms encircling me."

"I'm just playing devil's advocate here . . . maybe the unconsciousness affected your recall?"

"No," said Power. "Of this I am certain. Now, how can he talk to me on a phone and suffocate me at the same time? How can he never leave England, but commit a murder in Spain?"

"I would assume that he was the same man travelling on a fake passport and in Spain then in England."

"Once upon a time you could hire a forger to make up a passport like in the films, like in Casablanca with Bogart; but producing a passport nowadays, that's getting very difficult, isn't it? The images are digital now, on different watermarked papers. Not photos stuck on pages with a smudge of cow gum, an old world passport that any craftsman could cobble together. And anyway, the people who knew Doyle in England, they all vouched that he never left. So somehow he was always in the country, but he was also able to kill in Spain."

"That's the puzzle?"

"That's the puzzle."

"And the dream that you say is the solution?"

"It was unearthly. Things I could not easily comprehend or correspond with – no faces, no people, no animals, no plants, nothing familiar, no up, no down, no sky, no ground. Just movement and spinning electrons, with feelings – intimations of charge. And the tiniest particles, quarks, neutrinos whatever they were, changing like numbers on a cash register, but somehow all linked. One changed and I saw, across the universe, another changing in the same way at the same time."

"Did you have the cheese last night?" Lynch was frowning.

"You don't get it?"

"Frankly, no," Lynch looked wistfully over at the warm bed he had been in before. "Do you want to wait until the morning before you try and explain to me further? My brain might be in a better state to . . ."

"Twinned particles," said Power. "Separated by distance, but linked and identical."

"I remember that Ramon said something about this, but . . ." Lynch paused and tried to make some sense of the puzzle and the dream. "You are saying that there is more than one priest called Doyle?"

Power nodded.

"That there was one Doyle in Spain. And an identical Doyle in England?"

"Yes, yes," said Power.

"Twins? Criminal twins. That's extremely rare."

"It is not unusual for twins to share the same profession; to both be saints or sinners together. The Kray twins for instance. And identical twins are about sixty-five per cent concordant for crime." Lynch looked blank. "Concordant means that if one twin is a criminal that there's a sixty-five per cent chance that the other one will be too."

"Explain it to me again," said Lynch. "Slowly. It's late, or it's early and my brain can't take much at this hour." He sipped his coffee, which was a little cooler now and tolerable to his mouth.

"Twins," said Power. "One in Spain. One In England."

"One bad, one good?" asked Lynch.

"Both as evil as each other," said Power. "But they each can use their two identities, designing them for many years, making the one in England a paragon of virtue. A man who never leaves home, never goes abroad. He is their alibi. Both can share the good priest's identity because they both look the same. The twin in Spain can afford to be bad, to indulge his desires, to fall as far as a man can go.

He is the bad priest who runs an organisation that catches, grooms and exports children for abuse by members of the group. The twin in Spain can afford to be bad because he can always flee to England and assume the identity of a saint. And they can swap over and use either identity. So then both can indulge in their perversions, but only in one country. The one twin in residence in England must continue the pretence of sainthood. But they can swap over when they need. Only one twin with one passport travels to England, and the other uses the same passport to go back to Spain. The good identity is preserved. Until we disturb the nest, and then it all goes wrong. They feel the need to destroy me because I have discovered both twins, because I have seen them in both places. That shouldn't happen according to their plans. That's the thing that should never happen, but it did . . . and so one twin brings the girl over from Germany and murders her in England. Then he tries to kill me. And I don't know, the other swaps over, back to Spain, where he encounters the Count. And dies."

"So there are two of them. Twins. And the problem that all prosecutions face, is that the accused twin can say he is innocent – that it is the other twin who is guilty. And this other twin, if accused in turn plays the same game. Both reflects guilt on the other. And so neither twin can be convicted because no one can be sure which is the guilty twin. And of course, if you are right, there is this apparently blameless priest living in England, ready to claim innocence for the pair. And no jury will convict . . ."

"But now one twin is dead."

"Sad for the remaining twin, of course" said Lynch. "But ever so convenient. The dead twin can absorb all the blame."

"Does my dream make sense? The solution I mean?" Power braced himself for Lynch's sceptical disbelief.

"You know, Carl. It may be the lateness or earliness of the hour,

but I believe it does. It makes perfect sense in the cold light of day."
Lynch looked over to the window where the harsh first light of dawn
was peeking through the curtains. Dust motes danced in the beams
of sunrise. "Twin particles," said Lynch as he watched them. "The
twins work together across Europe using mobile phone technology.
They preserve one good and virtuous persona for emergencies in
one country. The other persona unleashes its desire and lusts as it
likes in another country. And they swap between the two just as they
please, like changing a suit of clothes. And the twin that is left alive
will play the innocent, wherever he may be."

"And that is the question – where is he?"

"Precisely," said Lynch. "He could have fled to anywhere in the
world."

"Or he could be here in Spain," said Power. "And who will he
blame for his brother's death?"

"The Count," Lynch replied. "And he, or his twin, has threatened
the Count before." Lynch frowned. "We must phone the Count and
warn him – now."

Chapter Twenty

Paradela to Alta de Poio

Traveler, there is no path to follow; you make the path as you go
Antonio Machado

In the end, Power waited until seven o'clock to phone the Count, who was up in the bedroom trying to put a sock on one foot and cursing his imposed disability when his wife handed him the phone.

"Hello, hello. Is this Dr Power?" the Count spoke testily. "Let me ask you, Doctor, why can't they mend bones faster? Some kind of glue, something like epoxy resin, would be an idea. This bone-healing is taking ages, and it makes me feel old!"

"You sound frustrated."

"The process of getting washed and dressed has taken on a whole new dimension," said the Count.

In the distance Power could hear the Countess commenting, "And he won't accept any help, the stubborn donkey!"

The Count grunted and scowled at her irritably.

"How can I help you, Doctor?"

"I wanted to tell you something," said Power. "To warn you."

"Ah," said the Count, smiling, "you have been thinking?"

"Yes," said Power.

"Well, you go ahead," said the Count, "and tell me what you think, and then I'll tell you what I've done."

"How do you mean?" asked Power, puzzled.

"You first, please," said the Count.

And Power launched into a description of how he had woken Lynch with his dream, and the interpretation of that dream, that there were probably two priests acting in synchrony. And he finished with a re-telling of his time in the priest's dungeon, and how before he had ebbed his way into hypoxic unconsciousness he had spoken with the priest through the cell door, and how the priest had admitted to his paedophilic lusts and to colluding with others in authority, but when he was challenged as to being a murderer he had also said, 'I'm not going to incriminate myself. But what if I said that I didn't do those things? Would that make any difference to your last few hours?'

"And I thought at the time, Count, that he was telling me the truth, that he personally was not a murderer of children, but that he was part of a conspiracy."

"You say *not* a murderer?" said the Count. "But he did leave you to suffocate, didn't he?"

"I meant that he had not killed the girls."

"But you think he was talking of his brother instead, the twin who had killed the girls?"

"Yes," said Power.

"I see," said the Count. 'Well, I have been lying down a lot and not allowed to do my job." He glared at his wife who was sitting in the corner of the room. "And with time on my hands, thinking and thinking, and the solution to the puzzle presented itself in a similar way."

Power could hear the Countess deliberately speaking loudly in the background so Power would hear. "Thinking when he should be resting! Running round the countryside at his age, brought home by gypsies. The indignity!"

The Count carried on regardless of his wife's displeasure. "The twin that tried to kill me also said something, which kept coming back to me again and again, as I lay here. When I tracked him down in the forest, he said, 'You can threaten me with jail, and you can say what you like, but I tell you that no court in the world will convict me. For which of us is innocent and which guilty?'" The Count paused. "And I thought he was being clever, twisting words about, like a priest evading blame and saying we are all guilty; aren't we all sinners? You know what I mean; *'Qui sine peccato est qui primum lapidemmittat.'"*

"I'm sorry?" asked Power.

"'Let he who is without sin cast the first stone,'" translated the Count.

"I am sorry, it's a long while since I did Latin at school."

"Even longer for me," said the Count. "But there you have it, the priest was preparing his defence even as we spoke. It was not me, it was my brother. I am not my brother's keeper. Creating enough doubt to defend himself, creating that shield of doubt – when all Courts need certainty to convict."

"It's not the court case I am so worried about," said Power. "It is that the other twin is still alive. He might run and hide abroad. The Church might even shelter him abroad in South America. They have done that before. Or he might be closer at hand, waiting to take revenge. And that revenge would serve two purposes. Pay back for his dead brother. And elimination of a witness."

"So," the old man said. "You are phoning to tell me that the game is not yet over. That I am not safe in my bed, eh?"

"I am sorry, but no, I don't think any of us are safe."

"Well, I have been thinking too, as you know, and I came to the same conclusion. And so I have taken what steps I can, and made some phone calls to get us the help we need."

"What do you mean?"

"When it is necessary I will tell you, of course, Dr Power." The

Count was mindful of his wife sitting opposite him. Her expression was unfathomable, but the Count was anticipating a difficult conversation after he put the phone down. He was already mentally preparing for this.

"Can't you say?" Power sounded mildly irritated.

"Not at the moment," said the Count, under the baleful eye of the Countess. "When it is necessary I will tell you everything, but don't worry for now; all will be well. We have friends on our side too."

And with that the Count finished the call with Dr Power, and turned round ready to face his wife. He took a deep breath. He had decided to tell her once and for all what had motivated him to track the priest down. Courage is not always about facing a physical threat. Courage can be needed to face the fear of rejection and misunderstanding. Courage to face down inappropriate guilt and shame. The Count summoned all his courage and began his tale.

* * *

"I've been thinking about twins, "said Lynch. "You said that identical twins are so genetically similar that if one is a criminal then they can both be criminals?"

They were walking along a path made of plates of irregular, broken granite. On either side of the path were dry-stone walls that would not have looked out of place in Cumbria or Yorkshire. There was a tunnel of black branches and verdant leaves above their heads. It was silent but for the sound of the feet on the path, and the clacking of the metal tips of their staffs as they walked.

"You are probably right in that identical twins share personality traits," said Power. "But is that because the twins share the same genes or because they've shared the same upbringing? Twin research is known to be difficult and contentious. The results often seem to depend on the beliefs of the observer, if you see what I mean. A bit like looking at particles in quantum physics – the very act of observing them changes what is seen. Identical twins are called monozygotic, because the two twins come from one zygote – sharing one hundred per cent the same genetic material. As opposed to non-identical twins who are known as dizygotic – from two zygotes, sharing around fifty per cent of the same genes."

They paused and drank water from their flasks. There was a pattering of rain starting up again on the canopy of leaves above their heads.

"Rain again," said Power, diverted from his theme. "At least we're under cover. I suppose it keeps Galicia so green." He paused and listened to the pitter patter of the raindrops. The earth around the path under the leafy umbrella had that moist, loamy smell that people call petrichor. "Anyway," Power said, as they set off again. "The twin studies of the nineteen-thirties showed that monozygotes nearly always shared characteristics like criminality. But they were German scientists and perhaps they were more than a little affected by the politics of the time. And researchers working in the liberal, laid-back Scandinavia of the nineteen-seventies found there were no links and they blamed environment for criminality. And perhaps they too were affected by the politics of their time. But later studies of monozygtic twins who were actually reared apart found great similarities in behaviours. And because they were reared separately, this kind of negated the idea that it was the environment."

"The identical twins were reared apart, like Ramon's twinned atomic particles at different ends of the Universe?" asked Lynch.

"Exactly, and they were found to have similar fingerprints, similar heart rates, even similar brain waves on EEG. And psychologically they had similar personality profiles."

"Even though they were reared apart. So much for nurture," said

Lynch. "Is it all nature then? Is our life just a playing out of various genes?"

"Probably not in every respect, I'm sure that we are shaped by life events too. But our susceptibility as to whether we cope with trauma or succumb to it, maybe that's genetic. And you'll be particularly interested to know that in the MISTRA study the same kind of religious faith – either strong or absent – was also usually found in both of the monozygotic twins reared apart. If one was a very religious Catholic then their twin was very religious too, even if it was a different religion."

"Religious behaviour? Determined by our genes? Then maybe we are determined to be religious by nature, by God."

"I can see that you might interpret it that way," smiled Power.

They had come to the edge of the leafy canopy that had been provided by the undergrowth, and the path ahead wound around the sides of some hills in the distance, like some country lane in the Lake District. The shower of rain had ceased and sheep stood in the fields watching them and munching the wet grass.

"Are we no more than computers directed by the program of our genes, no more than physical dust and shadows?" asked Lynch. "Surely it is not all genetically determined – 'Good wombs have borne bad sons' as they say. Surely our decisions are swayed by our upbringing, by the temptation of the devil, and not foretold by an array of amino acids in some spiral. Are we not made of more than this stuff? Is there not free will? And in the future will our genes be our defence in law? I don't think so, we are masters of our own decisions and it is only ourselves that will be held responsible."

The signs were now all in Gallego (Galician). They came to a village sign for Liñares and rested outside a twelfth century church called Igrexa de Santo. They drank water from a sparkling cold fountain and then made their way through the village to a rough track running parallel with the road. They climbed the steep track up to the Alto de San Roque. Here there were clear views across the mountains.

The clouds from earlier in the day were dwindling into mere wisps under the hot midday sun. There was a small chapel, and not far from this a tall bronze statue of a pilgrim facing Santiago. The pilgrim was holding his hat on to his head and leaning forward into the wind, carrying a staff adorned with shells and gourds.

They climbed up the path to another small village, where once there had been a hospital for pilgrims. The track wound on into the mountains, ever climbing upwards. By mid-afternoon they had nearly reached a village called Alto de Poio. A brown sign by the wayside said the village was a kilometre away and announced 'Altitud 1.335m'. They were crossing a barren plateau in the mountains and in front of them stalks of dry golden grass rippled in the breeze. Lynch was reading aloud from a guidebook, when the peace of the mountains was interrupted by a chattering, clappering sound, that grew in intensity from something like the lazy hum of a bee, to a clattering roar. It was Power that spotted it first, a light blue helicopter that had been moving at high altitude and high speed, and which had slowed, gently dropped lower and circled around the rim of the sky. Impetuously Power waved up to the helicopter, laughing into the breeze.

"They can't see you, surely," said Lynch.

"It doesn't matter," said Power. "I haven't seen a plane or anything like this for days."

Lynch shielded his eyes from the sun and looked up at the helicopter. "A Sikorsky," he said. "A naval rescue helicopter. I wonder what it's doing?"

"We're too far inland for a naval helicopter," said Power.

"Santiago de Compostela is only about thirty-five kilometres from the sea," said Lynch. "It could well be a Spanish naval helicopter on training manoeuvres."

Having circled Power and Lynch as they were walking, the helicopter came ever closer. The clatter of the helicopter rotors grew louder. "I think it's going to land," said Power.

As Power predicted, the helicopter began a further slow descent, its power blades causing a whirlwind that circled and flattened the grass of the plateau. The powder blue copter with black characters, SH-60B and EZ-EKL, stencilled upon its side, settled on its three sets of wheels perhaps five hundred metres in front of them. From nose to tail the helicopter was some sixty-four feet long, and dauntingly large even at a distance.

"They must be here for us," said Power to Lynch. He had to raise his voice to be heard over the incessant whirring of the whirling blades.

"It's probably just an exercise," said Lynch. "Let's walk on past." He so wanted to finish his walk in the way he had planned, but in his heart of hearts he also suspected the helicopter was there for them.

"There's someone getting out of it," said Power.

It was a slim figure, unfamiliar at first, in a white helmet and dark-blue flying suit. With head down, and slightly crouching, the figure ran forward until well out of the down-draught of the idling rotor-blades. Then he stood up, paused, and waved towards Power and Lynch, beckoning them towards him.

Lynch paused. "Maybe we should just walk on," he tried again. "Leave things alone for once." They had interrupted his journey one too many times, Lynch thought, and he was now full of foreboding that if they were tempted towards this figure from the helicopter, that they would never reach his goal at the end of the journey, Santiago de Compostela.

"I think it's definitely us he wants," said Dr Power. "Do you think they have been looking for us?"

"That doesn't mean we should go," cautioned Lynch, and he was even now turning towards the west and their route to Santiago.

Meanwhile, the helicopter blades on the Sikorsky were slowing as the engine had been cut. The figure had taken off his helmet, and was waving and smiling. He was a tall man, clean shaven with short, neat, reddish-brown hair. Power was the first to get within earshot of him. "Dr Power!" he shouted. "And Superintendent Lynch?"

"Yes?" said Power, amazed at the arrival of the helicopter from the outside world. "What is it? What is this all about?"

The man in the flying suit laughed and held out a hand to shake hands with Power. Lynch had walked behind Power, and now stood back, and shook the aviator's hand reluctantly. "Superintendent Lynch, Dr Power – so sorry to interrupt your walk. But somebody wanted your help," he gestured to the cabin behind the cockpit and pushed the door back so that Power could look inside. "Put your things in and climb aboard."

Dr Power clambered aboard. Lynch hung back, and then accepting this new turn of events, ducked and climbed into the cabin, a large space with five fixed canvas seats with frames and seat belts. Sprawled over two of these seats was the Count. His leg was raised up with a heavy orthopaedic boot resting on the second of the two seats.

The Count smiled at them, eyes twinkling and moustache bristling. He seemed in the best of health. "Good afternoon, both of you. I spotted you from on high!"

With a bang the cabin door clanged shut and the figure who had hailed them was getting back into one of the front seats. He was putting on his helmet. Something about him suddenly seemed vaguely familiar to Power. There were two men in the front, including the figure who had beckoned them in. Both had pilot's controls in front of them. There was a gabble of technical conversation between them, and an unseen person on the radio. There was a metallic shooting sound and the blades started to slowly turn outside.

"What's happening?" said Lynch, alarmed.

"We came to find you," said the Count. "I had to find you. Our friend here," he pointed at one of the pilots. "I asked him to help. It was urgent you see. And I could not find you myself," he gestured to his leg. "I am a cripple. But as they say, 'The wounds received in battle bestow honour, they do not take it away' . . ."

"Where are we going?" asked Lynch.

"To Santiago, of course. Don't worry. You will get to your final destination," said the Count. "Just not in the way we all expected, and for that I am sorry. But needs must . . ."

"And what is this great need, this great hurry?" asked Lynch again.

"The priest. The blonde priest. His twin has been sighted in Santiago, and we must get to him before he leaves for good."

"Doyle?" asked Power. He was staring so intently and closely into the Count's face that he hadn't noticed the cabin of the Sikorsky lurch first to the right, and then to the left and into the air, to hover a few feet off the earth before ascending fast into the sky. Lynch on the other hand felt the pit of his stomach slump deep into his pelvis. He looked uncomfortably out at the ground as it fell away from beneath them.

The Count nodded in response to Power's question. "Doyle again. Although which one? Anyway, he is there, hiding in the skirts of Mother Church, by which, I mean he is hiding as a pretended innocent, at the Cathedral. Shameless as ever. Hiding in sheep's clothing once again. And if we fail today he will simply slip away to a church in another country and hide, or rather be hidden."

"So we're flying to Santiago now?" asked Power. "To find him?"

The Count nodded. "Salazar's men circulated the photograph in the city. They found him, just like they found his brother before him. And I called up a friend," he reached over to the shoulder of the pilot on the right and patted it.

The pilot handed control over to his companion and lifted the helmet from his head, putting some headphones and a microphone on so he could still hear his companion. He turned to face Lynch and Power.

"Good evening," he said. "Shall I give you some pilot's chit chat – we're at a thousand feet and flying at a hundred miles an hour. We should be there in less than half an hour. We're touching down in the city itself in Plaza Obradoiro."

"Right outside the Cathedral?" asked Lynch. The pilot nodded. His eyes shone with excitement.

"Who are you?" asked Power, unnerved by the man's smile. "You look very familiar."

"I'm Simon, Simon Howarth-Weaver." He reached his arm out again over his shoulder, and shook Power by the hand.

"Howarth-Weaver?" Power's memory struggled to cope.

"The pharmaceutical company?" Lynch interposed. "The same Howarth-Weaver?"

"Exactly," said Simon. "Somebody has to finance our turbine-powered bird here." He pointed to the rotors above. "And the money might as well be doing good work as bad. I inherited it all a few years back. It's taken a battle to get what is rightly mine, but now it is, I will steer the money where I choose; where it can make a difference. And today is a day when we can make that difference, or rather you can. I'm just an enabler here."

Power was still puzzled. "The same Howarth-Weaver company that was involved in the malaria epidemic?"

"My father's time that. Before me. In my time we funded the

creation of the antidote, if you like. We manufactured the drug, the one you helped find on a hard drive, I recall." He chuckled because he could see Power was still puzzled.

"Your father ran Howarth-Weaver?" said Power, piecing ideas together. He frowned, struggling with a flashback. "I met the Chief Executive in Toronto once."

"My aunt. After that generation died they came a-looking for me. And it's been a battle with the corporate types. They don't give up control easily, even when it's your money! They tried to say I lacked capacity. But a change of clothes, shaving my beard off, cutting my hair as slick as theirs, and I can fit right in to their suited world, if I choose to. And when I don't choose to, well I go off in my yacht, or into the country, or even busking on the streets if I damn well wanted to. This chopper comes from my yacht by the way."

"It must be a big yacht," said Power, thoughtfully.

"The Sikorsky was a naval Seahawk from the Navy. So it's adapted for life on board. The tail section folds back, the blades fold too so it takes up less space once you land. It can make high impact landings on a moving deck. So many details – the rotor can go at eleven hundred rpm. It's powered by jet engines. I negotiated the deal myself. And as for the yacht, well, it was built for a Saudi prince, but he got bored of it, and so I negotiated the *keffiyeh* off him too."

Power was looking at the Howarth-Weaver heir – his clean-shaven jaw, and imagining him with a beard. He was thinking that the young man, who had been little more than a down and out when he had first encountered him years ago, had, after the death of his father's generation, clearly taken to business like a duck to water. "When we last met," said Power, "you had your beard, a tumble-down red beard. You said your name was Harker, Simon Harker."

"I always preferred my mother's name," Simon said. "An old English name, an old English family. I never really saw eye to eye with my father, you know. I studied music. I played music wherever anyone might listen, on the streets in this city and that city, wherever the road took me. 'There's no money or glory in that', my father always said."

"You were the Piper," said Power softly.

"I still am the Piper," said Simon. "Just with a bit more economic muscle and a bit more freedom to do what I want. Boy, how money opens doors."

They flew over the green earth, trees, and fields, skimming over the surface of the globe, travelling as fast as a giant in seven league boots. The hills fell from beneath them, and there was a sudden plain and a long, winding road leading towards to a low cluster of brown tile-topped buildings on the horizon.

"Santiago de Compostela ahead!" shouted Simon Howarth-Weaver. "Pilgrim's progress, but at a hundred and thirty miles an hour!"

Power noticed Lynch staring into the distance, his jaw square set. He knew that this was not the way Lynch had hoped to first encounter the city of Santiago de Compostela, a city that had been old even in Medieval times. Lynch had envisaged a climb up the hill called Monte de Gozo, where the weary pilgrims caught their first glimpse of the three spires of the Cathedral. The hill was still an hour's walk from the final destination, the Cathedral of St James, but the mere sight of the spires would cause the true pilgrim to sink to his knees and cry out in joy, hence the translation of Monte de Gozo, the hill of joy.

This very rapid twenty-first century flight, hurtling towards the city with blades clattering and jet engines whining was as far from Lynch's dream as possible.

"We'll go back and pick up where we left off," said Power. "Do the journey properly on foot. We'll get a bus back to Alta de Poio and walk this way again."

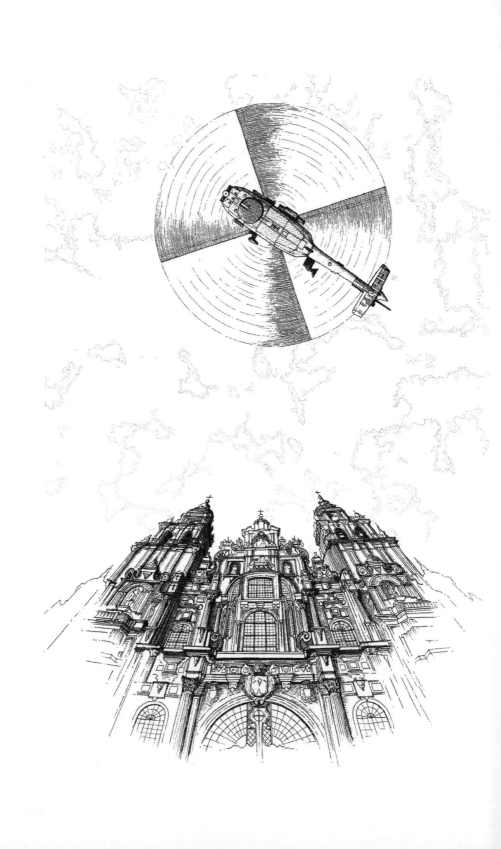

Lynch shook his head. "Let's focus on what we have to do." He looked at the Count. "Where is the priest exactly?"

"He's been working in the Cathedral for a few weeks," said the Count. "It's a busy place and they have hundreds of priests. Sixteen confession boxes for thousands of pilgrims running in a dozen languages almost fourteen hours a day. And at night he has wheeled a bed sleeping in the old Seminary building. There is such demand here, a priest from anywhere on the globe can just bring a certificate, a *celebret* from a Bishop – it's like a passport to a career anywhere in the world. You will have to find him in there, look carefully, for the Cathedral is heaving with thousands of pilgrims from early morning until late at night. All the roads, all the caminos from north and east and west and south all converge here at the Cathedral of Santiago, where everything ends."

Lynch was looking out of the side windows of the Seahawk. The green Galician fields had been replaced by low, whitewashed buildings topped by terracotta clay tiles. The whirring blades above him chopped at the air and as they rotated he could see a swirling shadow play as the helicopter's shade flitted from roof to roof below. The shadow, skipping from building to building, looked like the shape of some insect. Lynch imagined himself to be seated somewhere in the insect's thorax.

The pilot had slowed and the Sikorsky was hovering above the ancient city, spinning round in a lazy circling arc above the streets and buildings. Lynch could see the crowds of tourists moving like ants, and then as the helicopter lost altitude he began to see individual features; white hats and red tee-shirts in the distance, and within seconds they were lower still and he could make out upturned faces with compound eye sunglasses watching the Seahawk sailing past in the sky.

And then they were drifting above the three spires of the

Cathedral, above the thirteenth century roof. They were so low it almost looked as if they could just jump down on to the roof. The helicopter slid sideways and moved over the vertiginous walls of the nave to hover in the perfect middle of a vast square, bounded on four sides by the Cathedral, the old hospital for pilgrims; the Town Hall and the University respectively. The square centre of the old town is called the Praza de Obradoiro and once housed the stonemasons workshop for the Cathedral.

The helicopter dropped and Lynch could see a scattering plume of dust as the down-draught hit the granite stones of the square. As the dust scattered, so did the people as they vacated the place where the helicopter was coming down, right in front of the Baroque yellow stones of the west façade of the Cathedral. Two towers topped by spiky crucifixes soared up above the square. Lynch looked up at the ornamented swooping, curling curves of the Cathedral as the wheels of the Sikorsky touched gently down upon *terra firma*.

"This is it then," said the Count.

"I'm not sure what to do," said Power.

"Just go and get him, bring him here to me." The Count showed every sign of struggling up from the canvas seats to join them as they disembarked. Power started to protest, but the Count waved a walking stick at him. "I've come this far. I can stand here in the square while you go and get him, and we'll take him together to the police station; it's just over there by the Town Hall. I can walk that far." The Count pointed out of the helicopter to a corner of the square. "Just bring him to me."

Simon wrenched the cabin door open and Power helped the Count out of the belly of the helicopter. Lynch hung back for a second. He felt temporarily overwhelmed by the noise of the engines outside, and the maelstrom of sliced air caused by the rotor blades. A crowd of tourists and pilgrims watched at a safe distance as the trio disembarked. The Count staggered in his infirmity. Power took his arm and guided his hobbling body out of the down-draught of the still-spinning blades. The Count was pointing out the best door into the Cathedral to Power. "You go through there, through the archway at the other corner of the square – there's a tunnel or a passage. There's always Galician pipers playing there. The doors are on your right."

Lynch turned and looked at Simon Howarth-Weaver. He was poised ready to get back into the pilots' cabin.

"You're going?" asked Lynch.

The Piper nodded. "We can't stay here."

"Can you tell me something?"

"If I can help, yes."

"All this," Lynch pointed to the helicopter. "Your new wealth. Can you tell me if you were behind the job offer I received? Behind the idea of a Foundation? Are you bankrolling all that, Mr Howarth-Weaver?"

"Call me Simon, please."

Lynch frowned at the informality and the procrastination. "Mr Howarth-Weaver, are you behind the offer?"

Simon climbed into the pilot's seat and reached for the door. He called out to Lynch over the sound of the helicopter engines which were idling. "None of my business that; interfering in your life and telling you what you should do or not do. That's all your world. Your decision. Your life."

Simon put on his helmet and turned his attention to the other pilot who was shouting something at him. Lynch made ready to follow Power out of the down-draught. But before he put his visor down the Piper called Lynch back, just as he was closing the cockpit door. He leaned out of the cabin window slightly and called out.

"Mr Lynch? Whenever you're ready, just go and see Mr Berckley.

Now you'd better run, duck down and run and stand back over there. We're taking off. We have to leave. I can't afford to get a parking ticket!" he laughed.

As Lynch ran for safety across the stone square, the rotors swept faster and faster, buffeting him. The engine noise rose to a screaming pitch. The helicopter left the ground and began to ascend into the sky.

Chapter Twenty-One

Santiago de Compostela
Journey's End

*And that's why I have to go back
to so many places in the future,
there to find myself
and constantly examine myself
with no witness but the moon . . .*

Pablo Neruda

They left the Count standing on the stones of the square, watching as the helicopter slipped the gravity of earth, and escaped aloft, flying westwards to the open sea.

The Count, with one good leg and the other encased in a splint boot, gyred about as he watched the helicopter slip into the golden, late afternoon sky.

Power and Lynch hurried along the western edge of the Cathedral and dived to the right, into a tunnel that led east to the Cathedral's northern doors. The tunnel housed two pipers in Galician costume. Power saw their eyes follow him as he hurried past. He thought that they nodded almost imperceptibly to him and Lynch. The pipers' bagpipes let forth a skirling music that ascended with Power and Lynch as they ran up the stone ramp-way to the *Praza de Inmaculada.*

The square lay between the monastery of San Martiño Pinario, a seminary for Catholic priests, and the Northern door of the

Cathedral, the Azibechería entrance. This was the Cathedral entrance that all pilgrims had used from medieval times onwards.

The entrance had a series of ropes to guide the queue of pilgrims, but as the day was turning into evening, the numbers of pilgrims were less and the queue moved relatively quickly. Lynch sensed Power's impatience at his side. "Why is it taking so long?" Power asked. When they got closer, Power could see a pair of armed guards were examining the pilgrims' bags before they entered.

This reminded Lynch of something. "We didn't take our rucksacks out of the helicopter. We left them in there."

"They'll turn up," said Power.

It was their turn to speak to the guards. Power asked if they knew a blonde priest, "¿conoces un cura rubio llamado Doyle?"

They merely shrugged, saying, "Hay muchos sacerdotes," and smiling, waved them inside.

They entered and immediately faced a wall of people, three deep. There was no easy way through this. The pilgrims were queued up towards the left, along the narrow curve of the apse.

"What should we do?" asked Power. "Have you researched this place in your guidebook?"

"Go round them," said Lynch. "They're queued up to go into the roped off area beyond the altar. We can squeeze past. We'll go round the periphery of the Cathedral and try and orientate ourselves."

They excused themselves past the queue of tourists and pilgrims and pushed on towards the ring of chapels that circled round the outside of the curved apse. Power saw the pilgrims beyond the red velvet rope heading into a doorway that led down some stairs to the right beyond the altar. "Where are they going? The crypt?"

"That's the whole point of some people's pilgrimage," whispered Lynch. "The steps lead down to a special crypt where there are the bones of St James. The apostle, James."

They passed by the confused tumble of people that were herded in the semicircular apse, waiting to visit the crypt with its silver shrouded casket of St James's bones. Power and Lynch's eyes darted everywhere trying to glimpse the priest. They ran along the ambulatory and rounded the apse, and came upon a further throng of pilgrims, this time emerging from the central altar area, having descended steps to see the casket and then ascended further steps to emerge into a further queue on the other side of the apse.

The conga line of pilgrims faced away from Power and Lynch as they hurried down the other arm of the apse towards the nave. The pilgrims' line wound upwards through a turning of steps, which were concierged by an old shrunken priest handing out prayer cards. The steps led up to an area behind the altar and underneath a vast cupola supported by pillars formed into cumbersomely solid golden angels. In the space, behind a bejewelled statue of St James, the queue would pause and climb on to a step to hug the unyielding solidity of the Saint's shoulders, and after a few seconds' grace the line of pilgrims would move on.

They hurried forward at a pace just short of a run. The periphery of the vast space was full of pilgrims milling about. In the midst of the churning mass of people, queues of the penitent waited beside dark oak confessionals that sat around the edges of the great space like telephone booths to the Almighty. In the centre of the nave a service was going on, with a group of three robed-priests at the altar chanting Latin mass. Power looked, but could not see Doyle. Above the crossing a giant censer, called the *Botafumeiro*, swung majestically, spilling fuming white clouds of incense onto the seated worshippers. A giant thurible suspended high above the congregation had swung in this way every day since the seventeenth century. It was being tugged back and forth by eight men in red robes. They filled the censer with forty kilograms of charcoal and incense every day and pulled strongly so that the swinging eighty kilograms of thurible would almost touch the roof and reach nearly seventy kilometres an hour. Power looked back as they hurried across the Cathedral's crossing and took in the huge golden edifice of the altar, wreathed in sweet-smelling smoke. In the midst of it all the statue of St James stared out. He could just make out individual pilgrims from the queues they had passed, hugging the statue from behind.

Power was passing one of the wooden confessionals. It had a gabled roof, with an illuminated number '3' at the pinnacle of the gable. As he looked, he saw that there were indeed around sixteen confessionals scattered around the walls of the Cathedral, each in operation with a priest speaking a different language in each box. Italians would self-select to one confessional, French to another and so on. Above the opening where the priest sat was an inscription in dark gothic script carved into the wood of the confessional, '*qui tollis peccata mundi*'. The confessionals had doors flung open, like cupboard doors on either side, and inside, illuminated as the puppets in a Punch and Judy box might be, was a priest. This confessional had a balding white-haired priest in white and purple who offered confession in Italian. His umbrella was propped up against the ledge in front of him, and his beret hung up on the wall behind his head. He was blessing the head of a penitent, a small man who was kneeling contritely on a tiny velvet-covered step, right in front of the confessional. Power noticed the booth was fringed with white lace inside and lit internally by a chain of small white bulbs, which reminded him of fairy lights. Unfamiliar to such religious trappings, and having lived an entirely secular childhood, Power disrespectfully thought of a Christmas Santa in his grotto. "What an operation," breathed Power, trying to calculate how many confessions could be heard by sixteen priests in one day.

They moved through the thick, sweet air of the crossing into the nave of the Cathedral. The nave bay was filled pilgrims at prayer, but around the edges were more confession boxes. Power spotted two boxes offering confessions in English and pulled at Lynch's arm.

"What?" asked Lynch.

"Look," said Power, drawing Lynch through the milling crowd. "Could he be there? Taking confession?" They moved between the pillars of the nave, and all at once they stopped. There he was, under the confession box lights, his blonde hair shining like an artificial halo. Doyle was listening to a small man with a pinched nose who was reciting his sins. Doyle's eyes were closed and he was nodding intently, the very image of sincerity. Lynch stood stock still for a moment and glared, both fists clenched, as Power moved forward across the nave towards the confessional.

Dr Power stood in front of the confessional behind the penitent. Doyle was still focused on the man in front of him. Power looked at the threadbare coat around the man's shoulders and the worn soles of his shoes as he knelt. The queue of penitents had been waiting for the man to finish, eager for their own turn. They watched Power with some annoyance. He was outside the queue and clearly not obeying the established rules. They observed the doctor with some anxiety, because his motivation was not clear: he stood there an angry man, his face pale and brown eyes burning into the bowed head of the priest.

Power made his decision and laid a gentle hand on the pilgrim's shoulder. "I'm sorry, can you move please?"

The pilgrim was startled. "Do you mind? I'm confessing."

"Good, well, it's his turn now." Power pointed at the priest.

And seeing the quiet, but absolute determination in Power's eyes the pilgrim even stuttered an apology, rose to his feet, and stepped aside.

To prevent the priest's escape, Power stood directly in front of the confession box and pushed a knee against the lower doors of the booth.

The priest looked up slowly. Doyle had perhaps expected something like this may happen one day. He feigned astonishment at the interruption during confession, and was wondering whether to vocalize his protest, when Power put his finger near Doyle's lips. "I don't want to hear it, Father Doyle. We've no time for it."

Doyle looked up and saw that another figure had joined Power.

"Superintendent Lynch," Lynch said. "Would you come with us to the police station. I think there's something you should confess."

"And you wouldn't like to make a scene, would you?" said Power.

"Oh, I'm sorry, you're very mistaken, I don't mind making a scene," said Doyle. He suddenly stood, and with the advantage of a few inches height from inside the box, lashed out with his fist, punching down into Power's face. Power staggered backwards and collapsed into Lynch's arms. Doyle sprang forward. The confessional's wooden half-doors shot back with a bang and Doyle was running swiftly, like a hare, pushing over anybody in his way and barging his way through the crowd.

Still groggy, Power struggled up on one elbow on the stone flags. "Don't let him get away," he said to Lynch. "Run after him!"

But Lynch did not hear him because he was already running through the crowd after Doyle, and Power last saw him heading along the nave towards the crossing. Lynch had gone only a few yards before the crowd closed about him and Power lost all sight of the detective.

The pilgrims around him, bent down and picked Power up. "Are you all right?" they asked in various tongues. Others, new to the scene, were asking "What happened?" Still others were saying, "The priest stood and attacked him!"

Rubbing his bruised cheek, Power felt disorientated and confused by everyone's solicitude. He dragged himself to a pew and, as best he could, thanked people and waved them away. He felt dizzy and in pain, but could not bear to be a patient himself.

Lynch surged through the crowd as best he could, in the wake of the priest. He kept a steady eye on the priest in his vestments, as he scattered the people in his way. Doyle did not mind clashing with people, jarring their shoulders or pushing them forcefully backwards onto the stones.

All at once, at the crossing, the priest dived towards the right and round a corner, and Lynch lost sight of him. Moments later, Lynch too arrived at the junction and cast about trying to catch sight of the fugitive. The medieval Silversmith's Door lay open ahead, with golden evening light shining into the darkness of the Cathedral, but the door was too far for Doyle to reach it before Lynch could get to the corner, and yet there was no sign of him.

Lynch's attention was drawn to workmen's scaffolding over the inner walls of the transept. The stonemasons had been working on replacing eroded stones from centuries past. Grey, semi-transparent plastic sheeting covered the scaffolding, which towered high above the pilgrims up into the roof-space of the transept. Lynch ducked behind the plastic sheeting, thinking perhaps that Doyle might be hiding behind it, or had even climbed onto the scaffold to evade him. The scaffold was, though, a mere skeleton of metal and wood, uninhabited and desolate. Lynch scowled. He had lost Doyle, and they had lost any element of surprise.

There was, however, a dark and narrow wooden door in the corner of the walls, hidden away under a Romanesque archway. Lynch grasped the handle and pushed. The door yielded, and beyond Lynch could just make out a dark stairwell, ascending into the upper reaches of the Cathedral wall. What was more, Lynch could hear the sound of hurried footsteps reverberating on the stone stairs some way above him. Lynch began to run up the steps, two at a time. Above him, he heard a pause in the steps, as whoever it was stopped to listen. What they heard in their stillness was the sound of Lynch running after them, and alarmed by the sound of determined pursuit, they too began to climb again.

The steps were deep and after a minute Lynch felt his shins ache with the effort. Slightly breathless he switched to climbing just one step at a time. The stair wound round on itself in spiral fashion and Lynch remembered he had read that this had once been a 'fortress cathedral' that had survived bitter attacks by Normans, Vikings and Muslims.

The hidden stairway opened into a narrow secret tunnel that crossed over the nave and on to a still more narrow flight of stairs that ascended up into the roof-space.

Lynch burst out of the door at the top of the secret staircase. The setting sun blazed down upon him in a fanfare of red and orange. The pitched roof rose in a slope before him. The slope was composed of flat rectangular stones, arranged to form shallow steps that climbed upward to the ridge. Doyle had ascended the steps to the apex, and was disappearing over the other side. Lynch breathlessly launched himself forward and skittered over the same stone tiles that had sat patiently under rain and sun for over eight hundred years.

As Lynch reached the granite ridge he could see Doyle running down the roof of the transept and down to a flat pavement of lead that ran along the length of the roof, guarded by a parapet with stone pinnacles with small globes on top. Lynch shouted "Stop!", but to no avail. Doyle was running over to the right, towards a vast, Romanesque clock tower. He paused for a moment looking back towards Lynch. He shaded his eyes from the light. To Doyle, Lynch was a shadow of nemesis against the setting sun.

Doyle made for a door in the clock tower, hoping to evade Lynch by ducking through this, locking it behind him and escaping down a second flight of stairs to ground level, without anyone following him. But the door was locked, and Doyle suddenly felt his breath catch with fear. He could move round the roof ahead, but Lynch and Power had trapped him like a pawn trapped alone on a chessboard by two knights.

Doyle moved around the clock tower, but there was no way out there either. He looked through a vast rose window let into the wall, down into the Cathedral. The pilgrims were moving far below, like ants wholly unaware that they were being watched.

Doyle walked slowly beside the balustrade, along the leaden pavement, trailing his hand lazily along the parapet, feeling the warm stone under his palm. He patted each stone pinnacle as he passed it. He was smiling as Lynch, out of breath, hurried along the walkway toward him. About ten feet away Lynch paused. He could see that Doyle had reached a point from which he could not escape.

Doyle was slowly prowling back and forth in the corner of the parapet. He seemed taken by the play of amber light and shadow on the corner pinnacle, and almost caressed the stone. He was looking out over the roofs of Santiago as they reflected the fiery sky, his back to Lynch.

Suddenly he seemed to have made up his mind and he swung himself nimbly up so that he was standing on the very edge of the balustrade. His feet were on a ledge perhaps some eighteen inches wide and his right arm was hooked round the nearest pinnacle for balance and support. He looked round at Lynch and grinned, tauntingly. "Not a step nearer," he hissed.

"For goodness' sake, come down from there," said Lynch. "You might slip."

"I don't care," said Doyle. "You hounded my brother to death.

You're doing the same to me. Even though, of course, I could easily say it was all him. That he did everything. I could say that I am completely innocent. I am not my brother's keeper, as they say."

"And you'll have your say in Court, if you want to say that," said Lynch. "Just come down from there."

Doyle sighed. "Spare me your little speech about the wisdom of justice. I don't give a fig for you or your values. Look at them down there." He pointed with a free arm towards the pilgrims and tourists milling about a fountain in the plaza some fifty metres below. "Small-minded people with tiny lives, here for a brief stay on this earth and hidebound with their rules and laws. What does it all mean? We only live once, so why not do exactly what you want – take exactly what you want."

"What a curious attitude for a priest," said Lynch, taking a step closer. His hands were balled up into fists, so tightly his skin on them was white.

"Haven't you worked it out?" Doyle was mocking him. "Wake up! There is no God. It doesn't matter what we do here on Earth during our lives, so I take what I want. If people are fooled by a white collar and a bit of Latin, so much the better. It's a mask. It's just a passport to go where I want and do whatever I like. And it doesn't matter, because *now* is all there is, there's no heaven and no hell."

"And that's your philosophy? Your credo?" Lynch was about six feet away from the priest, and every time that Doyle looked down upon the plaza below, Lynch moved a little bit closer. He tried to keep his anger and loathing for Doyle out of his voice.

"My credo is 'take what you want'," said Doyle.

"I assume that's an admission of guilt. You knew what you wanted, and so you took what you lusted after from those who were too young to oppose you," said Lynch.

"Whatever," shrugged Doyle. He laughed. "Are you going to give me the little speech about getting down from here and facing Human Justice again?"

"Do you know what I think?" said Lynch, stepping forward. "I think I'd prefer it if you faced God's Justice."

* * *

Dr Power had stumbled his way through the crowd in a vain attempt to follow Doyle and Lynch. It had taken him a few minutes to regain any composure after the very solid and sudden punch he had taken to the skull. He made his way through the nave, along the transept and past the scaffold that Lynch and Doyle had run into earlier. Power passed the scaffolding by and emerged through the double arched Silversmith's Door into the plaza beyond. The golden Spanish sunlight was darkening to dusk. There were scattered groups of pilgrims with staffs and rucksacks. Power made his way down some steps. A party of tourists was crossing the plaza past a fountain, following a guide who held a folded pink umbrella aloft.

There was a shout from on high that echoed across the vast space between the ornate facades of the buildings. All at once, everyone looked up.

The priest fell from the parapet which was around the Cathedral roof. Power saw his black cassock spread wide by the rush of air around Doyle as he fell. There was no scream. He fell silently, apart from the rippling sound of his cassock, flapping about him. All the people in the square had stopped; wordless, silent witnesses.

The next sound was that of the body shattering on the granite slabs, only thirty metres or so away from the doctor. Power heard a popping noise as the skull exploded. It sounded ever so much like the sound you get when you drop a thin-walled glass jar of strawberry jam onto a tiled kitchen floor. The glass shatters and the

jar deforms and subsides, but the gooey red jam within dampens the sound, and smears the shattered glass.

Power watched, horrified and numb, as a pool of dark red venous blood spread out from the blonde-haired object that had been Doyle's head.

Then Power looked up, and saw Lynch looking down over the balustrade from which Doyle had fallen. Lynch's head and shoulders were a shadow against the darkening sky. And then Lynch was gone.

Power felt rooted to the spot. A crowd had gathered about the broken body. Some people were on mobile phones. In the distance there was the sound of a siren as emergency services began to respond.

At last Power freed himself from the stillness that had constrained him and he moved away, around the corner of the Cathedral towards the plaza where they had landed by helicopter only half an hour before.

On this side of the Cathedral, pilgrims were moving about completely unaware of the death in the plaza beyond, just a moment before.

Power moved towards the place where they had left the Count. He was still waiting patiently in the distance. The Count lifted an arm and waved towards Power, who waved back. A group of pilgrims were laughing as they marched past Power, elated at having reached the end of their journey. One of them saw him and clapped him on the back saying, *"Buen Camino."*

Power responded automatically, *"Buena vida."*

Epilogue

Power had been writing a chapter all morning, matching scientific points in the text with references and then double-checking everything. He took a break in his writing and brewed a cafetière of Blue Mountain Coffee. The aroma took him straight back to a small hotel in the lush green hills above Ocho Rios, where he had stayed many years ago. He was musing about the relative coolness of the hills compared to the humidity of Kingston town when his mobile rang. He answered the mobile at the same time as he applied gentle pressure to the plunger of the cafetière.

"Hello?" said Power.

"Carl?

"Yes?"

"It's Andrew here. What are you doing?"

"I'm in the kitchen, drinking coffee. Laura's making lunch and I'm actually considering whether I can . . . well, I'm planning to open up the door from the kitchen and try going down the steps again. You know about the secret door? I did tell you?" Power was sitting at the kitchen table. He took a sip of his flat white coffee. Laura smiled at him as she assembled a salad.

"You told me there were steps going down from your house, cut into the sandstone and an elaborate archway with gates, and a tunnel, going into the caves under the Edge. You got stuck there. In the dark."

"That's right. It's taken all that time, till now, for me to pluck up the courage to try again. Laura said she'd come with me after lunch.

We're taking at least four lamps, food supplies, water, some rope, matches, candles. You name it. I'm following the Boy Scout Motto and being prepared this time."

"You're going spelunking?" asked Lynch. "Is that the word?"

"I've no idea," said Power. "I wasn't planning anything beyond a little exploration. Not very far at all. Just a little bit further than where I got up to last time. I just was curious. Why did the Victorian architect keep a link between the house and the caves? The iron gate was really elaborate. The archway was superbly built. Did the owner ever make a habit of going down there? Why did he instruct the architect to make such a grand entrance to the caves? What did he do there? Why did someone cover it all up? There's no mention of it on surveys, or plans."

"Hmmm . . . be careful, Carl. Listen, we'll have to leave the mystery of the caves till another time, I'm afraid. I need to tell you something. Are you sitting down?"

"I'm drinking coffee at the table." Power suddenly felt uneasy. His heart was sinking at the potential idea of bad news. "Is it very bad?"

"I don't know," said Lynch. "It's not like someone you know has died, don't worry. And I will tell you in a moment, but I wanted to apologise first. For being sceptical when we were in Spain and after; for not believing you. I should know better by now."

"What do you mean?"

"Well," said Lynch. "You spotted the priest thing straightway. And I didn't believe that the man you accused here in England was involved."

"It took us all a while to realise that the explanation was a pair of twins, don't blame yourself."

"But I do," said Lynch. "Even more so now." He paused, uncertain how to proceed.

"Where are you?" asked Power.

"At my desk in Chester. I had to come in, even though it's the weekend. To receive a fax. I'm looking at it now."

"I'm not following you, Andrew."

"Ah, that's because you can't see the fax. If you could . . ." Lynch sighed. "I've made such a mistake in not listening to you. I was phoned at home by the Count, from Astorga. He is recovering by the way, and he sends his regards to you. His leg is nearly mended. He also told me that he has been doing some research in the Diocesan library in Astorga. They have documents going back to the third century. Vellum I suppose. Like those illuminated pages we saw, I suppose. Well he was digging at some paper files from the nineteen-eighties. A little more recent. He came across a private file about the brothers. It must have been kept by some member of the clergy in a private archive. It hadn't originated in any public archive. I think it was there by mistake. Overlooked by everyone including the brothers. They had expunged any official records of their being more than one of them. Some time during their training they had merged their identities into one. Only one emerged from the seminary. But as long as they looked the same, both could conspire and use the same identity, in different places, as we know. They had found it convenient to weed out any official documents about there being more than one of them in the seminary . . ."

"They trained together?"

"They went in to the same seminary, but only one emerged and they both used the same identity when they wanted to be a priest. What they used the other for, I don't yet know. They were masters at covering their tracks, but the Count has found something. A newspaper cutting from *El Pais,* from their Santiago office. It's in Spanish and I won't attempt to translate it. It's from nineteen eighty-nine and the Count says it documents our brothers entering the Irish College there. It was a seminary, founded in the seventeenth century, which took the boys from Dublin. They were a phenomenon, I suppose, being identical. There's a picture of them together. This may be the only picture of the boys together that still exists. They probably made a pact whilst they were in the College to destroy any evidence they could, including photographs."

"Did one of the twins fail his exams then?"

"I suspect that something happened at the College. Didn't they refer to being tempted, to falling into their ways, that in admitting their predilection they were initially fearful and ashamed, but that they were surprised to be . . . 'encouraged' by a section of people there? I think that their decision to merge their identities was a conscious decision, not something brought about by an event, like failing an exam. Some time during the five years they would have spent at the seminary as acolytes or deacons, whatever they are called, they merged and only one brother was ordained. But it's the picture I need to tell you about, Carl. You're sitting down?"

"You've been talking so long, I've finished my coffee. Laura's poured me out a glass of Rioja."

"Is it a big glass? Well, I hope it is, you may need it. The Count wanted to fax the picture over. He doesn't do email, like you. So I came into the HQ and it came through half an hour ago. There is a photo of the brothers in some courtyard, smiling and with arms around each other."

"So?" asked Power.

"There are three of them. They weren't twins. They were triplets. One identical pair of brothers and one non-identical. Two blonde brothers with blue eyes, and the other. At that time he had *two* brown eyes, and his hair was black."

"Cousins," murmured Power under his breath, horrified.

Music for Schrödinger's God

A set of music has been suggested by readers; these accompany some of the music that inspired the author, Hugh Greene, whilst writing the original novel.

If you would like to suggest further additions to this list please email the author via www.hughgreene.com

Queen Mab — Abel Korzeniowski
Clearing, Dawn, Dance — Judd Greenstein
Moon — Beth Orton
Eastsid — Heartbeat(s)
Queen Mab — Hexpero
Don Juan — Meilyr Jones
Rome — Meilyr Jones
Recomposed Vivaldi — Max Richter
Cantus in memoriam Benjamin Britten — Arno Pärt
Alborada de Veiga — Carlos Nuñez
A2 — Prins Thomas
Santiago Cuatro — Underworld
From our animal — Sarah Neufeld
Cadenza on the Night Plain — Terry Riley
Mile Markers — The Dead Weather
The Sticks — Burnt Friedman
Under My Skin — Peter Bradley Adams
Peacock Suit — Paul Weller
Kingdom — Julia Kent
Ebb — Julia Kent
Templar — deadmau5
Here Comes The War — New Model Army
House of Jealous Lovers — The Rapture
Conspiracy Theory — Harmonic Zoo
Gloucestershire Hornpipe/Mr Trill's Song — Morris On Band
Costa da Morte — Luar na lubre
Camiño de Ibias — Luar na lubre
Sanctus — Jacon Clemens non Pap

The Epiphany of Mrs Kugla — Shpongle
Sample This — Chilly Gonzales
Green's Leaves — Chilly Gonzales
Come again, sweet love doth now — John Dowland
Cordon de Plata — Gustavo Santaolalla
La taberna del Buda — Café Quijano
Moss — Claire Hamill
Cantaben els osells — Ramon Llull
Txalaparta — The Chieftains
Model — Balanescu Quartet
I'm in the Pink — Cliff Martinez
Bach Off — Nicolas Godin
Elfe Man — Nicolas Godin
Bach's Sonata No. 1 in F Major Op. 2. No. 1 — Glenn Gould
Bird — Billie Marten
Man of the World — Fleetwood Mac
Legions (War) — Zoë Keating
Schrödinger — Anakronic Electro Orchestra

SCHRÖDINGER'S GOD

Q & A with Hugh Greene

Why the title *Schrödinger's God*, and where did the inspiration to write it come from?

Most people have enjoyed a murder mystery, perhaps as a book, film or a TV series. Readers love murder mysteries, but the subject matter is, if you reflect upon it, so very dark, that it is difficult to reconcile this with the notion that the average person has a personality that is consistently peaceful, equable and reasonable. It is an uncomfortable truth that most adults privately seem to have a morbid fascination with death and murder. We are fascinated by the abnormal thoughts and thankfully rare behaviours associated with murder.

To balance out the dark and the light the Dr Power books are deliberately leavened with themes of healing and faith.

The Dr Power book that, to date, has the highest body count is *The Good Shepherd*. Deliberate acts of a conspiracy, driven by greed, lead to the deaths of thousands through disease. The evil of this, is offset by the deliberate goodness associated with self-sacrifice by key characters. Dr Power, as an agnostic takes a rather secular view of such altruism, but Lynch, a Christian, undoubtedly sees these as reflections of the divine.

Newton's Third Law of physics says, '*For every action, there is an equal and opposite reaction*' and so in the Dr Power Universe crimes explored in the books as events of profound negativity may therefore be offset by positive acts, or thoughts.

The problem of evil is something that Dr Power battles with throughout the books – how can a caring God allow abuse of children? – a reality recognised in many parts of the world in recent years – and Power sometimes finds his friend Lynch's faith in God a comfort and at other times he finds it incomprehensible.

In this book Power and Lynch meet a physicist and he discusses the quantum world. The notion that paired particles can act in synchrony, (although separated by a distance), is a physics-derived metaphor for the perpetrators in this novel. And the notion that particles can simultaneously exist and not exist attracts Power as it might offer an explanation for his alternating feelings that God may exist or not exist.

I have enjoyed reading several books on Schrödinger's physics and his life to research this book. An interesting man, who was for most of his life probably an atheist, but who glimpsed something spiritual, if not exactly divine, through his physics. I enjoyed discussing his ideas with my cousin, a physicist and doctor from Australia, in what was tragically the last year of his life.

And in terms of initial inspiration, before doing all that I was researching the Dr Power story *The Fallen Man* in Dublin. I was walking around Merrion Square and looking up saw a blue plaque to the effect that Schrödinger had worked there. I had assumed he had always worked in Austria, but he fell foul of the Nazis in World War II and was welcomed to Dublin. That started my research stream that formed into some of the elements used in *Schrödinger's God*.

A part of the book reads somewhat like a travelogue, what made you choose to write it this way? How factual is it?

Most of the details in the books are factually researched. So places and events referred to in *Schrödinger's God* are essentially correct. When Lynch and Beresford have a conversation referring to a recent child murder in the news, they are referring to the tragic murder of Sarah Payne in July 2000.

The *Camino* or walking route to Santiago del Compostela is a walking route that has been travelled by pilgrims for hundreds of years. The way was popularised again in the 1990s, and so this would have been something that Lynch was aware of. The places along the Way really are as described. The author walked the route in 2015.

The Camino is a special experience, and I hope that some sense of the personal transformation that can accompany it, is incorporated in the novel.

What were the highlights of writing this book?

I always enjoy weaving the research and experiences that lie behind the books into a working plot. There is a sense of being on a journey, rather like a pilgrim on the Way, and of course, one thing leads to another and one novel and its characters inevitably suggest the next. So, I enjoy the journey in many senses.

The Count is an interesting character, he is proud to be a Knight with ideals of chivalry and honour. Does the Order still exist today in this modern world?

The Order of St James of the Sword, or Santiago, was founded in the 12th Century and it developed to protect pilgrims on the Camino from terrorist attacks by Muslims at a time when Spain's cultural destiny was very much in the balance. The Order counted such luminaries as the Royal princes and Velázquez. The order co-existed with other orders such as the Knights Templar (1119–1312) and the Knights Hospitallers (1049 onwards). The Order of St James of the Sword was suppressed by the first Republic in 1873, but it was revived under the protection of King Juan Carlos. In the 21st Century the Knights of St James number just a few dozen.

The modern day Knights have more of a ceremonial or moral nature rather than a physical or military role in protecting

Christians from the depredations of Muslim attackers as in the past.

Was there a character you found particularly challenging?

The perpetrator in this book was a thoroughly unpleasant character to live with as the book developed. His selfish abuse of others is deeply repellent. Such perpetrators are not localised to any particular religion, or profession. They feed off power imbalance, as sense of their superiority, their own arrogance, a culture of secrecy, ignorance and their victim's misplaced shame. All adults throw a shadow as they move through life; all of us have a negative side; the trick is to have insight into that shadow, ensure that shadow is limited and that it does not harm others.

The Count was initially meant only as small character, but he took on a life of his own. He is in some ways an echo of Cervantes' Don Quixote, or is meant to be seen as such early on. He has a real strength and a determination. His motivation to be a hero perplexed me until I realised that he too had suffered.

Ramon, the physicist and astronomer, what was your inspiration for him? Is he based on a real person?

Ramon will have a part to play in future books and he is based on a historical figure, but I will leave it to the reader to research this.

This is a complex story, full of emotion, what was the most difficult part of writing it?

Earlier I did refer to Dr Power's struggle with the problem of evil, which would seem to be an intrinsic part of a murder mystery or thriller. Too often the murder is merely a device in such a book, and when this is so the reader and the writer are somehow insulated or detached from the sudden, jagged horror of the act, and the plight of the victim and their family. In this book the murders are supremely selfish acts to enable the abusers to evade punishment and continue indulging their desires at the expense of victims and society. The story necessarily includes victims that are children, and this is upsetting. I deliberately included no more detail than was strictly necessary to move the story forwards.

Did the story turn out the way you first envisaged?

Most of the twists and turns were clear to me when I began writing; for instance the epilogue was written in the first few weeks. Some characters surprised me along the way.

What would you like readers to take away from this book?

I'd be delighted if readers enjoyed the book and wanted to read another Dr Power book. More than that I'd like them to have been surprised at times during the read and inspired enough to act – to investigate the subject matter, to travel to the places mentioned, listen to the music, or drink the wine and eat the food described in the book.

How long did it take to write?

A year to research and a year to write. Then some months to let it settle and for me to read through critically. The editing advice, proofreading and illustration process allowed further reflection and fine tuning.

What will you be working on next?

Dr Power stories often contain clues as to the direction of future books in the series. Sometimes the clues are in the illustrations. So the stained glass window in the illustration of the chapel in *The*

Fire of Love referenced the next book, *The Good Shepherd.* The stories in *Dr Power's Casebook* link the first three novels with subsequent ones, for instance there are clues woven into the illustrations and text of *Dr Power's Casebook* to characters and plots in the next few novels. Much research precedes each book. I have been researching in Malta, Portugal and talking to academics about the archaeology of Alderley Edge.